Canada
United States
LUNAR ROCK
DASH'S HOUSE
RORI'S HOUSE
EVENTIDE
XANDER'S PLACE
JAY COUNTRY STORE
Jay Peak Ski Resort
Newport
I0694025

Also by

Veil & Shadow Series
**The Breaking*
**The Bleeding*

(**Prequel** to *The Anavrin Series*- Stand Alone)
**Little Red Rising*

The Anavrin Series
**A Kingdom Of Crowns And Malice*
**A Throne Of Chains And Fate*

Eventide Series
**Falling Even*
**Rising Tide*

Falling
Even
Anexa O Saphire

*A*uthor's Note:

Some Trigger Warnings

This book is a work of fiction. Any likeness to that of actual beings, living or deceased, is coincidental or embellished to tell a fictional tale.

It contains scenes that may be uncomfortable for some readers.

Including, but not limited to... violence, blood, explicit sex, alcohol abuse, and implied and/or unwanted sexual advances.

Some characters in this book are based off of real-world placement and classical works but do not strictly adhere to any one folklore.

The creative uses of such are fully fictional and not to be taken as fact.

Chapter One

It was another typical Friday night slinging drinks for the local riff-raff.

If I were a braver person, I might care about the fight that broke out in the corner of the bar. The scent of blood wafting through the air mixed with sweat and poor choices.

If I were a smarter person, I wouldn't work here in the first place.

Eventide was the kind of dive bar that any rational thinking person would steer clear of at all costs.

Neglected, small, and secluded, nestled into a dead-end road in the middle of nowhere Jay, Vermont, its location kept most sensible minded people away.

The highway here was notorious for swallowing up cars too caught up in the scenic beauty to notice they were lost until it was too late.

The *if you saw or heard something, no you didn't rule* was in full affect in these woods.

Strange things had a way of occurring up and down the mountain range.

Jay was isolated in the way all small towns in colder climates were.

Vermont was a beautiful place. The changing leaves in the fall. The skiing in the winter. Even the spring and summers had a nice way about them... if you were visiting. Living here, year-round, it wore on you.

People came and went from the ski resort not far from here all the time. Those were the only strangers that tended to occasionally wander into the bar.

There was no reward for coming to Eventide, except the promise of alcohol to numb the loneliness.

Fights were a regular occurrence, but lately, the uptake in their frequency screamed of some underlying reason I couldn't quite put my finger on.

"I hate to ask, but would you mind getting another keg from the backroom, Rori?" The petite, golden haired new hire asked as I came around the corner.

She'd only been here about three months. Somewhat on the clumsy side, she would drop drinks, bumping into tables and knocking things over in the beginning.

Her skills improved little by little each shift, but clumsiness must have been ingrained in her from birth.

Her small frame and pretty face came with a friendly enough personality. It was wasted at a place like this.

If it had been anyone but Kamie asking, I'd have told them to get it themselves.

Molly was working at the other end of the bar tonight and as usual, cared only about what was right in front of her.

My distaste for most people made the nights long. I'd usually put on a fake smile and power through.

Kamie was sweet though. With her positive outlook and tiny stature, she didn't belong anywhere near this place.

Catching a glimpse of myself in the mirror behind the bar, I pushed the strands of my blue streak of long, wavy hair behind my ear.

The streak's color was changed frequently, but royal blue was my go-to wax color for the natural silver thread that'd been the bane of my existence since I was born.

No matter my hair length. No matter how many times I dyed my whole head raven black. That silver strip of hair was always there.

Colored hair wax was the only solution that helped me not feel like a weirdo because of my premature silver hair strip.

"No problem." Lifting heavy kegs onto the handcart wasn't my favorite activity.

More often than not, I had to get one of the tipsy asshole males hanging around to help if Cody wasn't working.

Nothing ever came free around here. If you asked for help, they saw it as an opportunity to get handsy.

That was until I started dating the guy in town that everyone strangely showed deference to.

Dax hadn't shown up yet tonight.

It was still early. Lots of shenanigans for the regulars to get into before he'd make his appearance.

Having to put my foot down about four months ago to get him to stop scaring off the customers, his brooding possessiveness was messing with my tip intake.

We'd been seeing each other, if you could call it that, for nearly a year.

I'd known of him practically my whole adult life though. And at the ripe age of twenty-six, a decade was a long time.

Not one who usually liked burly guys, I was more of a lean muscled, afternoon shadow, kind of gal.

There was just something about Daxayrius Balodyn that revved my engine.

His chestnut-colored hair wasn't too long, but it had enough volume to get a good grip in when making out.

He had a tattoo of a moon, with some sort of runes. It looked like vines and thorns surrounding it on his left forearm.

Getting lost in those hazel eyes of his was one of my favorite pastimes. They had dark flecks that, sometimes, I'd swear they got bigger the broodier he'd become.

Maybe it was his undeniable take charge attitude that made my knees go weak.

In a town full of burly iron hammers, he shined like a polished silver axe.

Point be told, I initially started dating him because he made me feel safe amongst his not so gentlemanly friends.

I'd had enough of that in my past to last a lifetime.

Grunts and snarls filled their conversations more than words half-way through any given night around here.

Nurses weren't the only ones who notice the effects of a full moon. The bar was practically savage at that time each month.

"Ouch". The minute I got home, I was taking these stupid fake nails off.

That was the third time tonight one of them had snagged on something. I didn't know how I'd let Bitzy talk me into getting them in the first place.

She was off tonight. Of course. I couldn't remember the last time she was scheduled to work a Friday night shift.

Best friend or not, it was irritating.

"Where do you need this, Kam?" I'd asked without looking up first.

When she spotted me at the end of the bar, her relief was instantaneous.

Two of our rowdier regulars, Kazz and Gunner, had her practically cornered. Towering over her, they were muscular, arrogant, and drunk. A horrible combination.

Gunner looked up when he saw me coming. Eyes dark, his gaze ran the full length of my body.

Shivering internally, on the outside I showed nothing but cold indifference.

"Oh good." Kamie pushed passed Kazz to help me with the keg. "These guys were waiting for their refills. Can you put it under tap five?" Glancing up in my direction first, she turned her back on them. "You're a life saver, Rori."

Not really, but I had her back. That was nearly the same thing around here.

Not particularly caring for that little nickname from most people, I'd learned to live with it since grade school. Aurora was a mouthful.

Gunner still wouldn't move. With his body blocking my path, a smirk on his face, I shoved the hand truck into his legs.

Running him over with it, heavy keg and all, would be my pleasure.

"Do you enjoy being a bonehead or does it come too easy to you to notice?" The way his eyebrows rose was almost comical. "Get out from behind the bar, asshole."

If working here didn't give me a lesson in patience, nothing would.

My soft tone had sharpened over the last several years. My rounded edges had become points with teeth each shift I'd work.

Kazz and Gunner were not bad guys. And not bad to look at either. They were typical fun time drunks.

I had no idea how they were outside of the bar, but I only got to see them here. They hung out at Dax's place often, though he never had me over at the same time.

It was the cherry on my sundae whenever we'd have the house to ourselves.

Kazz's brown, shoulder length locks and golden eyes with green flecks fit his personality well.

Gunner had sandy blonde hair, cropped short at the top of his head and shaved on the sides.

With stubbly chin hair and a well-maintained moustache, his faded brown eyes had a steely grey appearance in low lighting that many women had flocked to over the years around last call.

It was their brutish behavior that was such a turn off.

Usually before the intake of the large sums of alcohol, they seemed to be decent guys individually.

Together, they were a menace.

"You sure you don't want a hand?" Gunner glanced over at Kazz and that fiendish smirk grew wider. "With the beer, I mean."

Backing away with his hands up in mock surrender, a shadow passed over his face. The beaming smile that was there only a second ago completely gone.

Shivering slightly, I turned to the open door. Dax stood in the reflection of light from the nearly full moon.

The guys shuffled out from behind the bar, casually making their way back to their table without a word.

Kyle, the athletic looking proprietor of Eventide, finally looked up from the paperwork he'd been stressing over since I'd arrived earlier tonight.

At twenty-eight years old, the loss of his dad put him in a position I knew he had never wanted.

He had big adventurous dreams in high school. I'd been a couple of years behind him, but his personality was larger than life back then.

His face fell when he looked in Dax's direction but in the next blink, he'd plastered on a clearly false smile for the crowd around the bar.

"Hey." Dax never said much.

His quiet, brooding personality was what drew me to him in the first place.

He was older than me. Out of school before I'd even entered high school.

When I was in school, I'd see him around town and not think much of it.

Everywhere I turned, there he was. The corner store. The post office. The gas station.

He'd never looked my way, but I noticed him.

When I came to work here a few years ago, he was always at that one half circle booth in the back, shadowed from the rest of the bar.

Our interactions were mostly me taking his order.

Two fingers of whiskey. Neat.

Him attempting a smile but falling short.

Me left feeling ... something... want? Desire? Fear? I couldn't say.

Whatever it was, I felt it calling to me every night as I laid down to sleep.

Remembering each of the few words he'd spoken. Imagining things I shouldn't. Wanting more than I should.

After a year or so of the same interactions, I figured he wasn't interested in me.

Maybe he didn't like that I was younger than him. Or maybe he preferred blondes, as opposed to my raven black, long hair with my colored streak.

Perhaps he thought of me as nothing more than a go nowhere townie.

It could have been any number of reasons that I didn't appeal to him.

My pale skin and barely blue eyes were my personal nemesis and maybe he found them lacking as well.

I didn't have the most beautiful face or body, but I could hold my own.

If he didn't like what he saw, I wasn't going to change me to fit his standards box.

I didn't know why I approached Dax's table that night almost a year ago. I didn't know what gave me the balls to ask him out.

When I looked back on it, I still laughed at my own forwardness.

Walking right up to him, I'd blurted out, "You know, if you're going to be everywhere I am, the least you could do is buy me dinner."

His half smile shattered my heart. It lit up his face, chasing away some of the dark bruises and crinkling in his eyes.

"There she is." Those were his only words to me before we whisked away after my shift to the twenty-four hour diner in the town over.

And now, here he stood. Tall and handsome. Standing in the doorway looking like a forgotten god of old.

Chapter Two

I wouldn't immediately go over to take his order. He preferred to sit and observe for the first half hour or so.

In the initial days of working here, I would come to see if he needed anything when he settled into his booth.

He'd wave a casual hand in my direction. Basically, shooing me off.

After a month of that, I stopped coming over and started waiting until he'd nod in my direction.

It irritated the hell out of me. I didn't know why... but okay... I did know. I just didn't want to give that kernel of knowledge recognition before I was ready to unpack it.

Everyone had a past. Mine was nothing special.

The hooligans around here acknowledged him and would tell me that they were all friends but the way they deferred to his subtle nods, or the curl of his lips, or the changes in his eyes whenever there was a ruckus, had me questioning their friendship.

It was more like he was in charge.

Thinking back on it, I realized that maybe that's what had me laying restless at night. The energy he maintained. The mysterious air about him.

It made no sense. Maybe I was too observant. I'd been read-ing too many dark romance novels, perhaps.

Or maybe all those fantasy books stacked around my room made me see things where there was nothing to be seen.

Shaking the cobweb of memories away, I headed back to the bar with another order for Kamie to make.

The dirty bar rag was clean just an hour ago. This place never got any cleaner. Washing it out at the sink behind the bar, I couldn't help but to think there must be more to life than living the same day in and out in this small town.

Dax dipped his chin in my direction as he walked towards his spot. He wanted a drink right away. Now I knew something was up.

"I need a double." His words were clipped, eyes troubled.

"What's wrong?" I had gotten use to his non-verbal ways. Learned to navigate the sea of grunts, hmmm's, and scoffs, as their own language.

We were not a touchy-feely couple. Hell, we were not even a couple.

I was using him for sex and protection. I still hadn't figured out what he was using me for, but I didn't care.

I'd never needed a heartfelt connection. Just a warm body that kept me safe. I couldn't remember ever connecting on a romantic level with anyone.

"Nothing of concern," he snarled from deep in his throat. My hands clenched at my sides, fisting at his cold reply.

Alright, maybe it would be nice to have someone who said more than three words at a time. Or someone who looked at me with feeling more than only when it was convenient.

I had caught him staring me up and down more than once, when no one was looking. When hunger wasn't the only thing in his eyes.

"Fine," my tone sharp, I turned away to go get his drink.

His massive hand snagged my wrist before I took half a step.

Turning defiantly slowly, I looked deep into his turbulent eyes. Sorrow and fear looked back at me.

"I'm not myself tonight." Short. To the point. No apology, as usual. "Forgive me." Not a question. A command, but softer than he'd ever said to anyone else.

The one corner of his mouth pulled up and something tugged at me, keeping my feet from moving away.

"You're not going to tell me what's going on?" If this was how it was going to be with him all the time, maybe I needed to rethink my choice in a companion. "A hint, even?"

After an audible intake of breath, he closed his eyes. Then let out an extra-long breath. Not a sigh, but resignation

"Eventide is being sold."

Yup. That would do it. Now, I needed a drink too.

My head snapped towards Kyle, who was purposefully not looking in our direction.

He could have told the staff before the public.

We'd be in a fine mess if the new owner didn't want to keep the current work crew around.

Or worse, if they wanted to tear it down to build some kind of tourist's destination.

Before I could storm over in Kyle's direction, with his hand still gripping my wrist, Dax dropped his voice to my ear, "He doesn't know yet." That stopped me short.

"How is that possible? He's the owner. If he didn't sell it, how..."

I didn't get a chance to finish my sentence.

A tinkling of glass snared my attention. The bottle that had smashed against the back mirror of the bar rained shards around Kamie's hunched body.

I caught the sight of green in the corner of my eye as another beer bottle came flying past my head. If Dax hadn't yank me back, it would have hit me square in the temple.

The growl he let out filled the entire bar and silence reigned in its wake. Every head turned to look at him, including mine.

People stopped playing pool. The dart players stopped mid throw. The dance floor halted. The troublemakers, who'd thrown the bottle, had the good sense to hang their heads and go sit quietly at their table.

"You idiots!" I shouted in their direction.

With Dax here, his presence gave me a set of balls that I didn't usually assert.

"You could have killed Kamie", I screamed, gesturing wildly at the broken mirror and the bartender. "Do you see what this place has become?"

Dax let go of me and I started toward their table.

With my anger leading the way, I scolded them further to alleviate some of it from my system. "If I wanted to risk my life, it wouldn't be to serve neanderthals alcohol!"

No smiles. No taunting me back. Gunner and Kazz didn't even lift their heads.

Turning back around, Dax had stood from his table, glaring in their direction.

Damn. I had thought I was the one they were kowtowing to.

I didn't suppose that two massive males like them would care what a twenty six year old bar waitress had to say.

After the initial shock, I stepped back to the bar and saw Kamie, shaking like a leaf. My temper boiled up again.

Clenching and unclenching my fists, I saw red. Figuratively and literally.

There was blood running down the side of her face. Her blouse was torn and hanging in shreds up her left arm. The fear in her eyes had me shaking with rage.

Cody was behind the bar and had rushed over to get Kamie sorted out.

Molly, the other bartender, was stuck. Her feet were planted, body swaying slightly. She was in shock.

Whirling to face the two brutes in their seats, I closed the distance to meet them face to face. A deathly calm distorted my emotions.

"If you two so much as breathe wrong in her direction again, I will rip your heads from your shoulders and place them on spikes at the edge of the road."

Whoa. Where the hell did that come from? That was graphic even for me.

"Aurora. Come sit with me." Dax's deep voice beckoned to me. Familiar. Soothing.

My head cleared the last of the poisonous anger from my system and there was pain in my right hand.

Hot liquid leaked down my fingers, dripping off my wrist. The steak knife I didn't even remember picking up was slicing into my flesh.

I'd gripped it so hard, I'd drawn blood without feeling it happen.

Shaking the cobwebs from my brain. I shuddered.

Dax extended his hand in invitation like a lifeline. Walking to his side, I let the knife clatter to the ground as I crumbled into his arms.

It had been this way all my life.

The trauma of my past was not something I liked to dwell on, but I knew where this anger, this wicked savage that lived under my skin, came from.

Most of the time, my temper was locked away tight, in a box, in the recesses of my head.

When it got past my defenses, it scared the shit out of me.

I felt like two totally different people.

The one who put on a smile, talked friendly chit chat with the patrons, and helped in any way she could.

And then there was the other one. The one who wanted nothing more than to watch the world burn.

If therapy were accessible and affordable around here, I'd seriously consider going.

"You okay?" His gruff tone told me that his rage wasn't nearly as contained as it usually was.

That thought was oddly comforting. I wasn't the only one who was not in control of themselves.

"I just don't understand how those twits continue to function. They're the reason warning labels are on laundry pods." I glanced over at the pair.

They had apparently decided darts were a better settler of their argument.

He scoffed. It was so rare that he showed any amusement.

Turning out of his arms and staring up at his face, the upturned corner of his mouth made my lower belly flutter.

"Want to get out of here?" He meant it.

He never said anything that he didn't mean but I needed tonight's money to pay my bills this week.

"How about you come stay at my place after my shift?"

It was only ten o'clock. I had to help clean up after closing.

Five hours was a long time to hold onto this heat. "I'll drive straight home."

Watching his face go from amusement to harshly cold was not my idea of a *healthy-balanced relationship*.

It almost reminded me of some of the toxic ones in those damned books I read.

If I was a smarter person, I'd stop this in its tracks.

I was a glutton for punishment though.

I still wanted him. I wanted to feel his massive hands running their way down my ass. I wanted to feel them tangle in my hair as he yanked me closer, kissing me with reckless abandon.

Looking in his eyes, I felt the distance between us, and it only made me want to rip his clothes off.

If this was all there was to us, so be it. We could destroy each other's bodies without a single care. Lack of feelings be damned.

Shaking my head to clear the lust, I stepped away. "Never mind. I need to get some sleep tonight anyway."

I turned out of his arms and began to walk back to the bar to finish my shift.

Say something. Anything...

Of course he didn't. He just let me walk away.

It was going to be a miserable shift.

A long, hard... nope. Not going there!

Chapter Three

Three more fights had broken out by 1 am. Eventide reeked of sweat and alcohol.

The last hour before closing always dragged by painfully slow.

Dax left once the majority of the problem customers had.

With half the patrons gone, I figured now was my chance to corner Kyle.

Picking up a wet rag and casually cleaning the table next to where he'd slumped over that spread of papers all night, I glanced in his direction.

"You've been cranky tonight. What's with all the ..." I gestured to the stacks in front of him. "... well, this?"

Pushing the calculator away, his fingers ran through the mop of rusty copper hair on top of his head. Kyle wasn't much older than I was.

If I remembered correctly, he'd only graduated two years ahead of me.

His dad died a few years ago and he'd begrudgingly taken over the bar.

As far as I knew, all that he'd ever wanted growing up was to leave this town behind and make for a warmer climate. That never happened.

"Just bar paperwork. It's nothing." His words didn't match his tone.

Walking over, I glanced down at all of the invoices. There were a lot of larger numbers. And they looked to be in the red. Not good.

"If it was nothing, you'd be working in your office."

There was an elegantly handwritten note to the side of his laptop. The few words I caught made my heart drop.

"You know, you can talk to me. I'm a great listener."

Taking a long pull from his drink, his eyes assessed my face.

Whatever he saw there, he must have agreed because his subtle nod is all confirmation I got before he let out a long, breathy sigh.

"Don't tell anyone, but I hate Eventide."

Looking around to see if anyone heard or maybe his ancestor's spirits were hovering close, he shivered.

"It's been in my family for four generations. I don't want to let their legacy go but this was never my dream. I've missed out on the adventures I wanted to take, and the bar feels like a financial noose around my neck." His shoulders sagged with the weight of his confession.

Pulling out the chair next to him and sitting, the night's long shift settled heavy in my bones.

"Look, I know you wanted to travel and hike and what have you, but Eventide is a local treasure."

Taking a second to put myself in his shoes, the thought of being chained to a life I didn't choose had me changing direction.

"How bad is it, Kyle? The finances? The upkeep?" Blowing out a breath and setting my hands on the table to keep them from fisting at my sides, I looked up at his face.

The sadness and despair were overwhelming. "How draining is it on your soul?"... because really, that should be the only question I asked him that matters.

"It's bad, Rori. I don't even know how I let it get this bad. My dad never let on that the land, the building, the inventory." Pale faced, he looked like a specter as he spoke.

Shaking his head, he reached over and took my hand, and I gave him a gentle squeeze.

"I never knew what he was going through. I never really considered it. We all have our burdens. And when he'd gotten sick, I still thought nothing of this place."

Shifting his hair forward to cover his eyes, I knew he was fighting back tears.

"I took care of him, sure, but... I let him continue to take on the responsibilities of running this place. I don't know. Now I think that maybe the stress of that caused him to die early. Maybe it's what made him sick in the first place. I don't know anymore."

Hanging his head, I could tell he was waiting for my judgement, but I had none. He was right. We all had our burdens to bear.

Dropping the gross rag to the table, and reaching for him with both arms, I pulled him into a hug.

I'd wanted to rage at him earlier for putting all of our livelihoods in jeopardy, but that was selfish, not considering anything he was going through.

I was not good at the friend thing on a normal day, but this... *Damn, I suck.*

He hugged me back so tightly that I thought he might be as lonely as he was stressed. It wasn't a romantic hug. Just a need for contact.

"It's not your fault. And it wasn't like you planned to be stuck in this town forever. Your dad knew that."

No tears leaked onto my shirt, which I was grateful for, but his unstable breathing told me that he was trying to hold back the emotions he'd been fighting alone.

After a few silent moments passed, I said, "I'm sorry you've felt you had to go through this alone. I should have asked you if there was anything you needed over the years."

As usual, he tried to take the burden of everything on his own shoulders.

"No. It's not your fault. I had to grow up quick when he died." He huffed out a throaty laugh and pulled back. "I don't know if you remember, but I was kind of a tool before he got sick."

The corner of his mouth drew up on one side, but the smile didn't quite reach his eyes.

"I don't think of it that way. You were young. You still had grand ideas of what life would be." Releasing him and leaning back, a flood of memories rushed me. "I will never forget that time you and that asinine friend of yours... what was his name?"

"Bobby. God, I miss him." I didn't miss the gleam in his eye.

That was his best friend in high school. The guy was built like a twig. Always laughing. Always up for anything.

"Yeah, Bobby. When you and he road to the ski resort and handed out all of those fliers. The ones warning people of the dangers of the woods. Of the werewolves, doppelgangers. and changelings." I smacked him lightly on the arm and shook my head. "Whatever made you guys do that, I'll never know."

A shadow passed over his face but was gone in the next instance. Maybe I was seeing things.

"Where's Bobby now, anyways?"

Color rose to the apples of his cheeks as a grin lit the inside of his eyes.

Pushing aside the papers, he pulled a different note from the other side of the laptop. It was messily scrolled out.

"He wrote me a few months ago. He has a place in Costa Rica." His cup was nearly empty but the way he was drinking from it made me think that he was searching for words. "He's asked me to come stay for a while." Kyles eyes met mine. "I think... I think I'm going to sell Eventide."

It wasn't that I didn't know this was why I'd come over to the table in the first place. Hearing it out loud was just awful. Like a bell that couldn't be unrung.

My mouth opened. Then closed. Then opened again like a freshwater bass, only to snap shut. I had no words.

There was a pressure inside my head and my heart felt shredded. I'd never realized what this bar meant to me before now. And gods, did it hurt.

"Say something, Rori." Laying his hand on top of mine, the heat of the connection jolted me out of the cold I was drifting through. "I got a letter from someone, a stranger, who wants to buy her. I'd never really thought it was an option before it came."

He gestured to the paperwork. "If I'd have had any clue that she was sellable, I'd probably would have done it right after my dad passed."

Hmmm. Eventide did have an *Old Girl* feeling to it.

Like my truck, Matilda. Maybe that's why each of his ancestors couldn't part with the place.

They were... attached.

"Why wouldn't you think it's sellable?" I looked around. The bar had mostly cleared out.

Kamie left around midnight, leaving Molly to close the till and Cody to clean up the tables with me.

I noticed glass still laying in small piles around the floor. The peeling wallpaper on the wall by the bathroom. The derelict state of the place in general.

Kyle's face held all of the emotions he had. Not a poker player, that one.

"It's remote. No potential for investment. No growth." He shook his head like he was trying to dislodge the harsh reality of his legacy. "Look. I don't want to lie to you and say that I'd like to keep the place, but I get it. The way you feel. This has been my family's home for over a hundred years."

It meant something to him. Just not enough.

"This letter," he handed the elegantly scripted one to me. "It gives me an opportunity I thought I would never get."

Taking the letter, I read it quickly.

Basically, this stranger said he was moving to the area and would like to buy the place. That he'd lived in the area a long time ago and that Eventide held a special place in his heart.

That was weird but okay. It went on to say that he wanted to keep the staff and the local "feel", but wanted to freshen it up, make it a touch safer.

I could see why Kyle is thinking about selling.

"I want adventure, Aurora. I want to see other cultures. I want to surf instead of ski." He'd certainly thought this through. "I wasn't going to sell, but I dragged all these papers out here tonight to watch the place. Really see it for what it is. Not what it was back in the day, when we were growing up and had kid-colored glasses on. Even beer goggles can't help this place."

Sighing, I turned over the note and my eyes bugged out of my head. "Dear Gods. How many zeroes is that?"

A sheepish look and a youthful smile lit up his face.

"Yeah... that's the other selling point. I can live happily, not just comfortably, for the rest of my life." Finishing the last drops from his glass, he pushed it over to me. "You see there where it says that the staff will be well taken care of? I don't think that someone with this much to offer won't going to make a good owner. Hell, you might even be able to afford wants and not just needs if I sell."

A faraway look took over before he turned back to me. "Not if... When I sell."

"I don't like change, but that's my issue, Kyle. Not yours." Giving his hand a quick squeeze, I grabbed his empty glass and headed toward the bar.

Looking back over my shoulder, I smiled. "I'm glad you're taken your life in a new direction. We all need that at some point. I wish you all the luck in the world."

With a wink, there was nothing more to say.

Molly was behind the bar scrubbing out the glasses as I added his to the mix. Her hands were weathered and cracked.

Soapy water dripped from her long fingers as she finished up doing the bar glasses.

In her mid-thirties, she'd been working here for about a decade.

"It was a shit night," she said. "If these assholes don't start tipping more, I'm going to have to look for a new job."

That threat of hers was on repeat.

We all knew that there were not enough jobs here. And the ones at the resort outside of town didn't last long for the personalities of us A-type townies.

"You may want to in the coming days. Kyle is selling Eventide." Coming up from behind me, Cody's tub was full of dishes as he set them at the edge of the sink. "The new owners want to keep us on, though. And from what I understand, they are going to make sure we're taken care of. Whatever that means."

"Are you serious?" Gathering the trash together, Cody's voice stood out.

The dulcet tenor tone usually hovered above the gruff bass a lot of the local male patrons had.

It helped during busy nights when we didn't have time to do anything except holler across the bar to each other.

He turned to the end of the counter and pulled the bag closed. Without missing a beat, he yelled down to the couple at the end of the bar. "Last call was ten minutes ago. Finish that up and get out."

Kiah and Jayana, a couple of our regulars who were here most nights of the week, grumbled but tossed back the last of their drinks without a word.

Gathering their stuff, they headed out the door into the freezing night.

"Who closes tomorrow?" Molly turned to the board with a huff, like it was the most inconvenient thing she's been asked to do all night.

Typical. Her selfish attitude was insufferable.

"Looks like Hannah and Bitzy open tomorrow. Cody's scheduled at 5pm and you're scheduled to start at 7pm," I said.

Her face fell. "Well, damn. That means I'll have to stock the bar when I open Sunday. I freaking hate working by myself."

Saturday nights were generally the busiest. If the bar wasn't stocked after closing, she'd end up actually having to the work instead of pushing it off on one of us.

Bitzy didn't give two shits in regards to Molly. They'd both started working at Eventide around the same time and had never liked each other.

We often made wagers on what would piss Molly off today. And Bitzy did her best to hedge her bets.

It wasn't uncommon on Saturday nights for the tourists from the ski resort to venture out. Exploring the town.

They'd usually ended up here. Lost. In need of directions. Not having the good sense to pick up on the "Locals Only" vibe.

Dax was here most of those Saturdays if Cody wasn't working.

Out of all of Dax's friends, Cody was the most likable. I felt almost as safe with him having my back as I did with Dax.

Cody wasn't nice, but he was kind. He was cute. I thought of him more as the brotherly type of cute. With his double dimples and his playful smacks to my arm while we worked and joked, I couldn't see him any other way.

I'd seen women and men both flirt with him in the times we were inundated with patrons from the ski resort.

I could see it. That innocent smile. The way his brown hair fell in front of his eyes, playing bashful, when he was trying to get better tips.

He definitely knew how to play to his strengths.

I'd never seen him have more than a couple of beers, though. Maybe he was as rowdy as the rest of Dax's friends when he got drunk.

"Well, if we're done here, I'd like to go wash the stench of this place off me. 'Night guys."

Not giving Molly a chance to rope me in to doing her shift tallies, I grabbed my things and headed for the door.

Chapter Four

The parking lot was almost empty. Janie and Kiah were in their truck, letting it heat up or heating it from within, I couldn't tell.

It was the coldest night we'd had so far this season, and the wind was licking up the insides of my legs through the gaps under my pants.

Bitter cold. Freezing my nether regions cold.

Shivering, I took my gloves off to put the key in the door.

This old truck of mine might be a classic but it got me from point A to point B just fine.

It took a few minutes to get her revved enough to start producing heat.

The frost on the windshield was stubborn and the fresh powder covering Matilda's green hood told me that it was going to take a bit of time to warm her up.

She was the only good thing my dad ever gave me. It used to be only backhands and his temper that I got.

The old house we owned had to go through probate after he died.

I'd never expected it to be passed to me in his will, but it was.

However, he wasn't smart enough to put it in a living trust for me. I had to go through the mess of paying the capital gains taxes on the place.

That monthly fee was as bad as rent in some places around the area.

It was a run-down dwelling, like a lot of the places were this far north, but it had a working hot water tank, a fireplace to keep me warm, running water, and a comfy bed with four thick blankets to climb under.

It could be better. It could also be worse. I'd count my blessings for the solid roof over my head.

Finally warmed up enough to see out the windows, the parking lot was completely empty.

Thanks for the concern, guys. Geesh. The least they could have done was check to make sure I got Matilda moving before they took off.

She grumbled as I put her into gear. Sputtered. Then roared to life.

Yes! That's my girl.

Slowly scooting forward, the snow crunched under the new tires I'd spent the last couple of months saving for.

Ice had made several glossy sheets around the outer perimeter of the parking lot and there were a couple of slick spots along the main drive.

Tire marks and slush showed where some people must have had a few problems, so I stayed clear of those.

The woods along this stretch of mountain road leading to the highway had an "otherly" feel to them. It was late, or early, however you wanted to look at it, and an eerie quiet blanketed the snow.

I'd never encountered anything that the rumors said lurked in these trees, but I swore, I felt... something.

The highway had recently been cleared. Only a thin layer of snow laid ahead.

My house wasn't far, maybe ten minutes. Ten minutes if I wasn't crawling but look at me, the only turtle in the mountains.

I sped up just a bit. I didn't want to go too fast and slide off the side of the road in the dark.

There wasn't much in my truck to keep me warm if that should happen.

I'd been meaning to put some emergency supplies in here, but I always got distracted.

Headlights from another vehicle were a good five hundred yards behind me.

Glancing in the rear-view mirror for a split second too long, I looked in forward time to see something darted out in a blur in front of me crossing the road.

Shit!

What they didn't tell you in *how to drive in these conditions* videos was that instincts almost always overrode knowledge and common sense.

I'd hit the brakes. Big mistake.

A patch of ice made my back tires slide towards the embankment.

Steering the other way, heart racing, I managed to correct but it was an over correction and spun once. Twice. Halfway a third time before coming to a stop.

Crunching metal rang in my ears and I turned to see what I'd hit.

It was the middle of the road. There was nothing there.

What the hell?

A blur of movement caught my attention.

The passenger side window creaked but stopped as the headlights that had been behind me, caught up and stopped off to the side of the road.

Nothing was out there to see, but I felt eyes on me.

"Rori!" Dax opened my driver's side door and yanked me to his chest. "You're okay." Not a question. I'm not sure if he was comforting me or himself. "I've got you. You're safe."

My heart began to slow. The cold leached in from the open door and the shock of the situation started wearing off.

Looking around, I didn't see anything. No animals. No carcass. Nothing that could have made that blurred movement that had me nearly sliding off of a mountain. Or the sound of crunching metal that brought me to a stop.

"Where'd it go?" He was in the vehicle behind me. He might have seen what happened. "Where's the thing I hit?"

Dax squeezed me tighter. "Aurora, there's nothing out here. I saw you slide on the ice and start spinning."

My head whipped around in all directions. The boughs of the trees hung heavy with fresh snow, making it impossible to see anything in the forest on either side.

It couldn't have been my imagination.

What was he even doing here?

Shoving off his arms and walking to the back of the truck, a patch of ice nearly had me slipping onto my ass, but I caught myself on the side of the bed.

There was a small dent by the tail end that I didn't remember being there before.

It was difficult to see anything in the shade of the trees, even with a nearly full moon.

I must be losing my mind.

Dax made his way to where I was standing and placed his hand at the small of my back.

"Might have grazed a deer." His eyes warily glanced around the perimeter. "Come on. Let's get you home."

There was no wind and yet the tree's leaves were rustling. A shiver that had nothing to do with the cold ran the length of my body.

Leaning into his touch, I felt safer.

Still, there was an odd sense that I was being watched.

I shivered again before letting him guide me back to Matilda's cab.

Grabbing for the driver's side door, he opened it but had me scootch across the seat. "I'll drive you home."

"What about your Jeep? You just going to leave it here?"

I appreciated his concern. It was more attentive affection than he'd ever shown me.

I couldn't help feeling there was more to why he was being so gallant. Maybe overprotective might have been the better word.

"I most certainly am." The corner of his mouth curled up but the hardness in his eyes told a different story. "I'll call the boys to come and get it."

Fifteen minutes later we we're at my house. We'd made the drive in silence as I watched his eyes roam in every direction the entire way.

Coming to open my door was a first. I didn't even know he possessed those kinds of manners.

The door lock was iced over, and it took me a few extra minutes to get us inside, but once over the threshold, he relaxed his stiff posture notably.

"I'll get us a fire going." With the last of the firewood outside in the woodshed, I turned back to the door. "I have to go get some more wood."

Snagging my arm quickly in his grip, he stopped me in my tracks. *What the hell?*

"You've been through a fright tonight. I'll get it."

This was getting weird. I couldn't remember a single time where he'd ever offered to do anything domestic for me. For anyone.

I couldn't shake the feeling that he didn't want me outside tonight.

"Okay." Releasing my arm, he headed back out without another word. "Get extra for tomorrow, if you don't mind," I called after him.

With his slight nod, I closed the door and made my way to the kitchen.

The adrenaline wearing off made my mouth feel like the desert.

It was taking longer than usual but ten minutes later, Dax banged on the door. His arms full up to the top of his chin with firewood.

"Where would you like this?"

In the basket next to the fireplace was the obvious answer but my smart mouth couldn't let the dumb question go.

"In the sink is fine." I deadpanned.

If I thought he'd laugh, I was wrong. Tension rolled off him in waves, crashing harshly through the room.

Seeing that he wasn't in the mood for my usual Rori sarcasm one oh one, I said, "Over by the fireplace."

Striking a match and opening the flue, a fire roared to life. The heat filled the small space quickly and Dax motioned for us to sit on the decade old couch.

Grabbing two small pillows and a throw cover to drape over us, his chest heaved up and down as his arms wrapped around me.

"You lost control, and I thought you'd be hurt. And I... didn't like it." My heart stuttered. The words were said like a shameful confession. Touching even.

"I saw something dart out in front of me and then I must have hit the ice wrong." Tightening his grip, a brush of a kiss grazed the top of my head.

The sound of him breathing in my scent sent ripples of desire down between my thighs. I was a sucker for simple things like that.

Try as I might, I couldn't turn. I wanted to kiss him and tell him thank you and a million other emotional things that might lead to something more than just physical, but he had me pinned.

If I didn't know better, I might think him being here with me had nothing to do with *us* and everything to do with whatever had been in those woods.

"Want to go upstairs?" The lust in my voice made it clear where my mind was.

Another moment passed in silence. Dax grabbed another blanket from the back of the sofa and threw it over the both of us.

"I think I'd rather sleep here, just like this, if you don't mind?" A question. So rare for him to ask anything.

Something was off but I'd wanted closeness for so long I couldn't bring myself to deny his request.

With my thoughts still wrapped around more adult themes, the sarcasm in my tone leaked out in full force. "Alright. We'll just sleep together. Here. In front of the fire."

Another kiss to my hair, gentle, tender... weird.

The next morning, I awoke alone.

He'd slipped out sometime after the sun came up.

I knew this because when the light poured in around the curtains earlier, I'd shifted and buried my head into his chest to block it.

Or maybe I'd dreamt the whole thing.

It wouldn't be the first time.

Chapter Five

Saturday morning meetings were super rare.

Kyle must have signed on the dotted line last night if he was calling all employees in at 10 am.

I hated getting up this early, but he'd left a voicemail asking that I try to make it in on time.

He knew me well. I couldn't even blame him for texting the message too.

I was not exactly coherent before noon. And if I knew him, he'd be texting again in the next few minutes, just to make sure I was on my way.

Matilda was warming up while I finished my coffee and brushed my hair out.

It was a rat's nest from sleeping on the couch but dolling myself up for a work meeting at the bar wasn't going to happen.

Everyone there had seen my no-makeup, messy hair, bags under eyes look anyway.

Going to the window and looking out to check Matilda's progress, something dark jumped in front of me.

I startled so bad that I dropped my dirty cereal bowl and unused milk splashed all over the floor.

Stupid cat. I loved him, but the mischief he liked to cause, kept me on my toes.

Aries' black fur and green eyes locked on mine as I grabbed the rag off the counter.

"You're just going to have to wait now, aren't you?"

That little meow got me in the feels, every time. Cocking his head to the side and rubbing on the sill, I could hear him purring right through the glass.

"Oh, alright. Get in here, you little brat." I couldn't help spoiling him. He was too cute for his own good.

As soon as I pushed the window open, he smacked at the snow, covering the back of the sink and counter, then slinked in to head butt me as he passed.

If I had a nickel for every time his roguery caused me undue angst, I'd be able to afford my monthly bills.

I kept his food in the pantry, because let's face it, if he had opposable thumbs, I'd need a second job to support his eating habits.

Glancing at the clock after feeding the damned cat, I was running late, as usual.

Bundling up properly, the coffee pot was turned off. Keys in hand. Wallet secured. Alright, checklist was done.

Grabbing my trusty granola bar and travel mug, the last thing to do was lock up.

The air smelled clean, crisp. Fresh snow blanketed the roads, so I would have to be careful.

Learning to drive in treacherous conditions was Vermont 101.

Last night's ice incident was nothing new but there was an underlying element to my nervousness I couldn't explain.

And the way Dax acted didn't freak me out, but it did put me on edge.

He'd never been chivalrous.

It was nice but, out of nowhere? It was peculiar, to say the least.

And there was Kyle. My pocket vibrating pulled me from my thoughts.

"OMW", I shot back my automatic response, and inched Matilda forward passed the heaping pile of snow the plow truck pushed to the corner end of my street.

The plow trucks had been out early this morning.

My house wasn't far from Jay Country Store, maybe a mile or so. Eventide was about a mile in the opposite direction.

This main thoroughfare had to be cleared as it was a main vein for the area.

Pulling into the parking lot, there were more cars here than there should be for a before open employee meeting.

Nice cars. Cars that weren't equipped for this kind of terrain.

The bar was dark compared to the bright sun shining outside and it took more than a few blinks for my eyes to adjust.

"There she is," I heard Bitzy call out. "Here I was thinking that I might have to go drag you out of bed."

Glancing around, Kyle was standing in front of the online jukebox.

There were two of the most beautiful people I'd ever seen in person sitting in chairs to his left. Movie stars didn't even compare. They certainly didn't fit in around these parts.

Scanning the room, with a quick inhale of surprise, I drank in the sight of Dax sitting in his booth. Cody and Kazz were sitting with him.

Kazz didn't look hungover, but how could he not be? The dude drank his body weight in alcohol last night.

Molly was being her impatient self. Tsking and rolling her eyes. Trying to make sure everyone knew that she was annoyed.

Being the ass that I was, I walked even slower towards the other employees, watching her arms fold over her chest in frustration.

"We don't have all day. Some of us have things to do, Rori."

The way my brain worked sometimes brought a tear of joyous wickedness to my eyes. Anything I could do in opposition, even in the slightest, felt right when she was acting like a superior bitch.

Kyle cleared his throat and drew my attention back to him as I took a seat between Bitzy and Kamie. Dylan was as silent as ever, but Hannah's mouth popped open in surprise.

"Good morning, Rori. Nice of you to join us."

My smile was genuine when our gaze connected. "I'd say good morning, but I'm not a liar."

I loved that responding grin. I'd be sad when he was no longer here, but I was happy for him. He deserved to get out of this town.

"Okay guys. On to business." The downcast of his eyes denoted his nervousness.

As far as I knew, only Molly and Cody knew about the situation. Maybe I shouldn't have told them last night, but he never asked me not to.

"I've sold Eventide." Gasps went up from Bitzy and Kam.

Ouch. My head smarted from the smack Bitzy landed to the back of it. Somehow, I was to blame for not telling my bestfriend.

I was kind of surprised at how little of time it took from Kyle making the decision last night to the sale apparently this morning.

"That fast? I mean, is it all finalized already?" Gods, I knew this was coming and it was still not easy to believe it was real. "I'm happy for you and all. I just didn't think it would happen overnight."

The beautiful female cleared her throat. "We're not the new owners. We're his..." she looked back at the male sitting next to her and he subtly nodded his encouragement. "... associates. Friends. He should be here soon. Just wrapping up some paperwork with the attorneys."

I hadn't heard Dax move closer. His tone full of contempt. "And what? He just sent you ahead like good little pets?"

Starting forward to apologize on his behalf, he snagged my waist, pulling me to his side.

"Really, Dax? What are you even doing here?" I chastised.

Yanking myself free, I stepped from his side and started forward again. This time he didn't stop me, but he did shadow me.

The female's hand was freezing as we shook.

"I'm sorry about him." He growled his disapproval. "I'm Aurora, but people call me Rori."

Her eyes met mine and the intensity of her gaze held me captive.

Kazz growled this time from Dax's side.

What the actual hell?

"I'm Karalissa, but I go by Lissa" Ushering the male forward, she gestured to her side. "And this is Seiran."

He was handsome. Clean cut. Nice jawline. He had a calming way about him. Innocent, yet still masculine.

I couldn't decide if the way he diverted his eyes from holding mine for too long was timidness or respect.

Either way, it made him feel less imposing and I liked him more because of it.

Most of the males in my life were domineering. This was a refreshing change.

Kyle fake coughed loudly, trying to return our attention back to him. Molly was still bitching. The rest of them had quieted down.

"Anyway, like I was saying, I sold Eventide and I'll be heading out on my new life's adventure on Wednesday. Mister Doraglia will be here to meet you all shortly. We wanted to greet you guys together and let you voice any concerns you might have."

Cody came to stand beside me while Dax and Kazz hung back to their table. I appreciated Cody as a fellow employee.

It did seem odd that yet another one of Dax's buddies was standing close enough to me for it to feel overprotective.

If I hadn't read another good enemies to lovers fantasy book last week, I'd have thought they were guarding me... but that was just silly.

"Are we all keeping our jobs?" Bitzy was more than a little bit cranky.

I probably should have called her and given her a heads up when I got home last night.

So much had happened within a span of a few short hours, I'd just wanted to sleep once Dax and I made it back to my house.

Whoa. All of a sudden, my insides felt wonky.

Dizziness washed through me. Swaying on my feet slightly, I stumbled.

Cody gripped me under my elbow and kept me from falling.

The front door swung open.

The most scrumptiously magnificent looking man I'd ever seen stood just inside the doorway.

And to my surprise, he was staring straight at Me.

Chapter Six

T he winter sun poured in from behind the male, lighting his broad shoulders, down to his well-dressed feet.

Bits of snow clung to his dark hair. The smallest bit of salt and pepper peeked through the sides, but his face looked no older than late twenties, early thirties.

No breath misted in front of his lips. A crisp, fresh scent rushed to me on a sudden wind from the opened door.

Two hands wrapped around my waist, pulling me back, while another wrapped around one of my wrists.

I hadn't even realized I'd been walking towards the stranger.

Shaking from my stupor, I regained myself... somewhat.

Dax's arms remained a vise around my middle but the hand on my wrist was Cody's. He released it as I pointedly stared down at his fingers.

"Geesh, guys. What a way to make a first impression," I said, but Dax didn't move.

Low growling rumbled from his chest.

Yanking hard against his arms, he wouldn't relent. "Dax! Let. Me. Go."

The hair on top of my head warmed as he loosed a huff of breath. I'd bet he didn't even know he'd been holding it.

When I turned my attention back to the new owner, his lips were turned up, gritting his teeth. *Well, this is going swimmingly.*

Dax let me go but stayed at my back. Cody side stepped me, landing between Bitzy and Kamie.

Eyeing his two associates... friends... whatever they were to him, Karalissa's chin dipped slightly.

Kyle rushed forward to welcome him inside.

The room wasn't small by any means but as he fully entered, the air became non-existent.

I couldn't take my eyes off him. There was something all-consuming about his presence.

No one else in the bar appeared to have any problems making their feet and mouths work.

Here I was, staring. Unable to put a coherent thought together.

"Mister Doraglia. Welcome to Eventide," Kyle said.

Motioning around to all of us, he took a step into our ranks, pointing us out individually.

"Molly, Kamie, Hannah, Dylan, Bitzy, Cody..."

Mr. Doraglia gave a small sneer as Cody was introduced but I didn't think anyone else noticed.

"...and Rori." I'd never seen Kyle so business like. It didn't suit him.

"Hut hum." Dax piped up, pretending to clear his throat. If he was any closer to me, we'd need to be naked.

Kyle grumbled under his breath but didn't mix words. "These are a couple of the regulars... Kazz and Dax."

With darkness swirling in his obsidian eyes, they had a red tint that went all the way through. His lashes were long and feathery, yet somehow, masculine.

I found myself mesmerized each time the light hit just right.

The bow of his lips had a slight, natural pout that drew me in. Like a moth to a flame.

"I guess going by Daxayrius is a mouthful." His voice was velvet raked over coals. Sultry, deep, and confident.

I thought I might actually swoon.

Snapping out of my stupor when my mind caught up to his words, I subtly shook my head to clear the daze from my train of thoughts.

"Wait. Do you two know each other?" Now my head was really spinning.

This might explain Dax's behavior the last few days. I'd been wondering why he didn't like this guy. Maybe he'd known who the buyer was.

Mister Doraglia offered his hand to me and instinctively, I took it.

It must have been freezing out there. His hands were artic.

"Nice to meet you. Rori, is it? I'm Alexander but you may call me Xander." Throwing a casual glance around the room, "You all may. No need for formality here. We'll be one big, happy family before long."

His throaty legato voice. Smooth. It rang with authority.

"I'm Aurora, but people call me Rori." I didn't know why I felt the rush of embarrassment fill my cheeks. Or the heat of other areas clouding my senses.

Dax was right here. I enjoyed our Not relationship. I knew I'd feel disrespected if the situation was reversed and needed to get a grip.

"I get the sense that you don't care for that nickname," Xander said. It was a small wonder that he'd taking an interest in me at all.

Clearly, he and Dax had history. Maybe that's why he was showing me attention in the first place.

Pulling away from the over-grown wall of muscle at my back, my eyes traveled back to the newcomer in front of me.

There was definitely something familiar there, but I simply couldn't place it.

"It's fine," I said on a sigh. "It just..." Sighing again, I shrugged my shoulders.

"Just what?" With Xander's full attention focused solely on me, the intensity of his stare sliced through my non-committal response, and I leaned in to tell him the truth without thinking.

"Well, it doesn't fit me." My feet were planted firmly. Raising my chin and shaking the cobwebs from my thoughts, I tried again. "I mean... even Aurora doesn't ... fit." *Gods, kill me now.*

That gaze of his speared right through me.

I owed Dax more respect than standing there making a fool of myself. I was practically drooling.

"Hmmm. Perhaps you're right. What would you prefer me to call you instead?" Crossing his arms and cocking his head, he studied my face like he was actually interested in my response.

A growl from behind me told me Dax was at his limit. I stepped back into the circle of his arms. I wasn't being fair to him.

Lifting my chin, I said the only thing that made sense. "Rori will be fine, Xander. I don't need a special nickname."

Bitzy came forward, dragging Kamie with her. "I'm Elizabeth, but Bitzy is fine."

I couldn't help noticing the lust in her eyes. Irrationally, I wanted to lash out at her. How dare her single, eligible ass lust after the same guy my tongue was waggling for?

He was a god of old, standing in the dankest of gloomy places. He shined so brightly that... wait. Stop it. Get a grip. *Damn it! ...*

I had been casually seeing Dax for nearly a year now. I wasn't some bed hopping, small town hussy.

Kamie blushed as Xander gently shook her hand.

That bouncy long hair of hers came forward to hide her embarrassment a bit too late.

The dimple in her right cheek made her innocent face show like a child. I'd often found it endearing.

As Seiran came to stand next to Xander, his looks mirrored hers.

He, too, had an innocent face with a dimple on his left cheek. Though, in all fairness, he still looked very masculine. Not boyish, just innocent, gentle.

Kyle wanted us all to feel comfortable with the new way of things before he left. That's why he'd called this meeting.

He wanted to make his exit with a clear conscience.

I had a few hours of notice to wrap my head around it. So did Molly and Cody, but for everyone else, it might take some time...

Or maybe not.

Hannah, Bitzy, and Dylan looked at the new owner and his two counterparts. Their expressions were as awed as mine.

Maybe the situation hadn't had time to sink in yet, but I didn't suspect that Kyle would be missed too sorely.

Not that he wasn't a good boss or anything.

I just had a feeling that the new ownership was going to shake things up.

And sometimes change, for better or worse, was just what small town folks needed.

Even if they railed against it.

Kyle brought all of our attention back to the front.

"Listen up guys. I want to turn over the reins to Mr. Doraglia." With a quick glance over at him, he corrected himself. "Sorry... to Xander. I know things will be different around here over the next few weeks. I'm trusting you all with my family's legacy. So don't be dicks to him."

Smiles crinkled in his and Xander's eyes, but Lissa pressed her lips tight.

Perhaps she wasn't relishing the idea of arguing with employees about the changes they were planning to make. Or maybe she didn't like the use of profanity.

If that was the case, I'd say she was in for a rude awakening. Eventide was a bar, after all.

"Right." Clapping Kyle on the back, Xander took front and center. "Kyle's right. I want to keep the local feel, but I am making changes. This whole place needs a makeover. And I can understand that a few of you may take issue with that."

Glancing at each one of us in turn, his tone turned more serious.

"However, I've paid good money to acquire this place and I'm willing to let all of you keep your jobs. I'm even going to be paying you a lot more to help make the transition. Not just from Kyle to myself, but from dive bar to a local bar that will be serving food."

Some protests went up around the room. Dax swore behind me. Of course, Molly started her bitching right away.

I didn't see a problem. More money. More customers. That meant more tips.

I was going to assume we wouldn't be working overtime because he didn't seem the type to make our lives miserable.

I could be wrong, but I didn't think I was. It was apparent that he had enough cash to throw around. He'd just hire more people.

Staring out over all of us, he quietly waited for the others to settle down.

No yelling. No raising his voice. Simply... waited.

It was so at odds to what I'd grown use to my whole life. I was kind of unnerved by his stillness.

Once everyone had thrown their individual hissy fits, he started again. "As I was saying. I will allow you all to continue your employment here, with raises, but this is now my establishment. If you have suggestions, great. I will be more than happy to hear them."

His eyes traveled to Molly. Kyle must have given him a heads up about her. And that thought had me smiling fiendishly.

"I will not, however, listen to grown, well paid men and women gripe or have fits when something new is introduced. If you find that you are unable to keep this workplace positive, you won't be employed here for long."

The sultry undertone in his command triggered a low rumbling in my nether regions.

Firm, kind, and confident. If this guy ended up being an asshole, I might just fall in love.

Dax jerked me back by my neck...

Painful? No... Embarrassing? Absolutely!

"What the hell, Dax?" I exclaimed.

Xander's glare snagged on the hand still holding me.

Growls erupted from both Dax's group and to my surprise, from Xander's group as well. Literal growls... from grown people.

It felt like I was in some bad B movie.

Dax snarled from just behind the shell of my ear. A shiver ran the length of my spine. "You were walking towards him... Again!"

I couldn't tell if that was jealousy in his tone... or hurt.

Either way, I was furious.

Chapter Seven

Pulling away from Daxayrius Balodyn might have been a bad move from others, but I was over controlling males.

My hands clenched into fists at my side, and I strode to the door. Kicked it open.

Not bothering with my jacket or Matilda's keys, I couldn't go far but, at least, I could leave the testosterone filled atmosphere behind me as I walked to Eventide's side patio.

Ashtrays and cigarette butts were littered around tables and in the grass. Out of town smokers tended to be a nuisance.

You couldn't smoke indoors in Vermont. A law which I greatly appreciated, but some of them gave us a hard time because they'd have to take their nasty habit outside.

I could sympathize with their dilemma. Addiction must be hard if you were willing to lose feeling in your extremities just to feed it.

We didn't cave into their demands to smoke indoors just because we were an off-the-beaten-path dive bar though.

Kyle and his late father had always put their employee's health before the all mighty dollar.

I didn't think I could work here if I had to breathe in the poisonous toxins from other people's exhales all night long. This job was difficult enough already.

Wiping some snow off one of the small tables, I sat on the cold, wet bench seat. Even the overhanging tarp didn't provide much cover from the elements out here.

Rustling trees to my left caught my attention. I knew off the wildlife that roamed these mountains. The thought set my nerves on edge.

Whimpers and snarls sounded deeper into the woods and all of a sudden it didn't feel like a good idea to be out here by myself.

Pushing away from the table, I stumbled backwards but Bitzy grabbed my elbow just before I fell. I hadn't even had enough awareness to realize she'd followed me.

"You okay?" Her tone was annoyed and concerned at the same time. "It took me a minute to get out here because I didn't want any of those guys following you out."

Brushing the debris from my pants, I straightened up and took the jacket she offered me. It wasn't mine but it would do the job for now.

"Men!" I said, throwing my hands in the air. "When will I ever learn?"

Her golden brown eyes locked in on mine. The blue rings that encircled her iris's glowed brighter whenever she was feeling emotional. They were a telltale sign of her frustration right now.

"Never. Apparently." Letting out a hefty breath, the mist was thick around her face.

If she crossed her arms any tighter, they'd probably be able to squash melons.

"You sure know how to pick them. Don't you?" her tone admonishing. She wasn't wrong.

I loved that little smoosh she got to her nose when she was lecturing me. It made her words less sharp. I knew she loved me.

My returning ear to ear grin broke her attempt at chastising my choices.

With a light chortle, she plopped into the seat I'd just vacated.

"What was all of that about anyway? Dax was rather over-protective back there." Tapping the seat beside her, she asked me to sit.

"I don't quite know. I nearly wiped-out last night on my way home from work." *Oops.* I forgot to tell her that. "He stayed with me at my house last night, but we slept on the couch."

With a deep breath in. And then out again, she gathered her thoughts in that way she did whenever I'd annoyed her or hurt her feelings.

"First. I'm glad that you are okay. Second," she raised her voice and smacked me on the arm at the same time. "Why didn't you tell me!?" I started to answer but she silenced me with her hand. "Third, how was it on the couch?"

Leave it to Bitzy to care more about my sex life than my actual life.

"We didn't do anything." At her incredulously raised brows, I added, "Honestly, we just slept there while he held me."

It wasn't just me. Dax was acting out of sorts. At least, out of sorts in relationship to us.

Today's antics were a continuation of last night's craziness between us.

"I'd better go in and break up the fight. Xander just bought the place this morning and Dax is already throwing around his machismo."

"It's fine. Kyle kicked him and his cronies out right after you went out the door."

The way she refers to Dax's friends always cracked me up. Who uses the word "cronies" anymore?

I'd just remembered the snarls and whimpers in the woods. I'd forgotten them when Bitzy had shown up and I'd fallen.

Glancing around warily, I pulled her up by the elbow.

"You ready to go back in and face the music?" I knew that playful tone.

Her amusement would be at my expense once we were face to face with Sir Dreamboat in there.

"I suppose we have to." I threw my arm into her hands. "Go on then. Drag me in to die of embarrassment at the hands of the hunky new owner."

She laughed. "He is rather handsome, isn't he?" *Understatement of the century*. "His friends are nice to look at too. It seems a bit unfair to us townies. We'll have to don makeup and clean ourselves up better just to fit into our own bar... Oh, sorry. Pub."

"Pub? Is that what he's changing it in to?" I must have missed that part of his speech when I was swooning.

"Isn't that what you call a bar that serves food but isn't quite a restaurant?" She might be right, but I couldn't say for certain.

Before we reached the door, Bitzy hauled me to a stop.

"Now, don't go getting mad or defensive or anything. And don't bite my head off, but..." The way she hesitated made me feel like a monster. Was I really that bad? "I think that you should pull back from Dax."

I didn't know what else I thought she might say. That definitely wasn't even in the stratosphere.

As far as I knew, she liked Dax.

At least, she liked living vicariously through me in the sex life department when it came to him.

"All I'm saying is that when it was just a good time, he was a god. It seems like he wants to be more now." Shrugging, she opened the door and dropped her voice. "He just proved to be another one of those asshole males that you tend to go for."

She had me there. I obviously had a type.

"I think you might be right. There's more beefcake in town now and I am suddenly starving!" Waggling my eyebrows at her, she giggled.

"You shouldn't play with fire, but damn! What a way to burn." Those knowing eyes looked through me as she waggled her brows now too.

Gods, I loved this crazy woman.

Shuffling through the opened door, hanging our jackets on the rack, and heading over to a couple of seats behind the others, I sighed dramatically.

"I could see myself fancying a buffet." Looking at Xander, the hairs on my neck rose. Leaning in and whispering, I said,

"Ya know, smorgasbord style. Who says I can't have steak and prime rib too? A girl can't live on batteries alone."

Looking to the front where Xander sat while Lissa was going over the upcoming plans, the corner of his mouth pulled up on one side.

If I didn't know better, I'd swear he'd heard us.

It might just be time to grab a fork.

Chapter Eight

L ast night we sent Kyle off with a bang. Hannah ran the bar and Luke bar backed but we all helped out.

Tuesday nights were usually slow anyway.

There'd been a dozen or so patrons throughout the night, but it was primarily just us staff and Kyle.

My head was pounding this morning.

Okay, afternoon. If I woke before 11:00 it was a miracle.

I was built for nights. From dusk to dawn is where I thrived.

When I was little, my mom used to tell me that I was her little night owl. She would hoot at me and tell me how wise I was for such a little girl.

After she died, my dad resented me for looking like her. The pain of her loss was too much for him.

A few days after her funeral, the casseroles ran out. The pantry was empty. The neighbors stopped coming by to check in on us.

I was seven years old and had to learn to take care of myself. Feed myself. Wash myself. Get myself to school. I missed her so much and he was no help.

He would drink himself into a stupor and pass out wherever he happened to be.

The porch. The woodshed. The middle of the living room floor.

As I got older and grew to fill out, fate was my enemy.

I loved that I look like my mom, but my drunken father sometimes couldn't remember that I wasn't her.

The first time his hands found places they shouldn't be, I was thirteen years old.

Once he realized I wasn't her, his hands became angry. They'd make their way across my face, my back, around my neck.

My brain still tended to disassociate his hands and the acts he would commit from him as a person.

The child in me clung to the daddy he'd been before my mom died.

It put me off alcohol for a long time. I had never even had a drink before I started working at Eventide a few years ago, so I didn't drink often, but when I did, gods did I pay for it.

Aries' meow was loud and obnoxious when he was hungry, and it raked the raw nerve endings in my swollen head.

Hoping the aspirin and my coffee would help the pounding subside, I opted for a greasy bacon, egg, and cheese sandwich fresh from the freezer to the microwave.

Patience was only a virtue when you had endless amounts of time.

The construction crew would begin at the bar today and I was glad I wasn't working. The sounds of demolition were not my idea of a good time.

Dax needed dealt with, so maybe I'd head over to his place after my shower.

The sooner I got this over with the better.

I could stop by the bar to see how Kamie, Dylan and Bitzy were holding up afterwards. They'd be working today through all of that mess.

Dylan hadn't worked there for that long, maybe six months. He was nice enough. Kept to himself.

He was okay to look at, with his rusty copper hair and green eyes.

I'd never really thought about him because he was so quiet. He did his job and left after each shift. No fuss. No muss.

Secretly, I wanted to have a peek in on the new owner too. There was just something about him that made my kitty purr.

I was going to have to be delicate. Men like Dax weren't used to being cast aside. As long as he used his words, not his fists, I'd consider the conversation a win.

Matilda was all warmed up. Gassed up. And ready to hit the pavement.

I loved this old gal. She'd been the closes thing that I had to family left since my dad died.

Bitzy was like a sister, but she'd only been in my life for a few years. We'd met at Eventide after I was hired.

She'd walked right up to me, crossed her arms over her chest, looked me up and down and said, "You'll shadow me. And don't think about taking advice from Molly."

I was only three hours into my first shift before I realized why she'd warned me about Molly. We'd been thick as thieves ever since.

I loved how she'd mother hen me. I could push back but mostly it felt nice to have someone in my life who truly cared about me.

She saw all of my flaws and didn't push me away. I loved her even more for seeing me, not the mask I'd wear.

Bitzy saw everything. I'd sometimes felt like her observational skills were a sixth sense the way she'd wield them.

She was my ride or die but, Matilda had been there since I was born.

There were times I'd have flashbacks of my mom in the driver's seat, doing the air ride with her hand out the window.

Or her in the passenger side of the bench seat. Me in the middle between my dad and the blackberries we'd all gone picking.

It would hit me from time to time that I had no family left.

Matilda filled that void the best an old truck could. She was Auntie Matilda. And I wouldn't trade her for the world.

Dax's house was nice. It wasn't overly big or grand, but it was roomy and fairly nice to look at.

A couple of cars were in the driveway. His was under the covered carport. Heavens forbid it be exposed to the elements.

There were usually at least three or four people hanging out around there at any given time.

I didn't understand how he could stand it. Alone time was a big thing for me. The way his friends were always around wore on my nerves.

Kiah opened the door half a second before I knocked. He and Janie were at the bar most nights of the week. Or at least, when I was working, that's what it seemed like.

I hadn't known his name nickname was short for Hezekiah until Dax and I started hanging out and he yelled it across the house.

At first, I thought his hollering meant he was mad, and I'd instinctually cringed back into a tight ball.

After seeing my fear and we'd been dating a bit longer, he learned about my past and didn't yell anymore when I was there.

"Come on in, Rori." I so rarely got to hear his voice. His face was always attached to Janie's. "Dax is in the game room."

"Thanks, Kiah. Where's Janie?" Glancing around the foyer, I didn't see her anywhere.

"She and Loxy needed a few things. They drove to Stowe. They'll be back tonight." *Interesting*.

I wondered at why he didn't go with them, but it was none of my business.

It didn't matter to me if he was here. I was just glad that Loxy wasn't at the house.

Loxana was Dax's cousin. When she was in town, I'd usually tried to make myself scarce.

It wasn't that I didn't like her, but I got the feeling that she didn't like me.

She was pretty, curvy and tough. Dax said that her feisty attitude didn't mean she didn't like me. That it was just how she was.

I didn't know if I believed him, but I gave her a wide birth whenever she was in town, just in case.

She only visited about once every four months, so it wasn't like I had to deal with her on a daily basis. And I didn't want Dax's family to not like me. Kazz was his cousin too and he'd never made me feel the way Loxy did.

When I made myself too busy while she visited, it was about self-preservation more than anything.

"Everything okay?" Not that Kiah had ever confided in me, but I couldn't help my curiosity in asking.

A quick, low chuckle was his only response. Motioning for me to go find Dax, he shut the door, cutting off the cold air that had been seeping into the room.

The house was quieter than normal.

The game room hosted a 65-inch tv. A few different gaming systems. A large couch. And a pinball machine. The whole thing was set up like a man cave.

Dax sat at the one end of the couch, a book in hand. *I didn't know he was a reader.* Whatever the book was, his rapt attention was consumed in the story. I didn't think he noticed me come into the room.

With a quick intake of breath, his eyes flashed dark for a split second. Laying his book aside, I stopped at the way he patted his knee.

"Am I a dog meant to heel?" The hairs on the back of my neck stuck up as goosebumps rose along my arms.

For someone who couldn't fight and was as fearful as I was, my sarcastic mouth and flippant attitude threw my hat into the ring way too often.

Glancing at the title of the book he was reading, I understood what he'd been attempting. "Hey! Is that one of mine?"

"I didn't think you'd mind. It's quite illuminating." The stray hair that hung to the side of his face fell across his eyes and he swiftly ran a hand through the soft locks.

Heat rose to the apples of my cheeks. It was one of my "why choose" fantasy novels. I liked reading them but that didn't mean I wanted to be in one.

At least, I didn't think I did. My mind wandered to Xander without my permission.

"Make sure you return it when you're through reading. That's part of a series." I couldn't tell if he was intrigued or perhaps aroused from reading the book. This wasn't going well so far. "We need to talk."

"That doesn't sound ominous or anything." I sometimes forgot how his voice alone could send me over the edge as he dropped it down and made each word sing in the back of his throat. "Sit." Not a command. An invitation.

Fidgeting with the zipper on my jacket, I took a seat next to him on the couch. *Gods, why does this have to be so hard?*

"I have fun with you, Dax. And the sex is great. And you're a great guy and..." I couldn't stop babbling.

The way my stomach roiled it felt like it was trying to escape my body.

Taking a deep breath, I blurted it out. "I don't want us to date anymore."

Not so clean cut but at least I got it out. I didn't know what to do with my hands. Time was stretching on, and he hadn't said anything yet.

Maybe I should leave; pick my guts up off the floor, stuff them back inside, and head out the door.

"I was thinking the same thing." Taking my hands in his, he brushed a kiss against my knuckles. "I think we should be exclusive. Not simply dating. Not just sex and fun."

Wait... what? *Oh no.* How did I get myself into these things?

Bitzy was right. I was a disaster.

Gently pulling my hands from his, I tried again. "That's not what I meant, Dax. I meant that things like that scene back at Eventide a couple of days ago won't be happening again. I meant that controlling, possessive males won't be dictating my life."

Sitting back and rubbing his chin, I could see the clockworks turning in his mind.

This hadn't gone to plan at all. I should have stayed in bed and read all day.

Snatching my keys out of my pocket, my legs wobbled from nerves as I stood and headed for the door.

Before I made it two whole strides, he was in front of me.

I closed my eyes and waited for the shove or the back hand, but they never came.

Curiosity got the best of me. Peeking out of one eye, the calculations racking around his face were almost comical. Almost.

"How about this? What if we..." With a finger under my chin, he lifted my eyes to his. "Open your eyes, Rori."

I flinched and I felt his notice. My fists were clenched in front of me, ready to push past him if I had to.

"I would. Never. Hurt you, Aurora!" Dax knew of my past. Of my father and of my less than stellar boyfriends.

I could see that I'd hurt him by thinking he was the same.

A crack fissured my heart. I'd wanted us to move forward for months. And now that I was ready to put some space between us, he was the one pushing for a relationship.

"I.. I'm not... I'm sorry, Dax. I know you wouldn't. Old habits die hard." What else could I say? I didn't come here to accuse him of anything.

His chest rose and fell, trying to regain his normally calm demeanor. After another moment or two, he composed himself again.

"How about we start over?" When I cocked my head in question, he tried again. "I mean, why don't we pretend we've only just met? We go on some dates. Dinner. Coffee. Things like that."

Running his hand over his facial hair again, his distress was clear, and I couldn't help but want to sooth it.

"I don't know. We've already done things that might make that newness feeling of dating feel not so... thrilling... without the sex aspect."

It was an intriguing idea. We'd missed that build up stage and went straight to the sheets.

"Okay. I've got some courting to do. I can appreciate that. If excitement and the thrill of the hunt is what you're asking from me, then that's what I'll do."

I'd never heard him speak so many words at one time. The heady feeling it brought me was a rush.

To start over. No strings attached. That sounded... amazing.

"I want to be free to date other people too. I won't be caged by our dating. You'll have to win me with your acts, not by default of our previous arrangement."

A true smile lit his eyes all the way to his soul. "You've got yourself a deal." Hauling me into a tender hug, his lips brush the top of my head. "Just so you know, I'm playing to win."

Chapter Nine

Sorting out the Dax situation didn't go quite as planned.

Actually, dating would be something new for me. My hopes weren't high, but it was exciting all the same.

Sex had always been my driving force. This wasn't going to be easy, for either of us, but I'd never had that lead up before.

The wanting. The yearning. A playful desire with little teasing pay offs.

Dinner and outings would mean talking. What if we didn't like each other as a person?

I was not the most easy-going person. I had many flaws. What if he thought I wasn't worth the baggage?

Stop it. *Ugh*. We were just dating. No strings or rings.

Besides, I was free to date other people. One person came to mind in the most delicious of ways.

Xander and Dax appeared to already have issues with each other and if I started dating both of them, there was a chance that this small town wouldn't be big enough for all of us anymore.

Of course, I still had no idea if Xander would even be interested in me that way. Perhaps I was putting the cart before the horse.

Matilda rolled into the parking lot, crunching gravel and the ice that formed in the wake of the melting snow.

There were already bulldozers, a dumpster, and other equipment that I had no clue what they were called, filed into the area around the building.

My head still felt a like drumbeat but a bit less painful. I needed to hydrate more.

Bitzy must have heard my truck from inside. With a bottle of water in hand, the front door swung open, and her hips sashayed towards my driver's side door.

Slipping slightly on the ice, she caught herself before she fell.

One look over her shoulder to the construction crew and I understood the sashaying. *Damn flirt.*

"Have you picked a target yet?" That look. I couldn't help but to laugh. If she could set me on fire with her mind, I'd be in trouble.

"Shush you! Here I am, bringing you some hangover relief, and you out me? For shame." The wrinkle in her forehead and the tightness of her lips betrayed her embarrassment.

That did it for me. The laugh that bubbled up from the soles of my feet had me grabbing my sides in pain.

Sliding in place from shaking myself silly, my arms flailed. My feet swooshed in opposite directions. Time slowed. Reaching quickly for the side of Matilda's bed, I came up short. This was going to hurt.

Before my ass hit the pavement, strong arms swept under the back of my knees and around my back. The scent of evergreen and copper hit my nose.

Looking up at my savior, my heart dropped into my stomach. The heat in my face was from equal parts embarrassment and sudden lust.

"Careful there, Ms. Evolet. I wouldn't want you to hurt yourself on the first full day of my ownership of this place." Xander's obsidian eyes crinkled in amusement.

If voices were sex, I'd be naked and ready for each word that left his sinfully salacious mouth.

Bitzy tsk'd to my right and he placed me on my feet, waiting to remove his hand until the ground was solid beneath me.

"Thanks. I..." I what?

I was glad you caught me before I went splat? I wished you weren't there to see how clumsy I was? I wanted to lick you from head to toe?

"I don't know what to say. Thank you, I guess." *I guess? Idiot.* Could I have been any more lame?

Handing me the bottle of water, Bitzy linked her arm with mine. "I've got her from here, Mr. Doraglia."

"Xander." He still hadn't stopped staring. "Call me Xander."

Without another word, he walked away to talk to the construction crew.

Dylan dipped his chin to me as we entered Eventide.

My coat hung open and I shivered slightly. Not for the first time, I noticed him go immediately over to the thermostat and turn the heat up.

He didn't ask if I was cold. He just acted. It was sweet.

Kamie wasn't behind the bar. She must have been in the back.

Wiping down the counter for her before she got back was a little game we had going on. She'd do it for me. It had become a running tit for tat.

The mirror behind the bar had yet to be replaced.

I wondered if Xander would be changing the layout of the place.

If I were him, I'd move the bar to the opposite side of the room. The flow would make more sense.

"What are you thinking about so hard over there?" Lissa was seated at the table were Kyle had all that paperwork strung out a few nights ago. It had the perfect vantage point to see the whole place.

"I was speculating on the changes. Wondering if the bar was going to be moved. Thinking of the better feng shui if we set things up a bit differently."

The shrewd twinkle in her eye told me that she'd been sitting there contemplating the same thing.

"How would you set it up? Keep in mind that we will be serving food now too. The liquor storeroom will be converted and expanded into a kitchen," she said.

It gave me pause. I'd never had anyone care what I thought on any matter of importance. What was her angle?

Ink from the red pen in her hand dripped onto the table as she continuously tapped it against the edge.

I didn't know this woman from Adam. I didn't think she was mocking me, but I also didn't like most people enough to care.

Xander trusted her with his business. As his friend. As his associate. I wondered if she'd been his lover as well.

Dang it. A dark hollowness filtered in behind my ribs.

"Oh, I'm just a barmaid. You don't need my opinion gumming up the works."

As I started to walk away, her nails drummed on the table. The broken pen laid discarded on the side of her notepad.

"Don't do that." There was no malice in her tone. Simple command. Direct. "Don't sell yourself short. You are not Just anything."

Taking a sip from the mug in front of her, I was caught in her predatory gaze.

Time stretched on as she stared me down. She went from giving me advice to hunting for weaknesses in the blink of an eye.

Sarcasm was usually my first response, but no clever witticisms left my mouth. There was a sense of danger in that stare of hers.

I turned to walk away again before I heard a snarl from the other side of the room.

"Karalissa! Please go instruct the demo crew to where you want them first." Xander's face was pinched.

If I knew him better, I might say that he was angry. Why? I had no clue. "Take your... coffee... with you."

A smile played at her lips, but she pulled the mug close to her mouth. "Mmmm. Yes. I wouldn't want to miss a drop."

Licking the top of the black mug, lips smacking, I watched bewildered as she walked out the door.

"Aurora. What was that all about?" There was a fire burning in his tone I didn't understand.

I couldn't figure out if he was mad at me or her. Either way, nothing happened.

"Lissa was asking me about how I think the new layout should be and I told her that I am just a barmaid. Even if I have ideas, they're probably not any good."

His eyes darkened a fraction at that. I felt that same disappointment from him that I'd felt from her.

"Then she told me that I wasn't *just* anything." A bit of my usual self-loathing crept into my thoughts. "I'm not use to people seeing me as worth anything. So, I froze."

I shouldn't say anymore but with his eyes piercing into me, I couldn't help myself. "Then it got weird. Creepy, even."

"Hmmm," he mused. "I see." Gesturing for me to sit in the chair Lissa had been in, I sat, and he sat beside me. Close enough for our shoulders to brush. "Tell me what you envision this space looking like."

Looking out over the area, I turned back to him, shocked at his closeness. His nose was practically at the shell of my ear.

And when I turned his way, we shared a breath. Hunger peered out from beneath his long lashes.

Backing up to put a foot or so between us, my heart beat faster. Heat pulled in my lower belly.

I needed fresh air to clear my head, but he persisted with his question.

"Well? How should I reshape this place?" The question curled around his tongue, and I leaned into the space between us.

That was definitely longing I heard in his voice.

Or maybe it had been my wild imagination mirrored in my waking thoughts.

The words were out of my mouth before I'd thought to pull them back in. "I think the bar would flow better over there."

Pointing to the far side of the room, he followed my gaze.

"And if we put seven tables in the center and a long bench seat against this wall," I motioned to the spot we were currently sitting in. "and put a couple of tables in front of it, it would encourage more mingling and dancing. We'd need to get rid of the booths."

That thought made me rethink it for a moment. Dax would be pissed. "Some of the regulars won't like it."

Xander glanced around the room. His eyes landing back on me, longing in his gaze.

My imagination wasn't that good. He must have felt the heat between us too, right?

"And why do you think we should encourage mingling and dancing?"

My mind snapped back to reality at the question. Surely, a businessman would know that. What was he playing at?

"Have you never owned a bar?" Pulling back another foot, I grabbed up a coaster off the table and picked at the edges apprehensively.

If he meant to belittle my confidence, it was working.

"People dancing, sweat. Sweat equal's thirst. The more they drink, the less they think about how many they're having. I thought everybody knew that."

The silence was awkward as I waited for his assessment. Those dark obsidian eyes digging deeper into me.

"And the mingling?" The way he asked the question gave me my answer.

Underneath the mask of ignorance, he was cunningly evaluating my intellect. *Well played.*

"People who mingle in a bar generally either know one another," I said, swallowing my nerves. "Or are trying to get to know each other on another level."

Shrugging off the indifference of anyone's judgement, I went on. "Mingling males buy potential hook ups drinks until the drunk goggles get them closer to their prize."

Heat colored my cheeks as he continued to stare. Usually not one to embarrass easily, for some unknown reason, every time we talked, I was reduced to a blushing schoolgirl.

"You are more astute than I first thought." A grin plastered his too handsome face but mine fell.

I bristled at the backhanded compliment. Seeing my reaction, he tried to brush past the remark, but my guard went up faster than a spark to kindling.

"I just meant that you are bright. I didn't mean any offense." His back peddling did no good.

"Then maybe before you assume that a person is some small town dullard, perhaps have a full conversation with them. Make small talk. Oh, I don't know, be here for more than a week before you judge someone's worth!"

Standing abruptly, I spilled the open water bottle I'd put on the table.

"Aurora, I didn't..." I cut him off with a look.

I meant it when I said I was over males like this. I'd told Dax that this very morning. I had a type and now was the time to change that.

"Do me a favor... don't pretend to care about the employees here. You've already made up your mind anyway. It will save us all a lot of trouble if you're the boss and we don't have to be *friends.*"

Heading over and snatching a clean rag from the counter, I headed back, fully intending on cleaning up my mess but Xander was still standing there, mouth opened wide. Looking at me with the most incredulous frown on his stupidly beautiful face.

"Aurora." I didn't understand the level of pain I saw in his eyes, but I was too mad to give in.

"Rori! I told you; I don't want special treatment." *Why don't men ever listen?*

After wiping up the water, I headed to the back to see if Bitzy wanted to come over tonight. I was in dire need of some girl talk. Maybe I'd ask Kamie to join us.

I could feel Xander's eyes still on me. A quick glance over my shoulder confirmed he hadn't moved an inch.

Guilt. *Good.* Let that eat at him for a while.

Chapter Ten

O nly two daiquiris in and I was already tipsy. With just a splash of alcohol in them, they were practically strawberry smoothies.

I had such a low tolerance. Not just for alcohol, but for sugar as well.

Kamie had decided to join Bitzy and me for some girl gossip tonight. Hannah had plans and we didn't invite Molly to do much of anything with us.

They weren't much better in the liquor department than I was. Neither of them could drink a thing without getting overzealous quickly.

Kamie's laugh was boisterously loud when she drank compared to her delicate disposition.

Bitz told her about me nearly falling flat on my ass in the parking lot and Mr. Sex on a Stick catching me.

They'd barely stopped cackling long enough to catch their breaths before starting up again.

My living room wasn't big enough for a whole lot of guests to sit comfortably, but the cozy space around the fireplace made a great spot for this evening's shenanigans.

Grabbing a makeshift charcuterie board of some things I already had in the kitchen, I headed back in to let them rib me some more.

"So, what's new with you, Kam? Anything exciting going on in the dating game?" She had told us a few weeks ago about a website she'd joined to try and meet people from other towns around the state.

I couldn't judge her for that. The pool here was shallow. Especially when we'd all gone through puberty and awkward stages together.

There was nothing like being on a date and them remembering you for being the one who's underpants got yanked down in front of the whole school by a bully.

"Hey, can you bring me a soda on your way back in?" *Geesh. Sure Bitz.* It wasn't like my hands were full or anything.

"Here." Shoving a bottle of water at her instead of a soda, the red blotches on her face were evidence of the alcohol flowing through her system. "You shouldn't drink anymore tonight."

"I'll have you know that I am perfectly sober." Kamie burst out in a fit of laughter. "Hey! I am. I'm not tipsy at all."

The stitch in my side ached so bad my ribs hurt.

With turned up lips, a crack appeared in her armor.

Kamie was still doubled over with laughter when a knock on the door caught all of our attention.

It was after dark. No one came here without an invitation when we all feared the things that went bump in the night this far north.

The woods on either side of my street were usually enough to make me uneasy at the best of times.

Someone at my house without an invite put my anxiety into overdrive.

If I'd been alone tonight, I would never even consider opening the door at all.

Bears and other critters had been known in this area to accidently ring doorbells but knocking?

As I made my way to the foyer, the atmosphere shifted. Both girls were quiet, waiting to see who was there.

Picking up the fire iron before I opened the door, I heard the female's voice. Ease washed through me, and I opened it out of pure relief.

Standing there on her phone, in all of her natural beauty, was Lissa.

"Let me know. I'll talk to you later." She hung up and smiled with all her teeth. "Sorry to bother you at home, but I need to get this paperwork in order before the courier picks it up in the morning and you weren't answering your phone."

She didn't say anything more. I didn't know if she'd heard about mine and Xander's little tiff and was here to check up on me. Or if she had actually tried to call.

Grabbing my phone out of the bag on the foyer table, there were three missed messages, two calls, and one voicemail. *Well shit.*

"Come on in, Lissie." Kam and Bitzy waved, blushing from in front of the fire.

"You're inviting me in?" I don't know why it surprised her.

Other than that one small bit of weirdness between us earlier today, we'd gotten along famously this week.

"We're doing the girls night thing. You're welcome to join us."

Entering the room cautiously and looking around, I couldn't place the emotions running across her face.

Sorrow, happiness, longing? I didn't quite know.

"It's Lissa, by the way." I took her coat as she shrugged it off.

"What?" I really needed to pay more attention when people were talking. My mind tended to do its own thing most of the time.

"It's Lissa. Not Lissie." Casually slipping her phone into her pocket, she stopped before entering the living room. "You girls seem to be having a cozy friend's night. I don't want to intrude."

Kamie was holding in one of her cackles behind where Lissa was standing and Bitzy was conspicuously sipping her cocktail.

"I'm sorry." That name didn't suit her as well. "Can I just say..."

I shouldn't say anything. I must have been more tipsy than I thought.

"Go on. Say whatever it is that has your glabella scrunching up so much." I had no idea what she meant. It must have shown on my face because she clarified. "That space between your forehead and eyes."

A genuine smile lit her face giving me the courage to boldly state my opinion.

Handing her a cocktail and sitting on the couch, I patted the seat next to me for her to join me there and she reluctantly made her way into the room.

"I don't think Lissa suits you." I giggled at her expression. Now she was the one with the scrunched up nose and brows. "I mean, it's pretty and all, but it's not fun. You seem to be more of a Lissie."

"Here, here," Bitzy saluted, holding her daquiri high in a cheers. "To Lissie. The newest member of our girls only club."

The slight hiccup aside, I agreed with her sentiment. We needed fresh gossip. Ours was all old and tired.

"I second that. Here's to Lissie. Our sister in arms. And our employers... Cousin?" She spit her drink just as she brought it to her lips. "Okay. Not cousin. Sister, hopefully?"

"No. Sorry. Long time friend and associate." My face probably belayed my disappointment. "Just for the record, not that anyone asked but, Xander and I have never been in any romantic linking's."

The unladylike snort that spilled from me made Bitzy spit her drink and Kam cackle louder than she had all night.

So, she was as smart as she was beautiful. My jealousy reared its ugly head for half a second.

They'd never been together, but Lissie was definitely a force to be reckon with when the dating pool was already so limited. Poor Kamie.

"Okay then. To Lissie. The Not competition for our new devastatingly handsome boss." *Gods.* I needed to stop drinking right this minute.

Pulling a hunk off of the bread and a chunk of cheese towards myself, I noted how little food was left on the board.

Bitzy was trying to sober herself up some. Kamie had no such compunction.

"How about Seiran? Do you have dibs on him, or is he up for grabs?" A slight blush colored Kamie's face as she realized she'd said that out loud.

Sipping from her drink, it didn't look like Lissie's contents had gone down any.

Maybe it was my over observant silliness again but, I would swear that she wasn't actually drinking it.

"Seiran isn't *up for grabs*, but he is single." She pretended to sip again. "He's a gentle soul. A person would be damn lucky if he chose them."

Kamie bristled in her seat.

Bitzy set her glass down and stared at Lissie with the fire of a thousand suns before she spoke. That temper of hers to defend those she cared about rearing its ugly head.

"Kamie is worth the pot of gold at the end of a leprechaun's fucking rainbow! He would be lucky if she even glanced his way."

Woah. My girl had that whole big sister, protector thing going in full swing.

Standing and putting myself in front of her, I turned back to see Lissie grinning.

"Okay then." Tipping her glass in salute, she winked. "I guess it should be worth mentioning that Seiran is my brother."

The tension in the room turned instead to laughter. Kamie perked up and Bitz sat back down.

"Younger brother, I'm supposing." With a wink of her own, Bitzy smiled. "We always look out for our tribe, don't we?"

That overprotective streak of hers was going to get her in real trouble one day.

When she loved someone, she loved them with her whole heart.

That was why I loved her the most.

"Are there any more beautiful associates we should be on the lookout for?" Bitzy was in full on brazen mode.

Where she got the alcoh'balls from, I had no idea.

After another fake sip, Lissie put the glass on the table and stood up. "Actually, yes."

Taking her phone out of her pocket, she brought up a picture of a few people standing beside Xander. "Gav, Nik, and Mina should be here by Friday. Then the real party will start."

Bitzy's eyes couldn't bug out of her head anymore even if she was a cartoon character.

"Put your tongue back in your mouth," Lissie said to her, laughing. "Gavriel and Nikolai are a couple. If Mina is more your tastes, go ahead. Give it a swing but I'll warn you... she's abrasive no matter what team you're batting for."

Xander's friends certainly all had great genes. Him being the hottest out of their little group was a feat all unto itself.

Another couple of comfortable minutes passed with no one saying anything. The fire snapped and crackled peacefully, making my eyelids droop.

"Alright, it's time for some dancing." Kamie's rosy cheeks grew redder as she turned the music up and grabbed Lissie by the hand.

"Hey Karalissa," I hollered over the music. She grinned over at me but didn't stop dancing. "Just so you know, I broke it off with Dax but we're going to give dating a try. Also, I think our new boss is a hot dish."

With a laugh that sounded like tinkling bells, she shot me a knowing look.

It gave me the courage to up the ante.

"And Lissie, I'm feeling rather peckish."

Chapter Eleven

Dax was picking me up in less than half an hour. There was a restaurant at the ski resort I'd always wanted to try but never had.

It would be a fancy first date but not too over the top. Just some food and conversation in a moderately nice setting.

All of the dresses I owned, all three of them, were draped across my bed waiting for some big revelation as to which one would look best.

I really needed to go shopping for new clothes sooner rather than later. If we truly were going to be getting raises, I'd have some extra money to afford that simple luxury.

Right now, I only made enough to pay my bills and eat a little bit of something weekly. I wasn't starving but I wasn't ever full either.

It would be nice to buy groceries enough to fill the pantry every week. And name brand shampoo and toiletries.

Snatching the long-sleeved blue dress from the bed, I'd realized that I had no shoes that would match it.

The only dress shoes I owned were the ones I wore to my father's funeral.

They were black and clunky and not really a dress shoe that would wow anyone, but they would have to do.

My mother's necklace was the only piece of jewelry that I owned.

The pendant was two pieces that pulled together into one. Silver metal made an almost figure eight that one larger sapphire sat center of while several diamond chips surrounded the sides.

It was the only thing that my father hadn't gotten his hands on to sell for booze. I'd hidden it in a bag of frozen broccoli when I was younger.

Realizing things around the house were disappearing, I was old enough to understand my father's drinking habit was the culprit.

He didn't eat vegetables by the time I was eleven. His diet mostly consisted of a hotdog from the gas station on his way to work and a case of beer after work.

Learning to fend for myself, I knew from Health class that people needed fruits and vegetables to grow properly.

Thank the gods for Mrs. Hutchison. She helped me learn a lot of the basic life skills. If not for her, who knows if I'd have lived past my teen years.

She was an elementary school teacher, but she never hesitated to give me advice or direction whenever I showed up at her classroom.

When I had my first menstrual cycle, I freaked out.

It was in my second class of the day in middle school. I'd gone into the bathroom, saw the blood, and bolted towards the elementary school down the street.

The wild look on my face surprised her enough to halt class and run over to see what was wrong.

The blood on my hands must have given her a heart attack, but her level-headed presence helped me to calm down.

Telling her what happened, she took me to the school nurses office to get supplies and explain things.

After that incident, Mrs. Hutchison gave me her home address. She was there for me, always.

I hadn't realized how much she'd done for me or how much I'd loved her until she passed away five years ago.

The grief that I'd felt had been like losing my mom all over again.

With no one to turn to, I was aimless. I had no friends. No purpose.

Just a twenty hour a week job to buy groceries and keep my father's habit going.

He passed a year later. The yellowing of his skin was all the coroner needed to see.

I'd met with the attorney, got the insurance money, and took possession of the house. With more bills than income, I found my way to Eventide.

Kyle remembered me and my sad life from high school and gave me a job on the spot with no experience.

I'd never really thank him for that. I'd have to write to him soon. Check and see how he's doing.

Latching the necklace in place, the rumble of a truck sounded out front, and I chanced one more look in the full-length mirror beside my bedroom door.

Not fabulous but still decent. It would have to do.

The snow was all beginning to melt from the latest snowfall, but we were forecasted to get more this weekend.

Grabbing my phone and keys off the entry table, I snagged the lighter of two jackets off the coat rack by the front door and headed out to meet him.

"No, no," he said. "Get back in there." Laughing at his command, I stepped back inside. "Close the door missy."

I did as he asked. If my cheeks cracked from grinning, it would totally be his fault.

Him knocking made me giggle.

Opening the door, my jaw dropped. Dax stood there with a big bouquet of flowers and a box of chocolates. *Gah*.

He was playing the part of courter to a tee.

"These are for you. Though they aren't nearly as beautiful," he said.

Heat rushed to the apples of my cheeks at his compliment, and I didn't know what to do with it.

"You didn't have to." One eyebrow raised on that gorgeous face, and I backtracked. "Thank you. They're perfect."

Setting them in the vase on the entryway table, I'd made a mental note to put water in them when I got home.

Offering me his arm, we strolled over to the truck. It would be a bit awkward to climb in with these shoes and a dress on. "Where's your car?"

"Loxy and Kazz needed it. I would have preferred to have it for our date, but Loxana insisted. She didn't want to use the truck for the long ride to Burlington."

Questions stirred and swirled in my head.

First Loxy and Janie, then Loxy and Kazz. If she came here to visit him, why was she traipsing all over the state with the others instead?

"So, what do you plan on getting?" The thought of the meal pulled me from my musings. "I heard they serve caribou. I might try some."

"You want to eat Santa's reindeer? You'll be on the naughty list for sure."

Venison was never my favorite but the thought of those big, gentle giants being a slab of meat on my plate made my stomach churn.

"If it's going to bother you, I'll have steak instead." Dax was making every effort to put my needs first. I liked this courting side of him.

He still had that in charge persona but the shift in his personality, at least towards me, was noticeably more gentlemanly.

"And dessert?" The coyness in his expression was there and gone in a flash. "Decidedly chocolate. Of course." I giggled. It wasn't a question. He knew how much sweets, especially anything chocolate, called my name.

He was making the effort. Something I appreciated more than he could know.

The hostess led us to a table by a window overlooking one of the lifts.

There was a fire roaring in the fireplace in the back of the room and the sunlight poured in from every tall pane of glass that encircled the place.

The views were stunning.

The sun was just beginning to set, and the sky was painted with oranges, purples, and soft shades of lavender.

Bread rolls and fresh fruit were placed in the middle of the table. Wine glasses sat ready to be poured into.

The ambience was more than any of the romance novels had prepared me for.

Daxayrius looked dashing. The dressier attire suited him.

A hand knitted sweater that was white at the top, light blue in the middle and ended in a darker blue at the bottom hugged his muscular form. Dark blue jeans showed off his strong, round ass.

Yup. I was ogling him.

Even though the room was bright and airy, it had a cozy, romantic feel to it.

I had to admit, as far as first dates went, this was the best-case scenario so far.

When are food came to the table, I barely noticed my surroundings anymore. Dax had been talking, something he hadn't previously attempted often, but I didn't pay attention to what he was saying.

The food was so unbelievably good, I lost myself to its consumption, practically drooling.

"It's good, right?" I loved that twinkle in his eye. The way the light would hit it made a galaxy of stars vie to outshine one another.

Taking a sip of my wine, I swallowed the last of my coco van. I'd wanted to try the dish since I was a teenager.

Watching Emeril Lagasse after school was a guilty pleasure and when he'd made the dish, I couldn't stop thinking about it for weeks after.

"It was... divine. Thank you so much for bringing me here, Dax. I didn't think this date would live up to the expectations I'd always envisioned a date would be but, you've made it..."

The air went out of the room. I stopped talking mid-sentence.

Dax's nose twitched and I could have sworn he was sniffing the air. A low growl rumbled in his chest as Alexander Doraglia came up to stand beside our table.

"Ms. Evolet. Mr. Balodyn. Funny running into you here." Dipping his chin, he gestured to the beautiful woman attached to his arm. "This is Kosmina."

Her long lashed green eyes smoldered. Whipping her long, auburn hair over one shoulder, she extended her hand to Dax like she expected him to kiss it. "Mina is fine."

Dax didn't miss a beat, gingerly grasping her fingertips and giving them an odd shake.

I giggled again. He'd held her hand like he was touching a venomous snake that was poised to bite at any moment.

"Yes. We've met. It's been some time ago, but My memory is long," he said, making me wonder again at how Dax knew Xander and his associates.

Standing and coming around to my side of the table, Dax scooted my chair back, for me to stand, I realized.

The gentlemanly gesture set butterflies to fluttering in my stomach. "I'm Aurora but, everyone calls me Rori."

"Is that so? I'll have to remember that, Aurora." *Passive-aggressive much?* "I'll be seeing you around Eventide. I'll be overseeing the restaurant side of things. Including the waitstaff. I guess that makes me your new boss."

If I could wipe the stupid smirk off her face and not ruin this perfect date Dax had set up for us, I would.

Seeing as how we were in the middle of a nice restaurant and Xander wasn't contradicting her, I could only assume that she was telling the truth.

Lissie had told us that Mina, Nik, and Gav were due to arrive soon, but she never said what they would be doing for Xander.

Just fucking great.

Dax put his hand at the small of my back, guiding me back down to my seat.

The infinitesimal squint of displeasure on Xander's face at the sight of that touch killed all the butterflies squirming around from before as he and Mina made their way to their own table.

He showed up to a nice restaurant with a gorgeous redhead and was what, upset?

Was he jealous? That made no sense.

Dax drew my attention back to him with a few snaps between us.

Normally, I'd think that was rude, but I could tell that he'd been trying to get my attention for some time.

"I'm sorry. What were you saying?" I needed to be present more. My mind always strayed, even in the middle of good things. "You have my undivided attention, Dax. I swear."

"I was asking if you'd care for any dessert? They have this amazing chocolate covered cheesecake that I think you'll absolutely love."

Cute. Manly. And trying to be what I wanted. How could I not fall for him?

The bigger question was, how come the only place my mind wandered anymore was in the direction of the mysterious guy walking away right now with another woman on his arm?

Chapter Twelve

The construction over the last two weeks had been a royal pain.

Lissie made sure the bar was functional, even when it had to be moved to one of the booth tables temporarily while they remade that area.

They'd been working practically non-stop. If all went to plan, Eventide's remodel would be finished within the next ten days.

Some of the locals had stayed away during the noise and mess, but the die-hard day drinkers showed up every morning and the hardcore night drinkers showed up every evening.

Tips hadn't been stellar. I had been hoping that the raises Xander talked about would go into effect from the first day he'd taken over, but they hadn't.

With only a few customers a day right now, my bills were going to be late.

At least it was winter. If they shut off my power, the cold stuff could go out in the lockbox outside. I'd just have to add snow to keep it from spoiling.

I had plenty of firewood for the fireplace. And like most people this far north, I kept a cast iron pot that would hang from a hook over the flame.

My soups and stews would be hot. Peanut butter and jelly sandwiches were always an option too.

Reading wasn't easy to do by lantern light, but it was still better than doing nothing on a cold, long night, bundle in blankets in front of the fire.

Dax and I had one other date since the restaurant. We took a long ride to Stowe, but he insisted it would be worth it.

The small mom and pop shop he'd wanted to show me was great. I'd gotten the feeling that it meant something to him, though he didn't say what.

It had been a pleasant day trip. He knew I'd never been an early morning person but nine o'clock wasn't too bad. I still grumbled about being tired most of the way back to Jay though.

When we'd gotten back to my house, I thought I'd offer him to come in, but he'd said something about needing to see Loxy off.

I hadn't even caught sight of her this trip. Every time she had a moment, one of his friends would drag her away for a shopping trip, or a movie, or another activity.

I'd always got the impression she would like to rip me apart, so I didn't mind not seeing her. I'd never done anything to her, but she clearly had an instant dislike for me when Dax introduced us.

Loxy usually showed up at least a couple of times at the bar, while I was working, each visit.

The way her eyes stared daggers at me throughout those nights left an uneasy feeling with me for days afterwards.

She'd never stopped in once this trip, and it was starting to feel like Dax had set it up that way intentionally.

His nose skimmed the shell of my ear, heating my body all the way to my toes. I raised on the balls of my feet to reach for his lips, but he pulled back before I could.

Leaning away slightly, his fingers traced from my ear, down the side of my jaw, coming to rest on my bottom lip.

Seeing the yearning in his eyes, it was reflected in my own.

We were supposed to be taking this dating thing slowly but, I wanted nothing more than to wrap myself around his body and climb him like a tree.

With a gentle kiss to my forehead, he stepped out of my personal space.

"I have to go. This has been a great day, Rori. Can I see you again?"

I almost laughed. I'd been the one who wanted to date. I wanted to experience the build-up, the longing, the desire of the dance.

Yet now, I was the one who wanted to push for more intimacy.

"Yes. Of course. When?" It felt awkward. I'd also liked it a lot.

The newness of it. The no expectations.

"I never want to Not see you." His forehead pressed against mine. "You work Friday night, so how about another day date on Saturday? Maybe we could go for a hike?"

I didn't relish outside activities in cold weather, but a hike might be nice.

It would keep me warm enough and hiking nature trails had been a spring and fall time passion of mine since I was an angsty teenager.

"That sounds great. I may need some warming up once we're through though." Batting my lashes once, he caught my drift.

With a seemingly uncomfortable chuckle, he grinned. "We'll get some hot cocoa afterwards."

I gawked at him. *Seriously?*

"I better get going. Loxy will be pissed if I'm not there to see her off." And with that, he'd left.

Saturday's hike was nice, and it tired me out sufficiently enough that hot cocoa in front of the warm fire was all I had energy for. It was almost as if he'd planned it that way.

We hadn't made any plans for upcoming dates before I'd fallen asleep, and he'd left sometime after.

Today, Xander had called a staff meeting for 2pm.

I hadn't seen but glimpses of him in his comings and goings for the last week or so. He was away more than he was here.

The new kitchen equipment had come in a couple of days ago and was installed yesterday.

Gavriel met with us a few days after I'd met Mina. He would be the kitchen manager and head cook.

We weren't going to be a full-blown restaurant. He said he'd add items here and there and we'd see how it went first.

Serving burgers, pizza, and odds and end appetizers would still be a new concept for the staff.

Gav was nice to all of us, and he didn't seem to share Xander's animosity towards Cody. He'd been nothing but inclusive towards all of us.

If anyone else noticed these types of things, they hadn't mentioned it.

Mina was a thorn in my side from day one. She tried to boss us all around like servants rather than employees.

Lissie tried her best to apologize for her friend's behavior and keep her away from me, Bitzy, and Kamie but, I'd found myself on the ass end of an argument with her more than once over the last couple of weeks.

I came to this meeting today with the intent of keeping my mouth shut.

Alexander Doraglia hadn't yet proven to be the savior Kyle had promised us at all so far.

His associates ran the show while he came back into town every few days with something else new that he'd want to implement.

From the moment he'd arrived, about an hour ago, he sat in the owner's box. That's what he was calling the only booth that Eventide had now.

He'd had it built in the corner at the far end. There were three steps up to the box and it overlooked the entirety of the place.

The curtains that surrounded it were thicker than blackout curtains. They could be pulled closed like a four-poster bed but only three sides were necessary because it backed up to the wall. No sound escaped those curtains.

Bitzy and I were playing around with them when they'd first been installed. We found out by accident when she closed them, and I wasn't able to hear a word she'd said.

I wasn't sure why Xander wanted them in the beginning but thinking on it over the last week, I'd realized he must have business he didn't want overheard.

The curtains were all open now. Mina, Gav, Lissie, Seiran, and Nik sat around the large table with him.

Gav and Nik sat close, fingers entwined. They were definitely a couple.

Lissie had told us but somewhere in my drink addled brain that fact got lost.

I wasn't sure at first, but I'd walked into the new kitchens to get a clean rag and caught Gav with his arms around Nik while he washed dishes.

It had been a sweet moment I didn't mean to intrude upon, but I really needed the rag. Gav had dropped his arms when he saw me, and I just smiled broadly at him.

After that, they hadn't hidden their relationship from the staff anymore.

I'd asked Gav earlier this week if he was embarrassed. He'd told me that, where they came from, it was frowned upon.

Feeling all kinds of ways about that sort of backwards thinking and taking a few deep breaths before I blurted out word vomit, I assured him that here... love was love. And if anyone hassled them, I would personally see to their come-upping's.

I sure talked a big game for someone who'd been a spicy disaster her whole life. I wasn't strong or formidable but, I was scrappy.

I could wriggle and worm my way out of most situations. I'd learned to slink away from my father's grasp and had been doing my best to keep that streak going.

Mina, Gav, and Lissie stood from the table and called us all to gather by it.

Chancing a glance at Xander, he was staring back down at me.

Quickly averting my eyes, I tugged Kamie to stand between me and his direct line of sight.

"Next week, we start new scheduling." The sound of Mina's voice grinded my gears. "And today we're going over how to waitress properly."

Molly hmphed and for once, I was with her. All of the staff here knew how to do their jobs.

Bitzy bristled beside me. "We know how to wait tables. Maybe we could go over the menu instead?"

With a woosh of air, Mina was in front of Bitzy. The venom in her eyes had Bitzy stepping back and me seeing red.

I stepped in front of her, putting myself between them. "Back. The Fuck! Off. Kosmina!" Our noses were only an inch apart.

Lissie stepped to my side and Seiran shuffled out from the booth to stand beside her. I could feel every eye in the place on me, but I didn't dare drop my guard.

"Vicious as ever, Aurora. You will learn your place around here or you'll be eliminated." Mina's fists clenched at her sides, but she didn't advance.

After she turned away, I let the breath I'd been holding loose.

Xander hadn't intervened. He looked on with a mask of indifference. His demeanor pissed me off even more.

Taking a step towards his booth, Lissie and Bitzy's hands held my shoulders from going any further.

"You're just going to sit there while your employees are debased?" I spit on the floor in front of him. "I'm not working for her! If your associate can't treat us with respect, I'm done!"

He set his drink to the side of his plate. The steak knife was tinged with blood and pieces of the rarest meat I'd ever seen someone eat, cut in small bites next to it.

"Mina. A word." Not a single change to his mask. Not one emotion flickered across his face.

"You can't be serious!" she demanded. With another whirl of wind, time felt like it sped up and slowed in the same instance.

Lissie stumbled to the side and Seiran grabbed for my arm, but something drove me to pick up the knife.

The moment my fingers curled around the handle, I'd brought it up to rest against Mina's throat. Her teeth had been a hairs breadth away from my neck.

Catty fucking woman! She was really going to bite me.

A small bit of blood rose to the surface just under the edge of the knife, but it didn't feel right. Only the surface skin had any give. It was hard like stone underneath.

The shock on her face was priceless.

I didn't know I had it in me. When push came to shove, I'd been more than happy to dish out the karma.

It scared me a little. Like muscle memory kicking in. I'd never been trained to fight. And I'd never hurt anyone on purpose.

I'd only taught myself enough self-defense to escape harmful situations. I'd had a few classes in martial arts at the community center over the years, but this felt wholly different.

My hand didn't shake. The poisonous rage in my system pushed for me to dig the blade in farther.

Xander's voice was a bucket of ice water over my head.

"Aurora! Please do not kill my friend."

Bitzy's sob snapped me out of my stupor. Dropping the knife, it clattered to the floor.

Mina stepped towards Xander holding her hand over her neck. When she pulled it away, there was no mark. Only drying blood. *What the hell?*

"Mina, I'm sorry. I didn't mean to..."

Sticking her nose in the air, she turned away from me without another word.

Xander's gazed burned through me. Gesturing to the booth, he moved aside. "Ms. Evolet. A word." *Well, shit.*

Chapter Thirteen

"Before you start, I want to apologize. I don't even remember picking up the knife." It had been a blur of adrenaline filled rage that had taken over.

Defending myself or those people I'd cared about had always been my instinct... but this? Violence should have never been the answer.

My smart mouth and flippant attitude were a defensive mechanism I'd adapted to cope with my childhood trauma. I'd never wanted to cause pain to anyone before.

Xander still said nothing. His eyes pinned me to the seat and his hand hovered over mine. I couldn't discern the look on his face. Anger? Concern? Fear?

After another few seconds of stilted silence, he blew out a long breath. It brushed my face, and the scent of evergreen and copper hit me full on. My train of thought lost.

Absentmindedly leaning closer, my hand lifted to brush his and he pulled back like it was a snake poised to bite.

Talk about a wakeup call. I hadn't been able to keep my thoughts from drifting his way over the last few weeks.

Dax was being wonderful and all I could think about in the quiet moments before sleep was this brooding asshole.

Swallowing loudly, his mouth twitched at the corner. Anxiety rolled off him, but his mask stayed firmly in place.

"Are you alright?" Genuine concern colored his tone. "I need to hear you say that you're okay."

Fidgeting with a napkin, I pulled pieces off in strips. "I've been better. I've also been much worse. I'll live."

His stoic expression shifted to one of anguish. If I'd thought my confession would help, I'd greatly underestimated the situation.

"I didn't intend to hurt Mina. Bitzy is my best friend. And when Mina advanced on her like that, I just lost it."

Picking up the glass and lifting it to his lips, I could smell the whiskey. It rolled over his tongue and my mind wandered to places it shouldn't be. His pensive gaze was intimidating. It was also hot.

"What, exactly, do you mean by you've *had it worse*? That incident out there was dreadful. She nearly bit you." His voice trailed off towards the end.

"That's what you're focusing on? I had a knife to your friend's throat and you're worried about the girl fight part of the situation?" *Unreal.*

I jumped as he slammed his fist down on the table. A crack appeared under his hand and the dishes clanked as they rattled.

"You don't understand!" his voice nearly yelling.

I'd coward instinctively, never seeing him lose his cool. Then other emotions flooded in.

The forcefulness of his voice had the butterflies in my belly waking up while the insolence of it put my hackles on end.

"Then explain it to me," I yelled right back. "Why do you even care? What does it matter if Mina and I don't like each other? I can find work elsewhere. Or do you think I'm too helpless to support myself?"

Taking another slow sip of whiskey, his gaze held me captive. I was powerless under its scrutiny.

A lethal calm settled over his face allowing me time to take in his features up close.

A pair of rings that dangled on a necklace. One hand clutched onto them, too deep in thought to have been a conscious decision.

"It matters because I don't want you to go." Leaning forward, his fingertips pressing into the table, he pushed up and crouched above me.

Well, that caught my attention. Maybe this attraction I'd felt for him wasn't so one sided after all.

"It matters because I don't want to replace you." His mouth was hovering a few inches away from mine.

Quieter now, the intensity of his words brushed a warm breath across my face.

"It matters because she could have hurt my chances of ever being close to you." His eyes smoldered and my insides melted.

The curtains were closed. No light except for the candle on the table. No sounds but ours.

His large hands gripped the tops of my arms and pulled me in. Our mouths met with a bruising force. I wound my fingers in his hair, pulling him closer.

Opening my lips, granting him access, and melted into the scent of him, I gave in to the yearning. Gave in to the... coldness?

I'd thought heat would fill his skin, but it was cold. Outside, in the snow, cold.

That couldn't be right. He'd been here, inside, for over an hour.

The bar was comfortable. Something was off. The sense of being in the woods after dark, off.

The heat I'd initially felt had been all consuming. Now I realized that my tongue was swirling inside of a slushie machine.

It wasn't unpleasant. Sweet and enjoyable even.

His evergreen and copper scent clung to him, pushing through the recesses of my head. Clouding my thoughts.

Hunger for him grew with every passing second. I wanted more. I needed him closer.

If I could just crawl onto his lap and explore every inch of him, maybe I could satiate this need I felt for him. *Fuck.*

Reluctantly pulling back from the kiss, I needed to put some distance between us.

Fantasizing about him was different than the reality of diddling my boss. Especially at my place of employment.

"That was..." I began.

"Unexpected.," he finished my thought.

I didn't know if he regretted it, or if it was simply a surprise. Either way, I needed to get out of this booth before I did something that would have the rumor mill churning.

Nik yanked the curtain back. "Oh, sorry. Gav had a few questions for you. I told him I'd come find you."

"I'll be right there." Scrunching up his nose, he grabbed his drink and brought it to his lips but didn't drink. Just sniffed it. *Weird.*

I didn't understand the pained look. All I knew was that I needed to head to the ladies room and deal with the puddle between my legs.

"We'll talk things through later, Ms. Evolet. Thank you for staying."

I didn't need a crystal ball to tell me this wouldn't end well.

Dax, Xander, dating, new customers and a whole new life all waiting to become a Shakespearian tragedy.

What could possibly go wrong?

Rounding the corner, Bitzy and Kamie yanked me into the alcove off the new bar.

It was already stacked with liquor bottles and cases of beer. There was a cooler to one side and a few kegs along the back.

With barely enough room for one person to move around, three was pushing it.

Smack. Right to my upper arm. I couldn't say I'd been surprised. It was Bitzy's go-to move.

"What the hell was that? A knife, Rori!" She pulled me into a hug.

Squeezing the breath from my lungs, I sputtered out, "Can't. Breathe," and she let me go.

Only for Kamie to do the same. Her arms weren't as strong. Her grip not as tight but, the sentiment was identical.

"You really know how to make a statement, don't you? She's your boss. What were you thinking? The trouble you could get into. " *Geesh*. A thank you might have been nice.

"I was thinking that no one should ever treat you poorly. Or maybe the only thing crossing my mind was that she was in your face over a simple question!"

In through the nose, out through the mouth. Bitzy didn't do anything wrong. It wasn't fair of me to take it out on her.

"We shouldn't be being treated like servants. We are grown people. They may employ us but that doesn't make them superior to us."

Kamie whispered, "Don't you go getting yourself fired on our account. I like you working here with me."

"Why are you whispering?" Looking over the space and the way they'd made this a little secret clique, I'd realized they were afraid of being overheard. "What are you afraid of?"

"We just don't want to get in trouble is all. I need this job. I'm pretty sure you do too." She fidgeted with the rag in her hand.

Bitzy reached over and gave her a reassuring squeeze.

I counted to ten in my head before I responded. If I took my frustrations out on them, I was no better than Mina.

"Okay. I'm going to say this one more time. We are grown people. We can't get in trouble. We can only be reprimanded for work related issues. Standing up for yourself against a bully shouldn't make you fear losing your job. If it does, it's a hostile environment and we shouldn't be working where we feel impending doom. Capiche?"

She nodded and Bitzy rolled her eyes.

"I mean it, Bitz. If you don't feel comfortable, we'll figure out a way to fix it."

"My hero," she said, putting her hand on her forehead and pretending to swoon.

Huffing out a laugh, I smacked her arm this time. "You are a bitch... but you're my bitch."

Bumping shoulders, we walked out of the alcove and Seiran stopped in my path. "What's up, buttercup?"

Arching an eyebrow at my remark, he said, "Can we talk?"

I hadn't had much interaction with him over the last few weeks, but he seemed nice enough. Levelheaded. Quiet. Not really the right type of personality for a bar though.

"Of course," I said, motioning for him to lead the way.

Steering us to the back office, it was the only spot that hadn't been fully remodeled yet.

The only thing that was different now was the placement of acoustic sound-proofing tiles covering the walls, door, and ceiling.

Privacy appeared to be high up on Xander's list.

The fact that he hadn't remodeled anything in this room except soundproofing it told me he had secrets. I couldn't be sure if that thrilled me or annoyed me more.

Noticing the new, solid oak desk, I supposed he was finally getting around to making the space more of his own than I'd thought before entering.

As soon as the door closed, he was already speaking. "I can't apologize for Kosmina but I want to. She's had a tough time for quite a while now. Her best friend died. Murdered actually."

My hands flew to my mouth as I gasped. Of all the things I thought he might want to discuss, this was none of them. The surprise must have shown on my face.

"I don't tell you this to excuse her actions. I'm telling you so you might understand her better. She's in pain."

"That's horrible. Still, she shouldn't treat my friends the way she does. And she seems to take out a lot of her anger on me. Why?"

I'd felt it from that first encounter at the restaurant. The way she'd said my name. The way she looked down her nose at me. It was how Loxy acted too.

"You remind her of the friend she lost." His head hung slightly, as if trying not to look at me while he spoke.

If that were the case, shouldn't she be nicer to me?

"I'm sure this isn't the right way to go about it, but I thought you should know... You're her, that friend, I mean. And you're not her. You're so much better than our friend ever was. And you're no match for her in other ways."

I glanced around the room. The only window in the office was small and sat high up on the wall. Surely, it wasn't sound-proof, but I didn't think anyone would be sitting outside listening.

"You knew her, this best friend?" He nodded. "And you agree with that assessment? I'm too good and not good enough for her to give me a chance?"

"I do, but for my own reasons. They're not the same as hers. Annastasia was a special person. She had many flaws, but her aura shined brighter than the sun. We were all devastated by her loss. Alexander the most. And when she was gone, Kosmina blamed Stasia's wicked ways and swore she'd never forgive her for the pain she'd caused when she'd gotten herself taken out."

It was a lot to take in. The fact that this Anastasia had been killed. The fact that he and Mina, at least, thought she'd been the cause of her own murder. It was overwhelming.

Add the problem of me reminding Mina of her friend, and we had enough ingredients for a full-on stew. *Well shit.*

Then it hit me. He said Xander was hurt the most.

I knew it would only pain me to hear the answer, but I had to ask the question.

"Seiran, who was Annastasia to Xander?"

Sorrow filled his eyes. I wanted to reach up and take away his pain, but I remained still.

"His everything. Stasia was his everything."

Chapter Fourteen

Dax and I had just gotten back to his house after the afternoon matinee. It was some romantic comedy he'd picked thinking I'd like it.

It was fine. I'd have rather gone to see the new action film with that hunky British actor.

Gods help him, he was trying. While I appreciated the effort on his part, I kind of missed the brooding asshole side of the Dax I'd come to know.

We'd settled in front of the big screen in his mancave.

Cuddling up to his neck and running my fingers through his hair was all it usually took for him to pounce but he wasn't taking the bait.

"What are you doing, little demon?" His voice took on that sultry thrum that revved my engine. "We're taking it slow, remember?"

After several of these nice, gentlemanly types of dates, I'd figured out that this whole wholesome thing wasn't my cup of tea.

Leaning forward, with my lips pressed against his ear, I doubled down.

"You wouldn't want to leave me unsatisfied, would you?"

The bulge in his pants screamed the answer but I wanted him to say it anyway.

Brushing casually against it with my elbow, he hissed.

"You're going to be the death of me. I just know it." Without warning, he yanked my legs out and around him, so that I was sitting in his lap. "Tell me, is this what you want?"

Gulp. Using my hips, he ground my center along the ridge of his restrained length.

Heat built in my core at an alarming rate. Puddles. Hot, wet, puddles. My panties soaked through.

We hadn't done more than kiss and neck in weeks. Ever since I'd tried to break it off. Ever since Xander bought Eventide.

Thinking of that bruising kiss shared with Xander, the yearning we'd both felt. My mind kept wandering to it.

Even now, sitting on Dax's lap, the cold taste of his Xander's taunted me.

"Release." Breathlessly, I snuggled into his neck. "I want release."

Firm but gently, he flipped me to my back on the worn-out couch.

The giggle that escaped me instantly brought a smile to his lips. "That, I can do."

Yanking up my skirt, he ripped away the red laced panties that dripped with my arousal.

Cool air hit me with the sudden exposure. Instantly, I was erect. That bundle of nerves zinged with a throbbing ache.

Pushing my knees wide apart, he knelt on the floor in front of me, staring.

"Damn, Rori. Have I ever told you just how beautiful you are? I don't think I appreciated you enough before."

He put his hand on my mound, firmly holding me in place, and licked in a long lap from entrance to bean.

The moan that action dragged from me was nothing less than ecstasy. Wriggling and squirming, trying to bring his tongue to heed my demands, he held fast to keep me in place.

"Whatever am I going to do with you?" Lick. "You wanted to end us." Lick. "You wanted us to take it slowly."

Adding a finger, I groaned in pleasure. Dax knew how to drag every one of my nerve endings into a tight knot.

"And before we can get to know each other, heart and soul," he said, adding a second finger and curling just so. "You have me on my knees, worshiping at your altar."

His long tongue made vigorous strokes as his fingers worked their magic inside me. It was too much, and I couldn't get enough.

Losing control had never been easy for me but with Dax, I never had a choice. My body always gave in to his demands.

Bringing the other hand to my clitoris, thumb circling over and over again, my climax built with each curling of his fingers. Each passing of his tongue.

He devoured me like he was starving, and I was a buffet. And I couldn't take a single second more.

My muscles clenched. Knees shook. Body trembled.

His rough guttural voice held nothing but pure command. "Come for me, baby. Give me all you've got."

I broke into a million pieces. The winter light coming from the window refracted into a diamond of prisms, dancing along my nerve endings, sparkling within my very soul.

Withdrawing his fingers and rubbing them up and down my sex, he didn't miss a single drop of honey. His tongue was still mercilessly lapping me up and I could do nothing but shake and pant.

My eyes rolled back in my head as a second wave ran its course. A hand on each of my knees grounded me to the spot.

"Mmmm. Simply beautiful," he growled. "You are the perfect dessert, little demon." I watched as he licked his fingers clean.

It gave me a secret thrill to know he thought I was delicious. I'd been ravished before, but those times were always from the pleasure of the act.

I'd never had someone connect with me. This felt too intimate. Too meaningful. It scared the shit out of me.

Pulling my knees together, I sat up. If I could reciprocate, maybe I wouldn't feel so stripped raw.

"What are you doing?" As if it wasn't obvious.

Trying to pull back out of my reach, my hands were fumbling with the button at the top of his jeans again before he could stop me.

"I don't think so, darling. I gave you the release you craved." He said it like it was a simple transaction.

"And now I get to have my fill," I said, dejectedly.

Deftly pulling my hands away, he gently pulled me closer and kissed my head.

"Not now. Not today." I tried to shrug him off, but he clung tighter. "This wasn't a tit for tat. I only wanted to give to you. I'm trying really hard to be the good guy you deserve. It's not my nature, Rori, but I'm trying."

Feeling irrationally rejected, I lashed out, looking for a way to hurt him back.

"I kissed Xander." He let me go and I sat back against the sofa. "I pulled a knife on Mina and when Xander and I talked in private, I kissed him."

My past was my only guiding force. I waited for the strike. For the retaliation... It didn't come.

Chancing a glance at him, his eyes shimmered. Not with tears. Not with anger. Sorrow looked back at me.

Finally, he spoke. Quietly. Calmly. "We're dating. Not exclusive. You're free to see whomever you'd like."

Guilt gripped me. I was stupid. A stupid, rotten idiot.

"Dax, I'm sorry." I didn't want him to hurt but I also like being free to do whatever I pleased. "I can't say I'm not going to do it again but I'm sorry if it hurts you."

Quietly taking my hand, he brought it to his lips. "I'll have to try harder to be all you need. No worries."

If guilt were a ship, I'd be sinking.

"Xander has a way about him. I don't know what it is, but I want to find out. I know I'm being selfish. I know I don't deserve you too." I hid my face in my hands.

Pulling them away, he smiled. It didn't reach his eyes, but at least he wasn't yelling or hitting me. In some ways, it felt worse.

"Rori, I only want you to be happy. If you say you need to find your bliss and you're willing to keep trying with me, I'll be glad for it. I'm not giving up. I'm only just realizing how amazing a person you are. If this is what you need to do, do it." Bringing our joined hand to his mouth, he kissed mine. "I'll deal. I promise. Be warned though, I may not fight fair, but I'll be bringing my all to the brawl."

"That doesn't mean really fighting, does it?" The idea of them physically fighting terrified me... but it also excited me.

Gods. What the hell was wrong with me?

"Let's hope it doesn't come to th..." He cut off mid-word and glanced towards the door.

Jumping to his feet as Loxy burst through the door to the game room.

"Alexander is here? Where you ever planning on telling me?" She and Dax stood face to face, inches apart. Finding me, her glare was deadly. "And you? Has Xander claimed you already?"

Dax snarled in her face. She tried to inch around him in my direction, but he wouldn't let her pass.

The hairs along my neck stood on end. I'd been in a few scraps in high school, but Loxy would tear me to pieces. I was sure of it.

"No one has a claim on me." My mouth would be the end of me one day. I'd never been able to master its control. "I'm seeing Dax and playing the field. Not that it's any of your business."

She tried one more time to get passed him before turning and leaving without another word.

"Grab your coat. We have to go!"

The fact that he commanded me to do something, like he usually did to his friends, told me he wasn't the same guy he'd been earlier.

This was the leader of their little rat pack.

My panties lay shredded a few feet away. There was no saving them.

The thought of going out into the cold with nothing under my skirt was a twisted thrill.

He must have been thinking along those same lines. I didn't understand the concern on his face but maybe he didn't like having me exposed.

Anyone could flip my skirt up and see. My lips were swollen. My inner thighs covered in my juices. Again, that thrill rushed through me.

Snagging my coat off the hook, I pushed past him. "Well, let's go already. If you're this upset about her, I'm sure we can find her and make amends."

When I turned back to make sure he was coming, he was on the phone. Clipped words. Loxy. Xander. I caught my name too.

Anger coursed off him and I instinctively slouched my shoulders in, making myself smaller.

A second later, my chin snatched in his hands, his eyes pleaded with me.

For what, I had no idea.

Kissing me once. Twice. A third placed to my forehead, we headed out the door not speaking.

Chapter Fifteen

"Where are we going?" Dax hadn't spoken in more than grunts since we'd gotten in the car.

We'd driven to Jay Country Store. Around the bend to the ski resort. Past my house. And now we were heading back on the main road.

"I haven't seen her anywhere. Have you?" I didn't care for his tone, but I tried to take it with a grain of salt.

He wanted to find Loxana. Why? I couldn't fathom.

She was livid when she'd stormed off. Who I dated was my business. Not hers. Though, I could see her side of the situation.

Loxy cared about her cousin, and I was, essentially, toying with his emotions.

Well, damn. I hated seeing it from her point of view.

"You think she's going to stay mad?"

I'd already hurt his feelings once today. I didn't want to be a source of stress between him and his family.

"I think maybe," he said. Knuckles white on the steering wheel. "She's going to do something brash. Vicious even."

Looking out the window as we drove slowly past my neighbors, I realized he was looking for her to be on foot. Not driving.

"Dax, why does she hate me so much?"

He didn't entertain the question. Brooding and worry had been his only emotions over the last couple of hours as we'd driven in circles around town.

I couldn't understand all the energy she'd put into hating me. I'd never done anything to her.

Being her friend was never an option, but I tried to be as cordial as possible towards her whenever she was in town. It had no effect.

This trip, I'd barely seen her. All of his friends entertained her. She'd hardly been around, and I'd let my guard down. Honestly, I'd thought she'd already left.

I wasn't comfortable hanging out at his house when she was around, and he knew that. So maybe, she'd come back, and he hadn't realized it.

We pulled into the parking lot at Eventide, and I got out of the car as it slowed down before he could drive off.

Stumbling as it still moved, my boots squished in a slushy spot and slipped on the ice that was hidden underneath.

When my legs slid apart, the cold air rushed between them, hitting the slick heat at my center. "Ooph!"

I grappled for the door before I could fall, and Dax slammed on the brakes.

"Where are you going? Get back in the car!" Anger sang in his tone, pissing me off more.

If he thought he could boss me around, he was in for a rude awakening.

"No. I'm going inside. You find her. I don't even like the bitch!" I wasn't being fair to him, but I was over Loxy and her bullshit.

I expected him to follow me in, but he didn't. *Rude.*

I would have to find a way back to my house on my own since I'd left Matilda at home when we'd gone on our date.

Warmth enveloped me when I'd open the door. Molly was behind the bar. Hannah was bussing a table. And Dylan was gathering the trash to take to the dumpster out back.

"Are you scheduled today? I could use a hand."

Of course she could. Anytime Molly could do half the work and get paid all the tips, she'd push for help.

"I'm not here to work, Molly. Can you make me a Captain and Coke? Just put it on my tab."

Sitting on the new barstools with no underwear had been interesting.

They were tall enough that I'd had to use the bottom rung to get up in the seat. My feet dangling a few inches of the ground.

"Since when do you drink?"

As usual, her cantankerous attitude rubbed me wrong. If she was having a bad day, I could deal.

But this was her character. Bitchy and snarky were her default.

"Make the damn drink and grab me a menu, will ya?" *Geesh.*

I wasn't a mean person. I'd always strived to put a friendly mask on, but liking people was not how I was programmed.

And when my mask slipped, it was hard to put back in place.

Cody came walking out of the new kitchens with a personal size pizza. He wasn't scheduled to work until tonight, but I had the sneaking suspicion Dax called him.

He been on the phone before we'd left the house, and it made sense that we'd end up here eventually.

I supposed a babysitter was inevitable when Dax was worried about what Loxy might do.

"Look at this. The cheese is perfectly melted. The crust crisp." He pulled it apart and moaned. "Oh man, look at that melty goodness."

I laughed. Cody liked simple things. It was evident in the way he spoke, worked, and talked. He made just as good a day drinking buddy as any.

"Have a seat." With a shout that I knew would annoy Molly, I hollered down the bar. "Molls, get Cody here the same as me and put it on my tab."

"Molls? You want her to spit in our drinks?" That cute smile of his dropped slightly when I grabbed a slice of his pizza. "Hey! Order your own."

Shoving it in my mouth, his eyes grew wide.

"I only want a slice, but I'll order you a second one."

Winking and chewing slowly, I downed the drink in front of me to wash it down.

Big mistake. It burned in the aftermath, but it was too late to remind myself alcohol should be sipped. Not gulped.

Coughing and sputtering, he rushed forward to pat my back until the fit stopped. "Easy there, tiger. It's not spring water."

Knowing I wasn't much of a drinker, Molly'd done me dirty and made it mostly alcohol with a small hint of soda.

"Is she okay?" Lissie popped her head out from the hall.

I didn't even know she was here. My throat stung too much to answer her.

"She'll be fine. Big drinker, this one." At least Cody and Lissie didn't have a problem getting along.

Unlike Xander, Lissie treated everyone with the same respect they showed her.

Dylan stopped in front of me, trash in hand. "You good, Ms. Rori?" *So sweet.*

I appreciated how he looked out for me. For Bitzy, Hannah, and Kamie too. It was rare to meet such a non-assuming, gentle soul.

Most of the time, he faded into the background. There when you needed something. Not in your way when you didn't.

Voice raspy, I said, "Thanks Dylan. I'll be okay in a few minutes. You're a good friend."

He beamed at the word. I didn't think he had many friends, if any.

Introverts only tended to come upon a new friend one of two ways. By sheer luck. Or they were adopted by an extrovert without any choice in the matter.

Redness crept high into the apples of his cheeks. "I'll take this to the dumpster and check back on you in a few."

Molly brought me a new drink and set Cody's down but didn't let go. "Can you grab me a keg before you sit down?"

I had to hand it to her. She did her best to work the bare minimum.

Shaking his head ruefully, with a two-finger salute, he went to go get it.

Lissie plopped down on his stool as he left. "I saw Daxayrius drop you off. I thought you'd broken it off with him?"

I couldn't tell if she was judging me or simply curious. Either way, she saw my spectacular exit from a moving vehicle. *Just wonderful.*

"We're dating. Like, really dating. Going out to dinner and to the movies. The whole nine yards." Pressing my legs tighter together, I took another sip of my drink. Her nose scrunched up. "We've only kissed and necked a bit since we broke up."

Her eyebrow practically met her hairline. Okay. Definitely judging.

"Today, we went to see a movie and when we'd gotten back to his house, I may or may not have pushed for a little more. We didn't do it though." My thoughts returned to Loxy. "His cousin showed up and got pissy. She'd overheard me telling Dax we weren't exclusive. She's a piece of work, that one. Like it's any of her business. She's just never liked me."

"Where is she now?" Concern crossed her face.

It was the same way Dax had looked when we were back at his house.

"I don't know. That's what we were doing, riding around looking for her. But when we'd gotten here, his attitude made me mad. So, I got out and he left."

Drumming her fingers on the countertop, I could have sworn her other hand was breezing a message across the keyboard on her phone.

It was so fast. There was no way it could have actually been words.

"I should go check on..." A scream sounded from the direction of the back door.

Dylan's voice yelled and cut off. Lissie took off before I could blink.

Cody dropped the keg and ran after her. Beer burst from a sharp dent that pierced a small hole in the side.

Gathering myself together, I knocked the stool over in my haste. That drink hit me harder than I'd thought.

Sliding for the second time in less than an hour, I fell on my ass. Beer coating my skirt and nether regions.

Hannah, Molly, and the few customers sitting at the tables didn't move. No one offered to help me up or go see what was happening.

It struck me again how there were two different types of people in this world. The ones who acted. And the ones who observed.

Getting to my feet and running to see what was going on, the back door stood wide open.

The largest wolf I'd ever seen had Dylan by the neck.

Time didn't slow down like in the movies. It was more like my mind worked faster to calculate what was happening.

The closer I got to the door, the more I could see.

Cody was running, full stride, one minute. The next, he was gone, and an even bigger wolf was lunging at the first.

A loud crack exploded the air around me. Dylan's neck. That was the crack.

Nooooo! I tried to scream but it got stuck in my throat. No sound escaped.

A half second before the second wolf was on the first, it ripped through his throat. Blood splattered the ground as his body fell, limp and unmoving.

Snarls and tearing noises engulfed the area. Lissie was watching but stood with her body slightly angled in front of mine.

When it looked as if the second wolf would lose, she took a step towards the fight.

I grabbed at her arm, coming up empty.

Watching in horror as she grabbed the first wolf by the neck, she used both hands, pulling it off the second wolf.

She began ripping into its fur, her hands fast and unrelenting.

The wolf who'd killed Dylan snapped its powerful jaws in her direction, but Lissie sidestepped just as the second wolf limped in to help her finish the job.

There was a large wound on the second wolf's chest. Blood flowed freely.

Another crack ripped through the air. The first wolf's body dropped to the ground beside Dylan. The second wolf collapsed to the ground a few moments later.

My legs wouldn't work. I tried to make them move to Dylan's side, but they trembled too much.

Shock. I was in shock.

Looking back to where the second wolf had been, Cody's naked body laid shivering. Blood covered his chest.

As I glanced towards the first wolf, Loxy's mangled body laid in two, crumpled and bloody. She was dead.

Screaming came from all around me.

Then, I realized... It was me. I was the one screaming.

With a forceful shake, Lissie snapped me out of it. "Call Dax... Now, Aurora! Tell him to get here. Cody needs him."

I still hadn't moved. My brain was jumbled, couldn't make sense of what I'd witnessed.

They were wolves. Cody and Loxy were wolves.

Lissie wasn't but she'd ripped through fur and flesh like it were butter. *Gods, what was she?*

Loxy was dead. Dylan was dead.

Dylan! Sweet, quiet Dylan was dead.

The smell of evergreen and copper hit my nose, breaking me from my thoughts. Strong arms wrapped protectively around me, pulling me close.

"What the hell happened?" That voice. Rage and fear.

Home.

Chapter Sixteen

My eyes refused to open. The scent of Xander curled around my mind, holding me captive in its grip.

There were quiet voices talking in hushed tones. All familiar. All angry.

Keeping my eyes closed, I tried to gather as much information as I could.

There was a semi-comfortable couch beneath me. A jacket lay cushioned under my head as a pillow. Xander's jacket, I realized.

Warmth. I was warm when it was still cold this time of year.

I didn't remember leaving the scene. I must have passed out and he'd carried me inside.

The way the voices seemed to be absorbed the moment they were spoken was odd.

The office. We must be in the sound-proofed office.

Everything started flooding back in and I struggled to keep from alerting them to being awake. *Think.*

"I'll bury him close to the den. He doesn't have any family to miss him. I don't think anyone will go looking too closely at his absence." That was Dax's voice,

"And what about Loxy? What are you going to tell Thane?" Xander's voice had an edge to it. A fear in it that rattled deep inside me. "He'll notice her absence soon. We'll have to be prepared."

There was more grumbling as my head swam from the alcohol, adrenaline, and shock.

Taking deep breaths as quietly as I could, I remained still with my eyes shut. They would all probably clam up if they knew I was listening.

I'd seen wolves fighting and Lissie rip one apart with her bare hands.

Cody had been standing there one minute and gone the next. I swore he turned into that second wolf, but that was crazy.

Loxy's dead body laid where that first wolf dropped to the ground dead. She'd snapped Dylan's neck.

Oh gods. Dylan! Dylan died. In the jaws of an oversized wolf. *Fuck! Fuck! Fuck!*

Nothing made any sense. People who were wolves. People with superhuman strength.

This was a bad nightmare. *Gods.* This couldn't be happening.

Common sense told me I should get as far from these people as possible. That I should be scared out of my mind.

Only... I wasn't.

Lissie and Cody were my friends. They might be the stuff of myths, but they were kind to me.

Would it be right not to hear them out? They'd never done anything to me. Was I going to push them away because they were different?

No. If living in a remote area had taught me anything, it was that kindness mattered. Friendship mattered.

It wasn't the body you wore but the character of your soul.

Taking another deep breath, a tingling sensation ran from the top of my head to the bottom of my feet.

Try as I might, I couldn't stay perfectly still.

"She's stirring. What are we going to tell her?" Lissie's concern for me was endearing.

I couldn't wrap my mind around the Lissie I knew being the same one that killed that wolf.

Loxy. Lissie killed Loxy with her bare hands. Bloodied up the forest doing it. She'd stepped in to save Cody. *Oh gods.*

Sitting up too fast, I gasped, clutching at my throat. "Cody? Where's Cody?" The room spun.

"Easy. You're okay, Rori." Dax rubbed my arm, trying to sooth me.

My breaths were coming to quick. I was hyperventilating.

A snarl sounded from the other side of me. "Remove it or lose it."

Dax's hand became tense against me at Xander's command, but he didn't argue.

His toned soften before he spoke to me. "Breathe, Aurora. Everything is fine. There's no more danger."

That snapped me into anger. Fine? Dylan and Loxy were dead. I didn't know if Cody was alive or not.

Werewolves and... *Oh my god!* Lissie's strength. Mina's near biting me. Xander's fear at that. His cold touch.

Vampire. *Holy shit!*

Lissie and Xander were vampires. Were all of his associate's vampires?

And what about Cody and Loxy? They were werewolves. Were Dax and all of his friends werewolves? *No. No. No. No. No!*

I'd been intimate with a werewolf and kissed a vampire. This couldn't be happening. There had to be some logical explanation. *Right?*

Deep breaths. Again. In through the nose. Out through the mouth.

With one final exhale, I managed to get myself under control. Sort of.

"Where's Cody? Is he alright?" I didn't miss the shared look that ran around the room.

"How are you feeling? Any nausea? Dizziness? You bumped your head pretty hard when you fell off that barstool." Xander's soothing voice was enthralling. It made me want to... *Damn it.*

Enthralling. Wasn't that one of a vampire's gifts? To make people compliant. Forgetful. And I almost fell for it.

"Do not patronize me. Where is Cody? He lost a lot of blood. We need to get him to the hospital." Their lies weren't going to work.

Lissie smirked. "Obstinate as ever. He's fine." If looks could kill, mine would have had her falling over dead. "He will be, at least. Kazz and Janie are tending to his care."

"There was so much blood. How is that possible?" *Were-wolf, duh.* "Never mind. I'm going to take a shot in the dark here and say that werewolves heal fast."

Dax tried to pull me closer and Xander snarled, smacking his hand away.

I stood and swayed but remained on my feet. I wasn't going to be in the middle of some supernatural tug of war.

Looking to Lissie, she raised her eyebrow at me in that friendly challenging way of hers. "You're a vampire, I assume. So are Xander and the rest of you who came with him."

With a smile, she dipped her chin in confirmation.

Turning to Dax, he had the good sense to look guilty. "And you and your lot are werewolves. Why didn't you tell me?"

Xander's expression was unreadable. I couldn't tell if he was afraid that I was in shock or thought I'd run, screaming for the hills.

His head cocked to the side like he was trying to figure out the answer to some unknown puzzle.

"And you," I said pointing my finger at his chest. "Why'd you really buy this place? You could go anywhere. Why here?"

His amusement pissed me off but also made heat pool in my core.

Remembering I was in a skirt, no panties on, I knocked my knees together.

Both males' faces abruptly changed from concern. To desire. To challenge.

Oh gods. Those damned books I read were right.

They'd scented my arousal and then each other's in turn.

Lissie yanked me back behind her, caging me into the corner.

Growls filled the air. I couldn't help the laugh that escaped me. Maybe I was in shock after all.

Everyone looked at me like I'd lost my mind.

Peeking around Lissie, the crestfallen faces they wore were comical.

Big, tough males doing big, tough things.

"What? Am I not supposed to laugh at the absurdity of a vampire and a werewolf fighting over me?"

Sheepishly, they both lowered back down onto the couch. Xander rumbling under his breath. Dax looked towards the wall.

A light knock on the door drew our attention. Gav sauntered in, hands in his front pockets.

"It's done. Lots of comp coupons and no one remembers a thing. And Janie asked me to get Dax. Cody's awake."

"You erased everyone's memory? You can do that?" My accusation was directed at Xander, not Gav. I figured he was just following orders.

"What should I do, Rori? Let them go run through the town screaming about it? We may not kill when we feed but make no mistake, I will kill anyone who threatens the existence of the people I care about." He'd never spoken like that to me before.

Dax smirked, thinking that it would make me angry with Xander.

I found it did just the opposite. His protectiveness over his friends made him more attractive than ever.

I must be broken. That could be the only explanation as to why danger excited me so much.

Dax stood to leave but I grabbed his arm. "Who's Thane?"

Why wouldn't they want him to know what happened here?

"Loxy's boyfriend." His head hung in sorrow.

I'd been calloused. He'd lost his cousin, and I hadn't given her a second thought.

He added as an afterthought, "And the leader of another pack. He's the original werewolf."

Well, fuck. Out of the frying pan and into the fire.

Chapter Seventeen

Lissie drove me home and came in to check the house before she left.

I didn't think that Thane, whoever he was, would have heard about Loxy's death already.

Why they thought he'd target me made no sense, but I didn't want to talk about anything right now. I did want answers about the things I didn't know. Just not yet.

The shock was wearing off and a deep cold radiated through my bones. I didn't want to make a big deal out of the fact that some crazy asshole might be hell bent on my demise, but how the fuck could I not? Especially since Lissie said we couldn't be too careful where he was concerned.

"Don't forget to eat and drink plenty of fluids." Lissie's caring side didn't match up with the vicious display I'd witnessed from her only hours ago. "Here." She draped the cover over my shoulders and tended to the fire. "I can sit with you for a bit if you like."

I wasn't sure if that was what I wanted. She was easy to like but the fact that she was a vampire sat heavy on my chest.

The whole world was sitting heavy on my chest today.

"I think I need some alone time. No offense." With sadness in her eyes, guilt pushed me back further into the couch. "I have some things I need to think through, Lissie."

That nickname had stuck since our girl's night shenanigans. We'd become closer over that bonding time. And in the time since.

Now I had to wonder if any of it was real. The thought made me sad.

"I understand. I'm sorry about Dylan. He didn't deserve what happened to him." Patting my shoulder as she passed, the cold of her skin was a reminder of what she was.

"Liss, how old are you?" I had to ask. I needed to at least know that much.

Even if I couldn't fathom it in reality, I had to start processing what I was dealing with.

Picking imaginary lint from her jacket, her face was half hidden in shadow. The only light was coming from the fireplace, and it did little to illuminate the space.

"Are you sure you're ready to know that? It may be too much for today." The recliner creaked as she extended the bottom.

I had a vampire in my house. Relaxing by my fireplace in a recliner. That thought alone struck me funny.

"I think I can handle it." Sarcasm dripped in my voice. "It's not every day that you find out not only do vampires and werewolves exist, but that you've been seeing one of each." She laughed. "So yeah, I can handle the idea of elderly friends."

Holding her sides, she laughed harder. "Gods, I've missed you."

That was an odd thing to say. We'd been together half the day.

"I guess you should rip the bandage off quick. Give it to me, grandma." I still found it easy to be around her. All things considered.

"I can't divulge things that aren't my story to tell but I can tell you my tale if you'd like." I nodded. "Okay. Try to let me get it all out before you pelt me with questions."

In the weeks since we'd met, she already knew me so well.

When she began her tale, the cadence of her voice changed, and I found myself drawn in.

"I was born in 1497 in a small village south of Poenari in Romania.

When I turned fifteen years old, my mamma grew sick. Poppa was never home, working tirelessly to save money to take her to a healer in the biggest town development at the time.

That left me, as the oldest of four siblings, to take care of our family.

Every night, I waited for my poppa's return. For him to tell us he'd earned enough.

Momma was wasting away and my tending to her was making little difference anymore.

Only, one evening, he never came home. Me and my siblings went on about our chores and waited for the next night to come.

Still, he didn't come home. After three weeks of waiting, momma passed away.

Her grief claimed her as much as the sickness that riddled her body.

I did the best I could to take care of my siblings, but it wasn't enough.

Seiran was two years younger than me and the twins, Astar and Celeste were only six years of age.

Five years passed slowly. Lots of struggle and strife.

I found menial work throughout the surrounding villages, but it never paid enough to fill all of our bellies.

The hovel we lived in was crumbling around our ears and I didn't know how to take care of it and them too.

I raised my siblings with the hopes of making a better life for them somehow.

Marriage wasn't an option when I couldn't afford clean clothes to make attempts at catching anyone's eye. I didn't even know what I was supposed to do as a wife or how to become a mother.

Momma had never gotten to that talk before she passed.

One day, I had been to market to pick up the few provisions we could afford.

A couple of handsome men gathered looks from all those in attendance. Milling around stalls. Dropping coin willy nilly.

It wasn't something that happened very often in our small neck of the woods.

One of the men caught me staring and smiled. My clothes were ratty. Dirt marred my hands and face that never seemed to come off.

I couldn't understand why he looked my way. He was still smiling and staring as I turned away, heading for home.

Sitting down with my brother and the twins to a meager supper, a knock came to the door. No one ever came to call on us.

I had Seiran take the twins to the room we all shared and close the door, with instructions not to come out until I called to them.

The two handsome strangers stood on my doorstep, rain pelting them. Drenching them through but not damaging their smiles in the least.

"Sorry to intrude but we seem to have been caught in a deluge. Could we trouble you to shelter us until it passes?"

I remembered his smile at the market and something low in my belly stirred. I didn't understand that feeling at the time. I'd never experienced it before.

"Yes, of course." I stepped aside so they could enter but neither of them moved.

The other one asked an odd question, but I thought little of it at the time. He said, "Are you sure you want to invite us in?"

Later, I'd realized that saying yes wasn't the same as an actual invitation.

I didn't call my siblings out of the room yet. Instead, inviting the men to sit and eat the meager amount of food we'd had.

They declined, looking around at the hovel we lived in. No judgement. No disgust.

They were already ten times better that the villagers we called neighbors.

We made conversation and I nibbled on the food. I told them about momma and poppa.

I waivered on whether or not to tell them about my siblings but Astar sneezed, and I couldn't keep them secret anymore."

She stopped talking for a few minutes and I thought she may not start again. Just as I started to speak, with a far-off look, she began to tell the rest.

"The smiling stranger asked me if I wanted to make enough coin to forever take care of my family.

He said that I wouldn't ever be able to see them again, but he'd leave enough to get a new house, horses, and livestock.

He'd also make certain that they had enough to buy clothes and food for many years to come.

My heart swelled. I was ashamed to admit, I'd considered giving up only a week prior. If never seeing them again was the cost of their prosperity, I'd gladly pay it.

It wasn't until we'd said a tearful goodbye that I realized how much I was giving up.

My siblings were all I had, and I'd never understood that I was rich for having their love.

After three days of walking and chit chatting back and forth, I still had no idea why they needed me or what they wanted me to do.

I resolved to do anything they asked to keep my family safe, fed, and taken care of.

We arrived at the front gate of a castle.

There were no spires. No guards. Only one gate that blocked the entrance of a walled in courtyard.

The metal work was extraordinary. A bat in flight was fashioned to one side and one in sleep hung on the other. Dragon heads on each post to either side.

As they creaked open, I couldn't imagine why I would be needed here.

I could cook some. Possibly clean. But the exorbitant amount of coin they'd been willing to pay didn't make sense.

Then I thought darker thoughts.

That maybe their carnal pleasures were unbecoming, and they required someone no one would miss if things went awry.

That was when I began to regret that I'd resigned my life away.

I wearily entered the castle behind them, looking around, taking in the dreary decorum.

There were no servants bustling around or merriment carrying on. The castle was cold in more ways than one.

A beautiful man and woman glided down from a winding staircase in the center of the large entry chamber.

I remembered thinking, "If this is to be my death, I'll gladly accept it."

Little did I know, my thoughts weren't far off.

I was ushered to a dining room off the main living area.

My smiling stranger pointed to the long table that stretched the length of the room.

When I pulled out a seat, he snatched my wrist and pointed to the table again. "Remove your garments and lie on your back, Karalissa."

A lone salty tear running down my cheek was my only tell. My innocence ran along with it.

Thinking of my family being safe. Keeping my eyes shut tight. I didn't understand the pain in my wrists, my neck. The feeling of teeth on my inner thighs and the top of my breasts."

I wiped at my own tear as she recalled her pain.

Her face stoic as she spoke. As if remembering the strength it took to endure being made into a banquet.

"But you didn't die. You're here." I realized my mistake the moment the words left my mouth.

"Didn't I? Even if I were never turned, would I still be that girl? The one who took care of her younger siblings and let strangers into her house? I can't imagine being that girl anymore." There was more to the story.

Afraid to push, I sat quietly waiting. If she wanted to tell me the rest, that would be up to her. I wouldn't force it from her.

"My human life didn't end that night.

They feasted their fill of my blood and then showed me to the biggest bedroom I'd ever seen. It had its own bathing chamber and a balcony overlooking a field of peonies.

I was well fed, clothed, and taken care of over the next several years. They saw to it that I had a tutor and learned all sorts of new things. They made sure I had relations with different people too.

They wanted me to be well versed in various subjects, including carnal pleasures.

The beautiful Lady of the castle had taken a liking to me. She'd seek me out for tea with her best friend.

I'd never enjoyed their idea of fun sports, but she was always good to me.

Funny and witty and totally in love with her mate.

They were sickeningly in love and sometimes viciously ruthless with their prey, but that's not my story to tell.

I was their ward. Their consenting food source. And believe it or not, they'd become my friends, my family.

On my twenty-sixth birthday, I'd been summoned to the dining room and hadn't thought anything of it.

That's where they usually fed when in the house and just because it was my birthday didn't mean they didn't need to drink.

There was a multi-layered cake with candles aflame on top and a glass of red wine.

They sang a traditional song of name day celebration, and we sat around the table making merry.

The moment I emptied the remnants of my glass, the Lady stood to make a speech.

"Karalissa, my sweet girl. You are aging too fast. We will blink and you will have left us."

I didn't know what to make of her salute. She lifted her glass to toast, and the others did the same.

"When next we meet, you'll be family forever."

I registered her words only a second or two before a knife was plunged through my heart from behind.

I remembered the cheers that went up and the smiles that filled their faces as the light left my eyes and darkness consumed me.

When I awoke, everything was brighter, sharper. Scents filled the air that I'd never noticed before.

And the Lord and Lady sat at the foot of my bed like adoptive parents, waiting for me to be born into my new life."

"That's awful. How could they take that choice from you and think that it was love?"

I'd thought I'd had it bad after my mom died. But this? *Gods.* I couldn't even begin to imagine the trauma.

Coming back to the present, she turned to smile weakly in my direction.

"So, that's my tragic little story. All in all, I'm grateful for the change."

Something connected then. "Wait. How did Seiran come to be with you?"

Her smile fell slightly but she recovered it quickly.

"Ah, ah, ah. I told you my story. If you want his, you'll have to ask him."

If Seiran was the biological brother that she'd left behind with the twins, his tale to find her was something I'd definitely be following up on.

"Where are they today? The Lord and Lady? Why didn't you stay with them?" The words rushed out of me before I could think them through.

Getting up to tend to the fire, the smell of the pine log she'd tossed on top brought memories of Xander's scent to the forefront of my thoughts.

"She died. It was a long time ago." I thought if I waited quietly, she'd tell me of the Lord too, but she didn't.

Poking the front of the fire, the logs snapped and crackled.

"I still miss her, you know? You never stop missing your sire." Replacing the poker to the rack, she turned from the fire.

"Sire? Is that what you call the person who killed and turn you?"

If someone killed me, I didn't think I'd be okay being their friend anymore.

"It's the blood. Whoever's blood you've consumed to transition. If you'll remember, the knife that killed me came from behind." Without another word, she tucked the blanket up under my chin snuggly, turned and left.

The Lady facilitated her death. I couldn't envision any scenario in which I would have forgiven the person who murdered me.

Lissie was my age when she'd been cut down. Five hundred years later, she still looked my age but the image of everyone I cared about withering away and leaving me alone didn't paint vampirism in a comfortable light.

Entangled with supernatural creatures, I could only pray my time wouldn't end so soon.

Chapter Eighteen

It had been two weeks since Dylan was killed.

Dax wanted to talk the day after, and I told him I needed time. Surprisingly, he listened.

Janie and Kiah hadn't been hanging out here during my shifts. Neither Gunner nor Kazz had made their usual weekend appearances.

I suspected they were still close by during each of my shifts, but I'd seen not hide nor hair of them.

Leaving me fully unattended while this Thane character could show up at any time wouldn't have been wise. And Dax had always been the overprotective type.

Cody was fully recovered. I didn't know why, but I didn't feel like anything had changed when I worked with him. He was still just... Cody.

If anyone should feel like a different person to me, it should be the person I saw turn into a werewolf right before my eyes.

He'd been more reserved. Not as quick to joke around with me. Not so carefree or smiley. It gave me the impression I was an animal he didn't want to spook.

If I were in a better mental space myself, I would have pushed for him to talk it through, but I wasn't ready to. Not yet.

Expecting Xander to bombard me when I'd come back to work, I'd taken off for a couple of days to get my head on straight.

The night before returning to Eventide, I had slept barely a wink.

Coming to the realization that I worked with vampires and hung out with werewolves, it all pushed me to re-evaluate how reckless I was still willing to be with my life.

That first shift back, my anxiety was at a new high.

I needn't have worried about Xander. He had only popped in a few times in the last couple of weeks. Not once did he approach me or even look my way.

As much as I wasn't ready to talk to him, his ignoring me hurt for no good reason.

We'd only kissed once. If he wanted more, I was fairly certain that my finding out his secret pushed me from his mind.

Mina hadn't relented her bossiness though. And knowing what she was now, I was reluctant to push her the same way I had before.

Lissie said I shouldn't give her any ground, but I didn't have that same fire for the fight after finding out she could rip me in half without much effort.

I couldn't shake Lissie, no matter if I wanted to or not. She'd practically never left my side since Dylan's death.

She did her job. Stopped by my house afterwards if I wasn't scheduled that day. And was always within shouting distance if I was working.

It made Bitzy irrationally irritable. I asked her why a few days ago and she snipped at me.

"You're my best friend. Not hers." Without another word, she huffed and walked away.

There had to be more to it than that, but I had no clue what it could be. I tried to talk to her later that evening when we'd had a lull in customers.

"Hey Bitz. Got a minute?" Without bothering to turn to look at me, she motioned to Kamie, and they took off to the ladies room.

Bitzy called over her shoulder, *"Not tonight, Rori. I'm not feeling up to it."*

That was what I'd said to her the day after Dylan "moved away unexpectedly." I had been at home when she called and gave me the news Xander had told the staff.

I hadn't realized she and Dylan were close. She'd never mentioned it to me, but the fact that she and Kamie shared a secret set my teeth itching.

I wondered if perhaps she did it to make me feel the same way she did about how close I'd become to Lissie. She'd never been jealous or envious of anyone.

Something wasn't right. And I didn't know how to make it any better.

I'd come in a couple of hours early today to have a drink before my night shift. Having one, sometimes two, before every shift since finding myself in the middle of a supernatural hub of activity.

Lissie had been forthright about any question I'd asked. Maybe too forthright if I was being honest.

Some of the things she'd told me sent chills up my spine, but she never held anything back that was hers to tell.

Even the reason Xander wanted Eventide to add food service.

It was to bring people from the ski resort to feed from.

She'd said that humans consuming only alcohol right before they fed on them didn't satiate the thirst the way it didn't if they'd had full stomachs.

The skiers would be healed and compelled to forget and then sent on their way with a coupon for their next visit.

I'd almost laughed at that last part. Almost.

Realizing that they didn't intend to kill people had made me feel a tad bit better about having all the vampires in town.

I'd asked her why, but she'd just told me Xander had decreed they not kill when it was avoidable ever since Anastasia died. And that if I wanted to know more, I'd have to ask him.

I'd grown up with a lot of the folks around these parts.

Bearing the weight of their deaths wouldn't make working with the vampires any easier.

Even if I understood the food chain, it didn't mean it was acceptable.

So, I took comfort where I could. Vampires with a conscience... I could live with that.

Hannah was working the bar until six tonight. Her flare for picking a new drink for me to try each time she'd worked endeared me to her even more.

She'd figured out that sweet drinks were more my forte than bitter or harsh tasting alcohols.

She'd also helped to figure out that beer, lagers, and wine were not for me.

Rum or amaretto-based drinks were my favorites. While whiskey and anything with tequila in it made me gag.

She was having fun with my alcohol naivete. The way her lips pursed when I'd scrunch my nose in disgust or lit up when I delighted in a new concoction bolstered my spirits into trying more varieties.

When Molly was on duty, I stuck with Captain and Coke. I wouldn't want her to strain her brain trying to look up and follow a recipe off her phone.

Today's offering from Hannah was a colorful frozen drink with an umbrella.

The bar must have obtained a blender when the vampires took over because we'd never had one before.

She waited for me to take my first sip.

"What's in it?" I was all for trying new things but some of her concoctions I needed to be prepared for.

"It's a classic. I'm sure you've never had one before so just drink up. I promise it's sweet." Her earnest grin had me biting back a sarcastic remark and bringing the straw to my lips.

With one long pull, the slushy, sweet drink reminded me of a certain males kiss.

The flavor hit my tongue in a tropical explosion. I wanted to savor it going all the way down.

"That's absolutely delicious. What is it?" Taking another long pull, brain freeze slammed its cold fist in my head.

Clapping her hands together proudly, she bounced on the balls of her feet. "Excellent! It's a Bahama Mama. I just knew it would be right up your alley."

The drink was almost like fruit punch. It went down way too easily.

If I was going to make it through my shift, I'd need to eat something to absorb some of the alcohol.

"I think I'm going to order a burger. Is Gav busy back there? My shift starts in half an hour."

The fact that I'd already nursed a ginger ale and peach schnapps for the last hour and a half left my tongue fuzzy.

That combination was a miss, but I hadn't had the heart to tell her.

"Actually, Gav and Nik have off today. I think Seiran is in the office and Cody is restocking the liquor storage. With Dylan gone, it's just us until Luke and Kamie come in."

"Luke?" I'd only worked six out of the last fifteen days.

Replacing Dylan had to be done but for his life to mean so little here hurt deeply.

She shouted over the water while washing the blender and glasses.

"Oh, you haven't met him yet? He's the new helper. The fact that he knows his way around a kitchen is a bonus. I don't know what we would have done for tonight if he wasn't able to cover for Gav and Nik."

Already feeling the weight of the upcoming Friday night before me, I threw the straw to the side and gulped down the icy Bahama Mama. Brain freeze took hold again immediately, and I couldn't see straight.

Registering in some distant part of my brain the sound of the front door's chimes, I tried to clear the fuzziness from my mind, but the pain wouldn't be rushed.

My head was still reeling when the seats on either side of me became occupied.

"You okay there?" The male's voice wasn't familiar, but mirth rang in its deep timber.

"Brain. Freeze." I muttered without taking my hands away from my head.

"That's almost the worst," said the male on my other side. "Not quite as bad as being found and ripped apart by a pack of werewolves, but it's right up there."

My back stiffened and the blood drained from my face. I still couldn't see straight.

With no one around to help, I prayed to all the gods these weren't who I thought they might be. *Please, not now.*

Hannah came back to grab my empty glass and take the newcomers orders. "What can I get ya?"

My eyes widen at her with alarm. To her credit, her smile didn't faulter as she made small talk while taking their orders.

"Refill hon?" The way her fierce eyes pierced into mine, registering my dilemma.

"Can you make me one more of those?" Without missing a beat, her subtle nod told me she understood.

If nothing else, I wanted her to get as far away from them as possible.

"Sure thing... Oh shoot, I need to go get some more grenadine from the back." Pouring their drinks before heading to find Cody, she set them down, giving me one last *hold on* glance.

Leaving the glass in front of me, I absentmindedly picked it back up. The remnants of the sweet syrup clung to its sides.

"You should try one of these. This was my first, but it was amazingly good." Running my finger along the rim to scrape the last vestiges of the whipped cream that clung to the top, my mind turned to Xander and then to Dax.

I'd never figured out what to say to them. I'd never gotten the chance to hear their tales or come to grips with this whole fiasco.

If one of these males were who I'd thought it was, I never would.

The one on my left was big, burly even, but his disposition felt kind. Tranquil even.

"How 'bout it? Care for a taste of the tropics?" My attempt at nonchalance while my hands trembled coming off just shy of believable.

Taking the glass from my hand, he stuck the straw into the bottom and sucked up the tiniest bit of juice that remained. "You're right. That is pretty good."

I turned to the one on my right. "How about you? Want to try some?"

Looking me up and down, a shiver went through me to my core. Whether it was fear of something else, I didn't have the space to examine my twisted excitement.

"Depends on what you're offering." He glanced down at the skirt I was wearing, my thighs on full display.

Smirking, he took another sip of his beer. Then turned back towards the bar. As if deciding I wasn't worthy of his attentions anymore. *Dick!*

The alcohol was making my head begin to swim. Slightly dizzy, I set the glass back onto the bar and glared at him.

Chuckling under his breath, he turned back to give me his attention again and I'd swear, the malice in his eyes burned brighter.

"You keep your fru-fru drink to yourself. I'll stick with my beer." His voice gruff, animosity roiled just beneath his skin.

I stood from the stool and set the glass back on the counter. Swaying, my legs felt like jelly. I hadn't managed to get that burger before these two brutes had shown up.

"Right. Okay then. I need to get ready to start my shift. If you gentlemen will excuse me?"

The hairs on the back of my neck stood on end as the male on the right's hand shot out, wrapping his fingers around my wrist in a vice like grip.

"I don't think so. We need to have a chat about our mutual friend, Loxy. Know where she is?" A cruel smile played at his lips.

Oh shit. Not just friends of Thane. Thane himself.

Cody came around the corner from the opposite side of where the storage room was. Hannah must not have seen him come out of it before she'd gone to get him.

Thankfully, she was still somewhere in the back. I didn't want her to be a part of this mess.

His gaze landed directly on the hand still wrapped around my wrist and a deep rumble vibrated through his frame. His growl unwillingly bringing me back to that night.

Coming to stand behind me, he pushed its bearer hard in the chest. The force yanked me back into the bully and his arms snaked around my middle.

The one that had been sitting on my left stood. His calm demeanor felt out of place with the situation unfolding around us.

"Cody, good to see you again." He hadn't made any threats. but with the way Cody stiffened, there definitely was one hidden in those few short words.

Without taking his eyes off of the male holding me captive, Cody dipped his chin. "Bram. It's been a while."

Stepping towards me, he stopped a foot away.

If I'd never thought of Cody being menacing, his voice now made the fact abundantly clear. "Thane. I highly suggest you don't do anything stupid."

The beard that was clean shaved on either side and hung well kempt two or three inches past his chin grazed along my jawline. His mouth coming to rest at the shell of my ear.

"I think kitten here might be interested in doing something stupid." His tongue darted out, skimming the flesh at the nape of my neck. "Isn't that right, kitten?"

Pulling me back flush with his body, the bulge of his manhood rubbed against my backside. Dark thoughts crept into my mind of their own accord.

Childhood trauma made me lean towards the more dangerous side, but I didn't know I had a death wish.

The thought shocked me into action.

Rearing back, I slammed my head into Thane's jaw. Hard.

That was going to hurt tomorrow. It was painful now, but not nearly as much as it would have had I not been drinking.

He swore but didn't loosen his grip one bit. His snarl crawled up my back, his cock at my back jumped in time with it.

"Mmmmm... Kitten has claws. Purrrrfect."

My nipples pebbled as his hot breath blew across my ear as he spoke.

I didn't hear Seiran approach, but I saw Cody's posture relax a fraction. He wasn't on his own anymore.

They might even be on even footing but not knowing enough about either species left me wondering for my life.

If I survived this, I'd make it my mission to learn everything I could about the people who surrounded me.

If I wasn't ready before, I was now.

"Bram, Thane. Welcome to Eventide." He glanced at Cody with a slight nod. "I see you've met Aurora. Her suitors will be joining us momentarily."

Suitors? What the fuck?

Chapter Nineteen

Thane's hard on pressed into me with a thrust, rubbing it up and down slowly. His nose skimmed my neck as his hand wrapped securely around my throat but didn't tighten.

"Good. We have much to discuss." Directing his next words to me, he purred in my ear, "Don't we, kitten?"

Running his fingertips down my arm, around to my breast, and lingering down my side, leaving me breathless, he released my arms and shoved me forward.

I slammed into Cody's chest and turned to face him. "Prick!"

"There's those claws. If you're going to call me names, I'm going to show you what they mean." His voice low and rough, sultry in its allure.

My core tightened and I had to squeeze my legs together to help squash the sudden ache.

Getting myself killed if any of them scented my arousal was not high up on my list of things to do today.

Dax, Gunner, and Kazz came busting in from the back at the same time Xander and Lissie walked through the front door.

With the alcohol still running rampant through my system, my thoughts muddled.

"Now, it's a party," Thane said.

Bram stood straighter but still remained calm. *Interesting.*

The tug in my chest split, pulling into opposite directions.

Dax stood behind Thane. Xander stood in front of him.

Whatever that was about, I didn't have the time or energy to deal with it right now.

The biggest threat to my life was standing a mere three feet in front of me.

Why did I feel the need to inch towards the dangerous male rather than away from him?

The spinning in my head doubled and I was suddenly exhausted.

Thane's eyes met mine before Dax and Xander reached me. Both of them placing a hand on each arm and stepping slightly in front of me with their bodies.

My scent must have reached them in the same instance as growls, snarls, and curled lips baring teeth had me pulling backwards trying to flee.

Bram didn't snarl or growl. He was taller than any of them. Muscular in a way that spoke of loneliness.

The bulk of which was earned by throwing yourself into lifting weights and working to feel better about yourself.

I'd learned a long time ago what it meant to try and earn companionship. To try to hide from the pain of not feeling worthy.

I'd found myself staring at him with understanding.

Bram laid a hand on Thane's shoulder and murmured words too low for me to hear. Thane surprised me by straightening with a smirk.

"Hello brother. There was no need for you to show up."
Brother? Was he talking to Xander or Dax? "I was just getting
to know Kitten here. And she was enjoying my company."

My face heated and I looked away.

The timber of his voice held his amusement in a near yowl.
"... But I guess you can smell that."

Turning back to look at him with all of the distain I could
muster, the moment our gazes connected, my nerves sputtered
out and I dropped my eyes to my feet.

Still feeling his stare on my neck, there was another rush of
heat in places it shouldn't have been.

What the hell? My body was betraying me. My mind wasn't
attempting to intercede.

Xander straightened but Dax remained in a semi crouch,
ready to spring into action should Thane attack.

"Why don't we take this in private?" Xander's words were
clipped. I doubted he cared. If looks could kill, Thane would
be dead ten times over. "Daxayrius can join us."

"Bram and oh yes, kitten here will be *coming* too." Thane's
inuendo wasn't lost on me.

When Dax and Xander both started to protest, Thane
shrugged his shoulders.

"Or we can air everything out right here. It's up to you." The
threat was thinly veiled

There were only a few humans in the building right now,
but his intentions were clear.

Lissie took my hand, giving it a quick squeeze of reassur-
ance.

I knew what she was telling me. She would be here to talk, no matter what I learned from this meeting.

I squeezed back with a faint smile. Then turned to the males around me.

Kazz and Gunner were tense, hostile even. Not their normal overzealous drunken aggression. More like wanting to rip apart and destroy the world type of energy.

Bram and Seiran had such similar dispositions, I'd nearly forgotten they were here.

Both relaxed. Both unassuming. Calmness wafted off them like a gentle breeze along a babbling brook.

Whether they had turmoil on the inside, I couldn't say, but their presence was a balm to my wrecked nerves.

"Fine. Let's go." Xander snapped.

His strong fingers found the small of my back, pushing forward as Dax grabbed my hand in his.

All eyes were on me as I swayed slightly. Yummy fruit punch sweet and creamy on my tongue. The smell of the tropical drink lingered in my nose.

The bemused look on Thane's face was priceless. I may have been vacillating between my vampire and my werewolf but that was none of his business.

Entering the office, Seiran shut the door once we were all over the threshold.

The new leather couch and the chair behind a solid mahogany desk took me a minute to adjust to.

I hadn't been in this room since Seiran and I had that talk.

Oh wait! I had been. The day Dylan had died. I must have blocked out the memory until now.

The smell of the leather was intoxicating... or maybe it was me.

My mind was slightly fuzzy. I was sure my slurred words and swaying gave me away, but I refused to acknowledge that with everything going on.

Thane went straight for the Scotch bottle on Xander's desk, pouring two fingers without offering the rest of us any.

"Get out of that," Xander said, snatching the decanter from his hand. "Anyone else like some?"

"I'll have one." My request falling from my lips without thought.

Dax looked at me like I'd grown three heads.

He and I hadn't spoken in weeks, and he didn't know that I'd started drinking a few drinks every time I'd come to Eventide since Dylan died.

"Rori, are you sure?" His challenging tone was enough to make me yank the glass from Xander's hand and down it in one go.

Big Mistake. I coughed and sputtered and coughed some more as Xander patted my back lightly, swearing under his breath.

"Maybe leave the *hard* stuff for when you've had more... experience." Thane's comment brought the heat of embarrassment to my cheeks.

I wasn't some novice. Drinking might be newer to me, but his insinuations about my sexual prowess graded on my nerves.

"If I wasn't so sure you'd disappoint, I might be willing to give you a go." Bram tried and failed to hold in a smirk at my drunken retort. "But you know what they say about those who boast?"

Sticking my pinky up, I let it slowly curl down. Then shrugged.

He growled, making Xander and Dax roared with laughter.

"Come closer and we can put that theory to the test." His vitriol ran through to my core.

It unnerved me how my body leaned towards him.

"Why are you here, Thane?" If Xander were an actor, he'd be well paid.

Feeling his angry energy gave away the lie in his performance.

I'd almost forgotten the reason for the visit. His girlfriend was dead.

"Well, brother. When one of my pack doesn't return within a couple weeks of when they were expected to, I find out why. Where's Loxy?" Thane's hard glare landed on Dax. "She came for her quarterly check in and never returned."

"You lost my cousin?" Dax demanded. "Why didn't you send word sooner? We could have picked up her trail."

Apparently, it was a supernatural trait. Dax should have received an Academy Award.

Surrounded by liars. Fangs every which way I'd turn. Secrets by the bushel.

How was I supposed to navigate these waters when I'd no idea where my rutter was or which way to sail?

"Do not test me, pup! You were in charge of keeping Alexander far away from her." His displeasure was there in the set of his perfectly bowed lips.

When his accusing finger landed on me, my shoulders curved in protectively. Instinctually.

My experience with testosterone and the male ego wasn't a pleasant tale.

I'd learned to make myself small whenever it reared its head. Stayed out of the way as long as possible.

Every stride I'd made to become a stronger, more confident person, always fell to the wayside whenever angry males were present.

Rough and cocky weren't the same as the lethal kindling of the male flame that came with fury.

I didn't understand why, but my body inched towards Bram. When he saw my fear, his expression shifted, and he subtly put me behind him without being noticed.

"Tempers are running high. Loxy being missing has kept Thane from releasing all of his pent-up energy. I'm sure you can understand that, Xander." Understanding dawned on me at Bram's words.

Loxy was Thane's girlfriend. She'd been gone two weeks since she'd been killed, but she'd been gone two weeks prior to that. A month in total. *Well, damn.*

Thane's werewolf side must need to dominate something and release all of his built-up tension.

I looked to Dax. We hadn't done anything in the months since Xander arrived, and if he needed to dominate someone too, it made me wonder who he'd been with.

Dax and I had loads of trysts before I'd ended it to start dating. Thinking back, never once had he let me take the lead. I'd never thought of it as dominating, but it was, wasn't it?

I hadn't been fair to him when I asked that we be able to see other people.

I'd known that he was free to see others too but realizing that I wasn't the only one to have the option made me irrationally jealous all of a sudden.

Then another thought took the forefront of my woozy mind.

What did Bram mean that Xander should understand? Was it the same way for him?

Oh gods. Was he tearing people's throats out because he wasn't finding his release?

Grabbing the decanter from Xander's hand, I poured myself another two fingers. Not particularly caring for the taste, I needed something to quiet all my racing thoughts.

His cold hand brushed against the back of my arm, sending an electric tingle shooting through my body.

"You're safe, love. No one will hurt you. I won't allow it." His voice was quiet, but I knew the rest of them would hear anyway.

"Are you sure about that, brother?" Thane's arrogance rubbed me the wrong way and I wasn't sure why I didn't fear him more.

"We haven't officially met, I'm Aurora."

"Aurora, this time, is it? Well, Aurora. I'm Thane Valsidalve. Prince and second born son to the House of Basarab. First and Original werewolf cursed to fate." I shuffled on my feet, trying to keep my balance. "I'd say it's a pleasure to meet you but I'm not a liar."

Prince? Xander tensed beside me.

I had no idea what he'd meant when he said, *this time,* but I was done being in the dark.

With alcohol clouding my judgement, I leaned towards him. "You... are a dick!"

Wobbling forward, my arm swung out, fist connecting with the side of his jaw.

Oops.

Chapter Twenty

Xander and Dax pushed me behind them. Even Bram stepped a foot towards his alpha but didn't dare touch him.

Closing my eyes shut tight, I waited for the hits to come.

One second. Two, three. After a full five seconds of tense quiet, not even any snarls, I peeked one eye open. Then the other.

The drinks had taken their toll. My vision was blurry. My posture wobbly.

I'd been sure that at any moment, Thane would explode into a wolf and kill me.

Laughter rumbled through his chest. Not the dark, humorless chuckles he'd given before. It was actual mirth that made its way past his defenses.

I couldn't believe what I was hearing.

Bram fully relaxed but Dax didn't so much as shift his footing.

With Xander's protective stance in front of me, I'd succumbed to the alcohol, falling with a plop onto the couch.

With my eyes heavy, I'd mumbled. "You're all ridiculous. I guess I'll get my buffet after all. Bitzy will love that."

Were they normal people, no one would have heard my ramblings.

These were anything but normal humans and they heard every word.

Darkness claimed me. The last thing I remembered was them all chuckling, passing around more drinks.

I couldn't have been out long. We were all still in the office. I could smell the leather couch and each of these testosterone driven males around me.

When I'd woken up, I'd heard voices and kept my eyes closed to listen in.

If they'd known I was awake, I couldn't be sure they'd be honest with me.

I had questions that had been rolling around my head for the last couple of weeks. This was my best shot at hearing the truth, whatever they were saying.

My head was laying on someone's lap. The scent of evergreen and copper filled my senses. Xander.

"A pistol, that one." I recognized Thane's voice. "I don't know why I let you convince me to let her live this time. Great job you did keeping him from finding her, asshole."

I'd faded slightly in and out for a few minutes.

Dax's scent of musk and pepper came from nearby. "... the first three lifetimes, you killing her as soon as she was located only brought her soul back faster. And last time was a fluke accident."

Thane gave a hard, unamused laugh. "You really think that, don't you?"

It was quiet for a moment before he continued. Or maybe my dizzy head added time that wasn't there.

"Loxana figured out that I was letting her live the last time. Who do you think the hit and run driver was?"

Dax swore. With my eyes closed, I could feel the angry heat coming off his body from somewhere to my side.

"Are you fucking kidding me? She killed her against your wishes, and you didn't punish her?"

I couldn't believe what I was hearing. Dax was outraged but he didn't sound all that surprised.

"Oh, I punished her. Took weeks dragging it out. I dare say she liked it, the masochist she was." Thane replied in turn.

Xander's quick intake of breath at that tid bit of information let me know he hadn't any idea of how horrible Loxy had been. I was weirdly comforted by that fact.

He'd promised no one would hurt me and he'd watched over me as I'd slept.

Snuggling into his hold as he ran his fingers through my hair, I let the gentle brush of his fingers ground my trepidations and slip away.

With my eyes still closed, I could hear the grumbling sounds issuing deep in Dax's chest.

"So, what the hell is going on here, brother? Why are you even tolerating Daxayrius near your mate." Mate? Thane had to be mistaken.

Squeezing my eyes shut tighter, trying not to give away my awareness, and I could swear that Xander snickered only low enough for me to hear.

"This is Aurora. Not Anastasia. Her soul is still mine, but this woman doesn't know me. Even if she feels the pull towards me." Xander's kind voice stirred something behind my ribcage.

His fingertips lightly grazed the side of my face, and it took everything in me not to lean into his touch.

He was practically humming with tenderness. "I want to earn her love. I will not turn her unless I do. And as you know, mating bonds only snap into place for super naturals. I won't do that to her again."

Again? What he meant by that would have to wait for me to ask at another time.

Dax had stopped snarling. Now he was whimpering quietly.

I wanted to go to him. Comfort him.

The next thought crossed through the darkest parts of my mind before dragging itself into the spotlight.

As irrational as it would be to have feelings for not just one. Not just two mythical creatures. I'd found myself wondering at all three of these fierce males.

"How selfless of you." The distain in Thane's tone brought on my anger again.

Why was he able to get under my skin so easily? It was infuriating.

"Tell me, brother. If she chooses to give her love to another this lifetime, will you stand by and watch as she spreads her legs for them? Bears their offspring? Will you sit ideally by as she grows old, withers, and dies?" The smirk in his voice was as clear as if I'd looked into his face.

With his hand resting now on the underside of my breast, Xander's tone turned melancholy.

"I remember everything, Thane. I remember finding her. I remember turning her. She never had a choice. I took that from her the first time. She became a monster the longer the years waned on."

He brushed the hair from my face. My nose tickled and I scrunched it up to soothe the itch.

"I remember how you always tagged along. Always coveted her. And I remember you taking the choice from me to end her life." There was a darkness as he spit those last words. "Ask me again if her choice matters?"

No one spoke for a few minutes. I could hear glasses being emptied and Bram clearing his throat, but he didn't add to the conversation.

"If it's between the three of us then?" I didn't know why Thane put himself into the mix, but I couldn't help the thrill of excitement that quivered low in my stomach.

Dax huffed his defiance but didn't interject anything to the conversation.

"If it's between the three of us," Xander answered, "I may not be so understanding. If she wants a human life, I can accept that. You two are not human. And if either of you wins her hand and turns her, I will fight for her with everything I've got. Rori may not be mine.... but Anastasia's soul certainly is!"

Bram spoke up for the first time since I'd stirred. "Have you ever considered that her soul may decide to go in a new direction this time?"

His voice held no contempt. Just questioning, and perhaps a little concern.

"I suppose time will only tell. For now, I will take whatever she decides to share with me. Whether it be everything, only her company, or nothing at all. After all, that's what love is, right?"

The others were quiet for so long that I must have drifted off for a few minutes. When I'd roused again, the conversation had taken a different turn.

".... it's been nearly four hundred years. You seriously have had no trysts with anyone? Your balls must be bluer than the deepest ocean." I couldn't be hearing Thane correctly.

Was he suggesting that Xander hadn't had sex in four centuries?

"When you lose your other half, no one fills that gap. I would sooner rip the beating heart from my chest than lay with all the velvet in the world. She was my everything. And I loved her beyond reason. So no, brother. I haven't lowered myself to take another since you killed her."

I stirred, unable to sit still any longer.

Reaching up to cup Xander's face, his obsidian eyes bore into mine. Something familiar laid in their depths.

Dax, Thane, and Bram disappeared for the briefest of moments.

There was only Xander. There was only us.

Chapter Twenty-One

Noticing I was awake, Dax came and knelt beside me, drawing my attention away from Xander.

"Hey there, little demon. How you feeling?" His touch firm, but gentle.

Xander smacked his hand away from my arm and stood to stop him from addressing me.

"Do not touch her, mongrel! Not in my presence." Spit flew from his mouth with each word.

The pain in his voice softened my normal sarcastic remarks. I'd only wanted to ease his suffering, but when I'd looked at Dax, my heart fell.

Of course, Thane couldn't let it go. *Asshole*.

"Looks like I'll be picking up the scraps in this tug o war." I'd made the mistake of looking his way, only to find him licking his lips. "All the better. It's the only kind of leftovers worth having."

My head was pounding but that didn't stop the heat from rising at his words.

"You're a pig." If I'd thought calling him names would deter his behavior, I'd been wrong. It only pushed him farther.

As he leaned closer, I got a whiff of honeysuckle and clove. His scent was scrumptious, and it had my toes curling inside my shoes.

"Oh no, kitten. I'm the big bad wolf. The better to eat you with, my dear." He was incorrigible.

The room was suddenly too small for all of this machismo. The urge to flee overwhelmed me.

Pushing passed Xander and Dax, I headed to the door. They didn't stop me, but they did start shoving each other around before I'd had a chance to open it.

Bram was up and at my side in an instant and as I'd flung the door open, Seiran quickly yanked me out of the room, tugging me behind him.

"I've got her from here, Bram. Thank you." As grateful as I was to be out of there, Seiran's territorialness gave me pause.

The gentle giant that Bram was, inclined his head and headed back in, closing the chaos off from sight.

"You really know how to liven things up, queenie." That dimple of his lit up his face, bringing me back down from the anxiety that had built up back in that room.

Lissie came to join us as we re-entered the bar area. With a nod in Seiran's direction, he headed back towards the office.

"Are we talking about anything yet? I'm all ears when you're ready, Rori."

She'd become a close friend in the last month or so. Her confident attitude and firm, but caring character helped me open up about a lot of things that I'd normally kept bottled up.

Very few people knew so much about me. That might be why Bitzy was upset with me. I couldn't be sure.

It'd only taking Lissie a few weeks to learn as much about me as Bitzy learned in over four years.

"What did you tell Hannah? She's the one who went to find Cody when she sensed I was in trouble."

If she'd come back to see that stand-off before we'd went into the office, the whole situation could have been much worse.

Suddenly fascinated by her nails, she played off the question.

Thrumming my fingers along each of my crossed arms, I waited.

Figuring out over the past few weeks Lissie's weakness worked in my favor.

She wasn't comfortable with awkward silence.

We could sit for hours in a peaceable silence, but when it came to questioning her with things she didn't want to answer, any pregnant pause was her undoing.

"Okay, but don't be mad. I compelled her to forget what happened. She's happily out there tending bar and upset that you're not in yet."

My face must have showed my confusion. If she'd compelled her to forget everything she'd seen, then why was Hannah upset with me?

"She thinks you're running late and worried that you won't have time to set up before the night crowd comes in. It's Luke's first shift cooking and she's frustrated that she may have to do everything."

I snorted. "Well, we can't have that now, can we? We don't want another Molly on our hands."

Her posture relaxed. "You're not mad at me for using my bloodsucker woo-doo on her?" Wiggling her fingers in front of my face, I smacked them away playfully.

"Of course not. I don't want her to be anxious or scared. You did the right thing, Liss." My wink was a little over the top, but it lightened my mood as well as hers.

We continued walking and as soon as we came in view, Hannah's look of relief at the sight of me had me feeling guilty for no reason.

"I'll catch up with you later. I'd better get things sorted out." Prep work wasn't my favorite part of the night, but neither was clean up.

She giggled quietly. I didn't understand the shit eating grin, but she walked away without another word.

Making my way to the beer case to take inventory before I headed to the stock room, I noticed it was full.

Checking the kegs, full. Fresh bar glasses washed and ready. Tables wiped down.

What the hell is going on?

Just as I'd started making my way around the bar, a sandy blonde-haired male came bounding out of the kitchen with a tub of filled condiment bottles for the tables.

The smell of garlic and spices wafted out of the kitchen in his wake, and I realized I'd never gotten my food before everything happened with Thane. *Too late now.*

"Oh, hey. I'm Luke," he said without preamble.

Wiping his hand on the dish towel he had hanging from his front pants pocket, he stuck it out to me.

"I'm the new floater. I'm quite excited to try my hand in the kitchens tonight."

Taking his hand and giving it a weak shake, I said, "I'm Rori. Are you saying you've never cooked before? You do realize this is a Friday night shift? It's going to be slammed."

I didn't mean to bust the guy's balls, but I needed my tips tonight. working only six days in the last two weeks left my bills unpaid and my stomach empty.

With the new raises came a new payment schedule. Our hourly wages were paid bi-monthly. Our tips were ours to keep that day, but I hadn't quite learned to make mine stretch until pay day yet.

"No worries. I'm a quick study. I've made my own food for a very long time. I've got this." With no more than a wink, he finished the tables and shuffled back into the kitchen.

The regulars started filling the bar area and some out of towners from the ski lodge made their way to the tables, asking for menus without even a glance at the bar.

This was only the second Friday night since Eventide opened the kitchen.

We'd all been testing the pub style foods for a couple of weeks and the locals were offered that opportunity for the last week.

Mina called it a **soft opening**. I guessed that meant a trial run.

I didn't like her, but begrudgingly I had to admit her skills as a manager were good.

She was mean and looked down on all of us. I wouldn't cross her in her area of expertise though.

Her people skills might have sucked but she knew how to do the other aspects of her job well.

Bitzy and Kamie came waltzing through the door all dolled up for a night out.

I waved at them both. It was good to see them out to have fun.

Kamie beamed and waved meekly, but Bitzy sneered, giving me her back.

Things had been strained between us, and I didn't know how to fix them.

I needed Lissie. I needed someone I could confide in when it came to the supernatural things going on.

If Bitzy couldn't accept that Lissie and I had become good friends, I didn't see a way around our problem.

If this day had been long, the night would be longer. It dragged on like a badly subtitled movie.

And now, watching Bitzy hang all over a couple of rough looking guys in the corner while she threw back drinks like she could handle them, I'd been saddled with babysitter duties.

Kazz and Gunner showed up tonight. The new dart boards were being put to good use.

Kiah and Janie sat at their usual spot at the end of the bar, though it wasn't in the same position anymore.

With Thane showing up today, it seemed Dax called in reinforcements to watch over me.

Kamie was casually dancing with Seiran on the edge of the dance floor, but his attention swung to Bitzy more often than I'd thought was necessary.

Then it hit me.

He wasn't watching Bitzy.

His hands clenched at his sides. The glare in his eyes focused.

He was leering at the strangers she was with.

Fear peaked my senses. Scanning them fully, I felt the danger.

I didn't know if they were wolf or vampire. but Seiran knew. And the evil eye he was giving them spoke of familiarity. He knew who they were.

If I had any common sense, I'd leave it to him to handle... but I didn't.

My protectiveness overrode my fear and when I yanked on Bitzy's arm, she swayed.

"What do you want, Rori? Can't you leave any scraps for the rest of us?" *What the hell*? I had no idea what that was about, but she was definitely drunk. "Go back to your guys. Where are they, anyway? Trouble in paradise?"

Taking a calming breath before I'd say something I'd regret later, I glared at the two guys with her.

If I'd had any doubt before about them not being human, the volatile atmosphere that surrounded them made it perfectly clear now that I knew what to look for.

"Rori, isn't it?" the one with the hazel eyes took a step around Bitzy.

Brown hair covered more than just his head. A tuft of it shown from the top of his vee necked shirt. His arms thick with it.

"I've heard so much about you." The sneer was saturated with sarcasm.

Looking to Bitzy, she threw up her hands and stormed off.

"Oh, fuck me. They're all yours, Rori," she called over her shoulder.

Then it dawned on me. He hadn't heard of me from her.

That must mean...

"Thane. Man of the hour." Pushing passed me, knocking me to the side as he went. "Orders?"

Part of Thane's pack then.

Thane came from the back office with Dax. Xander was nowhere in sight. When he spotted me, he made a beeline.

Kamie must have gone to look after Bitzy but Seiran and Lissie were only a few yards away.

They didn't let on if anything was amiss, but I'd gotten to know their tells. Tightness around her eyes. No dimple showing on his face. They were alert, troubled.

Kiah had stood from his barstool, but Janie took hold of his arm, keeping her by his side until necessary.

Smart. No need to call undo attention unless things went sideways.

Kazz and Gunner finished their game loudly.

The other patrons didn't notice the tension filling the room and for that, I was grateful.

With a casual arm wrapping around my waist, Kazz lifted and twirled me in a circle. "Did you see that? I wiped the floor with him."

Gunner huffed and sat bodily down at the table beside us.

Taking a drink of ale, it slopped down the front of him. "You got lucky, that's all."

If I hadn't known them so long, I'd have assumed they'd not been paying attention to what was going on around us... but I did know them.

Setting me on my feet and deftly blocking me from view, Kazz leaned in and placed a playful kiss on my cheek. He whispered in my ear as he brushed back. "Stay behind us."

Gunner stood. Smacking him on the shoulder. "I bet you won't beat me at pool. After we order some food, I'm going to kick your ass."

He too made his move to stand in front of me so nonchalantly that I almost bought it myself.

Peering between the two giants, Thane met my gaze for a moment before turning back to Dax.

"I'm leaving Zeth and Fitz here. I'll be back in a week or so to check in on the ... situation."

If his insult was meant for me, it fell short of its mark. I could care less if he checked in on me as long as I got to keep breathing when he did.

"They're not staying at my place. There's no need for your dogs to be around." I'd never seen Dax so out of sorts. He tried to play it off, but his usual commanding nature seemed like child's play next to Thane's dominating presence.

Thane didn't acknowledge the disrespect. Taking a step in my direction, he peered over the wall of muscle standing in front of me.

"I see you, kitten. Play nice or it'll be my turn to play rough." With a wink, he left.

I had no idea what he'd meant by that little quip.

All I knew was that life in this small town just got a whole lot more interesting.

And that excited me more than it should.

Chapter Twenty-Two

It'd been almost two weeks since Thane had shown up at Eventide.

It'd been just as long since Bitzy even glanced in my direction.

There had to be more to why she was mad at me, but every time I'd tried to coax it out of her, she'd thrown up a wall and told me not to worry myself.

Cody's schedule now lined up with mine, except for today apparently. And either Gav, Seiran, or Lissie were always working during my shifts.

Zeth and Fitz were there every shift I'd worked.

While Fitz wasn't a total dick, he also wasn't the friendliest guy. Zeth, on the other hand, was a dick.

He'd made lude comments, not bothering to keep his voice from carrying.

Doing his best to provoke me whenever I was in ear shot, my patience was now at an all-time low.

And today, he tripped me while I was bringing a full tray of food to a table.

Those patrons didn't bother leaving a tip. As if it was my fault the werehole made me spill their food all over the floor.

My temper got the best of me, and I stepped up, toe to toe, with the werewolf.

I was in front of him before I'd given myself permission to move. "You cost me money, asshole!" My finger waggling in his face.

Luke had been stocking the bar and came around to stand by my side.

"Let's get you a cheeseburger. On me," he said to Zeth.

Wrapping his arms around the tops of mine, he led me away while Zeth sneered.

I didn't protest. I knew it was for the best. I knew the situation must have been alarming if the only other human working with me today sensed danger and intervened.

Bringing me into the kitchens, he helped me up onto a stool next to the chopping station.

He put his hand under my chin, lifting it to meet his eyes. "You okay? What was that back there?"

I couldn't very well tell him the truth. That it was a vengeful werewolf pack doing their best to intimidate me and make my life miserable.

I couldn't really tell him much of anything.

Like how his bosses were all vampires and he worked at a place that another pack of werewolves hung out, trying to protect me.

I didn't want to go back out there with Zeth and Fitz to finish my shift.

They had become a constant thorn in my side. Hanging around the bar. Stalking the woods outside my house.

Lissie stayed with me many nights of the week anymore. Though Dax had offered, I didn't want to give him the wrong idea.

We hadn't been out on anymore dates since the movies the day Dylan died.

I couldn't decide if that was a good thing or a bad thing.

All I knew was that I'd missed him... or at least, I missed who I'd thought he was.

Xander was a totally different matter.

He'd escorted me home after my Sunday night shift.

When we'd gotten to my door, I'd thought he'd press to come in and stay.

He didn't. He leaned in to kiss my cheek, never crossing the threshold. Got in his car and left. Tail lights fading into the night.

Ten minutes later, Lissie showed up sporting an overnight bag and a thermos.

I could only assume that it contained blood. From where, I had no clue.

Luke dropped his hand from my chin and snapped his fingers in my face a few times before I'd remembered he was talking to me. "Rori? Anyone home?"

I'd nodded. "I'm alright. I must be hungry. I'm not a morning person"

He grinned. "It's 2pm, Rori. That hardly qualifies as morning."

Stepping back and picking up the menu off a nearby counter, he handed it to me.

"Pick something. I'll get Gav to make it when he gets off break." Walking away to do more prep, he didn't push me for anything.

I liked that about him. He hadn't been here long, but our interactions felt comfortable.

Wondering where Gav went, his absence unnerved me for half a second. *Get a grip.*

He'd probably only stepped out the back for a moment but from some unfortunate twist of luck, he'd missed my outburst.

I'd have to tell Luke to keep this between us. I wouldn't want Xander to take it out on Gav because I couldn't keep my temper in check.

Once I'd given my attention to the fact that I hadn't eaten anything but the supplements I took with my coffee, I became ravenous.

Luke came back with his arms full of boxes. I didn't bother to offer my help. He'd refuse it anyway.

"I don't get up until around noon, Luke. This Is my morning," I'd deadpanned. He laughed. "I'm starving. Let me look this over for a minute."

As I'd scanned the items available, I'd remembered the arrogant wolves out in the dining room.

"You'd better get on that cheeseburger. Wouldn't want some overbearing dickhead barking down your neck." I'd chuckled at my own joke.

Zeth was nothing but a stray dog.

"Gav will be back in a minute. That guy out there can wait. I've gotta get back to the bar. I'm still learning the ropes with some of those fancier drinks the ski resort folks have been ordering lately." Waggling his eyebrows and biting his bottom lip, that half smile lit all the way to his eyes.

Luke's happy-go-lucky attitude was a breath of fresh air in my current stagnant mood.

"Figured I could work on it before this weekend. Three days should be enough time." He'd taken to everything and anything we'd thrown him into.

I'd been skeptical but he'd been right when I'd first met him. He learned rather fast.

Why he wanted to be here, I didn't know. With talent like his, he could probably do or be anything he wanted to be. *None of my business.*

I'd written my order down on the order pad and shoved it into the cook's line up wheel.

Begrudgingly, I'd put in an order for two cheeseburger platters for Zeth and Fitz as well before I'd headed out to face the music.

This shift couldn't end fast enough.

When I'd returned to the dining area, a woman with flowing white-blonde hair was seated with them.

I'd never imagined having anyone who'd want their company, let alone a beautiful woman like her.

Something about the set of her jaw, the shape of her eyes, and the confidence she exuded was familiar.

There were only a handful of customers around the room.

The lunch shift hadn't quite taken off yet the way the dinner crowd had.

The skiers at the lodge usually grabbed a quick bite from their dining area before heading back out to the slopes.

I'd checked that everything was still good and that no one needed more drinks or anything before walking over to where the newcomer was sitting between the werewolves.

"Zeth, Fitz. I put in an order for your cheeseburgers." Turning to the female, I'd nodded to the menu on the table. "Is there anything I can get you? A drink while you browse?"

Her carnivorous smile made the hair on my arms stand on end.

Glancing over the menu, she'd handed it back to me. "I don't see what I want on the menu."

The venomous drawl of her tone set my teeth itching. An unwarranted antipathy wrapped around my core.

"So, tell me, where Is that fine specimen at today?" Her words were a coo.

I couldn't put my finger on it. I'd never met her before, but I instantly wanted to slap the shit out of her.

"I'm sorry? Who are you looking for?"

I almost didn't want to know but with the hateful way she'd looked at me, I had a pretty good idea of who she'd meant.

"Alexander, of course. Where is my former lover? That handsome mate of yours?"

Chapter Twenty-Three

Irrational anger coursed through my system.

I didn't know what she'd meant by mate. Thane had said the same thing when I'd been in the office, feigning sleep after I'd awoken from passing out drunk.

It didn't matter. My body reacted anyway.

Seething, my words were more harsh than they should have been. "He's not on the menu. So, take a look to see if there's anything else you'd might like."

It took everything in me to not flip my hair over my shoulder and turn my back on the lot of them.

Tsking in my direction, the female smiled a devilish grin. "Come now, Anastasia. Surely we can share."

I'd launched myself towards the table unthinkingly.

An arm caught around my middle, but I was in a blinding rage.

My vision was tunneled to focus only on her. Images of my hands, pulling her hair, biting her face, ripping her head from her shoulders ran through my mind. Bloody. Brutal images.

The feminine voice at my ear hissed a string of curse words. Her arms were a vice that squeezed harder with each of my lurches forward.

"Calm yourself, queenie. She's not worth it." The venom in her tone seeped into the recesses of my mind.

It was familiar and settled me in a way I couldn't explain.

Expecting to see Lissie when I turned my head, the sight of Mina holding me drained the anger from my system entirely.

Anger turned into unease. I felt the blood rushing under the surface of my skin and secretly wondered if it called to her.

Sensing that I was finished with my tantrum, she let me go but stayed close.

"Kosmina. It's been a long time, sister," the female at the table said. "I see you still keep abhorrent company."

Mina straightened her posture, brushing down the front of her shirt to erase the creases holding me back had put in her blouse.

It might have been my imagination, but I could have sworn the corner of Mina's mouth pulled up ever so slightly on one side.

"Korrina. Sister is a stretch now, isn't it? You're hardly more than a dog chasing memories to me anymore." With a swift glance at Fitz, and then to Zeth, she'd huffed an unamused laugh. "If my company is abhorred, yours is downright repugnant."

I had to hand it to Mina. She might have been a bitch at the best of times but in this moment, it made my heart happy.

"Oh, come now, Mina. Is it really so bad to see me? I've missed our little get togethers." Zeth chuckled, but Fitz sat up straighter in his seat. "This could be another rather entertaining bonding experience."

"Kori! Thane doesn't want her hurt," he glanced in my direction, "yet." Fitz's nervous fidgeting had me fidgeting myself.

I had no idea what games Mina and Kori usually played but if the werewolf was nervous, I should be categorically terrified.

The smirk Zeth had been sporting wavered. Thane didn't seem like the forgiving kind to me.

Thinking back on it now, he'd punished Loxy, repeatedly over a few weeks.

The twisted wolf she'd been, she'd liked it, but that didn't mean it was anything less than painful.

"Relax, Fitz. I wasn't going to damage her. She doesn't need all of her fingers, right?" Kori was fast becoming the person I hated most in the world.

Cody came from somewhere in the back. Noticing our little group, he made a beeline straight to my side.

"Fitz, Zeth," he said with a dip of his chin. "Kori, to what do we owe the pleasure?" His tone implied he found her company anything but pleasurable.

As Kori came around the table, Mina casually stepped in front of me.

I didn't know if I trusted her enough to protect me but with Cody here, I felt mildly safer with her backing him up.

"Come now, Cody. You and I have certainly had our fun in the past. How about you go fetch that boss of yours and we can have a grand old time." Licking her lips, her full body perusal of my friend made me sick.

I wasn't sure what she was, vampire or werewolf, but I suspected she would think it amusing to have one of each in her bed at the same time.

If the vampire in question was Xander, I didn't know if I could keep my murderous intentions to myself.

Leaning around Mina, Kori's eyes met mine. Fitz stiffened.

I barely recognized my own voice when I spoke through my teeth. Deep. Full of acid. "We reserve the right to refuse service. Take your skanky ass out of my bar!"

I didn't hear it, but I felt Mina's exasperated sigh at my side. Cody chuckled under his breath, but Zeth growled.

I also didn't know what gave me the balls to talk back to someone who could tear me limb from limb, but there was no way I would serve Xander up to her.

He wasn't mine. He had every right to bed whoever he wanted. I shouldn't be this angry, but thinking of him with another female made me see red.

Why did I feel so damned possessive?

And poor Cody. He had come to protect me, and I couldn't even keep my smart mouth shut.

"Rori," Mina said. "Let's go into the office."

My determination was set, and she could tell I didn't want to budge.

When she added, "Please" my resolve waivered.

I let her lead me away, leaving the trio and Cody to their bickering.

Korrina called out to us before we got to the hall. "Aurora, do make sure you knock on doors before entering. You wouldn't want to see my body being ravaged by one or more of your... friends."

Struggling against Mina's sudden grip on my arms, she dragged me into the office and shut the door to the soundproof room.

Blood was draining from my fingertips with how tightly she'd gripped the tops of them.

I snarled at her, and she huffed out a laugh but let go, pushing me down onto the couch.

"Look at you. Not even turned and already as vicious as ever." Pouring herself a drink, she motioned to the bottle, and I shook my head.

I didn't need my judgement any more clouded than it already was.

"Suit yourself."

Pursing my lips, I refused to give her the satisfaction of my sarcastic retorts that laid behind my teeth.

She'd never liked me. Her opinion hadn't mattered. At least, that's what I'd told myself whenever people criticized or judged me and my choices.

Secretly, I overthought ever single negative energy thrown my way from everyone and anyone.

Broken people often put on a devil may care attitude. but privately chastised their every interaction.

"Nothing to say? That's so unlike you." Sipping her Scotch, the sound of her nails drumming against the glass grated on my last nerve.

"How would you know? You know nothing about me!" My sudden outburst seemed to amuse her.

Accidentally opening my mouth, the flood gates were now wide open.

"I haven't done anything to anyone and now I have supernatural enemies. What the actual fuck am I supposed to do with that? And you... you're supposed to be on the good side? You act like a bitch to everyone but especially to me. Why?"

Swiveling the last of the Scotch around the bottom of the glass, she downed it and slammed the cup onto the desk.

The shattering glass caused me to jump back in my seat.

"I know nothing? No, Rori. You know nothing."

With a deep breath in through her nose and out through her mouth, she pinched the bridge of her nose.

"I'm bound to my own story. If I overstep my own tale, I do no one justice. So, I will talk, and you will listen. Understand?" Mina wasn't someone who mixed words.

I'd known that from the first week. And while her temper had flared moments ago, she was relatively calm now.

Giving her the opportunity to tell me why she was the way she was might answer some lingering questions that kept me awake at night.

"One question first," I said, and she rolled her eyes but smirked. "I'm assuming Kori is supernatural. She called you sister."

"That's not a question," she said smugly.

It was my turn to roll my eyes at her.

Gathering my courage to hear the answer, I pushed forward.

"Is she your actual sister, or a sister in the sense of what you are and who made you...," I motioned to her beautiful form, "...this way?"

"Are you sure you want the answer to that question? I can only tell you so much. For the rest of that particular tale, you'll need to have a chat with our boss."

I respected how all of these vampires would only reveal what was theirs to reveal.

Never imagining people with fangs with blood as their main diet could be so civilized. It was all so very honorable.

And it kind of creeped me out.

She took my silence as affirmation. My intrigue must have been written all over my face because her resigned sigh ended with an eye roll that left me feeling like a tick in an unreachable spot on a hounds back.

The smell of the new leather couch surrounded me in a warm embrace.

Settling into its depths, my mind wandered to the last time I'd been in this room.

Xander's lap under my head. Dax standing close enough to touch.

Thane and his ridiculously handsome face standing across the room. The way my belly dipped with each male who spoke...

"Rori!" Mina was snapping her fingers at me. "Honestly, if you're not going to listen, why should I bother talking?"

She had started her story, and I'd missed it with my daydreaming.

"Sorry, Mina. I promise, I'm here. I want to understand your tale." Criss-crossing my fingers over my heart, I mocked zipping my lips and a twitch appeared at the corner of her mouth.

"Very well then. Korrina was my sister." I began to interrupt and stopped instantly at the severe glare she gave me.

"Korrina was my older sister, by nearly three years. We'd been close but when she'd hit puberty, she didn't want her little sister tagging along with her and her older friends."

"We lived in one of the larger villages in Romania.

There were plenty of boys to court her and when mama would send me along with her to run errands, Kori wouldn't hesitate to pinch me over and over again whenever we'd meet up with her friends and I'd do something she deemed childish."

"I'd always had a careful eye. I noticed more than the average person from a young age.

Kori would flirt her way around the market on every outing mama sent us on together.

I hadn't hit puberty yet, but I knew what it was to attract the eye of wanting males."

When I gasped, she laughed. "Oh, don't look so scandalized. Females back in the fourteen hundreds were often married off around their first bleed. We were well off compared to most of the villagers. That allowed us a bit more time to come into our own."

It was difficult to not pelt her with all of the questions that bubbled up on my tongue, but I sensed that if I'd interrupted her now, I wouldn't get another chance to hear her tale.

"One afternoon, after the market had been closing up for the day, I had wandered off to the bakery cart to see if the young woman who ran it had any leftover wares she'd like to part with for a fraction of their price. When I'd returned, my sister was chatting with two overly handsome males.

They'd struck me as something more than noble. More than human.

Korrina didn't have the good sense the gods gave her. She didn't feel anything amiss.

At fourteen years old, I felt like the more mature of the two of us.

Trying to warn her away, she stood fast to her flirtation and bid me to go home.

It was getting dark, and mama had forbidden us from staying until the market closed but Kori hadn't wanted to leave.

I had a choice... stay and watch over my sister. Or go home as our mother told us to.

I begged her to come but she shooed me away like a mere child to her seventeen years.

When I arrived on our doorstep, father demanded to know where Korinna was, and I told him.

Without another word, he grabbed his sword and left to find her.

His efforts were fruitless. She'd gone with the strange males without a trace.

A few years went by. I missed my sister terribly. I'd never allowed suitors to court me. My head filled with grief at her loss.

And when I turned twenty-one, father insisted I find a noble male and marry. He couldn't understand why I wasn't willing to settle down.

If I'd have given in, if I'd moved on with my life, it felt like I was meant to give up on ever seeing her again.

I couldn't let that happen. So, I left home to find her or whatever happened to her.

Traveling village to village for nearly a year, there was no sign of her and there were no leads as to her whereabouts.

I stopped at every pub, every tavern. I talked to everyone and anyone who would listen.

Sometimes the stench of sweat and old ale would turn my stomach to the point of upheaval.

One evening, after interrogating nearly an entire village, I was having dinner in the tavern beneath the inn before retiring for the night.

A girl my age walked right up to me, clapped her hand on my shoulder, and downed the pint of ale that sat on my table next to the stew and bread the barmaid had just set down.

When I looked up, she wasn't alone.

Two males stood a head above her, casting her face in shadow.

When the shorter one moved back, Korinna smiled down at me like the cat that ate the canary.

She said she'd been living in a castle. That she was going to be young and beautiful forever.

Then she asked if I loved her enough to come with her and be granted the same fate.

I went along, not knowing that I'd be fed on. Not knowing that I'd find a best friend there a few years later.

I had been at the castle for a couple of years before I'd come to meet her. And it was another couple of years before I was turned."

I couldn't keep my inside thoughts to myself anymore. "So, that's why she looks younger than you... Mina, what happened between you and Kori?"

It was quiet. The soundproof tiles absorbed any and all noise.

I could hear the blood rushing in my ears as I waited for her to answer.

"Kori was jealous of my friend. I loved my sister, but she had always been a selfish, self-serving prat. When she'd seen how happy I was with my friend, the woman she'd thought didn't deserve what was hers; she plotted with ... someone else who'd felt the same way. In the end, their jealousy led to my friend's death."

She was silent for a minute or two, up inside her own head.

Reaching over to pat her arm in comfort, I pulled it back when she hissed.

With lips pursed, she became that cold bitch I'd come to know since I'd met her.

"My sister tore my happiness away from me and ceased being anything more to me from that moment on."

That made sense but I still didn't understand what I had done to earn her ire.

"Okay, but why do you hate me? I wasn't there, Mina. I haven't wronged you in any way."

Standing abruptly, she glared at me. Unshed tears in her eyes. "No, Rori. YOU weren't."

Without looking back, she went to the door and shut it behind her, leaving me with more questions than when we'd first begun her tale.

Chapter Twenty-Four

I t had been over a week since I'd talked to Mina. Knowing her story better, I still didn't feel any closer to her.

Kori made two visits to Eventide and caused all kinds of raucous with Zeth and Fitz while she belittled me and talked about Xander as loudly as possible.

Xander came in during that second visit.

His eyes landed on her right away and he didn't look happy about it.

He made straight for the office, but she'd caught up to him easily. When they'd come back out ten minutes later, her face was crestfallen.

She'd seen I was watching. So of course, her hands brushed casually over his arm, settling on the side of his face.

The low snarl that rumbled in the back of my throat surprised me, but I couldn't make it stop.

With his excellent hearing, his eyes widened, and he pushed her away.

It had been the first time I'd wished to be supernatural.

If I'd had their scenting abilities or their hearing, I could have known what was going on between them.

In that moment, I hated being human.

Neither Kori, nor Xander, had been in since then. Unless they'd come in before or after I'd gotten off, they'd avoided the place.

I worked every day this week so that I could have off this weekend. Dax had called and asked me to go out to dinner earlier in the week.

He was picking me up today around three.

Having a Saturday morning off to sip coffee, read a book, and love on Aries was a blessing I hadn't realized I'd needed.

With our date not until later in the afternoon, there hadn't been the stress of setting an alarm or worrying about rushing around.

Today turned out to be rather warm for upper Vermont this early in the spring. We were going on a hike to the wolfs den.

The temperature was in the upper 60's and there were flowers blooming and trees covered in a spring green for as far as the eye could see.

I'd worn a pair of comfortable capri pants. I knew the shade would be brisk and shorts would have made me colder while the sweat from my exertion glistened on my skin.

The bookish tee shirt I'd worn was of a fabulous series. It wasn't complete yet but the first three had made quite an impression on me.

Dax kept staring at the logo as we'd hiked until I'd finally snapped at him.

Apparently wearing a dragon was some kind of conflict for him. I had no idea why.

He'd just brushed it off but asked if I'd needed his light jacket a few times as we walked.

If I wasn't so hot, I might have taken it just to keep that hurt puppy look off his face.

We hadn't spoken much on the way here. It took every bit of my concentration to keep putting one foot in front of the other on the four-mile trail that wound up the mountain.

To call it a trail was a stretch. The actual trail ended at around mile one.

From there out, he'd gone ahead of me holding back tree limbs, helping me over fallen trunks, and keeping me from slipping down the embankment.

As we approached the cave at Lunar Rock, he sped ahead to ensure we didn't have any visitors.

I was as worried about Thane's crew as much as he was, but we needn't have troubled ourselves. No one showed up unexpectantly.

Cody had eyes on Fitz and Zeth. And Kazz and Gunner were running around the woods in wolf form to scent anyone else who might come our way.

Dax told them to stay away from the den but to keep their ears and noses honed in.

The den was bigger on the inside than it looked from outside.

There were a few chairs strewn about the space. A bed in one corner towards the back. And a makeshift counter that housed snacks like jerky, chips, and packaged cookies.

They were all locked up tight to keep bears at bay, but Dax told me that other animals tended to instinctively stay away from supernaturals of any sort.

I'd thought about Aries and how he'd never warmed up to Lissie. He'd skirt around the outside of the room if she was present.

He'd always been a bit stand offish with people at first, so I hadn't thought anything of it.

Looking back now, he did seem more put out by her than he usually would have been.

He was seldom in the house if Dax was around. Night was his prowling time and, in the past, Dax had been gone by morning.

"I know you have a lot of questions, Rori. I'm actually surprised that you haven't come knocking on my door, bombarding me with them."

Shuffling his feet, his energy was so shy, it was like some kind of body snatchers thing was going on.

I didn't want to hurt his feelings, but I owed him my honesty.

"At first, I needed time. If I had come to see you right after I'd found out, I would probably have been too overwhelmed to take in anything you told me. And after a few weeks had gone by, you never called, Dax. I expected you to reach out to me, but you never did."

The hurt must have shown on my face.

Taking a tentative step in my direction, I realized he was afraid I might not want to be near him.

I'd never thought I'd see the day where broody, commanding Daxayrius Balodyn would be reduced to a timid, unsure guy in my presence.

"I thought you'd need time, honey. I thought you might want to get your bearings." Reaching over and patting the chair next to him, I sat. "Honestly, when you never came around my place with questions, I thought you'd made your choice to be with him."

How foolish could I have been?

The whole time I'd been *getting my bearings*, this poor male had been suffering my absence.

I cared about Dax, and never once had I thought about what I was doing to him by not contacting him.

When Thane had shown up, Dax made sure to be there. Made sure I was safe.

Finding out that he did so while he'd thought I'd given up on him... I was an insensitive idiot.

"I don't know anything about who you really are, Dax. I'd like to, though. If you're willing to tell me."

He looked at me. Really looked at my face like there was something etched in the shadows.

"As for Xander, I've barely seen him in the last few months. I don't know any more about him than I do you. No one will tell me anybody else's story and it's becoming increasingly frustrating not knowing what's going on."

Laying his hand atop mine, warmth seeped into my skin. Brushing a stray hair away from my face, he sighed.

"Look, I don't know everything. If you're willing to hear me out, I will tell you anything and everything I know. No holds barred."

Giving my fingers a gentle squeeze, one corner of his mouth tugged up.

"I'm not some honorable blood sucker. I won't keep things from you," with my arched brow, he tacked on... "anymore. I won't keep things from you any more now that you're in the know."

If that was true, I might be able to sleep a bit better than I had in the past month or so.

The not knowing has been eating away at me in the small quiet of my room, night after sleepless night.

"I want to know everything. Anything you can tell, no matter if it's vampire or werewolf. I can't move forward. I can't breathe. I want to know who I was in the past, all the way to the present. Can you do that, Dax? Can you give me some semblance of peace of mind?"

The den was poorly lit but the way his eyes tightened slightly in the dim light spoke of his regret.

He might not be who I'd come to know. He was, however, still someone I wanted to know better.

"I need a drink. Want one?" His tone made it clear that he needed to steel his nerves.

There was a makeshift bar on the one side of the counter, next to the lockbox of food. Whiskey, rum, and vodka were in the front, but I glimpsed a pretty bottle just behind them.

"What's in that one?" I pointed and he huffed a laugh.

"That's a butterscotch liqueur. Janie made Kiah buy it to stash here for when she was on duty. It didn't take her long to figure out it needed a mixer."

I began to protest when he walked outside but he was back before I'd even opened my mouth.

There was still snow in the shadows, heaped along the cave's exterior. When he brought back in a soda of some sort, I'd realized it must have acted like a cold box.

After mixing the butterscotch with soda, he handed it to me, sat back down, and sipped from his whiskey waiting for me to try the new cocktail.

That first sip was heavenly. "Good gods! That's fabulous. What kind of soda is that?"

I took a bigger drink, rolling it around my tongue before swallowing the sweet mixture.

"Cream soda. Have you ever heard of the Harry Potter series? It's called a Butterbeer. Only it needs sweetened cream to be on top for it to be a true one."

He knew I loved reading fantasy books. Did he believe for one second that I wouldn't know the Harry Potter books?

I had a sneaking suspicion he set this up. I'd have to ask Janie later if she really was the one that made this drink her on duty go to.

"Good, right? I thought you'd like it. That Scotch back in Xander's office did you no good. The way your face squinched up was adorable though."

I loved that little half smile he'd only ever gave to me.

That had been the last time I'd seen him. With my head laying in Xander's lap. With Thane getting under Xander's skin. Dax's too, apparently.

I'd walked out on them and hadn't engaged with any of them in weeks.

Lissie had told me her story. Seiran hadn't.

Lissie had said that he was her brother but that didn't make any sense to me... unless...

"Dax, is Seiran really Lissie's younger brother?"

She'd left a brother and twin sisters behind. I'd known that and still didn't make the connection.

"I'll tell you whatever I know."

He took another sip of the whiskey before he went on. Steeling his courage or trying to remember, I couldn't say.

"Yes. I don't know the details, but I know he is her true biological brother. She'd already been gone and turned for nearly fifteen years when he'd found her. That's why he looks older than her. His human life went on longer than hers."

That made sense. He'd gone looking for her and when he'd found her.. what? She turned him?

"Why is he a vampire? She was turned without her consent. I can't believe she'd do that to him." Shaking my head, I tried to clear away those negative thoughts.

I'd come to like Lissie. I was beginning to think I might even know her a bit better since her tale. Something didn't add up.

"No, Rori. Karalissa didn't turn her brother." There was a deep thrum as his breath went in and out.

I couldn't understand the underlying angst he was pushing through.

Looking into my eyes, sadness dwelled beneath the surface.

"She won't tell you. None of them are telling you what needs to be said so I guess it falls to me."

Geesh. That didn't sound ominous or anything.

"Dax, who turned Seiran? Did Xander do that to him?" The thought gave me pause.

I was still getting know the hunky vampire. Feeling drawn to him every time I was in his presence. I liked him more than I should for the scant number of times we'd interacted.

If he took Seiran's life without his consent, I didn't know if I could forgive him.

His tone became somber. "No, little demon. It was you. You're the one who ended his human life."

Chapter Twenty-Five

My head was swimming. Not with the alcohol, but with the accusation.

I couldn't have done that. I couldn't have been that heartless. There must have been some kind of mistake.

Reaching over and taking my chin between his forefinger and thumb, he lifted my face to stare into my eyes.

With tears welling up and threatened to spill over, I did my best to reign them in.

"You're not her anymore. You're not the one responsible for your past lives even if you are the same soul."

I tried and failed to pull from his grip. It was gentle, but firm.

" Listen to me. You are not Anastasia. You are Aurora. Do you understand me?"

A single tear ran down my cheek. Releasing my chin, he gently brushed it away.

"How can that be? How could any of that have been me?"

I knew my temper could get the best of me from time to time.

I knew my childhood trauma played a big part in why I'd acted out my whole life.

It made me reckless at the best of times. It made me lash out or live dangerously on the edge at the worst of times.

I'd always had that as my excuse to myself.

If this was true, I had been a bad seed from the start. That thought was terrifying.

"I'm a bad person, Dax. I've been rotten from the start. You knew. You knew and you still went out with me. Why?"

I couldn't help the torrent of emotions from overtaking my mouth.

Did I really want to know anymore? *Oh gods.*

"I wasn't alive then. I can only go by hearsay and pack mind thoughts. If you want me to tell you about your past from the view of the other wolves, I will do my best with what I can, but it may not all be right."

Running a hand through his hair, he was even more handsome for his worrying.

With a steadying breath, I collected myself enough to respond.

"Please. Tell me everything... even if you think it will break me. I need the truth, and I don't want it sugar coated, Dax. Will you do that?"

I had to know about me before I could learn any more about him, Xander, or Thane.

I wasn't sure if they'd provide me that information along the way or not, but I needed to find out who the hell I'd been and why I was in this situation now.

"Okay, Rori. I'm going to do my best. If it gets to be too much, you will let me know. We can always go back to the topic later. Alright?" He waited until I nodded.

My body and head felt disconnected somehow.

It wasn't the drink. It was me. My overactive mind was running in circles with different scenarios.

"As you know, me and my friends are wolves. I say that so you understand wolves and werewolves are not a mutually inclusive or exclusive term. Technically, we're shapeshifters.

Our forms took the shape of wolves because that is where our line started; with Thane.

Thane was the original werewolf.

That term has been used to describe a half wolf/ half man creature that walks on two legs, only turns during a full moon, and has no human thoughts during the time.

That is what they portray in the movies, and I guess it's in some books too.

We aren't like that. Were is a word from the old tongue that means half man, half animal.

Thane had already had an affinity for wolves when he was tasked with the responsibility of creating a counterbalance to his brother's monster.

What we are is cursed. Cursed by a witch back when Xander was running amuck.

Back when that same witch was forced by his coven to correct his mistakes. To balance the magics of the lands after he'd thrown them out of whack by giving Xander's curse more power than he'd meant to."

I had more questions now than I'd had before. It was a lot to unpack.

Thane and Xander were brothers. Xander had been cursed by a male witch to become the first vampire.

And who knew how many years later, Thane had been cursed to keep his brother in check.

I thought I might be sick. Dax would stop if I wanted him to, but I needed to know more.

Swallowing the lump of unease in my throat, I gathered my resolve. "Please. Continue"

He looked unsure if he should. I couldn't blame him. Knowing if I looked in a mirror right now, I'd see a green tinge to my skin.

Nausea threatened to bring my drink back up and I fought against my own stomach to keep it down.

"We can stop, Rori. I can always pick this up later."

Shaking my head because I didn't want to ruin it by sounding as sick as I felt, my eyes bore into him until he gave in.

"Okay. I have no idea what Xander did to this witch to make him curse him.

Male witches magics are different from their female counterparts.

The way I understand it, females are fluid, have the ability of change. Their magics are fluid as well.

However, male witches, their magics are inflexible, steady. Their bodies don't change for childbirth like a female. Magics go the same way as biology."

Stumbling over his words, I could feel him struggling for the right thing to say.

"See, maybe I'm not the best one to get the answers from. Maybe you could ask Lissie."

I shook my head no. Reluctantly, he began again.

"So, from what I've gathered, Xander was turned into a vampire.

The witch's coven ousted him because of the mayhem he inadvertently caused.

And when Thane showed up on his doorstep to try and get help for his brother, he was cursed to pay the witch's debt of balance."

"Both Xander and Thane made new vamps and weres. There were no guidelines. No instructions on how to be what they were.

They fed and accidentally made new creatures by..." He hesitated.

Did he think I'd want to know the specifics so they could turn me into one of them?

"Anyway, there were several new creatures. And they too accidentally turned some people.

The were and vamp populations were growing too fast, too viciously.

Thane and Xander called a truce to get rid of the problem ones and made an agreement to limit who and how they turned others once they figured out how it was happening."

My face must have held all the tension I was feeling because when he started on the next part, he took my hand in his and gave it a gentle squeeze.

"Now remember, I wasn't there. This is what me and my pack have put together over the years from snippets of overheard conversations and pack mind glimpses."

"You were brought to the castle to be one of the blood maidens. I think Lissie told you about her own blood maiden time there?"

I nodded and he looked relieved not to have to explain that part to me.

"Xander was known for liking to feed from the femoral artery of maidens around the lands.

The ones brought to the castle in this particular group only had three girls to choose from.

You all came willingly. His looks, his wealth. It was a draw to lift you up in stature.

One night of whatever the king wanted in exchange for enough money to last your families a month.

Or if you were selected as a blood maiden, you were expected to give him anything he wanted, no questions asked.

Your families would be taken care of for the rest of their days, but you could never see them again.

Not one of you knew he'd want more than your bodies. No one, at that time, suspected anything unbecoming of their king.

You walked in like lambs to the slaughter. Willingly laying down in his bed and spreading your legs so your families could live well for a time."

Sympathy rolled off him. No judgement.

"Your innocence was taken the moment he sank his fangs into your upper thigh.

I've heard how his growl tore across the entire castle.

Once your blood hit his tongue, he knew."

My nails were bitten to the quicks. I couldn't contain the energy bouncing around my system.

I didn't want to hurt Dax's feelings, but this felt bigger than the both of us.

"What? What did he know? What happened to me... her?"

If he was upset by my excitement, he didn't show it.

He wanted me to know. He needed me to understand.

I was more grateful for his willingness to tell me than I could ever express.

Blowing out a long breath, he took another sip of his whiskey. The sun was starting to turn purple outside the den.

I didn't relish walking back in the dark, but I couldn't bring myself to mention it now that I was finally getting answers.

"You were his mate. His other half.

That witch's coven sought to bring balance back in their own way once Xander and Thane got things back under control.

It was their way of rewarding them for their efforts while ensuring that they had a reason to live for more than just the violence.

When a were or vamp finds the missing part of their soul, the world shutters.

Only death can split them apart. And even then, the one that remains feels incomplete until they find them in the next life."

That explained the pull to Xander. My soul recognized him as something more to me.

"If he's my mate or half of my soul, why aren't we together?" I said, biting my lip raw.

Did this mean I didn't get a choice with Dax or anyone else now?

No wonder he'd assumed I'd made my choice, and it wasn't him.

"You have to be supernatural for the bond to snap into place."

He picked morosely at a patch of hair on the side of his face.

"There's more but I don't know if you want to hear it."

Ugh. Just rip the bandage off already. My glare must have leaked with my frustration.

"Okay. Okay. Well, the thing is... you, well... she and Thane used to be lovers before Xander found her."

Chapter Twenty-Six

Gasping and spitting out the drink I'd just brought to my mouth, he patted me on the back to try and comfort me.

His half smile lit his eyes. The thought of Thane and Anastasia being lovers made me choke and that amused him.

"You weren't romantic or anything, from what we can tell. You and he used to have a few trysts here and there."

He took another long sip of whiskey. The twinkle in his eye held something like sorrow.

"Honestly, we all believe that Thane was in love with you but didn't want anyone to know because you came from a commoner family.

He was extended royalty, brother of the king.

A human with a vampire brother who was in charge of the lands.

No one outside of the castle knew that their king was a vampire, but that didn't mean Thane wasn't trying to protect the subjects of his kingdom.

He was their prince, after all.

He may not have wanted him anywhere near you for that reason.

We also believe that he loved Xander much more than he's ever let on.

Why else would he go to that witch to try and get the curse lifted?

Xander had been turned when Thane was around sixteen years old while Xander was twenty-seven.

His father had remarried after his mother's death and had Thane, whom we've learned he adored more than anyone.

Thane idolized his big brother. He lived with the knowledge of the blood and pain his brother created for the rest of his adolescence.

And when he too turned twenty-seven, he went to find the witch and end the curse that had started to become an issue for the whole kingdom.

They'd never known the source of their hardships.

Thane had disappeared for over a year, and more tales reached the ears of the king about wolves in the area tearing through villages.

It's been said that you were sad at the loss of your lover. Angry that no one had any answers for you. And desperate to keep your family afloat after your father died in a hunting accident.

You went to the castle after hearing from another maiden who'd spent the night doing the bidding of the king. Coming home with enough money to feed her family well and clothe them too.

She couldn't give any details, and we suspect compulsion was used on any of the maidens who weren't selected to be blood maidens, but we can't be sure.

When Xander took you, he claimed you that night."

Downing the rest of his drink, he slammed it on the counter harder than necessary, making me jump slightly.

"He turned you. He killed your human life without your consent, Rori."

I'd been so enthralled in the story that I'd gotten lost in the past. Memories itched just inside my skull, but I couldn't reach them.

"I understand," I finally said.

"I don't think you do. He made you into a monster. He took you from your family, from Thane, from everyone you'd ever known."

It seemed important to him to clarify the obvious, not wanting me to fall back in love with the idea of Xander.

"I get it, Dax. I saw what Lissie did to Loxy... but I also saw what Loxy was capable of doing to Dylan. And correct me if I'm wrong, but hasn't it been a werewolf who's killed me in all of my past lives? Isn't that what Thane had said?"

I didn't know why I was busting his chops. Maybe because it felt like he was chastising me for liking the vampires.

"Thane killed you. Not werewolves. Thane killed you when you were Anastasia. Thane killed you the next three times. And he was the one to get Loxy riled up enough to kill you the last time!"

He was on his feet, pacing around the room like it was a cage.

Normally, I would have been hunched in on myself. Male aggression causing my body to respond in its own way.

Now that I knew the truth. The fact that I'd been a blood thirsty vampire in a past life, something shifted.

Turning his body and kneeling in front of me, I saw the pleading in his eyes for me to understand the distinction.

"I would never hurt you, Rori. I swear it." Now I'd caught on.

His plea for me to grasp the difference. He was afraid I'd see him as the same kind of monster that Thane was.

Laying my hands on top of his and leaning forward, I kissed him.

The touch of my lips to his made him go still, like I'd come to my senses and bolt at any moment.

"I know that, Dax. I don't imagine you could. We have something real here. And I get that you're scared Xander's coming back might fuck that up, but I'm here, aren't I? I'm still giving this dating thing a go, right?"

He didn't look convinced. I took both sides of his face in my hands.

"I'm not giving you up just because I had some mating connection to him in a past life."

After letting go and sitting back, I needed to be clear. I was figuring things out.

Figuring out who I was and who I wanted had to be a journey. Not a destination.

"Look, I want to keep going the way we decided before. I may end up with him, or you, or Hannah for all I know. The future isn't set in stone. Whoever I end up with, it will be because they put in the work. I'm having fun. Aren't you?"

Now it was my turn to hold my breath. Playing the field had begun to feel more like working the field, but I wasn't so sure I could handle the rejection if he was done.

"I have one more part of the story to tell you, honey. And I know you're not going to like hearing it."

I thought I knew where he was going with what was next.

The tightness around his eyes, the pursing of his lips.

He was about to tell me why I turned Seiran. About why Thane killed me. About why I was such a horrible person in the past.

Nodding for him to get on with it, he sat back down in the chair next to me.

The cooler air was beginning to seep into the den now that the sun was starting to set further behind the trees.

"When you and Xander were mated. When you were turned... your emotions were all heightened. You'd been angry and maybe in love with Thane. We don't know.

All the extreme highs and deep lows you had when you died played a big part on who you became.

You became overly fun loving. A party of the highest order.

You let vampires get away with more than Xander had in the last few years and they'd loved you for it.

You turned ruthless with those you saw as unworthy. And you lavished those who befriended you with all of their greatest wishes.

Have you ever heard of Vlad, The Impaler?"

I had heard that name in history class years ago but never paid much attention.

"Well, anyway. Xander was that king. Tsar is what they called it back then.

His logo was dragons. They were on his gates, throughout his castle, and on everything from cups to armor.

He was only Vlad. The Impaler nickname came later, after you and he were joined together.

The lands became bloody. Heads of villagers and nobles alike, who had even minor infractions, were placed upon spears all around the castle.

*From all we've learned, surrounding countries were in talks of war to **stop the spread of your diseased lands**. Their words, not ours."*

"Xander did that? He was responsible for all that turmoil?" Then it hit me, Dax was telling My story.

"He took the rap for Anastasia's misdeeds. He'd loved her more than the air he breathed.

He took the name of Impaler on himself because he didn't want the people to hate her or the other counties to find out she was the one leaving a bloody trail in her wake."

Shaking his head, I could tell he wasn't thrilled about giving Xander credit for trying to keep my honor. *Damn it.* Her honor.

"Well, after some time, Thane made the decision that Xander couldn't... wouldn't. He killed you for the good of the land.

Thane loved you to the end.

We know it because even though you belonged with his brother. Even though you'd been turned into his rival creature. He killed you because he knew it was what the human you would have wanted."

I couldn't believe what he was telling me. I'd heard Mina's story. Her sister was involved. "I thought my death had something to do with Kori?"

"Mina's sister, Korinna had been in Xander's bed more often than any other blood maiden.

She'd thought that when he turned her, she'd be his Tsarina." Seeing my confusion, he added... *"It's what they called their queen."*

Well shit. That's why both Seiran and Mina had called me queenie.

"She'd sought Thane out and they planned it together. She felt she'd been owed retribution for Anastasia usurping her position.

Thane didn't need her help. He'd planned to end your suffering *himself, but he used her vengeance as a springboard to accomplish his goal. "*

Rubbing the five o'clock shadow on his chin, he slapped his hand onto my knee.

"That's all I really know. I'd tell you more if I knew it."

I couldn't help the laugh that bubbled out of me. The absurdity of it all.

I had been Vlad, The Impaler. I had been a ruthless, sadistic vampire who had been responsible for the deaths of thousands of people.

I couldn't stop laughing. Hysteria was filling like a helium balloon just below the surface.

Gods. I'd been a monster.

I didn't know when in the last few minutes Dax had scooped me up into his arms but the pressure of his hands patting me up and down my back kept me from floating away.

"It wasn't you, Rori. It wasn't you. You aren't responsible for who your soul used to be." The whispered reassurances in my ear did nothing to quell my raging panic.

How could I live with what I'd done? Who I used to be?

Whatever I thought I glimpsed with Xander was overshadowed but they were my horrible deeds.

He'd loved me so much that he let them make him out to be the bad guy when it was me, my fault.

Maybe I'd judged Thane too harshly.

If what Dax said was true, Thane had acted on my human behalf.

Though that didn't excuse his behavior now. Somewhere over the centuries, he'd turned sadistic.

Losing the woman you loved to your brother and then killing her over and over again would do that to a person.

Understanding my past a little better, it clicked as to why part of me responded to him the way I did. To his less than gentle ways.

Taking calming breaths, I leaned into Dax's support.

"I know it wasn't me, but it was. It was me in the past, but still me, Dax. How do I live with that?"

Handing me back my drink, I let the alcohol numb some of my pain.

It wasn't an answer. He didn't have one.

"I can't imagine what you're feeling, Rori, but I want you to know that I'm here. I'll be here for you until you don't want me anymore." He kept kissing the top of my head.

I'd always seen him as a commanding force to be messed with.

As of late, his caring side was all he'd been giving me. The gentlemanly side. The side he'd thought might sway my heart towards his.

And I wanted the arrogant asshole back in this moment.

"I want you, Dax. Make me forget for a little while."

Clawing at his shirt, I tried to strike a match to the timber of his desire, but he wasn't having it.

With both my hands held tightly in one of his, he kissed my forehead.

"Let's just sleep tonight, honey. We can figure things out in the morning."

Irrationally, I felt the ping of rejection and lashed out. "Do I not make you hard anymore?"

The evidence to the contrary pressed firmly against the insides of his jeans.

"You know that's not the case, little demon. I'm trying my best to be respectful of you." I gave him a scathing look and he blew out a long breath. "Truth? I'm trying to respect Xander. If you were my former mate and some other male was to fuck you once I'd known who you were, I'd want to tear them apart."

Oh gods. I hadn't thought of that. These males could scent my arousal, but they could also scent each other's if it mixed with mine.

Sensing that I'd finally understood things from his point of view, he kissed the top of my head.

I didn't protest him carrying me to the mattress on the other side of the den.

Emotionally exhausted, my eyes closed before he'd even settled in beside me, the darkness swallowed me whole.

Chapter Twenty-Seven

L issie met me at Eventide Friday afternoon. I wasn't scheduled to work until tomorrow night.

I wanted to see her before then to compare notes with what Dax had told me.

The air had turned crisp again overnight, but it was expected to be warmer later in the week and for that I was grateful.

"What do you want me to say, Rori?" She drummed her nails on the table.

We had the sound barrier curtains drawn. The only light in the booth came from a lantern at the center.

"Oh, I don't know, Lissie. How about how terrible a person I am. Or maybe, hey Rori, I don't want to be your friend because you turned me into a monster in your past life? You know I wouldn't blame you in the least."

After throwing my little hissy fit, she smiled. "I've missed you so much. If I thought for a second that telling you about your past would bring you closure of some sort, I'd have done it months ago."

Taking a drink from her mug of blood, she set it down and pushed it towards me. "Here, have some."

I practically fell out of the booth trying to scoot away from it.

"No way. Get that away from me. I don't drink blood, you know. I am a human, Liss."

Again, she smiled.

"Precisely! You, Aurora, do not drink blood. You are not her. As much as I sometimes wish to have her back, I think you're better."

The faraway look in her eyes told me she was remembering the past.

"I've missed my friend dearly. We all have, but the fact of the matter is she's dead. Your soul is one and the same but that doesn't mean that you, personally, did any of those things. I mean, the whole point of reincarnating is to grow as a soul, right?"

I had no idea. Shrugging at her question, her lips twitched with amusement.

"Anastasia was six lifetimes ago. That's a lot of time to become a better version of yourself."

I couldn't argue with things I had no clue about. The logic was sound.

The persistent loop of beating myself up eased a tiny bit.

This group of vampires sought me out. I didn't know them, but they'd cared for Anastasia so much that they'd never stopped looking for her... for me.

That had to mean something.

The smell of onions frying and yeasty breads penetrated our little bubble when Lissie's hand hit the curtain flap, allowing in the tiniest amount of air and light.

My stomach gave a loud grumble, making me realize how hungry I was.

Luke was on duty. His culinary skills improved so fast over the last few weeks, I'd have thought he was trained by some great chef.

Opening the curtains all the way, we slid out of the booth.

I stopped just shy of the kitchens, snagging Lissie's arm to hold her back a moment.

Whispering so as to not be overheard, I asked the question that had nagged me throughout the night as I laid in Dax's arms.

"And the Thane part. Is it true?"

The front door creaked open, and she tensed beside me.

With the sun coming from behind, the tall male was thrown into shadow. I couldn't make out his face, but my entire body reacted anyway.

"Finally asking the right questions, kitten?"

Thane.

Registering the pain in my arm, I looked down at the re-straining hand she had wrapped around my elbow.

I'd started walking towards him without thinking. My body betrayed my mind more and more lately.

"What do you want?" I regretted the words the minute they'd left my mouth.

Stepping out of the shadows, Thane's jawline, his rugged build, his dominating demeanor, all drew me in, but I refused to let him command me.

"What I want, I take." That rough voice did me in.

A shiver ran down my spine, lingering between my thighs. *Damn, sexy werewolf.*

Sniffing the air, though I tried to deny it, he must have scented my arousal.

A growl of desire rumbled in his chest, and I dripped.

At this point, Lissie might as well have been a statue for all of the notice either of us paid attention to her.

"Down, boy," she said, holding a hand out in front of us to stop his approach. "She's still figuring things out. Maybe you should go back to your territory and mount something."

I couldn't help the laugh that burst from my mouth, drawing me out of my lust filled haze.

The fact that she'd talked to the original werewolf like he was some hormone consumed teenager was just so ridiculous.

"I see you haven't changed, pet." Velvet over hot coals. That was the only way to describe how he sounded.

The heat coming off his body set the aching between my thighs into overdrive.

My nerves had been frayed for weeks. Here stood the reason for the danger signs flashing in my mind over and over again.

Dax had been my steady rock. I still counted on him. I knew I could shelter in his solid embrace.

And Xander was an ocean, waves rolling, leaving my legs shaky. Never knowing when the next dip or bob would lull me into a storm.

Thane was a hurricane. Even being able to track his path, the changes to his trajectory could carve destruction in the wake of everything he touched.

Kazz and Gunner came through the door, took in the scene, and casually slipped into seats just behind where we stood.

"How about I get us the first round?" Kazz said loudly.

Gunner stood, slinking up behind me and throwing an arm over my shoulder.

"What about you, killer?" My body seized up. That term took on a whole new meaning to me now. "Want to help wipe the floor with our boy? I hear you're a ringer at darts."

With Thane's eyes piercing a hole in me, and Lissie still staring him down, I was grateful for the out.

"Want to take him for money or for pride?" I said, turning my back on Thane.

A low growl reverberated from his chest, straight through me, leaving my nipples pebbled.

Before my next breath, his arm snaked around my waist from behind. The hairs on the back of my neck stood on end as he whispered, breath blowing out behind the shell of my ear.

"I know you didn't just turn your back on me for some low chain, third class wolf?"

Yanking me roughly against him, our body's lined up, his hard length pressed into me while teeth grazed the side of my neck.

Lissie stepped forward but Thane's other hand wrapped tightly around my throat.

"Uh, uh, uh. Move and I'll squeeze the life out of poor kitten here."

Even with his hand threatening to choke the breath from my lungs, my arousal heightened at the way he rubbed against my ass.

What the fuck was wrong with me? He could kill me before I could blink but my body wouldn't respond to my mind telling it to pull away.

Kazz walked back, feigning a smile and sporting a pitcher of beer. "Who's up first?"

Several things happened at once. I could only move so much, my vision blurring.

Gunner grabbed a glass, poured and downed the contents, then ran at Thane as he shifted into his wolf form from one second to the next.

Kazz swore. Lissie snarled as Luke came out of the back to see what all the commotion was.

The hand around my throat eased slightly and I gasped in delicious air. I could hear growls and snarls as my vision started to clear.

It was all happening too fast for my mind to capture each movement.

Letting go of me entirely, Thane transformed into a massive grey and white wolf. Bigger than I'd ever imagined was possible.

Kazz shifted next as Gunner and Thane clashed with both of them in midair.

I couldn't keep up. Lissie's fists were landing blow after blow in a whirl of colors I could barely make out.

The double trouble duo were coming in, snipping and biting in what seemed to be a rehearsed fighting style.

Thane was incredible. Dangerous, but incredible all the same.

He fought with a dominating presence. The three other supernaturals weren't enough to stop him.

That realization had me panicking. I wasn't sure what I wanted to happen.

I knew that Thane could and would kill me if the fancy suited him. It was a rush instead of fear and that scared me more than anything else.

Feeling a tug on my arm, I pulled away without looking.

Sounds all ran together.

A firm hand clamped down on my wrist, not letting go, yanking me towards the hall.

I yelled and kicked out trying to get away before realizing it was Luke.

The fact that he had his wits about him enough to drag me out of danger from the midst of a bunch of supernatural creatures left me flummoxed.

Some people are calm in an emergency situation, but this was beyond a simple emergency.

"Rori! Stop hitting me." I paused my assault, calming slightly. "You can't go back in there. There are wild animals attacking each other! Why didn't you run?"

Maybe he hadn't seen the werewolf's shift. That would explain his somewhat less than freaked out demeanor.

He'd thought that animals got into Eventide somehow and jumped into hero mode to save me.

"I'm sorry. I didn't mean to hurt you. I just thought..." Why was I blubbering?

I needed Luke to get to safety, but I had to go back and see what was happening.

Taking a calming breath, there was nothing I could do about my shaking limbs. "I'm fine. I got confused is all."

"That's understandable. I'd known coming to Vermont would mean run ins with wildlife but that," He pointed in the direction of the dining area. "I never thought they'd come inside of buildings for territorial fights. Should we call somebody? The police or wildlife officials?"

Picking up the office phone, he started to dial. Panic seized my system.

"No! I mean, they'd get themselves hurt trying to wrangle them back out. We should wait. Let them find the way out on their own."

Arching his brow as if I was crazy or maybe in shock, he shook his head in reluctant resignation.

The shaking in my hands started to settle, but on the inside, the trembling was like an earthquake.

"Really, we should just settle in here for a bit and wait it out", I said. "We can clean up afterwards."

I didn't want to sit in this soundproof office, not knowing what was happening. My skin itched to peek out there.

Thane had taken on two werewolves and a vampire. And while I knew he was not a good person, that didn't mean I wanted him, or the others hurt.

Making a split-second decision, I grabbed the phone from Luke's hand.

"I should at least call Xander though. It Is his bar getting trashed. Ya know, give him a heads up."

I couldn't decern the look on Luke's face.

Fear, disgust? If I didn't know any better, I'd think it was hate.

That wouldn't make any sense though. As far as I knew, Xander had only been in the bar a few times since Luke was hired.

Could he really have taken such a dislike to him in such a small time? How often had they interacted, I wondered.

With a dip of his chin, he handed me the dial pad.

Pushing me a glass with two fingers of the Scotch Xander had on his desk, he clinked his against mine before lifting to his lips and downing it in one go.

The phone rang twice before Xander picked up. "What is it? I'm in the middle of..."

"Xander?" Silence reigned on the other end. "Xander, the bar is being trashed by wild animals. Luke and I locked ourselves in your office."

Another beat of silence, heavy breathing. "Sit tight. I'm on my way." I started to hang up, then... "Rori? Is he there?"

"Yes. We're fine." I hoped he understood that Luke's presents was why I wasn't speaking freely.

A rev of an engine on the other end.

"I'm coming to get you." The line went dead.

Chapter Twenty-Eight

I'd called Dax after we'd been waiting for ten minutes or so.

Luke kept shooting me little side glances. He hadn't said much when I'd asked Dax to ride around the building to see if there was still noise or trouble.

It was the only way I could think to be able to call Dax without raising any suspicion.

Luke was on his third drink when a sound outside the door drew our attention.

Picking up the bat Kyle had left behind the door, he approached and lifted it to swing in case whatever was out there got in.

The handle jiggled. A few seconds of rustling sounds as something tried to get in and then... "Rori?"

I ran to the door, but Luke grabbed my arm. Mouthing, "Are you sure?"

Concern crinkled in his eyes, the corners of his mouth.

"Yes. It's him." I could feel it in my bones.

Unlocking the door with fumbling fingers, I gave it a yank and threw it wide open.

"Xander!" I was in his arms, wrapping my legs around his waist before he'd had the chance to open his mouth.

He smoothed the back of my hair as he cradled me to him. Pulling back, fear roiled in his eyes. Dark and penetrating.

"I'm alright. I'm alright." My reassurances did nothing to alleviate the tightness he held in his body.

Without waiting for more conformation than that, his mouth crashed against mine.

I opened to allow him access and heat blossomed low in my stomach as his sweet, frosty tongue danced with mine like a man possessed.

A cough interrupted our moment.

The heat of embarrassment burned in my cheeks as I remembered Luke's existence.

Xander didn't put me down though. He was reluctant to even turn towards him.

"Is everything good out there?" Luke didn't avert his eyes from our little display as he spoke.

I couldn't tell if he was annoyed or disappointed, but he definitely wasn't happy.

Maybe making out with the boss in front of another employee hadn't been the wisest move. I hadn't done it intentionally.

When I saw him, I fell into the safety of his presence and everything else simply melted away.

"Lissie has a few scratches. There's some blood on the floor from one of the animals and a few tables and chairs got broken. Other than that, everything is fine." Xander's carefully worded reply sent my heart into overdrive.

"I hadn't seen her out there. Shit! I left her out there with those animals." Luke scrubbed at his face as if it would erase his mistake.

He'd had no idea she'd been out there because she was a blur of movement as she fought, coming out when the chaos had already begun.

"Hey, don't feel bad. I was in here with you, remember? I didn't help her either."

With a slight tilt of my head, understanding registered behind Xander's eyes.

"Don't fret, Luke. She got here as the wolves were making their way out the door. She'd gotten scratched by a few broken boards as she jumped to get out of their way. No worries. She's fine."

Luke looked relieved but only a tiny bit. I didn't know if he believed him or not.

Heading towards the door, I grabbed his arm after Xander set me back on my feet.

"Thank you, Luke. I don't know what would have happened if you hadn't dragged me out of my stupor." It had been necessary. I could admit that much.

That hadn't meant I didn't want to scream and claw to get back out there to see everything going on.

Xander dipped his chin to him in thanks but said nothing.

"No problem. I'd better go start cleaning up before tonight's crowd gets here." With one last glance in my direction, he left Xander and me alone in the office.

From what Xander had said, Lissie had been hurt.

There was blood on the floor.

He hadn't mention anything about Gunner or Kazz, so I wasn't sure if they were okay or not.

My mind reeling, I asked the only question that pounded over and over in my skull.

"Is Thane?" Finishing the question didn't seem possible but he knew what I was asking.

Pulling me against his chest, he kissed the top of my head. "He got away just before I arrived. You're safe."

Safe was a relative term. How could I ever be safe?

I worked and lusted after werewolves and vampires.

I'd never been safe in my life but this... this was a whole other level of *not safe*.

Remembering that I'd called Dax too, I pushed him back and stepped away.

Dax gave me a feeling of safety. I trusted him to tell me things. I trusted him to do his best to protect me.

So why did I call Xander first?

It was a long ten minutes before I'd remembered to call Dax. To tell him I was in danger. To give him a heads up about his people being in danger like I did for Xander.

"I know about who I used to be, Xander."

I had only told Lissie an hour ago. It wasn't like I'd kept it from him, but his face fell as if I had.

"I know what you and I had been in the past. The hell I caused that you'd taken the blame for."

He'd stepped towards me, and I held my hands up to hold him back. I needed to get this out before I crumbled.

"I'm not your mate in this lifetime. You are still mated to my soul but I'm not her."

If being with him right now meant that he would put some kind of claim on me, I couldn't allow us to continue down this road. Not yet. Maybe not ever.

With a tilt of his head, his eyes narrowed in on my face. I couldn't be sure what he saw, but he came closer, brushing the side of my neck with his long fingers.

With him this close, heat rose like magma from my core, singeing the sensitive flesh between my folds.

"I know, Rori. I will love you forever, no matter what body you wear." Wrapping his hands around my wrists, he dragged us over to the sofa to sit down. "I do not expect anything from you. And you owe me nothing. Not even an explanation. I only wish to get to know this version of you better."

Melting at his words, my fingers curled into his hair. It was an inch longer than it was the last time I'd seen him. That was only a week or so ago.

It had me suddenly wondering if vampire hair grew faster than human hair.

Lissie kept hers in a pixie cut and Mina's hair was long enough that I'd never noticed if it grew fast or not.

The smell of evergreen and copper lingered on his skin, and I found myself leaning towards him, tracing the line of his jaw.

A satisfied hum resonated in the back of his throat. "If you keep touching me like that, I may have to leave in order to maintain control of myself."

Thinking back to what I had overheard in that meeting with him, Thane, and Dax, a question that has been repeating in my mind bubbles to the surface.

"Is it true you haven't been with anyone in over four-hundred years?" Immediately blushing, I looked away from his face. "I'm sorry. You don't have to answer that."

Chuckling with his whole chest, my cheeks heated even hotter.

"It's true. I've never had anyone appeal to me since Anastasia was killed."

I appreciated him separating me from her.

The vicious vampire she had been made me sick to my stomach every time I allowed myself to think about it.

If he could really see me as Rori and not her, maybe this could work between us.

I would never ask anything of him that he wasn't willing to give. And neither would I ever want him to take on any of my transgressions... should I ever make any.

"Why? It's not like you were cheating or anything. She was dead. She was..."

What? Horribly murdered after killing thousands of people and allowing you to take the fall? After you'd lived several lifetimes and never found her again?

Again, he chuckled. Laying against his chest as he pulled closer, I heard him inhale my scent.

"Imagine that your favorite food is spaghetti. There are so many different sauces that picking just one to be considered your favorite seems impossible. Then one day, you've found it."

Kissing the top of my head, he inhaled again. The whisper of breath blowing in waves down to the sides of my face.

"The taste explodes in your mouth in the most delicious combination of tomatoes and spices. You've thought of spaghetti as your favorite food for your entire life... but once you tasted this specific sauce, everything you thought you enjoyed about other sauces falls to the wayside. Only this one sauce will ever satisfy your craving ever again."

"So, she was your favorite spaghetti sauce? That's what you're trying to tell me." I'd leaned back to see his face. "What about a lasagna? You could have tried other sauce and pasta combinations. No one would ever have blamed you for still liking Italian food."

What was I even saying? I didn't want to think of him with anyone else. Why was I pushing this hard?

Perhaps I'd unconsciously felt bad about having sex with other people but that made no sense.

We haven't even seen each other's private parts. I owed him no loyalty.

"I'll stick with a blood diet if my favorite dish isn't available. Thank you very much." Picking up my hand and lifting my wrist to his mouth, I shudder.

Was he going to bite me?

I couldn't lie. The thought made my heart race, but it didn't make me want to pull away.

Placing tender kisses instead, he made his way up my arm, to my neck, behind my ear.

"I will take whatever scraps you give me, love. If you aren't meant to be mine in this lifetime, there is always the next."

More kisses along my jaw. Nips to the corner of my mouth.

"I will keep loving you and do my best to be worthy of you each lifetime until you deem me laudable of your love in return."

Capturing my bottom lip between his teeth and sucking it into his mouth made me ache in all the right places.

Reaching up and entangled my fingers in his hair again while pulling him closer, our tongues wrestled for control.

This kiss was passionate, tender. It burned hot enough that I failed to notice his frosty interior. I couldn't get enough of his scent.

Coming up for air, we broke apart, gasping. Intense didn't begin to describe what we'd just shared.

"When I called earlier, you didn't know it was me at first." Not a question. "You said you were busy but what were you doing? You've been away a lot."

There was accusation in my tone that I didn't mean to put there.

He'd said he wanted to win me over but how would he do that if we rarely saw one another?

"We've established that you've been informed of the past. How much were you told about me? About what turned me into this?" He motioned to himself. A vampire.

"A witch cursed you and you became the first vampire. I don't know the specifics, other than the same witch cursed Thane too. He became the first were... wolf. Well, shapeshifter."

Kissing me a few more times, he pulled back and shifted me into his lap.

Dax made me feel safe. Xander... he made me feel secure.

"Allow me to tell you my story. I have a lot to atone for in life but the tale leading to my transformation is perhaps the thing that will damn my soul forever."

243

Chapter Twenty-Nine

My focus was increasingly difficult to maintain.

The slow rising bulge of his cock underneath me while I sat on his lap was becoming more and more distracting.

The way Xander smelled seeped into all the right spaces of my soul until the desire was an ache so unbearable between my legs, I couldn't concentrate on his words.

He caught me staring at his full, beautiful lips and chuckled. It was quickly becoming one of my favorite sounds in all the world.

Gently prying me off his lap, he set me on the cushion next to him.

If willpower were a superpower, he'd be a god.

Four centuries of composure and here, I couldn't get through a conversation without longing to touch him.

"I was a tempestuous youth, having only a few true friends, though everyone loved my company.

I was loud and brash and fun loving on nights out at the local tavern... until I wasn't. My moods often flipped on a dime without warning."

Discomfort at some memory I couldn't see brought the few lines he had around his eyes into sharp review.

"My father didn't care for my shenanigans. I was meant to take over as king once he abdicated.

We'd had another one of our monumental arguments that evening and I headed out to drink away my responsibilities."

Taking my hand in his, he lifted it to his mouth and brushed his lips against my knuckles, sending a shiver down my center.

"That night had been especially boisterous and full of hijinks.

I'd danced, drank, flirted, and made friends with another male at the tavern I'd never seen in town before.

We'd had a grand time hanging out for the majority of the evening. Getting more sloshed as the night wore on."

My concentration was torn between his story and the circles his fingers ran up and down my arm. It was such a pleasant sensation. Familiar, yet excitingly new.

Kissing my temple, he sat back in the seat, pulling away from our contact. I instantly missed it as if it were a limb.

"My new friend was even more drunk than I was. He told me he had magics." Darkness filled his eyes, and I straightened, unsure whether I should reach over and comfort him or let him work through it.

Uncertainty gripped me. In the end, I leaned forward but refrained from touching him.

"I laughed at him and needless to say, he didn't take that well.

He showed me a little of his magics. The candles burned a bit higher.

The noise around the room hushed but the people were still conversing and carrying on. We simply couldn't hear it as much.

The smile on his face when I acknowledged his gifts was the most fiendish look I'd ever seen at that time.

I'd told him about my situation with my father and asked if he could help me do something to him.

Even in his drunken state, he declined. Said he wouldn't upset the balance.

I had no idea what he meant by that, but I kept pushing to no avail."

Registering the pain in my fingers, I pulled them from my mouth, not knowing when I'd started biting the nails back.

This was the story of the very first vampire in existence from that very same vampire's point of view.

I probably should have been more terrified.

At the very least, I shouldn't have been in a soundproof room alone with him.

Most importantly, the want to climb on his lap and feel his hands wander all over my body should have been the furthest thoughts from my head.

I needed to get a grip.

Dax would be here sooner or later, and I had to be out of this room before that happened.

Making him feel bad was never part of my plan when I'd called him.

It wouldn't be fair to find me making out with Xander.

"What happened after he told you no? Why did he curse you?"

The obvious answer would be because Xander knew of his magics, but I doubted the witch would upset the balance simply to prove a point.

"Like I said, I wasn't the best person back then.

*My answer to his **No** had been to push him every time we'd met up.*

Becoming friends, he knew how much I loathed my father.

And I'd found out he was one of only three male witches in his coven. His cousin and his uncle didn't have but a third of the power he possessed."

His hand scrubbed at the back of his neck. Turmoil lying just beneath the surface of his eyes.

I itched to soothe it, but I needed to let him work through the story on his own.

"Males aren't supposed to carry as much powerful magics as females.

They don't have the ability to change. They're solid rather than fluid.

And magics need vessels that ebb and flow instead of break.

His magics were seen as an omen by the females of the coven.

And I used that against him."

There was a pleading in his eyes. A desire for forgiveness that I didn't understand.

Dax had attempted to explain the same thing about the fluidity magics needed but Xander did it better.

"I found them. His coven.

After he wouldn't give me what I wanted, I found them.

And being the arrogant asshole that I was, I bedded his sister. And then his aunt. And then... his mother.

None of them knew that I'd bedded the other of course. I wasn't rubbing it in the females faces. Only his."

That darkness filled his eyes once again as he finished reliving that moment from his past.

"I sought him out at the cave he'd shown me after our first few times hanging out, relishing in his discomfort, his rage.

My selfish arrogance didn't care that I'd destroyed his sense of family. That when they would inevitably find out, it would weaken his coven.

I only cared that he'd had the ability to help me get what I wanted, and he'd refused."

Placing his hand on my knee, I wrapped my smaller hands around it in comfort.

"The witch had some kind of potion going in a cast iron pot when I'd arrived and I hadn't taken much notice of it.

That is, until he was angry and tossing dried herbs and chanting in a language I didn't understand.

Sparks rose from inside. My eyes swam with pain and colors. The gums in my mouth ached and bled.

I didn't know what was going on.

I ran from the cave straight home."

A single tear slid down his face and he let it lay there, unashamedly glistening on his cheek, tugging at my heart.

"When I awoke in the middle of the night, I cried out in pain.

I mouth hurt. My throat was on fire and my stomach cramped so hard I'd screamed out for my mother.

When she came in, I leaped on top of her, new fangs digging into her neck before I'd realized I was out of bed.

Her blood running down the back of my throat, barely extinguished the painful burning for more than a few minutes.

My father heard her silent sobs from down the hall and came running, axe in hand, to investigate."

Inching closer to him with every word, the beating of my heart raced along with the story.

It occurred to me that I'd must have left my common sense back in that coffin with my mother.

If I were smarter, I'd be making my way towards the door and away from this vampire.

So why was I still here?

"My mind was screaming at me to let her go but this monster inside of me refused to relinquish control.

My father swung the axe at my back, hitting me where my heart should have stopped... but it was already dead, unbeating in my chest.

The metal had no effect. And before I could wrap my brain around the situation, I lunged at my father. Killing him with long pulls from the vein in his neck."

If there was ever a time to run, it would be now.

I couldn't. I'd been transfixed by his tale and ensnared by his charms.

"My brother came in the room. Took in the blood and our parent's body's and picked up the axe to fend me off.

He was sixteen years old and loved me more than anything, but he was ready to die to stop me.

Seeing him like that was the only thing that pulled me from my bloodlust."

Poor Thane. His past was even more traumatizing than mine.

If there was ever a time to get the hell out of this town and away from these monsters, it was now.

With no money and nowhere to go, I'd always felt stuck. Stuck was better than dead though.

If only I could make myself stay away from them, the danger they inherently possessed, maybe I could be just a bystander like Hannah or Bitzy.

Why did I feel the buzz of excitement whenever I flirted with disaster?

Learning of my past life, I knew now it had never been a choice.

With my soul tainted, chasing thrills must have been in my programming.

Instead of pulling away, I wrapped my arms around his neck and cradle his head to my chest.

At first, the tension in along his back and stiffness of his torso warred with his desire to luxuriate in my comforting.

After a few seconds, he relaxed into me, arms winding around my waist, pulling me close.

A comfort for his loss. After centuries, the tears running down his cheeks spoke to how much sorrow he'd held onto for all of these years.

I had been ripped away from him too.

He'd done his best to keep it all in. I could tell.

Now that I was here, giving him the safe space he desperately needed, getting the poison of his story out of his system was cathartic.

With his head still resting upon my chest, I ran my fingers through his hair, reveling in its softness.

The scent of evergreen and copper hitting the back of my nose. Shoving its way into my throat. Taking me back to a past I'd never personally experienced.

An ache built between my legs. The warmth of his body pressed to mine.

Wetness pooling, rubbing against the silky lace of my panties, had me shifting in my seat.

Xander stiffened in my arms. The scent of my arousal reaching his senses.

A low growl rumbled in his chest as he cupped one of my breasts, rubbing circles around my nipple with his thumb through my shirt.

Arching my back, I slid forward, legs wrapping around him with delicious heat as my center ground against his hardened length.

Our mouths crashed together. No words were needed to understand what we both were feeling.

I craved him more than I'd ever craved anyone before in my life. My soul recognized his soul, and it took over my common sense.

There was no getting control of my body back.

He stood with my legs still wrapped around his waist, pushing me firmly but somehow still gently into the wall.

Tongues wrestling, I barely registered the coolness. To me it was all heat. Sweet and refreshing like sucking on peppermint candy and breathing in winter chilled air.

His hands slid over me everywhere he could reach, finally grasping the back of my head, bringing our passionate kiss to full focus.

I wanted more. I wanted everything he was willing to give me.

I'd given a tiny little thought to Dax just a bit ago but once Xander and I collided in this moment, nothing else mattered.

Trying to rip the buttons from his shirt, my weakness on full display, he pulled back and chuckled.

Deftly undoing them before bringing those luscious lips back to mine.

Before I knew anything was amiss, I'd been deposited on the sofa and he was across the room, shirt rebuttoned with hair still slightly tussled.

The door flew open in the next instant with a shuttering bang.

"Rori! Oh god! Are you okay?" Bitzy spotted me on the couch and scooped me up into a bear hug. "Luke said you were but... it's just such a mess out there. Are you hurt?"

She hadn't spoken to me much in the last several weeks. I was surprised to see her this put out by my possible demise.

I should have known better. Bitzy had been my best friend for a long time. Our little fight didn't mean she'd wish me any harm.

Guilt for even letting the thought cross my mind nipped little bites at my heart.

Hugging her back fiercely, I sobbed.

Not for what happened out there with Thane, but for the time that I let slip away from us. For the barrier I'd built to protect her.

I'd had no right to be upset with her and from here on out, I would do my best to include her in on my life without giving too much away.

"I'm fine. I'm so sorry, Bitz. If I'd come to you earlier, we could have talked everything through."

She patted the back of my head.

I was a blubbering idiot once I'd let it all start flowing. "I can't lose you. You know that, right? Those animals could have killed me, and I can't have you hating me when I go?"

Xander stiffened from the corner of my eye. I could tell he didn't like the thought of me dying anytime soon.

Trying to give him a weak smile, it fell flat.

"Hate you? Rori, I could never hate you." She threw her hands up in the air. "Good god! I'm sorry. I've been acting like a jealous brat. You're allowed to have other friends. I don't really know what my problem has been, but I promise I won't be making that mistake again. You could have died."

Releasing her tight hold on me, the look of devastation when she pulled back broke my heart.

"Let's vow to never go to bed angry with each other again. We talk it out. Or yell it out. Or throw things at each other until we deal with whatever issue it is, but never again. Okay?"

Her impish smile pieced together the cracks in my heart that her absence had left.

I was sure the thought of throwing things at me at some point was the cause of her current smirk.

Xander cleared his throat and Bitzy took notice of him in the room for the first time.

Grrrrr. She still had the hots for boss man, here. Too bad for her that he wanted no one but me.

"You two go on back out there. I need to call the insurance company and file a claim. Make sure they've taken a few pictures, will you Bitz?" His voice dripped with a seductive allure and my knees went weak.

"Of course. I'm on it." Giving him one last glance or her shoulder, she headed out the door.

Whispering quietly enough that she wouldn't hear, he asked, "We'll finish this later?"

The question in his eyes had been clear; did I regret what happened between us?

My center throbbed just looking at him. No regrets on my end.

"Count on it," I whispered.

Batting my eyes slowly, I heard the growl from behind me as I closed the door and headed down the hall.

Chapter Thirty

Kamie came bounding towards me the moment I stepped into the room. Her exuberance nearly knocking us both to the ground.

"I'm okay," I assured her, and she reluctantly let me go, looking me up and down checking for injuries.

Now that I allowed myself to take a good look around, I understood why Bitzy and Kamie weren't convinced of my well-being.

There were tables smashed to splinters. Chairs that looked more like kindling. And the blood... it was covering everything in the area.

Xander had mentioned that Lissie was fine. On the mend even.

Now I recalled that he'd never mentioned how badly any of the wolves were.

Did he not tell me on purpose?

"Oh good, you're ready to help us." Luke's tone was cold.

Maybe he was mad that I'd stayed in the room with Xander instead of coming right out here with him to clean up before the evening shift started.

I'd left him with the clean-up. Not something I'd meant to do.

Motioning to the side, he said, "Want to grab a rag and wipe down the walls?"

I didn't want to be anywhere near that blood but what else was I going to do?

I needed this shift's money to pay the monthly taxes on my place and buy some groceries and cat food this week.

My head hadn't been in the game for weeks.

While Xander had given us all nice hourly raises, I still relied a lot on my tips until my bills were paid down.

With everything going on, my hospitality was lacking, and it showed in my nightly take home pay.

Aries all but snubbed me this morning when I gave him only one can of food.

I'd been out of treats for over a week, and the little brat kept waking me up every morning around nine to complain loudly at his maltreatment.

"Sure. Where's the mop bucket?"

He pointed to the far wall where it was already full of soap and hot water.

Luke did everything around here. He was quick and efficient and rarely complained about anything.

To know he was put out with me made me feel more guilt than I was used to feeling from anyone other than Bitzy.

He had this way about him. I couldn't quite put my finger on it, but I could feel it.

A pull. A draw. His smile was joy. His words, a powerful charm. He could lift your spirits or make you loathe yourself.

"Sorry. I guess I'm still in a bit of shock myself."

He took the mop from my hand. I began to protest but with a smile and shake of his head, he brushed me off.

"You should probably deal with the bar set up. You were here too. I don't want you to touch that blood. Could you stock the beer coolers instead?"

If I didn't know any better, I'd have said he was embarrassed. Why? I had no idea.

He'd saved me. He'd seen the wolves and the fighting. And yet, here he was, trying to make everything okay for me.

Thoughts of Dylan crossed my mind. He'd been nice and helped me out. And look where that got him.

"I'll stock the coolers, but I am going to help with this mess before I do."

Bending down to pick up some broken pieces of table, he grabbed my wrist.

"Luke, let go. I've got this."

Awkwardly staring at me, I refused to drop his gaze.

He hadn't been rough. His grip didn't hurt, but I wasn't letting anyone else tell me what to do.

The warring in his eyes, the decision to relent weighing on his mind. After another few seconds, he nodded and walked away.

After finishing the clean-up and stocking the cooler, I checked in with Bitzy.

She and Kamie were working the bar tonight while Luke, Hannah, and I worked the floor.

Molly had worked the day shift, otherwise she'd have been scheduled tonight too.

There was a festival going on in town this weekend and we were expecting a lot more people to find their way to Eventide than usual.

If I could get my shit together, I might be able to make enough in tips to get Matilda that tune up and oil change she'd desperately needed.

Lissie procured a few new tables and chairs. From where, I had no clue.

They didn't match the rest of the sets around the room, but she'd artfully rearranged a few things and made them look like they'd belonged there all along.

Dax and the others still hadn't shown up. I tried not to think about what that meant.

He was their alpha. He needed to be with them if there were any problems occurring.

Selfishly, I wanted him to check on me. To make sure that I was unharmed first.

Chastising myself internally for the thought, it persisted anyway.

Dax knew that Xander was here. He knew I'd be protected with the vampire's very life.

Still, my stupid little heart stomped its foot at him for not verifying that I was safe and sound himself before running off with his furry friends.

The smell of garlic and various other yummy things wafted from the kitchens. Gav and Nik were on cooking duty tonight.

Nik made that noodle dish with the capers. I could never remember the name, but after he'd insisted that I try it a couple of weeks ago, I was in love.

Seiran sat on a chair by the front door that perched in the perfect position to observe the entire room.

We'd never had a bouncer when Kyle owned the place. Maybe that was part of the problem.

Now that Friday and Saturday nights were looked after by the mild-mannered male, I'd felt safer and able to do my job without always having to look over my shoulder.

"Rori, go fetch Luke from out back. I need him to do a couple of things before the night crowd shuffles in." Mina was still her overbearing, bossy self. Even after everything had been laid on the line.

I was trying to earn back kinship that I'd never had. It was important to me for reasons I couldn't wrap my head around.

"Sure thing. Should I grab a leash, or will he come on command?" Okay. My sarcasm might be a barrier that could use some work.

Rolling her eyes as she turned away, I could have sworn the corner of her mouth fought not to curl up. I would count that as a win.

The sun had begun to set. Darkness hadn't taken hold completely yet but the dim lighting cast shadows along the tree line when I stepped outside.

Luke stood at the table out there with his back to me.

There was a green light in front of him and smoke rising over his head as he spoke words I couldn't understand.

It made no sense. I didn't even know he was a smoker.

As I approached, sticks crunched and snapped under my feet. He stiffened slightly but turned a second later with a smile on his face.

No green light. No smoke to be seen. My mind must have been playing tricks on me.

Perhaps it was simply the filtering light through the trees swaying at odd angles. An optical illusion.

"Hey." His sheepish greeting left me with the impression he was embarrassed about something.

""Hey. Sorry about before." I didn't know why I still felt guilty about staying to talk to Xander, but I did. "I should have helped you out sooner. You saved my life back there."

The silence between us was awkward. He'd always had a ready smile. Good natured. Helpful.

Now, however, I got the feeling he'd rather be anywhere but here talking to me.

I'd never noticed how his eyes took on a purplish hue in the low light. They were captivating.

"No. I'm sorry. If I could use shock as an excuse, I would." He smiled at his own joke, but I wasn't in on it because I didn't understand what he was saying. "I'm not going to make excuses. I was an ass."

I laughed. It felt good to laugh with another human for no reason other than humor. It had been a long time.

Stress, a horrible past life revelation, and the original werewolf wanting to toy with me had me in a state of constant survival mode.

Laughing with another human didn't only feel good. It felt necessary.

"Mina sent me out here to retrieve you." He arched a brow. "You know how our pejorative overlord is. She probably wants you to rearrange all of the wine bottles by color or something."

His chuckle eased the knot in my chest a bit. Luke wasn't someone I thought I'd allow myself to like after replacing Dylan.

Standoffish as I'd let myself become over the years, he'd wormed his way into my inner comfort zone in no time at all.

"I love this time of day," he said, gesturing around us.

The sun was almost fully down, and the moon was hanging low in the sky. We could still make out everything around us, but color leeched away with the setting sun.

"In olden times, that's what they call this part of the day; eventide. I suppose that's where the name for this place came from."

I'd never really thought about it. It made sense though.

Nightlife only happened once the evening would fall. And what a better name for a bar than one that meant you could start your evening relaxation.

"Rori, I know it's not my place."

Those words never started any good conversation in my life, but I didn't stop him.

"I've been around the sun a few more times than you. And I've traveled across many countries and seen many things."

Reaching over, he took my hand. Not in a romantic way. It felt more big brotherish.

"Just promise me... before you go and make any kind of commitments, you'll think about the future. It's all out there waiting for you."

Looking up at the night sky, not saying anything more or pushing an agenda, he squeezed my hand once before heading back inside, leaving me to my rushing thoughts.

Chapter Thirty-One

The night had been lively so far. We had about thirty more people than a typical Friday night, but we were hustling right along.

The music wasn't my taste. If it were louder, that might have been an issue.

The jukebox Lissie had put next to the bar took dollar bills and only played one song per dollar.

It would only let a person purchase five songs at a time with a three-minute break interval after the last one to give someone else a chance to change it up if they wanted a different genre.

The group of skiers who came in a couple of hours ago monopolized the song choices tonight.

While sea chanty music was fine in small doses, the other patrons couldn't exactly dance to it, and I needed these tips tonight.

I knew the last song they'd just played was almost over and I could see the blue-eyed, blonde haired woman grabbing more bills off the table.

She hadn't headed this way yet, so I seized my opportunity while bussing the table closes to the jukebox.

After the last start of the group's music, I'd gotten Bitzy to exchange me a few ones for the fives and tens the night had granted me.

Slyly maneuvering to the front of the box. I pushed the override code and used ten ones to play dance music for the next hour or so.

The blonde didn't look too pleased, but I couldn't take it anymore.

Besides that, tips would be better if people got up to dance. Sweating people ordered more drinks after all.

Luke had been keeping up well with all of his tables. He'd even helped me out a few times with a lazy smile on his face.

It was nice to have him around. I'd guess that traveling from country to country gave you a different perspective on life.

Awhile back, I'd been saving up to take a trip. I didn't have any particular destination in mind. I'd just wanted to see more than Vermont.

Staycations were great when your state was bigger, but I wanted to get out and see more of the country.

A loftier ambition would have been to see more countries. I'd need my passport for that though.

And spending money on anything but necessities hadn't been a part of the picture for a long time.

The ten dollars a week I'd been putting away had gone into buying a new jacket and shoes that I'd desperately needed to survive the cold winter months here.

"Hey, Luke? Can you grab another keg from the back for Bitzy? She'd asked me a bit ago and I got caught up and forgot."

He was stronger anyway. I'd need extra time I couldn't afford to lose on the task. He'd have it changed out three times as quickly.

"Sure thing. Looks like we're low on a few bottles in the cooler too. I'll grab them if you'll watch my tables for me." Gesturing to the guys in the corner, I all but groaned.

Zeth and Fitz had a full pitcher on the table. Bram was sitting in the back chair.

The fact that he was here pulled up the corners of my mouth. I knew he'd keep the other two in line.

I still hadn't heard from Dax yet. And Cody didn't come in tonight like I'd thought he would, but Kiah and Janie sat at their usual spot at the end of the bar.

There was a tightness in Kiah's eyes. It made alarm bells go off in my head.

"I've got you. They've got a full tank right now, but I'll keep a look out." With an overly done large wink in his direction, he laughed at my antics.

The sound was wholesome. There was no other word for it. His laughter was like a balm to my system that I didn't know I needed.

Making my way to Kiah and Janie, my clumsy ass tripped, spilling the half empty glasses and dirty plates I'd taken off the last table.

The smell of ale and cheap whiskey covered the bottoms of my sleeves.

My knees had hit first, landing on a piece of glass that had broken.

Warm wetness spread out and slid down the inside of my pants, dripping down my shins.

Red stains spread quickly, leaking through the material. Blood

A growl reached my ears just before Bram's body crashed into my back. When I looked up, he was curled protectively over me.

Fitz and Zeth were both only a few feet away trying to restrain Kori.

I hadn't even noticed her here before her eyes locked onto mine.

There was no one home. Bloodlust had taken her so quickly she'd forgotten to act the part of human in public.

Janie, Kiah, and Lissie were there in an instant. Bitzy screamed something to me, but I couldn't hear over the cacophony of noise.

Pushing to my feet, Bram helped me up.

To all the onlookers, it merely looked like a catty girl fight.

They couldn't see her eyes or the way her teeth snapped in my direction while the lights were dim and the dance floor was lit up with color.

Taking a step in her direction, Bram attempted to grab hold of me, but I was done with being the victim.

Even if it got me killed, I was going to stand my ground.

Before I could think better of it, I swung my arm out as hard as I could, slapping her straight across the face.

Her head snapped back with a whimper. It couldn't have hurt. She possessed supernatural strength. It must have simply stunned her.

Lissie gasped. The corner of Kiah's mouth pulled up. They bolstered my confidence.

"Get. Out! This is the last time I will tell your skanky ass... We reserve the right to refuse service to anyone, and I want you gone before I come back from the kitchens."

Seiran strolled over to us like he had all the time in the world. "You heard the lady." He motioned to the door.

Kori's incredulous face told a story of revenge and wrath coming in the near future and I couldn't make myself care.

"You. And you." Pointing to Zeth first and then to Fitz, he pointed to the door again. "Out."

"We didn't do anything. Besides, we're not finished our beer. I think we'll stay." Zeth spoke big words for a guy outnumbered.

Being in Thane's pack, I knew he would be a force to mess with. The cocky attitude might be warranted but I didn't know for sure.

Luke and Gav had heard the commotion from the kitchens and now made their way to where we were all facing off.

I didn't want Luke anywhere near the rest of them, but it wasn't like I could say anything.

Kori had gained back her composure enough to calmly shake from Fitz and Zeth's grip.

"We don't want to be here anyway. Not with a whore like you breathing the same air."

I don't know what gave me the balls, but I leaned in towards her. "Like you actually breathe air, bitch!"

Curling her lips back, exposing pointed teeth, she hissed like a damn cat. "You'd better watch your back. I aim to take back what was once mine, slut!"

The temperature dropped around the room.

The smell of evergreen and copper filled my senses.

A quiet hush fell over the patrons still watching in apt curiosity.

I didn't turn. I knew he was there.

Kori stared over my head at his approach with fear and longing written on her stupidly beautiful face.

"What's yours?" I asked.

My tone dripped with only just contained contempt.

"Poor, delusional Korrina. Alexander has never been yours."

Holding my hand out behind me without looking, his fingers slipped into mine.

"You played with fate. You lost. Get over it."

Finally turning, with my other hand wrapping around Xander's neck, I pulled him in for a passionate kiss.

Vaguely, the sound of Luke's disapproving huff. Bitzy's amused laugh, and the stomp of Kori's foot registered in the recesses of my mind.

The chill in the air intensified as our tongues mingled in claiming and acknowledgement.

When we parted, he didn't need to say the words. He was mine.

If I wanted all of him or none of him. This magnificent specimen was all mine.

Looking back to the bitch in front of me, I felt the shift. I felt dangerous. I felt complete for the first time since before my mother had passed.

"I will say this one time and one time only. If I catch you near what is mine, you won't only lose the fight. You will lose your life. Do I make myself clear, Mutt?"

The well of cruelty rising in me would have been frightening if it didn't feel so right. My soul sang with its stroking.

What the hell had I said? That I'd kill her? That couldn't be right, could it?

Xander's arm swept me back, wrapped protectively around my middle.

Bram dipped his chin but remained quiet. I didn't understand how he could be Thane's second. Their personalities were so different.

Seiran stepped forward once again. "Time to go."

With a nod of respect to Bram, Bram's chin came up and towards the door. Fitz, Zeth, and Kori turned and left without another word.

With his head hung slightly, Bram reached out and clasped my hand in a quick goodbye.

"I'll let Thane know," he said to Xander.

Glancing at me one more time, he left too.

Janie moved away from Kiah to stand by my side. "Is this your final choice, Rori?" There was no judgement in her tone. Only sadness.

"What do you mean? What choice?" Then it hit me.

I'd claimed Xander as mine. I'd said it to get Kori away from him but apparently claiming in the supernatural world was a bigger deal to them than I'd realized.

Lissie turned me towards her, taking my hands in hers. Luke leaned in to hear better.

"If you are staking your claim on Xander, are you saying you're willing to complete the mating bond?"

Xander yanked me back and growled at all of them. His rage was a living thing.

"She will NOT be completing the mating bond! If any of you attempt to make that happen, I will end you!"

Ouch. I did claim him. I wasn't sure if I wanted to be mated. To be allowed only one person for the rest of my days.

The fact that he was so against it set my teeth itching. They did that a lot lately.

He'd forgone sex for over four hundred years because Anastasia was gone.

Wasn't I her? Wasn't I enough for him?

He'd told me I was, but when finally presented with the option, maybe he'd reconsidered.

Lissie didn't back down.

I would have kowtowed under the intensity of his glare.

"It's the only logical step," she said. "She deserves to make this choice for herself."

The way she'd laid it out, said I'd get to make a choice. It swirled around my mind, scratching against my skull. Then it dawned on me.

Remembering a hushed conversation on the brink of sleep between the three males my loins ached for.

Dax's words from a few weeks ago, when he'd told me why the bond with Xander wasn't complete.

A mating bond could only be completed once a human was turned. I had to die.

Well, shit. No wonder Xander was enraged. He didn't want me to die to complete the bonding process. Now it all made sense.

Luke grabbed my wrist and dragged me away from the whole group.

Xander's snarl was low, but I heard it as clearly as if his mouth had been pressed against my ear.

"What the hell, Rori? Fighting? And now they all seem to want you to choose between your boss or dating anyone else? That's..." The sudden hard press of his lips made it clear he was struggling for words.

Patting him on the side of his arm, I leaned my head against his bicep. "I know, right?"

What else was I going to say. Luke wouldn't understand any of it. Hell, I barely did either.

I wasn't ready to give up seeing Dax.

And I wasn't sure why, but I really wanted to rub up against Thane before making a lifelong, irrevocable decision.

After a few awkward minutes, all of us returned to our positions, finishing out the shift.

Bitzy cashed out the bar with Kamie wiping things down.

The vampires were going from patron to patron, having short, look you in the eye conversations that I could only guess were compulsion related.

"Well, kiddo. You Rori'd it up again. I hope you got the tips you needed first."

That smirk. I didn't know whether to laugh or punch her in the arm.

"I was serious out there." Luke wouldn't be put off his concerns. "Maybe you should take a vacation. Far away from here. Come back with a clear head."

A vacation sounded nice. It wouldn't be long enough to make any kind of decisions though.

Besides, where would I go? Who would I drag along?

Everyone I'd want to come with me would be exactly who I should be getting away from.

Except Bitzy but I knew she'd never venture far from here.

She talked a big game. When in reality, the world outside of our state filled her with anxiety.

"That's the kind of plan rich people make, Luke. I haven't the money or the sense of adventure you do."

The thought of being away from this place broke something in me I didn't want to dwell on for too long.

"I've got money. I could send you on a cruise. What do you say? Fourteen days around the Caribbean?" He was being earnest.

He would foot the bill for me to get away and clear my head if I agreed.

Bitzy looked between the two of us. Back and forth and back again.

"Is there something going on here I should know about?" Her tone made it clear what she was asking.

She'd just seen me kissing our boss and I could see the clock-works of her mind spinning to the point of breaking.

I didn't want to laugh but it slipped out.

Hurting Luke's feelings didn't sit right with me. He'd been nothing but nice. He wasn't bad to look at either, but I wasn't attracted to him in the slightest.

Before I'd time to apologize for my outburst, he chimed in. "Good gravy, no."

That shut me up. Him not being attracted to me was fine. The bluntness wasn't.

"She's more of the little sister type. Ya know what I mean?"

"Yes, actually. I've felt that way since she walked through that door all those years ago. I've been playing the role of big sister and have zero regrets about it." Her teasing tone tugged at my heartstrings.

She and Luke were smiling at each other in a devilish way.

I took that as my cue to leave.

"Well, then. Why don't I just leave you two older siblings here to discuss the how my precocious ways amuse you?"

Belly laughs. They both doubled over, holding their stomachs like I'd been a small child who'd told a horrible dad joke.

Their laughter carried from behind me as I left them to their beer and skittles.

Any customers who'd been lingering were on their way out the door.

Kamie put the last barstool up and after a quick goodbye, she'd left for the night too.

Xander caught my eye. Broad smiles on both our faces, we walked in the same direction.

Towards his soundproof office with that comfy couch.

Before we'd reached the hall, the front door slammed open.

Dax had finally arrived.

Chapter Thirty-Two

ax stormed over to where we stood.

He didn't look at Xander at all. That dark gaze was focused entirely on me, and I felt so small in its depths.

"Is it true?" The hurt in his voice made my heart ache.

My hand went up to touch his chest involuntarily, but he stepped back before it connected.

That didn't sting or anything.

The three of us glanced around the room. Hannah was counting out there till behind the bar. Bitzy's and Luke's quiet laughter rang out from the kitchens.

Without saying anything, we made our way to the office and shut the door to the outside world.

"Imagine how I felt, Rori? Hearing it from one of my pack while I was already in so much emotional turmoil over Gunner?"

I didn't know what he meant by that. Was Gunner hurt?

Running a hand over his haggard face, he huffed out a sigh and plopped down on the sofa.

Xander was already handing him a glass of whiskey.

"What's wrong with Gunner?" My chest constricted. The air wouldn't fill my lungs properly.

Dax's eyes went straight to Xander.

"You didn't tell her? What the fuck, dude? Didn't you think she'd want to know?"

Xander came to stand behind me.

Putting a hand over my heart and one around my waist, he took in a deep breath and then let it out. Then another. "Breathe, Rori."

He took another breath in, and I did the same. Then let it out, following his lead.

Slowly, I started to get a hold of myself.

Dax's expression shifted from one of anger to one of sorrow.

After Xander was sure I'd stopped hyperventilating, he turned his frustration on Dax.

"I didn't know the extent, other than what I'd been told. And I didn't want to uselessly worry her when there was absolutely nothing she could have done about it."

Xander reluctantly let me go as I tugged against the circle of his arms.

Now, I was the one becoming angry.

I may not want to know everything, but I needed to know the things going on around me.

All of this overprotectiveness was becoming a cage.

"Stop trying to protect my feelings! Both of you!"

With my hands on my hips, I was sure I looked like a chicken clucking at a coyote.

"You're both going to tell me everything from now on. Capiche?"

That earned me an arched eyebrow from one and a chuckle from the other.

Alrighty then. I must have been in my comedic era. Give me a funny hat and call me a jester.

Dax became serious again. "Thane hurt Gunner pretty bad. He tore a chunk off one of his hind legs. I don't know if it will ever fully heal." Shaking the image from his thoughts, he continued. "As it stands, before I left, the bleeding had finally stopped but he'd lost a big piece of bone just above the ankle."

Cliche as it was, my hands flew to cover my mouth. I'd had no idea that could happen.

I'd assumed that if they got hurt, the quick healing would heal everything.

Poor Gunner. He wasn't my biggest fan, but he'd stepped up to save me anyway.

I'd gotten him injured. He was hurt because of me.

Xander yanked me into the cradle of his arms, kissing the top of my head. "Stop. It isn't your fault."

Did I say that out loud? I couldn't have.

Pulling away from the hug, I turned to Dax. He stood and took me into his arms the same way Xander had.

"You couldn't have done anything. Gunner is a strong wolf. In body and spirit. He'll be mad if you try to take this glory away from him."

Sobbing, a small laugh bubbled to my lips.

Pulling back to lift my chin, he leaned down and gently kissed my tears away.

I'd thought Xander would growl but he must have known this was what I'd needed.

Reaching behind me, I pulled on his hand, wrapping it around my waist.

Dax looked up and stepped back, but I grabbed a hold of the front of his shirt with my other hand.

"I can't stop seeing either of you yet. I'm not ready. I know that makes me selfish, but I need you both. I want you both."

I was an awful person. Their feelings were clear. They wanted me. And for my part, I wanted them. They didn't want to share, and I totally understood that.

When Kori mentioned her and Xander together, I'd lost my shit.

Ugh. I really was a horrible person for putting them through this.

"I'm not asking anything of you, love." Kissing the top of my head again, Xander's evergreen and copper scent blew the tendrils of hair from my face.

It was cool and refreshing and made me long with the desire to climb that mountain of a cock he'd kept hidden under those trousers. They didn't restrict the way jeans did.

My nighttime fantasy often lingered around unleashing his hardened length and covering it with a fresh coating of white ... snow.

"Hey. Don't let it be said that I wasn't giving you the time and space you needed to make your own decisions. I may not be as suave as this asshole, but I won't push you either, Rori."

Dax's crooked grin set my heart galloping.

He used to be so quiet. Didn't string but a few words together at any given time.

Since the vampires had come to town, he'd been more verbal. Freer to speak his mind.

I'd wondered what had changed and had asked him over dinner one night.

He'd told me that before, he was always worried about letting the secrets of my past, of his werewolf side, and any of the other things he wasn't supposed to tell me slip past his lips.

That I'd wormed my way into his heart, and he'd had a difficult time keeping me in the dark, so he'd made a conscious effort to not speak too much.

It made me want to slap him, but I understood his side of things too. I didn't like it or appreciate it, but I'd got it.

Secrets and the supernatural world went hand in hand.

"I'm sorry. I know it's horrible to keep you both on the line. I know that I should make a choice to save you the pain in the end."

A small sob bubbled up from my chest and they both reached out to comfort me at the same time.

If I was a better person, I'd set them both free.

But I wasn't a better person. I wasn't even a good person.

If learning of my past life taught me anything, it was that a seed of cruelty sat firmly nestled in my heart.

"I just can't. I can't imagine not seeing one of you anymore. I ... I... I'm..." I didn't know what.

If hell opened a pit at my feet right this minute, I wouldn't have been surprised.

Lifting my chin with his forefinger and thumb, Xander stared down into my eyes.

"You're not a bad person, Rori. You owe me nothing."

The love for my past life's soul shown bright through his beautiful eyes.

"Your mind is not hers. You are not her. Even if your soul is inclined to want some part of me, you are under no obligation to seek it."

If he thought that would help me feel less like a piece of shit, he was sorely mistaken.

Because I did want him. Irrationally. Irrevocably. Covetous even. I wanted him to be mine and mine alone... but I wanted to be free to see where things lead with Dax.

And if I were being honest with myself, there was a pull in me towards Thane that I didn't want, but it was there, nonetheless.

Shifting uncomfortably behind me, Dax headed towards the door after kissing my cheek.

"Where are you going?" If he was giving up on me, I couldn't blame him.

He was allowed to protect his own heart.

Mine ached with the thought but that was my cross to bear.

"I'm my packs alpha, little demon. I shouldn't have left when Gunner needed me." Hanging his head, he closed his eyes. "I'm so wrapped up in you, Rori. I couldn't let you go without a fight. But I need to get back."

Crossing the small space quickly, I threw my arms around his middle.

Coming up to just under his chest, he towered over me, but his arms came around me all the same.

"Fight. Fight for them. Fight for us, Dax. Don't give up on me yet. Promise?"

The hesitation drove a knife through my heart. Xander said nothing. The tension in the room bore down like a fresh waft of hot steam in a sauna.

With a long inhale and an extra-long exhale, he too kissed the top of my head.

Being so much shorter than these giant males was giving me a complex.

"Okay. I'll keep vying for your affection. I may never claim your heart, but I'll do my best to be worthy of your company."

Opening my mouth to protest, he shook his head and walked out.

Shutting the office door behind him, I turned slowly to face the other half of my soul.

Chapter Thirty-Three

Xander and I talked for the better part of an hour before I'd decided that the day had been long enough.

He saw me to my truck and once Matilda vroomed to life, he'd gone back inside as I drove off to find comfort in my bed.

It was close enough to morning that he didn't feel the need to call Lissie and have her meet me at my house.

My street was dark. The sensored porch light by my front door wasn't on.

Either it burned out or the night/day sensor wasn't working properly.

The shadows it normally cast this early in the wee hours weren't there to make me suspect every bush or tree, but the total darkness played on my nerves all the same.

Fumbling with my keys, the door pushed open when I tried to put it in the lock.

Forgetting to lock it had been a bad habit I'd thought I'd put behind me but apparently not.

Wouldn't it be my luck that a bear or a moose rammed into it and tore apart my belongings because of my absent mindedness?

The moment the door opened, Aries mewed loudly.

Pushing at my legs, I slid off the top step.

"Aries! What the hell, dude? If I break my leg, who's going to feed you? Huh?"

His appetite was a constant thorn in my side, but I loved the little brat.

I made my way back to the door only for him to do it again.

His meow was like an alarm you couldn't shut off. Loud and obnoxious.

Normally he'd run out the door to prowl the surrounding forest the moment I'd open it and wouldn't be back until around noonish when I'd get up so he could be fed.

Smacking at the side of my pant leg, I admonished him with my "don't try me" tone but he continued to push at me and meow.

"Alright! Geesh." Setting my keys in the dish by the front door, I made my way to the kitchen, turning on the hall light as I went.

The cans of food were usually stocked next to the cabinet by the fridge, but they'd been knocked all over the floor.

If the boy had hands, he'd be as fat as a hibernating squirrel.

The thrum of the electric can opener burst through the quiet house.

When it stopped, there was still a noise I couldn't decipher. It sounded as if it might be coming from the living room.

Setting Aries can on the floor, I picked up the dull knife I'd washed yesterday morning after making myself some breakfast and leaving the dishes to air dry on the counter.

The hall light didn't cast much illumination into the room. I usually used the fireplace for that, but it wasn't lit.

There was a low hum, almost like a moan, coming from in the shadows. Perhaps a hurt animal. Or a...

"Don't just stand there, Kitten. Help your former lover out."

Dropping the knife to the floor, I ran over to turn the overhead lights on.

On the floor beside my sofa laid the male responsible for all of my deaths.

"Thane! What are you doing here?" My heart beat so fast, it could take flight at any moment. "Is that blood?"

Without thinking, my knees hit the floor beside him.

Ignoring the sting in my cut knee, my hands fluttered above his wounds, unsure what I was supposed to do.

Reasoning caught up with my panic and I grabbed the throw blanket from the back of the couch, pressing it to the open gash as it continued to leak blood all over my floor.

He cried out in pain. A few broken ribs for sure.

Growling in my face, saliva dripped from sharp, elongated teeth.

I didn't stop. If I didn't keep pressure on his wound, he'd bleed out.

"That hurts!" He roared at me.

"If you want me to stop the bleeding, then I have to push hard, asshole!" That earned me a hesitant smirk.

Today was the day my buffoonish sarcasm and wit wouldn't be kept under wraps.

Wonderful. What painful way would I like to die?

"I thought you were the original werewolf? Shouldn't you be tougher or something?"

Looking around the room for anything I could use as a makeshift bandage, I spotted one of my long socks next to the chair.

It was clean, falling to the floor when I'd brought the laundry in here to fold.

If I could get the fire going quickly, maybe I could cauterize the wound and wrap it until his healing took over.

Or you could let him bleed out and save yourself the terror of his obsession with killing you, a small voice said in my mind. *Tempting.*

Shaking the malicious thought from my head, I grabbed his hands and placed them over the blanket, on the wound.

"Here. Hold this in place while I start the fire."

His normally quick remarks failed him. It had been hours since the fight he'd been in at the bar.

Face scrunched up, color draining from his lips, he must have been in too much pain to bite back at me. That wasn't a good sign.

The fire roared to life, and I placed a poker in its hearth to heat.

If the bleeding didn't stop soon... *Ugh.* Not finishing that thought.

Running to the kitchen, I was back in two shakes with a glass of water, a dish towel, and some soap.

"I'm going to have to clean this, Thane. Do you think you can man up enough not to rip my head off?"

Through gritted teeth, he hissed, "You sure are cheeky for someone made of soft, delicate pieces."

Arching a brow, I waited for him to confirm that I wasn't going to die trying to save him from his own damned actions.

"Go on then. Fix me."

Wild laughter broke free from my chest.

"Fix you? There isn't enough time in the world to fix you, you jackass. I'll clean you up the best I can though."

Taking the glass of water, I poured it on the rag with a drop or two of antibacterial soap.

The cut was deep. Blood kept oozing around the opening. Unlucky for him, it was in a spot just out of his reach.

Noticing a whitish nub in the red, I pushed open the wound while his hellish snarl sounded throughout my small living room.

Teeth bared, he kept himself in check as I pulled out a sharp fang and pushed the broken ribs back into place the best I could.

Willing myself not to pass out from the grossness all of this was, I wiped at the wound again. It leaked, but the steady flow slowed dramatically.

My floor was trashed. I'd never be able to get all the blood gone.

It would be a constant reminder of the vicious male in front of me.

The fire was hot enough now. Grabbing the poker, I made my way back to him and his eyes widened as he tried to scootch further into the couch away from the red-hot metal.

"I need to close the wound, Thane. It'll only hurt a minute." Even as I said it, I knew it was a lie.

Burns hurt for a lot longer than cuts and bruises. One of my exes taught me that lesson first hand.

"Put the claws away, kitten. I don't need your superfluous healing methods."

Lifting my ruined sock that I'd stuffed against his side when I'd gone to get the poker, he wiped at the trickle of blood. The damaged flesh was already starting to knit itself back together.

It would probably be healed completely in the next fifteen minutes or so at that rate.

"That's amazing." The fact that I still wanted to stick him notwithstanding, the way these werewolves healed was incredible. I couldn't pull my eyes away.

A charged tension filled the space between us. The room became too small.

"Stop looking at me like that," he purred. "Or else I'm liable to bust it back open while taking you roughly against the back of this sofa."

The bass in his voice spoke straight to the center of my core.

Without thinking, my hand wrapped around my own throat.

Remembering his hands being there instead. Reliving how his hard cock pressed up against my backside, sliding up and down.

Swallowing the lump in my throat was made more difficult when his eyes met mine.

With a deep resonating growl, he sat up. Hand landing on the firm outline of his cock through his pants, stroking up and down. Smiling like a cat who ate the canary.

I stood frozen. With fear. With excitement. With a profound longing.

Wetness pooled between my thighs, and I tried to clench them tighter together.

Dax and Xander weren't the only ones my body craved.

My mind screamed at me to run but my feet were planted to the spot.

Thane was dangerous. He'd been hurt and came here. Came to find me.

For help of all things. It made no sense.

Now he was healing. And we were alone. Very alone.

Two adults with wants and needs crammed into the small confines of my tiny front room.

Scenting my arousal, his upper lip pulled over his teeth.

With a long intake of breath through his nose, I knew it was no use to deny that I'd wanted him to take me just as he had made me picture it.

Snatching my wrist, he yanked me towards the sofa. A meek gasp escaped my lips.

"Come closer, kitten. You know you want a taste of what you gave up all those years ago."

Run. Step back. My mind wouldn't shut up, but my body would not respond to the commands.

Gooseflesh covered my arms at his touch. My nipples pebbled so hard, they were painful.

I still hadn't uttered a word. Staring at the way his Adam's apple bobbed when he swallowed. Fascinated at the corded muscle that laid below the hair on his chest.

He yanked on my wrist again and my knees hit the floor with a shot of pain.

Kneeling in his blood, the smell turning my stomach. Somewhere inside me craved it more. Craved him more.

Get up, you idiot. As much as I knew I shouldn't want him, it only served to flame my desires to taste him.

With the hand that had been stroking his length, he popped open the button, unzipped the zipper, and freed himself from the restraint of his pants.

Not massive, but definitely above average, my core ached at the sight of it on display.

A small hand wrapped around its girth and the realization that it was mine shook me. I didn't remember giving myself permission to do so.

"You like that, don't you kitten?" I wanted to wipe that stupid smirk from his face, but my body wouldn't let me. It drove me forward. "Be a good girl. Take what you want."

Fingers closed around the back of my neck and pulled me towards it.

Screaming at myself to stop did no good. I wanted this. I needed this.

"I hate you." The words didn't sit right but I spit them all the same.

"Sure you do, kitten." With his fingers gripping tight in my hair, he pulled me closer. "Now, let's see just how much."

I deserved this humbling and humility for all I'd done in my past.

I deserved to have this pleasure for all I'd endured in my current existence.

As my mouth hovered over the head of his cock, he snatched my head back, not letting me take him in.

"What do you say?" he asked with no lack of authority.

I knew what he wanted. I didn't know how I knew, but I did.

Swallowing my pride, I allowed my desire to take the driver's seat. "Please... Please let me have a taste?"

The smirk that lit in his eyes was nothing less than gloating satisfaction and I couldn't make myself feel anything but elated that I'd been the one to bring it to him.

None to gently, he shoved my head down. His cock hit the back of my throat before I'd processed that it was in my mouth.

I was no quitter. I sucked and slurped as he pushed me down and up over and over again. Slobber dribbling down my chin.

Once or twice, he'd hit the back of my throat and held me there, gagging, struggling for air, until I'd tap him on the side and he released his hold.

"Such a wicked little thing. Mmmm... your tongue is as divine as it is vicious."

Horror and excitement rose within me in equal parts. Fear rose to the surface of my being, and I'd loved it with each choked plunge that cut off my oxygen.

The ache between my legs intensified with every stroke of my tongue around him.

Swelling beneath my touch, Thane threw his head back and howled as his release choked me into submission.

I slurped and swallowed every last drop.

Once he was finished, the fingers still wrapped in my flowing black locks released and he shoved me backwards.

I landed on my ass, slipping in the blood that was soaking through the floor. "You asshole!"

Before the words were out of my mouth, he pounced.

Ripping my shirt open, with a jerk of his massive, calloused hand, my bra tore free. Exposing my erect nipples as my chest heaved up and down.

His fingers bloody, he drew circles around each of my breast. It was disgusting and repulsive and I couldn't get enough.

Hot breath blew down my front. Teeth grazed each nipple to the point of mild pain, but I didn't want him to stop.

"What do you want now, kitten?"

Knocking my knees apart, he slid between my thighs. His hand came to rest right above my pants.

If he was going to make me beg, at least I'd make it worth it. Get what I needed from him before I'd kick him to the curb.

Rubbing my clit through the fabric. He groaned. "I can smell you from here. Do you want this cock, kitten? What is it you crave?"

I couldn't think with his hands tracing pleasure up and down my sex.

I knew this was wrong. I hadn't slept with Dax in months. I hadn't been with Xander at all.

The fact that Xander hadn't done anything with anyone in centuries because of me weighed heavily on my mind.

...But I wanted this. I wanted my own release.

I'd said before that I was over letting anyone other than me dictate my life and I'd meant it.

"I want you inside of me, Thane."

I knew I'd feel bad about it later, but right now I wouldn't let myself care.

A cruel laugh issued from the male stroking me. "As you wish."

The leggings I'd been wearing ripped but only in the center, giving way to my lack of panties from clit to asshole.

The bastard didn't take them off me. It somehow left me feeling more exposed than if I was laid naked before him.

Settling his head between my legs, the flat of his tongue pressed against that erect bundle of nerves until my back arched off the bloody floor.

Slipping a finger inside as he lapped me up. A wall shattering moan ripped from my throat. A second finger slid in, and both curled over and over again.

As my release built higher and higher, he snarled louder with each suckling of my clit.

I was almost there. My back arched, tightening the muscles all the way down to my knees.

Just before I could get there, he ripped the two fingers out and I screamed my frustration. "You prick! Finish me!"

A cold chuckle left him as his slick fingers rubbed against my asshole.

Flipping me onto my knees and elbows in one swift motion, my ass was fully exposed.

Before I could yell no, he slid his thumb inside and he returned the two fingers to continue their ministrations.

Bucking wildly against him, my body caved into the pleasures he bestowed me.

Pulling me onto my knees, flush with his body, he reached around to my front.

Franticly, his thumb circled back and forth across my clit, all while his thumb and fingers pumped in and out of my ass and honeypot.

His mouth at my ear, he purred. "Take it, kitten. Take it like the good little slut you are."

Sinking his teeth into my neck, I hissed.

Pain and pleasure engulfed my mind. Warm blood trickled down my neck.

Every spark of focus homed in on the building release inching towards my shattering.

I couldn't hold back. I came. Hard. Harder than I'd ever cum before.

I'd squirted everywhere. I didn't even know I could, but the evidence of it dripped all around me.

Spinning me around, my back hit the floor, knocking the breath from my lungs.

His mouth came down on my swollen mound and he nipped at the tender flesh before his tongue ran flat over my pussy.

Thane smiled as he lapped up everything I'd given him. "Mmmm. You taste divine, kitten."

Pulling myself away from him, I slid in his blood again.

The scene looked every bit of a horror story.

I was equal parts fascinated and disgusted as I looked down at my half naked body.

"Get out." I didn't know why I'd suddenly felt shameful, but I did. "Get out and go back to where you came from!"

Zipping up his pants, he smeared my juices mixed with his own blood across his face. It looked like the deadly consequences of my action incarnate.

"I got what I needed," he said as the corner of his mouth pulled up on one side. "And then some."

Winking as he reached the door, he added, "Make sure you tell that brother of mine how hard you came for me, kitten. He's gotta know the stakes if he wants to make you scream the way I did."

The shoe I'd throne hit the back of the door as it closed behind him. *Gods! What have I done?*

Chapter Thirty-Four

The next day, I called Lissie to help me with the floors. I didn't know what else to do.

I had to tell someone what happened, or I'd lose my mind. And Bitzy wouldn't understand.

It was becoming blaringly clear that my days of telling my best friend almost anything about my life were at an end.

My skin felt raw. I stood in the scalding hot shower for over an hour after he'd left. The hot water had turned frigid before I'd gathered myself together and gotten out.

"Hand me that rag." Where she'd gotten the cleaner from, I hadn't a clue.

Vampires certainly were quick. She had most of the blood cleaned up before I'd come back in the room.

To be fair, I'd taken an extra-long time feeding Aries and making my coffee. I had no wish to see the evidence of my betrayal.

How could I ever explain to Xander that I'd let Thane into my body willingly. After all he'd done to him over the years. After all that he'd done to me over the years.

There was some sick and twisted part of me that hungered for the depraved things Thane represented.

I could see the evil. Touch the evil. And it felt good to let go of the need to be moral with him.

If Anastasia had felt this way before she was turned, no wonder she'd given in and let herself indulge in the carnage.

Shaking myself from my ridiculous justifications, Lissie snapped her fingers in front of me. "Where did you go?"

Could I tell her? She'd been friends with, been killed and turned by, the monster I'd been in my past life.

I didn't want her to have to relive any of that, but she might have been the only one to understand enough to purge this poison from my thoughts.

"Thane isn't the worst part, Lissie. I am. My thoughts have gone dark on many occasions over the years but giving into them felt good. I'm a horrible person."

Staring at the stained floorboards, I cursed myself.

Thane had held me by the throat earlier that day. He'd taken a chunk out of Gunner. He'd trashed Eventide without an ounce of remorse.

"How am I going to tell Xander? How am I supposed to face Dax? They should get as far away from me as possible. I'm not good for either one of them."

If I'd thought she'd immediately rush to my defense, I'd been wrong.

Lips pursed, she glared at me for a moment, and I wasn't sure if I should be worried or not.

"Look, Rori. I can't tell you what to do. I can only ask a favor of you and hope you understand my reasoning."

Throwing the bloodied rag into the soap bucket, she stood up to face me. With a tightness around her eyes, I could tell she was having trouble articulating her thoughts.

"I owe you, Liss. Just spit it out." The smell of copper hitting my nose every few minutes.

The soap did nothing to mask it. I'd need new floorboards that my bank account couldn't suffer.

"YOU don't owe me anything. You need to distinguish between Stasia's actions and your own! But you're right. Stasia does owe me, so it is that part of your soul I'll ask my favor from," she said.

It was a relief to hear. Any more things to feel guilty over and I'd probably lose my shit altogether.

"Anything. She turned you. I stole... she stole your life. You can ask anything of me." I didn't know why I felt the need to make up for mistakes that were never mine, but I did.

"Alright then... don't take the light from Xander's eyes. It's been hard to watch over the centuries. He never moved on. He never moved forward." She patted my shoulder.

It wasn't like I wanted to hurt him. A part of me knew how wrong I'd been for trying to have my cake and eat it too.

I needed to give one of them up, but my mind immediately shied away from the thought.

"I'm not telling you that he must be who you choose. And I'm certainly not telling you whether or not to inform him of the Thane thing. I'm just asking that you fully think through whatever it is you decide. I don't think he'd survive finding you again only to lose you."

No pressure there. *Geesh.*

What she said made a lot of sense, but it also left me with more questions to ask myself than I'd had when we'd started the conversation.

If I told him about the Thane situation, he'd be hurt but he'd still stick by me.

If I told him about the darkness in my heart, he'd be even more concerned.

He'd want to keep me alive and unbonded to him to spare me from the person I'd become all those years ago.

Xander would suffer beside me if I asked it of him and that wasn't fair.

Thane needed to be dealt with and that would leave only my situation with Dax.

I couldn't push him away. No matter what I was feeling or who I had been in regard to Xander.

Selfish. Party of one.

Dax was going to hate me. The thought of not having him in my life brought tears to my eyes.

He'd been fun to have around for a long time. Then, he'd been my safe harbor.

And now, when he'd tried so hard to win my heart... I couldn't make a choice yet.

I was the worst person alive, but I would do what I could to safeguard all of our hearts before I had to rip one of them out of our chests.

"I promise I will do my best, Liss. Thanks for caring about him over the years." I couldn't promise any more than that.

Looking at the stains on the floor, she shook her head. "We're going to have to replace these."

"I don't think I have enough in my account to cover them and my bills too."

With an exaggerated sigh, I threw the rag in the bucket and walked towards the hallway.

"They'll have to wait. Let's take the throw rug from my bedroom and put it over the majority of it for now."

Rolling her eyes, she pulled a black credit card from the inside pocket of her jacket.

"Silly, Rori," she said, booping me on the nose. "Money is something that you don't have to worry about anymore."

I began to protest but she held up a hand to stymie my complaints.

"Even if you don't end up with Xander, he'll never let you want for anything for the rest of your days. THAT you don't have a choice in."

I wanted to argue but I knew it would be pointless. These vampires could be so pushy when they decided something.

If paying my way through life was on their agenda, I wasn't going to complain one bit.

A few hours later, we'd picked out some new floors and she'd insisted that we pick a new paint for the walls.

Shopping online had always been a luxury I couldn't afford. It was amazing the things that they'd ship right to your door.

After leaving me alone to my thoughts, hunger gnawed at my insides.

Eventide had a great pot roast on today's menu and the mashed potatoes were to die for.

By the time I'd dressed, gassed up Matilda, and arrived at the parking lot, the sun was beginning to set.

The smell of garlic and warm spices permeated my nose as soon as I opened the door.

Stomach rumbling loudly, it was all I could do not to head straight to the kitchens.

While my eyes adjusted to the dimmer lights inside, spots formed in my vision.

I didn't see the person in front of me until my head flew back and pain radiated along my cheeks.

A small dribble of wetness leaked from the corner of my mouth.

Mina stood hovering a couple of inches in front of me. "I should kill you myself!"

No one seemed to notice our exchange. Patrons were dancing around the dance floor. Eating meals at their tables. Playing pool over in the corner.

Standing in my personal space, she was so close to me that I needed to step back... but I didn't.

"You hit me! You fucking bitch!"

My arm swung out, but vampire reflexes prevailed.

Grabbing my arm at the crook of my elbow, she whisked us towards the hall between the kitchens and the bar.

Her temper slithering through the space between us, she hadn't finished her tirade.

"I should have killed you that first week I was here. You've gone insane," A small amount of spit glistened on her lower lip as I stood there rubbing my jaw. "Smacking the hybrid warrants my outrage, Anastasia!"

Chest heaving rapidly as she finished, the fact that she didn't need to breathe wasn't lost on me.

Yanking my arm from her strong grip wasn't easy but I did it.

"I'm not Anastasia, you daft cunt! Get that through your thick skull!" I yelled right back.

With lips swelling, I let the trickle of blood lay there in plain sight. Letting it sink into her what she had done... Or giving her more fuel for her outrage.

Really smart, idiot. Sure. Go on. Provoke the angry vampire with your blood.

My face stung from her slap, but I knew it could have been so much worse. She'd tempered her strength when she'd swung.

"No. You are not. You don't have half the gumption she had. Nor do you wield a fraction of her charisma. Kori could have killed you before you'd blinked. Do you realize how careless with Xander's heart you're being?" Her words struck home.

I was being more than selfish. If you looked up selfish in the dictionary, my picture would be plastered right beside it.

It may not have been any of her business what I did with my love life, but I empathized with her point of view.

She'd been Anastasia's best friend. She'd been there after she'd run amuck, and Thane had put her down.

Mina had been there to help Xander through losing his mate.

Then I'd thought back to what she'd said... Hybrid. Kori was a hybrid. What did that mean?

"You're right, Mina. I'm sorry. I haven't been thinking straight lately. I'll work on it."

If looks could end my life, this one could cremate me completely.

"Next time I hit you for being an insufferable dimwit, you won't walk away so easily. Am I clear?" If she pursed her lips any tighter, I'd worry that they permanently weld together.

"Crystal... Mina?" I called after her as she headed back towards the main room.

I didn't talk above a whisper, but I knew she could hear me.

"What did you mean by hybrid? I thought Kori was a vampire. The bloodlust in her eyes had been clear when she'd attacked me."

Before I'd gotten my answer, Luke walked around the corner and stopped in his tracks. "What the hell is going on here?"

Well, shit. His timing could have been better.

"It was a misunderstanding. I'm fine."

I'd forgotten about my swollen lip and the blood. The stinking in my face had turned to a steady throb.

"I'd insulted her family. I was in the wrong, Luke. It's okay."

Without looking back, Mina left us.

His fingers brushed the side of my face gently, but it tingled in his wake.

Stars popped in and out of my eye on that side and it looked like the aurora in my peripheral vision for a moment.

"You really know how to attract danger, don't you, kiddo?"

Embarrassment filled me for always needing to be rescued. He was only human, but sweeping in to save the day on a regular basis made him my real life hero.

Corny much? Snorting at my own folly, I rubbed my cheek again with a laugh.

Fisting his hands, he dropped them to his side. "You should head to the bar and get some ice to put on that. It looks like it's already going down. I don't think it'll bruise."

Concern had made the purplish hue of his eyes deeper, richer. I'd noticed them before but no one else had ever mentioned them to be odd or anything.

It must have been a trick of the lighting each time.

He was too nice to me for someone I'd only met a couple of months ago. I needed more niceness in my life.

"Thanks, Luke. You're the big brother I never wanted," I said. Sarcasm saturating my every word. "Overprotective and caring all in one."

Smiling my most winning grin, I batted my lashes playfully.

With a quiet chuckle, he turned to walk away.

Under his breath, I swear I heard him say, "If you only knew," but he was out the back door before I could puzzle out what he'd meant.

Chapter Thirty-Five

Molly's attitude was stellar tonight.

She'd flung the dirty bar rag at Cody when he got in her way while trying to change out a keg.

She'd practically chewed Hannah's head off for grabbing her the wrong beer.

And now she was tutting and pursing her lips because I refused to drink any faster while sitting at the bar.

It wasn't that I didn't understand. Turnover was how she made bank, how she got her register to ring higher.

Pushing paying customers to eat their grub, drink in abundance, and being a grade A bitch wasn't a good look for the staff of Eventide.

"Molly, you might want to tone it down a bit. You heard Xander when he took over. I don't think you want to go looking for another job."

Slamming the glass she'd been washing into the sink, soapy dish water sprayed down the front of her blouse.

"Is that a threat, Rori? I know you've been chummy with the bossman. Are you trying to get me fired?"

I hadn't been but it was a good idea. Xander wouldn't hesitate to do it if that's what I had wanted.

She'd never liked me. Well, she liked me even less than the rest of the people around her. Not a friendly bone in her body.

"No. Forget I said anything. Keep on being bitchy. It suits you."

If she wanted to keep up her asinine demeanor, it would be on her when Mina gave her the axe.

My sarcasm had been at an all-time high lately.

There was a crueler mischief in it's under tone that slipped in little by little that had begun to worry me, but I was having trouble reining it in.

Taking my first bite of my meal, I'd been right.

The pot roast tonight made me see stars. The potatoes were so creamy and buttery. And the new pop-over rolls that Luke introduced Gav and Nik to had my mouth crying out in pure ecstasy.

I didn't mean to let a moan slip passed my lips but the guy sitting next to me chuckled. "That good, huh?"

Normally, talking to other patrons wasn't high on my to-do list except when I was working towards better tips. Especially when I was off and not required to interact with anyone.

Lately, since Xander came into the picture, I'd become a Chatty Cathy.

I didn't know if that was because I'd found out about the supernatural world or because I'd felt safer on some level.

Humans weren't the unknowing threat they used to be to me.

"You should snag some before they run out. The mashed potatoes are heavenly."

I took another bite, and my eyes rolled into my head. He chuckled again.

"I guess I'll have to order some," he said, flagging Hannah down.

Wise of him not to bother with Molly.

"Can I get a plate of what she's having? And buy her a drink on me."

"Oh, you don't have to do that. I'm good."

It was my natural response, but Hannah was already pouring me another rum and Coke.

There was something familiar about this guy. I couldn't place him from anywhere though.

He was in his mid-forties. Dirty blonde hair. Not much of an accent as far as I could tell.

Wait! His eyes. They were dark in this lighting, but a deep purple hue shown through if I looked close enough each time the dance floor lights drifted our way.

"Do you know Luke?" I don't know why I didn't see it before.

He didn't look like Luke but there was a way about him that was all Lukish, for the lack of a better word.

Shifting on his barstool, he sipped from his glass, looking uncomfortable.

"I don't know a Luke." The sudden coolness from him was odd. "I'm just passing through. Thought I'd stop in for a few drinks."

Turning to face me again, lips turned up in an impish grin, his eyes twinkled in amusement.

"And now I have a plate of holy pot roast and the company of a pretty lady," he said with a wink.

I must have imagined the cool shift in him. Being around Thane was starting to make me see hateful things where there were none.

"Gotcha. Thanks for the drink. I wasn't trying to flirt my way to free booze." He chuckled again and heat rushed to my cheeks. "I mean it. It's this roast. It's killer. You'll see."

Hannah came back at that moment to tell him that we were out of pot roast and ask if he'd like anything else instead.

Another good-hearted chuckle before he declined. "If there's none of the roast left, I'd best be on my way."

"What? You're choosing to leave a pretty lady to eat alone because there's no more divine beef on a hot plate?"

Poking fun at his dilemma seemed like a good way to finish out the conversation.

As he turned to leave again, I said, "I never even caught your name."

Standing only a few feet away, the light had shined directly into his eyes. They were definitely the same type of purple as Luke's.

What were the odds of him being here and not knowing him? I didn't know why he would lie, though.

With another chuckle, he downed the last of his drink.

"Good night, ma'am. Thanks for the company."

That was it. He left without even glancing back.

Another week had flown by.

The sun was rising higher in the sky. The nights were beginning to stretch longer into the night.

Most of the snow had now melted from all over the mountainside.

With the melting snow came less visitors to the resort. Less customers to Eventide as we approached the summer months.

Hikers were a different breed than skiers. They didn't often drink much. Hydration was key to high altitude trail exploration.

We'd had more customers for this time of year than any of the years past. The addition of good food had been a draw that couldn't be denied.

Xander was in and out as always. Even knowing what he'd been doing didn't take away the want to see him more often.

If he were to find the witch and somehow get the curse reversed, we could live out a normal human lifespan.

I couldn't decide if that was a good thing or a bad. His friends would have to watch as he grew old and feeble and eventually passed away.

After all they'd been through together, was it fair of him to leave them that burden of grief?

We'd had two nights this week where we'd begun to make out in his office and gotten interrupted. Once by Cody. Once by Luke.

It was as if the universe didn't want the two of us to connect for more than a few stolen interludes.

Maybe it was right. The last lifetime that had happened, thousands of people died. By my hand.

Tonight, however, we'd actually planned a date. A time to spend getting to know each other better.

Excitement coiled in my chest and mind all day.

It wasn't about whether or not we'd be intimate. Though I was longing for that too.

I wanted to know Xander on a deeper level. Everything inside of me came alive when he was near.

I owed it to myself and to him to explore where our feeling might take us.

To discover all of his quirks. To see all of his strengths as well as his shortcomings.

It was a short drive to his house. He lived fairly close to me, and I was grateful for that fact.

If it had been a longer drive, anxiety would have held me in a tight choke hold. The more time I would have had to overthink, the worse my anxiety would have been.

As it were, I pulled onto the winding driveway less than ten minutes after leaving my place.

The house rose up in front of me and blocked my view of almost everything around.

It was enormous. Beautiful in that way old houses from a forgotten era always were.

New landscaping and fresh tilled earth spoke of renovation. Spotting a drop or two of paint on a few leaves, the freshening up of the property had to extend to the house itself.

If this house were here before, I couldn't recall it.

Stepping out of Matilda, the smell of tar wormed its way up my nose. The driveway had a new layer of asphalt that to have been recently done.

The snow had only melted in the last week or so. I wondered idlily if the driveway had time to set properly.

Evergreen trees lined the long drive right up to the house.

If the vampires stayed to decorate next Christmas, these trees would make for the perfect holiday setting.

I'd never had that. My father didn't bother. If he couldn't drink it, it wasn't worth his time.

After he'd died, I'd bought my first Christmas tree and put a few lights on it.

It was small and the needles all fell off before Christmas because I'd bought it too early in all my excitement to decorate.

That Christmas morning, all I felt was lonely. The lights brough me little joy.

The next day, I marched into Eventide and didn't give Kyle any other choice but to hire me.

And within a few weeks, Bitzy and I had become thick as thieves.

I was a little less lonely the next Christmas.

We'd spent it together, drinking virgin eggnog and dancing around in the lights of her tree to the tune of Holly Jolly Christmas.

We'd fallen asleep by the fire after watching holiday movie after holiday movie.

It had been the best Christmas of my life.

If Xander stayed, I wasn't above begging him to deck the halls and make this place look magical.

Lissie said they had money. Lighting this place up wouldn't break their bank like it would mine. I'd grovel if I had to.

Just once, I wanted to feel the spirit of the holidays like other people got to.

Just once, I wanted to live high on life and not merely in survival mode.

Xander opened the door as I raised my hand to knock. *Stupid vampire hearing.* That quirky half smile of his made my heart gallop.

I'd been so caught up in fantasizing, I hadn't realized I'd climbed the steps.

If he'd thought I was silly or daft, he didn't try to embarrass me.

"You look stunning, love."

My skirt was a few inches above my knees. The blouse I'd chosen was one that Lissie purchased online with that black credit card when we were picking out my flooring.

It had popped up in an ad across the bottom off the screen and I mentioned it was nice.

That's it. That's all I'd said.

When the flooring showed up at my door, there were several other packages with it.

All clothes and shoes. All in my size. All gorgeous and way out of my price range.

I'd tried to thank her the next time I'd seen her, and she'd waved me away like I was being ridiculous.

A gal could get used to that kind of treatment.

New floors. New walls. New clothes.

I'd considered mentioning how old my kitchen appliances were the next time she was at my house, but I didn't want to be too greedy.

"Thank you. Something smells delicious." The scent of garlic and oregano hung heavy in the air coming from the open door behind him.

Immediately salivating, I took an unconscious step closer.

Grabbing my chin between his forefinger and thumb, he lifted my face.

"You smell delicious." Our lips met briefly, tenderly. "You tempt me more than you know."

Swallowing the sudden lump in my throat, I tried and failed to avert my eyes.

I don't fear him... but I should.

A vampire who tells you that you smell delicious should elicit some sense of self preservation.

The heat pooling low in my stomach at his dangerous words spoke to how pathetically broken I was.

Dropping my chin, Xander stepped aside and motioned for me to enter.

"Your feast awaits, dragonfly."

Chapter Thirty-Six

Dumbfounded. Completely dumbfounded. My mouth hung open like a fish out of water.

Lissie hadn't exaggerated when she'd said they had money. Babysitting me at my house must have been like camping in a tent for her.

The cavernous entryway was bright and elegant but not ostentatious.

A staircase leading up to the second story wound along one side at the back of the room.

To the right, a fire blazed in the hearth tall enough for a grown man to walk in to.

The room was quaint, with bookshelves lining one wall and four cozy looking chairs in the center, facing each other in front of the fire.

In the far corner of the room on the left, a grand piano sat on a raised triangular platform. The rest of the room had a few high-top tables with finely made chairs along the wall.

"That's the ballroom. It's not big, but it does the job." He motioned for us to go through to the next room.

"Uh-huh. Sure. Not big at all." The high ceilings drew my eye up, to the artwork hanging above the piano.

Nestled in a wood frame the size of Connecticut was the most beautiful abstract painting I'd ever seen.

It had shades of blue and green running horizontally in splashes across the eight foot canvas. Crimson red dripped from an abstract set of wispy wings, landing in a puddle of the deepest shade of black.

It was awful. And beautiful. It reminded me of vibrant life and horrible death all at once.

I felt his eyes on me without looking. The thrum coming from his chest was like that of a lion's purr. The sound vibrating straight through me.

All my focus left the sights in front of me and narrowed down to the hand he'd placed at the small of my back to guide me forward.

The blouse came together with a single button in the back as two triangle pieces of fabric closed together at the points.

Bending down to kiss the top of my head, his scent engulfed me entirely.

The top of my shoulders and the bottom of my back were exposed, and I felt every breath he exhaled like a caress.

Entering a grand dining room, the table was massive.

Twelve place settings along each side and one at each end.

There were four candelabras stretched the length from one end to the other. There were no dishes currently on it, but the fact that it was that big tugged sadly at my chest.

Having this many people to dine with, it wouldn't feel cozy or friendly. You couldn't speak to the people at the other end unless you shouted.

Sure, it gave you a lot of elbow room, but at least four to six more chairs could be added.

It'd make it more family like. More inviting. More communal.

Moving on to the kitchen, there were all of the high end, newfangled appliances. An island that was large but right for the space. And a pantry the size of my bedroom at home.

Ushering us over to a large picture window in a space at the back of the kitchen, a nook with a much cozier feeling came into view.

"This is where we usually eat. That out there is for dinner parties or special gatherings."

That crooked grin of his would be my undoing.

Could he sense my sorrow back there?

I needed to find out what these vampires could do. What other abilities besides being bitey might they have?

Pulling my chair out, Xander poured me a glass of wine from the bottle he had chilling in a bucket on the table.

I hadn't found a wine I liked yet. I didn't want to squash his spirit though, so I took a tentative sip

The burst of sweetness on my tongue was pleasantly surprising. "What kind is this?"

It wasn't too dry or vinegary like the wines Hannah had me try.

"I thought you might like a nice Moscato. The lighter the color, the more refreshing and brighter it is. You don't strike me as a Merlot drinker."

I couldn't tell if that was a compliment or a dig, but I didn't suppose he'd go out of his way to poke fun at my naivete.

The way the corner of his mouth turned up on one side made my stomach flutter.

A timer dinged on the oven, and he went to retrieve what-ever was in there.

The smell was unbelievable. I'd hoped we could eat soon. I'd been too anxious to eat much of anything all day.

The aroma of tomatoes and garlic brought my hunger to the forefront of my thoughts

Even with a drop-dead gorgeous vampire who smelled heavenly and looked deliciously dangerous making me dinner ten feet away, the food itself was my main focus.

Coming back with a salad and placing a basket of fresh baked bread in the center of the table, my face fell slightly. My pout must have given me away.

I loved the low chuckle that sounded in his chest. It was a harmony that completed the song of my soul.

"The lasagna needs to sit for thirty minutes before it's ready to serve."

Handing me a piece of bread after buttering it, I snatched it up and shoved it in my mouth like a starving alley cat.

Amusement twinkled in his eyes.

"Sorry, I haven't eaten much today, I should have more etiquette but honestly..." *Wait a minute!*

Something I should have thought of before occurred to me all of a sudden.

"Xander, do you actually eat food? Or is it just blood you crave?"

In answer to my question, he picked up a piece of bread. Ripping of the end, he put it in his mouth and began chewing slowly.

"We can eat food. We can drink too. Everything tastes rather blase though. Only the strongest of flavors has any appeal."

Swirling the wine in his cup, he set it down without drinking it.

"Whiskey is preferable as far as alcohol goes. The notes are a lot more subtle than when I was human, but they still fill the void that some of my other preferences left.

A far off look took hold of his face. His voice turned into a low, thrumming growl. The corners of his mouth twitched with the whisper of a smile.

"As far as the other cravings... they're still there. Only one person, one soul, will ever be able to satisfy them."

Reaching across the table, I put my hand on his. Suffering through centuries of heartache could have brought out the worst of him, but instead, he held onto his hope rather than let the bitterness of loss claim him.

With a shake of his head, he dislodged the past and smiled. It wasn't the same lighthearted one he usually gave me.

It was tight. Forced but optimistic.

"Where are my manners?"

After a few minutes rummaging through the refrigerator, he brought us back a plate of arancini and a few different types of salad dressing.

"Here we go." Setting mine down, he took his own plate and sat across from me.

It was a good thing his heart didn't need to beat anymore. The amount of salt he'd put on his food had my heart stopping from the mere proximity.

"This is delicious. How did you learn to cook so well if you can't taste it right?"

I shoveled another bite into my mouth and the flavor exploded over my tongue in such a scrumptious way.

"Food Network." That smirk of his would be my undoing one of these days

After we finished with the salad and arancini, we retreated to the study to wait for the lasagna to be ready to serve.

I wanted to browse the shelves. See what kind of books he was into.

Tolkien, Tolstoy, Byron were there, of course. There was a section devoted to King and Koontz as well.

I was pleasantly surprised to see an entire fantasy section.

With him being as old as he was, I didn't think he'd be interested in newer authors.

Sanderson, Rice, Abercrombie, and Brown were in solid representation.

My gaze fell to the back wall. There were four bookcases along it with...

Oh my goddess! Alexander Doraglia, the original vampire himself, had romantasy sitting right here on his shelves.

Turning back to look at him incuriously, his easy gaze and impish smile lit up my world.

"It's a guilty pleasure. I won't have you giving me grief for it, *regina mea*"

Biting my bottom lip, I held in the roguish retort that had risen to my tongue. If I teased about having the same taste as I did, I wouldn't be able to borrow any of them from him.

Turning back to peruse the shelves, I'd lost myself for a good fifteen minutes or so.

Traveling from bookcase to bookcase. Touching them. Taking in their smell. Losing myself to my own thoughts.

He had the full collections of Maas, Clare, Yarros, and Armentrout books lining an entire case.

And if I wasn't mistaken, the shelf to the left of the fireplace housed indie authors.

Some who had gone traditional later on, but a lot who were still making a go of it on their own.

Broadbent, Tuli, and Jensen stood out to me. I'd read everything they'd written so far.

The other books on the shelves might as well be a "**Hey, check me out!**" sign flashing for my bibliophile brain.

I'd read a few of these authors. K J Sutton, Kay C. Rice, Geneva Monroe were all sitting on my own shelves at home.

Some of the others I'd be looking up the minute I got home. I loved to discover hidden gems that the socials hadn't found yet.

All of this time, he watched. Not saying a word. Just watched me as I picked through his massive collection. I could feel his eyes on me.

Here we were on a date, and I couldn't tear my eyes away from his book hoard...

Oh... Oh! Dragon hoard. *Face palm to the slow girl.*

His gates. His decor, His symbol. That's what Dax had said all those weeks ago.

Xander's symbol was a dragon. My mind swam in circles. The realization stole the air from my lungs, and I swayed.

"Rori!" He caught me before I fell, setting me down in one of the chairs next to the fire. "What's wrong, love?"

In through the nose. Out through the mouth. Stars popped in and out of my vision.

First, I'd stopped breathing. And now, I was hyperventilating. *Nice look, doofus.*

After a few more breaths, my gaze melted the fire dancing in his dark obsidian eyes. Burgundy laced the edges of the pupils.

"You're Dracula, aren't you?`"

It was blaringly obvious now that I'd put all the pieces into their proper places

He'd never lied to me. Not once. I'd known he'd covered for Anastasia and took on the moniker Vlad the Impaler for her sake.

Dax stated plainly that Xander's symbol was a dragon.

No one shied away from telling me that he was the original vampire. The very first in existence.

How had I not come to that conclusion already? Were my eyes so full of hearts, my mind blocked them out?

Oh hell. His last name even sounded like I should have guessed it right away.

It was impossible... but it was the truth.

I had been soulmates with Dracula.

Chapter Thirty-Seven

The revelation threw me for a loop.

Thrown into the supernatural world. Threatened. Thrilled. Witnessing death and doom.

Those had been my life the last few months.

Not once had my brain done the math. Not once had I ever considered the reality.

""What's wrong, Rori? Talk to me, love," he said as he came to kneel in front of me.

"I... it's just..." I blew out and exaggerated breath as his touch calmed my overactive nervous system. "Stupid me. I've just now put it all together."

"And what's that?" I'd never known him to be anything but confident. The uncertainty in his voice tugged at my heart-strings.

Leaning into his touch, I brushed my lips lightly to his. He stilled.

"It's silly of me." Cheek's heating, I felt small. Insignificant.

All of the vampire stories I'd read over the years. All of the tales of the legendary Dracula. My existence was a speck of dust in comparison to his.

"You are the original vampire." I couldn't look him in the face. The embarrassment was an elephant on my chest.

"You already knew that, love. I'm not sure I understand the dilemma." With his eyes staring into my soul, I shuttered.

"Xander, you are Dracula. THE Dracula." Foolish little butterflies lined my stomach.

The thrill that statement gave me went straight to between my legs. I'd been mates with a vampire of myth and legend. The rush was heady.

Shifting in the chair, I reached for him. Fingers clasping the front of his shirt, I pulled him closer.

Our mouths collided. The icy feel of his tongue a welcome balm to the heat of mine.

Passion poured from me. From him. If I could meld the two of us together into one being, my life would be complete.

A pull from the center of my chest, warm and insistent, drove every other thought from my mind.

Hunger. Awkwardness. Air. They were tiny blips on my radar as the kiss continued to reshape me.

The softness of his hair as it slipped through my fingers. The scent of evergreen and copper. The feel of hard muscle as his chest pressed to mine.

They all pooled desire in every cell of my body.

I may not be bonded to this male but my soul and his recognized each other. They longed for reconnection.

The push of his hardened length against my stomach told me he'd felt the same way.

With his fingers wrapped around the back of my neck, the heat of passion burned me through and through as we continued devouring our lust.

Somewhere outside of our little bubble of pleasure, a chiming was becoming more persistent. Louder and louder with each passing second.

Pulling his lips from mine, I pouted. I didn't want to be separated. We felt perfect as one.

The sudden air on my lips left a chill that burned as I licked the swollen flesh. The taste of him still on my tongue.

That smirk I loved so much lit his obsidian eyes to near glowing red around the rims.

When he stepped away, the emptiness in his wake threatened to buckle me over.

"It's the lasagna, love. It's ready to eat."

Walking back to the kitchens, my appetite was wet for more than just lasagna, but I shoved the thought into a filing cabinet in my mind for later use.

With skill and practice he had the piece cut, set, and plated before I'd even had the chance to offer my assistance.

If I weren't so damned hungry, I'd have pushed it to the side and demanded we continue what we'd started.

As it were, even with already eating those arancini, my stomach grumbled loudly as he set the delicious smelling morsel in front of me.

From the first bite, I melted. The way the tomato sauce blended wholly with the noodles and cheeses was beyond euphoric. I'd never eaten anything so good in my life.

My fork scraped the bottom of the plate entirely too quickly. The whole piece gone in mere minutes.

There had been nothing ladylike or dainty about it.

Xander's chuckle brought me up short. The heat of embarrassment rising in my cheeks once again.

"That was impressive." Humor colored his tone as he took my plate back to the kitchen. "Would you like another slice?"

I wanted more but if I could convince him to return to what we were previously doing, I didn't want an overfull belly to be a problem.

"That was extraordinary. Thank you."

Finishing off the last of the wine in my glass, I sauntered over to the island where he was washing the dish.

I didn't know where the other vampires were, but my guess was that he'd told them we'd wanted to be alone for our date tonight.

I liked that. The idea of "getting to know" each other wasn't something I needed spectators for.

Brushing my hand along the back of his neck as I walked by made him quiver.

Good. The desire to affect him as much as he affected me filled me with longing.

"How about we retire to the other room?" I said, pointedly looking him up and down, booping him on his nose and continuing towards the doorway.

The dish clanged in the sink behind him. His arms wrapped around my waist from behind, lifting me off my feet, and swinging me in a wide circle as I laughed at his enthusiasm.

Sweeping me up over his shoulder, the blurring speed in which he moved us to a room I hadn't yet seen, made me laugh harder.

The couch on which he set me was plush and comfortable. Trying to sit up to get a look around, his strong hands yanked my legs, causing me to fall flat.

"Hey!" The breath rushed from my lungs, but I giggled. "I take it you're okay with my suggestion?"

Nuzzling his head into the crook of my neck, he snarled below the shell of my ear.

It sent an immediate vibration along my chest, down my belly, and reverberating between my legs at my core. I dripped.

His nose scrunched and he sniffed deeply, scenting my arousal. The growl shook me from the inside.

"There was a name I use to call her. I can't help but want to know if you'd be worthy of it," he said.

Kissing below my ear. Along my neck. To the side of my jaw. My mind went blissfully foggy.

I'd never been more of a pile of goo. The throbbing of my core ached to the point of near pain.

"Worthy?" Biting the side of my bottom lip, my self-deprecating mind filled with worry. "Why? What did you call her?"

Knowing that I'd been Anastasia in the past did nothing to alleviate the trepidation that I wouldn't be good enough for him.

Xander was the original vampire. A prince among men. A god amongst supernaturals.

How was I supposed to live up to the memory of his lost soulmate? *Because you are her, dumbass.*

Inhaling my scent again, he brushed the stray blue strip of hair that had fallen in my face to the side.

I could practically see the cartoon hearts in his eyes. If I wasn't careful, I'd fall into a trap of my own making.

Sucking in a quick breath at the surprise attack, his hand came down between my thighs. My skirt hiked up, bunching just above my hips.

Gently cupping my center, he worked his thumb in circles around that sensitive bundle of nerves below my panties. The touch brought my body to life.

I knew that if he'd ever stopped, I would die from the lack of connection.

Lifting my ass off the sofa, I ground into his palm. My panties were soaked.

"Mmmm... I guess you are worthy."

The weight of those words eased an ache I didn't know I had.

The next kiss wasn't that gentlemanly, restrained kind he usually gave me. This one spoke to a place of hunger. Of desire and longing.

"Shall I slip these off, love?"

With a quick nod, they disappeared. The pressure of his thumb increased. It was bliss and agony all in one.

"What did you call her?" I couldn't keep the breathless question from spilling from my lips. My curiosity wouldn't be sedated.

Sliding a finger inside, he paused. His voice sultry. "Is this alright?"

Was he serious? I would self-combust at any moment. Lifting my ass to demand friction, I nodded but he didn't give in.

"I want to hear you say it. Do you want me to continue, Aurora?" My name on his lips set off a live wire deep in my bones.

He was with me. Here in the present. Not reliving the past with her.

"Yes. I need you, Xander." Grabbing the front of his shirt, I pulled him down into a kiss.

Without hesitation, a second finger thrust alongside the first. Curling and pumping, rubbing and caressing. It was all too much and not enough.

To my frustration, he never attempted to taste me. Kissing me with all of the passion of an erupting volcano, the thought consumed my mind through the pleasure.

I didn't know if he didn't want me that way or if he didn't trust himself so close to the vein he'd used to turn Anastasia and bond her to him as his mate.

With one hand helping me find pleasure, his other held a firm, almost too tight grip on my left leg, keeping me spread wide so he could look his fill as our kiss broke apart.

Feeling a bit exposed, I attempted to bring my legs closer.

His rumbling growl was enough to put a respectable amount of fear in me. It was also thrilling.

My walls clenched around his fingers. Release was so close.

"Look at me, Rori!" The demand powerful, I felt its call in my soul.

Looking into his eyes, I let out an earth-shattering cry of ecstasy as I came.

Liquid squirted, thick and sticky, coating his fingers.

"Good girl," he snarled. Fangs exposed. "There she is... My Puddles." Triumph reigned in his expression.

Puddles. That was what he had called Anastasia. He must have brought out the same reaction in her when she came.

I should feel jealous. I should be mad or, at the very least, upset.

He was thinking about another woman while staring at my swollen sex...

But I wasn't. The irrational self-consciousness I usually felt after a moment of bliss didn't come.

My legs still spread wide, shaking from the aftermath, I waited for the need to cover myself up. Hide from sight... but it never came. All I felt was satisfied.

Perhaps a better word would be complete. I felt complete.

My soul sang of rejoining. My heart pounded a steady beat behind my ribs.

Xander stared on in awe and my normal reactions didn't surface.

The boost that brought me made me bold. Wrapping one leg behind his back, I tried to draw him closer, but he was immovable.

Finally noticing my attempts, his answering smile stunned me.

He was gorgeous, no doubt, but at times I found that I could barely look away. Drawn like a moth to a flame.

"Beautiful. Simply beautiful," he said, still looking his fill.

Most males could be led around by the short hairs, but this felt more like reverence.

"It's been more than four centuries since I've last seen anything worthy of worship. I've lived too many lifetimes. Seen too much hate throughout the world."

His fingers grazed the center of my folds, and I shuddered.

"... but this? You? Mmmm."

Contentment rumbled through his chest, filling mine with the same warmth.

Rising from between my legs, he kissed his way up my stomach, nipping at each breast, before laying his head against my thumping heart.

My fingers wound in his hair, tugging his face up to meet my waiting lips.

Rubbing my foot across his hardened length through his pants, I snaked one of my arms down to cradle it. "My turn."

Jumping up and out of my reach, I pouted.

With a few breaths, his strained lips curled up at one corner.

"That's not necessary, love. Why don't I grab you another plate of food before you go?" He headed out the door before I'd had a chance to reply.

What the hell had just happened? Was he dismissing me?

I didn't think rejection would hurt quite this bad, but it stung hard.

First Dax. Then Thane. Now, Xander? Was I not good enough for any of them to go any farther with?

Sitting up and replacing my panties, I yanked my skirt back in place while I waited.

Coming back a few minutes later, he had my jacket and a restaurant style container for my leftovers.

"Xander, did I do something wrong?" Tears rimmed the corners of my eyes, but I refused to let them fall... Yet.

Running his hand over his face and back through his hair, a frustrated look donned his features.

Tightness around his eyes. Lips downturned and pursed. Angst wrinkled his forehead.

"Gods no, regina mea. I would love nothing more than to snatch you up and run you straight up the stairs to my bedroom. The things I've imagined doing to you could make the most experienced brothel worker blush." The hunger in his eyes went straight through me.

Heat rose high to the apples of my cheeks and that smirk of his I loved so much returned.

"Then why don't we continue this now?" Reaching for him, he stepped back.

Taking a breath, I looked towards the ceiling. *Gods, please grant me serenity.*

"I can't, Rori. I can't." Head hung, he stared at his feet.

It was so unlike him that it gave me pause.

I didn't know why I was pushing. Men were allowed to say no too.

I could respect that... but I still needed to understand why he'd been okay with pleasuring me if he didn't want us going any farther.

Barely above a whisper, my eyes staring at my feet now too, I asked, "Why not? Is it because I'm not her? You don't want my watered-down version of your soulmate?"

With his forefinger and thumb, he pulled my face up to look at him.

Trying to turn my head away, he wasn't having it.

"Silly dragonfly. I have searched through several lifetimes for your return. I have done great things and horrible things in equal measure. If there ever comes a day that I don't want you, my life would be forfeit."

I tried again to pull away. I couldn't understand what would make him keep this distance between us.

My instincts were telling me to hide, but as trauma ridden and stubborn as I was, I needed to hear him out.

"Don't you see? I can't lay with you, Rori."

He shook his head as I started to ask why again. His lips claimed mine possessively before pulling back.

"I can't lay with you and not declare you from this day forward."

Pausing to stare directly into my eyes, I let the tears slip over the rims this time.

"You wanted a choice. And I don't want to take that away from you. I want you to have whatever you want in life."

Wrapping my face in both hands, he kissed me softly. Softly and gently until my tears stopped flowing.

The salt taste mixing with his sweet, cool tongue.

Dropping his hands to hold both of mine, he took a step back.

"If I took you in that way... if I even tasted you, I'd never let you go. I am not a good man."

Shaking his head to dislodge thoughts I couldn't see, he took a calming breath.

"If you and I were to be together intimately, I would destroy anyone who tried to take what was mine. I am a vampire, love. And even unbonded, I do not share."

Kissing my forehead, I quivered at the brush of his lips.

Understanding resonated like a bell being rung in my head and heart that couldn't be unrung.

He wanted me more, not less. He was trying to protect me from him. From his possessive nature.

Only, I'd felt more tonight than I'd ever felt before. Emotionally. Physically. And on some level, I knew that I'd never be the same.

"See me home?" I asked.

With a woeful smile, he ushered us to the door.

Chapter Thirty-Eight

Xander drove me home in Matilda.

He said he could run home a hundred times faster than she could go and I smacked his arm playfully at the dig to my prize possession.

Upon coming to the door, I joked that I wouldn't invite him in, but he nodded seriously and turned to leave.

I had to practically drag him in the house after that. Apparently, ancient vampires like him didn't understand my humor.

We talked a lot that night.

About how he'd hated life for a long time before he'd met *His Puddles*.

He'd only called her that in private. He called her *dragonfly or love* in public.

He'd also call her *regina mea*, which some of the other vampires did as well. It meant *My Queen* in Romanian. That's where his brood were from.

We had chatted about what his life had been like over the centuries since her loss.

About his brother. About the time before his curse and the time that came after Thane's curse.

I'd kept quiet and let him talk through everything.

The feelings I'd had about Thane versus the feelings Anastasia had about him were vastly different.

He'd told me about how Thane had stood by his side into his adult years. How he'd tried to curb Xander's bloodlust.

How he'd thought that Thane had been keeping his affections for someone in one of the villages from him and how it hurt that his brother wouldn't trust him with the knowledge.

He'd spoken of Thane's demand to the witch who cursed him and how that same witch cursed his brother in revenge.

While Xander barely noticed Thane's year long absence, his brother was on a quest to find out who he now was as a werewolf.

The story that broke my heart was the part about Anastasia being a possible blood maiden until he'd turned her into his mate and broke his brother's heart.

Dax and the rest of the pack had it wrong. Thane and Anastasia had been in love, but it wasn't a love like mates experienced.

The mating bond was the other half of your soul. And as such, there was no one who could hold your heart tight enough to pull you from that bond.

Not even the lover who you had sworn you would spend the rest of your life with.

The other thing we discussed before my yawning brought our night to an end was his absences.

He had given me a small piece of the information before, but not enough. I was curious about where he'd been and what he'd been doing.

My selfish subconscious mind had been niggling at me for months.

Xander had just found the love of his life's re-incarnated soul and he'd been hardly around to try to get to know her... Me. *Gods.* The past life thing played with my head.

His explanation was more straight forward than I'd been imagining.

My mind had wandered to nefarious acts. To a lack of interest. To various things that all involved him staying away from me.

My face should have been on a poster about what overthinking and self-loathing looked like.

Oscar Wilde once said, "Sarcasm is the lowest form of wit but the highest form of intelligence."

In reality, sarcasm was a trauma and self-deprecating response if you were smart enough to use it.

My sarcasm started around the same time my dad and puberty began to hit. *Go figure.*

Xander had intertwined our fingers, running his other hand lightly up and down my arm while I laid against his chest on my sofa.

With a fire burning low that night, the cozy space had made my eyelids heavy.

Though my stubbornness refused to let him leave while I had him talking for once.

It was possible he'd thought I was nearly asleep when he'd answered. His voice was a lullaby of its own.

He'd been hunting for the witch who had cursed him.

He and the other vampires had found him a few times over the centuries, but he'd always managed to elude capture.

The last time Vincent had been spotted was six months ago. Right before their spies located me.

Their biggest problem when it came to the witch was that he could glamour himself to look like somebody else, making it hard to keep up with all of his changes.

Xander wanted to find the witch and force him to reverse the curse.

Finally finding me, he longed to live as a human. That was, if he were the one to win my heart. His goal was to age and die by my side.

I'd found it so romantic in my sleep addled brain.

It wasn't until the next day that I'd thought about all he'd said. Questions repeating over and over again in my skull.

Like how had a witch lived so long? And how would he force him to undo the curse if he hadn't had the ability to make him change it all those years ago?

And a bunch of other little questions that I'd probably never get the answers to.

I'd woken up in my bed not remembering how I'd gotten there. I must have really been out.

My sleep shirt and socks clung to my body, but I hadn't changed into them before he'd left.

Heat colored my cheeks at the thought of his hands roaming over my unconscious body to undress and redress me in comfortable sleepwear.

It was a few minutes before the fantasy running through my brain quieted.

Knowing Xander would never take advantage of me, the dirty images flashing in my head didn't care.

The rich aroma of coffee reached my nose, drawling me from my wandering thoughts.

I'd set the timer on the new machine last night before going on our date.

If I had a way to make the smell of bacon go along with it, it'd be the perfect alarm clock.

Aries jumped off the top of the cabinet and landed on my shoulder the second I'd walked into the kitchen. "Ouch! You little brat."

He could be such a pain in the ass. Staying mad at his furry little face wasn't easy though.

He and Matilda were my family.

I hadn't gotten her a tune up yet, but I could feed him. Taking care of his needs for today was the best I could do.

"Here's your breakfast, Sir Fluffy McMousington."

Purring loudly, he head butted me before jumping off my shoulder to eat.

I'd taken to calling him all sorts of silly names over the years, but he knew when I was mad or serious.

It was the only time I'd use his real name. Aries Xavier Evolet.

With him fed and watered, it was time to prepare for my day.

I had to be at work at 3 pm today. A half shift because Molly was scheduled to work but had a doctor's appointment.

Kamie agreed to do the first half if I'd do the second. She'd accepted a date for tonight from one of those online apps that we'd talked about.

The extra money would come in handy. Even if Lissie insisted I didn't need to worry about such things anymore.

Worrying about bills was ingrained into who I was once I'd become the person responsible for making sure me and my dad had a roof over our heads.

Every time I looked at my new floors and the new paint throughout the whole house it brought a cheek rubbing grin to my face.

This old house had never looked this fresh. This inviting.

If I were being honest, it never looked this clean either.

Guilt pinched at my chest.

Lissie not only painted and installed the floors. She'd cleaned the whole damned thing from top to bottom.

She, Seiran and Nik brought in new appliances a few days ago.

I had been sitting on the couch reading and there was an unexpected knock at the door. And boom... I had to invite the guys in so they could set up my new kitchen.

Xander never said a word about it on our date. It made me wonder if he even knew Lissie spent his money so willy nilly.

Her stance on me having old, outdated things was that she and the others were the only old things allowed.

I'd giggled my head off when she'd told me that while she moved the stove into place.

There wasn't much of a crowd when I'd arrived at Eventide an hour ago.

With the snow melting, skiing was out. And it was still too nice out for any hikers to come for a bite to eat yet.

This time of year we usually experienced to worst lag in customers.

Now that we had food service too, I wondered if the place would fare better the next couple of months.

There'd already been more customers the last two weeks than there had been in years past.

I'd thought I saw Luke earlier, but Gav was working the kitchen and said he'd not seen him in a couple of days.

Sometimes the remoteness of the bar played tricks on my mind.

I could have sworn Luke walked out the back door when I was bringing a round of beers to Fitz, Zeth, and Bram.

With Bram here, I didn't worry about the other two giving me a hard time as much since Kori wasn't with them.

She often bolstered their wicked antics. I hadn't seen her since that night I'd had her kicked out of the bar.

Nik told me a few days ago that Xander made it clear... if she came back to Eventide, he'd take drastic measures to remove her.

He hadn't said her head, but Nik wasn't one to give details about the vampire's dealings.

Xander would not be pleased if Kori threatened me in any way. Even if it was simply psychologically.

For whatever reason, Thane's second liked me. Bram had been kind and soft spoken over the last couple of months.

When he'd covered my body with his to protect me from that bitch hybrid, he'd spoken with authority to his pack, not violence.

There was a difference between aggressive and assertive. Watching him, anyone could understand what that meant.

In another lifetime, I would have liked to find out about his past. What made him how he was. I'd have liked to try and crack open his shell.

Piling anymore onto my plate wasn't happening though. Not now.

Not with my feelings for Xander growing.

Not with how I needed to sort out how I felt about Dax.

Thinking of Dax hurt. Knowing Xander held my heart hadn't made it any easier to face the thought of ending things with Dax.

He deserved better. He deserved someone who could be all in with him. He deserved to be free of me.

Especially not now with how I'd betrayed myself, allowing Thane to corrupt not only my mind, but my body.

He'd killed me. Over and over and over again.

The fact that he'd decided to "see how it goes" this lifetime didn't matter. Bitterness and violence had sunk their teeth into him over the centuries.

Thane wasn't that adolescent boy Xander had spoken about from all those years ago anymore.

He wasn't the male Anastasia loved before being turned onto a monster either.

He enjoyed being the villain fate turned him into. Embraced its deadly nature.

Circumstances be damned.

We all had a past. Some of us more horrible than others but a past none the less.

That old Native American proverb that talked about darkness said it all.

We all have darkness and light inside us. Whichever one you fed the most would win out in the long run.

I couldn't be selfish anymore. Someone was always going to get hurt in the end.

Talking to Dax wouldn't be easy but it needed to be done. I had to let him go.

Thane would need to be dealt with soon, but I didn't have the brain space at the moment to think about that particular disaster.

Speak of the devil and he shall appear. *Damn it.*

Thane walked through the door like he owned the place.

Spotting me over by the bar, he brought his two fingers up to his mouth, sucked them in, then ran his tongue along their center.

My face fell. I could feel it. His eyes never left mine as another figure walked in behind him... Dax.

Oh Gods. What had he told him?

When Dax pushed around him, he'd made a beeline in my direction.

I had the good sense to head towards the end of the bar, not wanting to have this conversation inside.

Going out the back door, I caught the scent of burning herbs. With a quick look around, there wasn't anything on fire. *Weird.*

Just as my ass touched the table, Dax came shoving out the screen door.

I jumped as it slammed with a deafening crack against the back of the building.

"What in the actual fuck, Rori?"

Gods. He knew.

Chapter Thirty-Nine

y hands instinctively went up in submission.

Male anger wasn't anything I wasn't used to, but it still made me tremble every time.

"Gods, Rori! After all this time you still think I'd ever put my hands on you?" The hurt in his voice was my undoing.

Dax had been a lot of things in our *not relationship* in the past.

He'd certainly been more of a gentleman than I ever expected once we tried giving dating a go.

And here I stood, cowering as if he were a brute.

Admonishing my own reactions, I took a tentative step towards him.

The fear was rooted in my core but the male before me had never so much as raised his voice to me, and I owed him better.

"Dax, I'm sorry. I don't know what else to say." I couldn't excuse my actions. I didn't think it would be right to anyway.

Thane held a piece of my heart from the past. I understood that now.

The thrill of being with him didn't lessen the hurt I'd caused to Dax.

Had he sought him out to rub it in his face? They'd practically walked in together.

It'd be the kind of thing Thane would do.

Over the last couple of weeks, I'd tried my best to put it out of my mind. The feel of him against my tongue. The feel of me against his.

Sometimes, late at night, my mind would wander back to all that blood. To the excitement it had mixed in when he'd devoured me.

I was a monster. Dax didn't deserve to be cast aside... but even the dangerous exhilaration Thane brought couldn't compare to the deep corded need I'd begun to feel for Xander.

And Dax was neither of them. I had to disentangle myself from him before he was hurt even more.

"So that's it? You're choosing the male who's killed you in every lifetime over the one who is bound to your soul and the one who loves you even without a bond?"

Wait... what? Oh shit.

"You love me?" If I could turn into a bat and hide in a cave, now would be the perfect time.

How had this happened? When did we go from having fun to him catching feelings?

He'd known from the begin how emotionally unavailable I'd been my whole life.

Shuffling his feet, his arms swung awkwardly at his sides. "I didn't mean to blurt it out like that."

A cool breeze drifted through the trees. The blue strand of my hair blowing in my face and blocking my view.

There was that smell again. Stronger this time.

"Do you smell that?" I couldn't place the herbs that were burning, but an acrid scent with a subtle sweetness whipped around us.

Ignoring my question, he took both my hands in his. Face serious.

"Rori, Thane's not right for you. I may not have Xander's money or his brother's commanding personality, but I assure you, I would protect you and cherish you with every breath for the rest of your days."

Gods. This poor guy. It couldn't be any worse.

Not only did I hurt his feelings in regard to being intimate with Thane, but for him to tell me that he loved me?

He still wanted me and thought that he wasn't good enough to match up to the **Original Brothers**.

"Dax, you've been nothing but perfect. I'm not choosing Thane over you. What he and I did was a mistake. A moment of weakness." Light re-entered his eyes.

I couldn't bear the hope beginning to dance in them.

Quick, like a bandage. "I'm sorry, but I need to step back from us... From you."

My words took a minute to register. When they did, it looked like I'd physically hit him.

That dancing light went out. The slight smile faded.

Dropping my hands, he stepped back, putting a foot of space between us.

The effort to not wrap my arms around him and take it all back was a physical pain.

Looking up at his touch, he used his thumb to gently brush away the tears I hadn't realized I'd let spill over.

"Don't cry, honey," he sighed. "I knew you'd choose him in the end."

I cried harder and he pulled me against his chest, wrapping me in those strong arms.

His musk and spicy pepper scent comforting all the holes in my heart I'd made by telling him I needed to let him go.

Truly, he deserved better than having to comfort me.

Yup. I was a monster. He was worthy of a great deal more than the likes of me.

"I do love you, Dax," I tried to say through my sobs. "But I can't fight what I feel for him. It wouldn't be fair to you."

Kissing the top of my head, he shushed me over and over again until I stopped crying.

It felt nice there in the circle of his arms and I was too selfish to let go first.

"Do you smell that?" he asked.

Dropping his arms, the sudden lack of warmth made me shiver, though it was light jacket weather in the shade of the trees this early in the evening.

Taking one of my hands, he pulled me around the end of the building with him, towards the edge of the forest where Loxy and Dylan were killed.

A cast iron pot sat on the ground few yards inside the trail. No fire burned under it, but the glowing green contents bubbled over the rim all the same.

Shadows danced through the otherwise still trees. No birds sang. No insects chirped. The eerie quiet poked at my survival instincts to run.

Pushing me slightly behind him, we walked forward to take a look.

Someone stood under the shadow of a tall tree, but I couldn't make out who it was.

Leaning down to quietly whisper, Dax told me to go back inside.

My stubborn curiosity had me clinging tighter to his hand rather than listen.

"Who's there? Show yourself!" The command in Dax's voice was all alpha.

The shadowed figure was chanting something in a strange language I'd never heard.

Sparks burst higher from the pot. Hissing and sizzling sounds filled the air.

Letting go of my hand, Dax stood fully in front of me.

With a quick glance over his shoulder, he ordered me away. "Rori! Go! Tell Cody I need him, honey."

That was probably the only thing he could have said to make me obey. He needed help.

Turning to run towards Eventide, I felt the air shift. A huge wolf now stood where Dax had been only seconds ago.

Stumbling back, I tripped over a root, landing hard on my ass. Pain radiated up my spine to the tops of my shoulders.

Growling bellowed deep from the wolf's chest as the figure stepped into the light.

My human eyes still couldn't see who or what it was clearly enough.

Scootching backwards like a crab, trying to put some distance between me and the fight that was sure to start, it was like wading through quicksand.

I needed to go get help, but I couldn't make my legs work. Every time I tried to right myself, I fell back down.

The adrenaline rush making my limbs flail pitifully. Crawling inch by inch back towards the opening in the trail.

Too dark in the canopy of trees, I still couldn't see who it was.

The figure advancing on Dax in his wolf form held a curved sword, symbols glowing in the blade.

They began chanting louder now with every step forward. The runes burning brighter.

With every lunge from the wolf, the chanting figure weaved sideways, just out of reach.

Tearing my eyes from the fight, I knew I needed to get Cody. Maybe Bram too.

Finally making it the ten feet or so to the opening, I had better control of my body.

Snarls and clangs sounded all around the trail. Dax diving forward time and again, only to be forced back by that blade.

I needed to get inside and sound an alarm. He needed help. *Gods*. I was useless.

Afraid to let them out of my sight, I stumbled in the direction of the bar, but my head swung around at the yelp that followed the loud clank of metal.

The sound drove me to my knees. Hands flying to cover my ears.

Reprimanding myself to get up, my brain screamed at me through a fog. *Get up now! Find help*!

Standing took all my effort. Snarls and whimpers stealing my focus.

A few more clangs of metal against tree and rock, and I found my strength.

The door was twenty feet away. *Move!*

Tripping again, I had to wonder if I was this clumsy or if it had something to do with that chanting?

"Cody!" I tried to scream out but the breath in my lungs was non-existent. "Cody! Anybody! Help! Somebody help!"

There were a number of supernatural beings in that building. I'd take any of their help at this point.

Saying a quick prayer that none of the humans in there came running out, I yelled again.

The next yelp turned my stomach. There'd been pain in its depths.

Dax's voice reached my ears. Low. Breathless. Stopping me in my tracks.

He'd had to turn back into his human form for that to be the case.

What if that chanting was meant for that? To turn him back? Make him weaker?

Oh gods! I wanted to scream at Dax to run but I didn't want to steal his focus.

Turning back and hurrying towards the trail again, I saw him. Bloody, naked, and on his knees.

If I'd still been a vampire, I could have helped him... but I was a hopelessly weak human. *Fuck!*

Barely making out Dax's words to the sword wielder, I listened with everything I had.

"You'll never win. He'll kill you before you can touch a hair on h..."

The figure swung the runed blade through the air. It glowed so brightly, I needed to shield my eyes for a split second.

A swoosh sound brought my attention to full focus on the scene playing out before my eyes.

Coming down in one quick motion, it sliced clear through Dax's neck in one swift blow.

His head fell to the side, eyes wide in a lifeless stare.

The scream that tore from my throat ripped its way across the distance.

The last thing I saw was the figure glaring my way. The last thing I heard were the sound of thunderous footfalls.

Then all went dark.

Chapter Forty

"She should be awake by now. We should do something." Cody's broken voice reached me through the darkness.

Something had happened. My brain wouldn't supply anything though. It wouldn't let me find the way back to open my eyes yet.

Hushed sobs came from a few others that I couldn't see. I could only smell.

Orange peel, jasmine... and leather. My head rested on Lissie's lap in Xander's office.

Why were we all gathered here?

Sorrow sat on my chest like a baby elephant, but I couldn't remember why.

"No. Give her mind time to protect itself." Bram's concerned toned brought an unexplained tightness to my chest.

Trying again, my eyes still wouldn't cooperate. Even my fingers wouldn't twitch.

I was trapped in limbo listening to the conversation around me.

The door burst open, slamming against the inside frame.

Kazz's voice thundered through the room. "What the fuck happen?"

"We're not sure." That was Kiah. Which meant Janie must be here too. They were so rarely separated.

Tension hung heavy in the room. Becoming fitful, Lissie's cold fingers brushed at my hair. Her voice a whisper, shooshing me in a soothing tone.

"I saw the area myself! You all were here! Feet away for fucks sake! How did this happen?" Kazz was barely holding it together.

A sob came from the direction I'd heard Kiah talk. It had to be Janie. Why would she be crying?

"Don't try to guilt us, pup." Thane's alpha voice rang clear. Ominous. "We were lucky to get to Rori before whoever it was got her too."

"Fuck Rori! My cousin is dead you asshole!" Growls went up around the room.

Oh no! Oh no, No, no, no, no. It all came flooding in then. The dam in my mind broke under the pressure of holding it back.

Eyes shooting wide, my scream was unending. Throat raw. Heart shredded.

Dax! Dax was dead. I couldn't breathe. Couldn't get any air in. Panic seized me.

Cody grabbed my hand and Lissie hissed at him. "Rori! Count with me."

The scream subsided only because I couldn't fill my lungs with air.

His eyes locked on mine, squeezing my hand with gentle but firm pressure.

"Come on, honey. Three things you can see." Cody's calmness helped my agitated state to focus.

Bram stood with a hand on Cody's shoulder, a second calm presence to keep me grounded.

Sips of precious oxygen slipping into place. "A desk... a couch... a room full of people." My answers were breathless.

"Good. Now two things you can feel." Under his instructions, I gathered my resolve.

"Lissie's lap... your rough hand." My mind settled but was far from relaxed.

With all of us crowded in here, he was surely dead. Dax was dead.

"Who was it? What did they look like?" Kazz had pushed Cody aside. Hands wrapped in my shirt, he shook me.

Before I could say a word. Before I could blink... Thane snatched Kazz from where he stood and tossed him like a ragdoll across the room.

He went sliding down the wall with a bone cracking thud, knocking several heavy wooden framed pictures to the floor.

"Never touch her again, pup! Don't talk to her. As a matter of fact, don't even look at her. You're not worthy!" If I'd thought Kazz would back down from Thane's command, I'd been wrong.

"She's the only one who saw what went down. We need answers!" His voice was fill with pain. With loss.

I felt it too. Dax would never smile that dimpled grin at me again. He'd never be my safe haven in a storm or a shoulder to lean on. He was irrevocably gone.

After my horrified scream, my throat felt like I'd swallowed glass.

Talking wouldn't be easy, but Kazz was right. If they were going to find the perpetrator, I needed to tell them everything I remembered sooner rather than later.

Barely above a whisper, I tried. "We'd gone out back to talk. After a few minutes, we noticed an odd smell. Following it to the opening just inside the trail, we saw a pot with some glowing substance in it and Dax told me to go find help."

Swallowing didn't help ease the lump in my throat. Tears ran down my cheeks in an endless torrent.

Kazz's impatience visible in the corners of his eyes. His cousin was dead. He wanted answers, but no amount of them would bring Dax back.

Grief was pain. Pain brought fear. And fear often made good men turn violent.

Gathering my thoughts, sorrow gripped my heart in a merciless hold.

"I couldn't make out who it was. They were tall but not overly. Dark clothes. Nothing showed from where I stood... Dax made me run to find Cody, but I kept falling."

Bram spoke quietly. "Why were you falling, Rori?" There was no judgement. A simple question.

"At first I thought it was the rush of adrenaline, but I'd never stumbled so much in my life. Even when I was afraid for my life in the past." Thane's eyes darkened at that. "The figure had been chanting. A different language. Could it have been that?"

I hadn't noticed Mina and Kori earlier. They were standing together in the corner. *Odd.*

Mina looked to her sister before answering me.

"Yes. If what you said about the acrid herb smell is true, it's more than probable that it was a spell." She said no more.

Huddle with Kori the way she was, it made me wonder about what had happen to make Kori a hybrid and if Mina still cared for her sister's well-being.

"He had a curved sword. There were runes running down the length of the blade. They glowed brighter the longer he chanted."

Lissie pulled me off her lap, sitting me upright before getting up herself to pace the room.

"A spell. Herbs in a cauldron. A runed blade." Reaching for her phone, her fingers flew across the keypad. "Xander is still a few minutes out. He'll be here soon."

I'd wanted to have him hold me since I'd first heard Cody's voice.

Remembering that Dax's fate had happened right after I'd broken things off with him, the guilt nearly pulled me back under.

My sole focus needed to be finding his killer. It shouldn't be needing Xander's comfort or Thane's presence.

The fact that I felt better with him here troubled my already chaotic mind.

"Where's Gunner?" I asked no one in particular.

"He's at the house. Still taking it easy. He wanted to come but..." Kazz didn't get to say any more than that.

Thane's fist connected with his face. Blood squirted. His nose broken.

"I told you not to talk to her!" Thane seethed.

If looks could kill, neither of them would be breathing.

I'd made my choice with Xander... but there was an itch I couldn't scratch when it came to the werewolf alpha. It made me tingle in places that had no business throbbing.

Bram sighed heavily. Mina tsked at the display of useless testosterone. Janie sobbed again.

Then stopped. Pulling away from Kiah's chest, she shook him. "Kiah?" He didn't respond. "Kiah, baby, what's wrong?" Grabbing his face, she shook it. "Hezekiah!"

His head lobbed to the side, body slumping against hers. The screaming started again but this time it wasn't mine.

Bram dashed over to pull Kiah into a sitting position. He checked several different things to no avail. Kiah was gone.

Janie's screams stopped as her head flopped down onto his chest. Her body going still.

I'd thought she'd fainted, but Bram again checked her over only to announce to the room that she was gone too.

"What the hell is happening here?" Kazz dropped to his knees before his two fallen pack members, eyes locked with mine.

A split second later, he growled. "You! You're the cause for all of these problems!"

Between one moment and the next, his wolf was midflight as the door crashed open yet again.

Xander yanked the wolf out of the air, slamming Kazz to the ground.

He hadn't landed that hard, but blood pooled from his ears. His body turned back into a human. A dead human.

Just like the rest of his pack.

Cody looked to me. Sorrow marred his otherwise handsome face. I saw resignation there. Acceptance of his fate.

His pack was dead. He'd be gone soon too.

"It's been my privilege to watch over you from lifetime to lifetime, Rori."

"No! Cody, no! Please..." I didn't know what gods I was begging but this couldn't be happening.

Xander's arms wrapped me firmly in a tight embrace. I struggled against his hold. "Shh, love. It's okay. It's okay."

Mina cried out as Kori slumped to the floor.

Hadn't she been part of Thane's pack? What the fuck was going on?

Bram's eyes flickered when he pressed his fingers against her neck. "She's still with us. At least, I think she is. It's only her vampire side that has the telltale signs of life."

Cody stared at her. And then at Bram. Shaking out the cobwebs.

Clarity spilling from his face that I still didn't have.

Thane and Xander exchanged a look that I didn't miss. If it was a brother thing or a supernatural thing, I didn't know.

"What is happening?" I demanded.

Thrashing against Xander's hold, this time he let me go.

Lissie had texted Xander everything that had happen so far. That was the only explanation as to why he was up to speed.

"Dax's pack died... because he was the one to turn them. Or in Janie's case, Kiah turned her, but Dax had turned Kiah. It seems that whoever it was that killed Dax used him as a test to see if he could end the line of succession."

Cody breathed a sigh of relief for the first time in the last few minutes.

I didn't understand what they were talking about but apparently, he did.

"Test, huh?" Thane looked to his brother for an answer and Xander nodded once. "For us, right? It'd make sense for them to try it out further down our lines before coming for us."

My brain slammed into the side of my skull. The pounding behind my eyes enough to make me nauseated. My stomach did a few backflips, and I swayed on the spot.

Xander's arms came up around me as Thane took a step in my direction but stopped himself.

Breathing through my nose, I gathered my thoughts. "Are you saying Dax was killed to see if it'd work to kill all the werewolves under him?"

It was so much worse than I'd thought. Killing off the other wolves without them being able to defend themselves was horrible.

Bram nodded once, confirming my answer.

Pulling away from Xander, I barely made it to the waste basket before losing the little sustenance I'd had today.

Strong hands lifted my hair, patting my back gently. Strong but feminine. Lissie.

She handed me a bottle of water. From where, I hadn't a clue.

"I figured this would happen when we'd initially brought you in here."

Right. To talk about Dax's death.

Back when I was naive enough to think I'd have only one person to grieve over today.

Knowing there was a magical evil doer running around in our mists wasn't enough from the universe.

This was karma. I'd been a horrible person in one of my past lives and karma was exacting revenge on my friends.

"I thought Kori was in Thane's pack?"

Thane snorted but didn't contribute anything to the conversation.

"And Cody? I know you were in Dax's."

Frustration clawed its way through me. I hated being in the dark when everyone around me seemed to be in the know.

"I turned Cody," Bram said, taking a seat in the chair behind Xander's desk. "I'd found him at the bottom of a ravine, broken and bleeding. He was in and out of consciousness, but I'd made sure he understood the life I was offering him before saving him the only way I was able to."

Cody smirked at me. The smile of my friend helped ease the smallest amount of my misery. He was alive. Thankfully.

Bram looked to Thane before continuing. He was Thane's second, but I got the feeling he was also Thane's moral compass. Or tried to be at least.

"Thane didn't want him in our pack. Cody was an adventurous, caring person and dickhead here," he thumbed at Thane, "was still in his hateful era."

"He's out of that era now?" It slipped from my lips before I could think better of it.

Xander chuckled and Thane smiled the first genuine smile I'd ever seen him make.

Janie, Kiah, and Kazz's bodies looked like they were sleeping. I knew if I went to Dax's house, Gunner's would be too.

Sobering reality hung heavy in the air. Dax's entire pack was dead.

He'd been beheaded by a magical sword. And now the bodies of those he'd turned laid at our feet around the room.

Lissie pushed the water in my direction again and Mina let out a small sob from the floor next to Kori.

"What about her?" I pointed to Kori's still form. "How'd she end up in Dax's pack?"

Thane fielded this one. Walking over and throwing his arm around my shoulder, Xander growled but took a step back at when I glared my disapproval.

"Korrina wasn't happy that our boy there chose you over her." His rough velvet voice scraped along the inside of my skull. A thrum of pure male.

Rubbing his thumb down the side of my neck did things to me it shouldn't but I ignored the ache it caused.

Xander's eyes darkened at my quiet exhale, but he stayed where he was.

"You see," Thane continued. "she'd gotten a taste of what it'd be like to reign by his side. Not only did she crave him. She coveted the power he held."

Tsking in her direction, he turned towards Xander and then towards me.

"He wouldn't return to her bed after meeting you, kitten. She thought plotting with me would get her a second prince, but I didn't have any interest in a cast-off vampire."

Mina hissed from the corner on her sister's behalf.

"How? I mean... how?" It still confounded me.

Could any of these werewolves turn a vampire into a hybrid? Or vice versa?

"There's the rub. She went to the witch that cursed us. She took a concoction he'd made, and he'd told her that a werewolf would need to turn her for it to work. When I wouldn't do it, she'd gotten Daxayrius so drunk he couldn't see straight. They fell into bed together and she'd used another kind of potion to force his hand in turning her."

My mouth was so dry, I couldn't swallow.

Dax had never told me. Kori was a hybrid because of him. She'd almost died because of being turned by him.

The office, full of living and dead bodies alike, felt too small all of a sudden. The stench of sweat and rot shoved its way up my nose.

I wanted to find Dax and yell at him for not being up front with me.

Then I remembered that I'd never be able to talk to him again.

Falling to my knees, Lissie cushioned my head before it hit the floor. Raw grief ripped from my chest. I couldn't find my eyes again.

Before darkness made me its bitch, Xander and Thane agreed it had to be the same witch who'd cursed them that killed Dax and his pack.

The same one Xander had been searching all over for.

The same one that had started this life saga of blood, pain, and death.

Vincent Luciant Cazan, the Breaker of the Balance.

Chapter Forty-One

When I'd come too again, I was in my own house.

The fire burned low in the hearth. Aries sprawled out across my chest.

Looking around, I couldn't believe I was all alone. Aries notwithstanding.

They'd left me to my pain, and I couldn't decide if that was better or worse.

After a few groggy minutes, my stomach grumbled and the ache in my bladder made it necessary to get up.

All I wanted to do was hide my head under the throw blanket and let the oblivion of sleep help dull the grief, but my body wouldn't allow it.

After relieving myself and feeding Sir Bottomless Pit again, I noticed a note propped up on the counter next to the coffee maker.

My Love,

Please understand how much this pains me. To see you in the throes of grief and not be able to comfort you will ruin me for the rest of my days.

If there were any other way to keep you for myself and keep you safe at the same time, I would.

My presence, along with all of my friends is a danger to you that I cannot allow.

Eventide is yours. I signed the deed over last night. There is a bank account with more than enough for several lifetimes in your name at your disposal.

I can't believe I've finally found you again only to have to let you go.

Know this... if there is a way back to you this lifetime, I will stop at nothing to get there.

We are on the hunt for that cursed witch.

Rest assured, he will pay for what he has done. None of us will let him live for the turmoil he has caused.

Thane has agreed to hunt him as well. His pack will go one way, and we shall head the other.

We Will find him, Rori. I swear it!

Live. Travel. See the world and have adventures. Don't hold back on living a full life, regina mea.

Fall in love. Have a family. Do all the things I could never do with you as a creature of myth.

Take care of yourself, Rori. Be sure to take your daily vitamins. Get some sunshine and go for walks.

I won't interfere. I would never deny you happiness.

If we haven't found him and dealt with him in the next year or more, consider this my goodbye.

My heart breaks as I put pen to paper. What could have been eats at my soul, but your happiness is more important to me than the air I breathe.

I love you. I have loved you since the moment I'd laid eyes on you.

Not Anastasia. You, Aurora.

Yours forever and always, Xander.

Big, fat tears rolled down my cheeks, dripping into the steaming bowl of soup I'd made before finding the letter.

They were gone. All of them had abandoned me.

I'd never hang out with Lissie or drink with Cody again. I'd never snap at Fitz or Zeth about being idiots again.

Xander and Thane left me. For my own good, but they'd left.

To grieve the deaths of my friends. To grieve Dax.

Now I would be alone, with a chasm in my chest, threatening to rip me into pieces.

I'd have to grieve their loss as well. All of them.

And with Eventide in my hands, I'd have to replace their positions while doing it.

I couldn't even explain to Bitzy or the others why I was sad or what happened to everyone.

Going back to the couch, I skipped the soup, shoveled a peanut butter and banana sandwich into my mouth, downed a glass of milk and took my vitamins.

Turning the ringer off on my phone, I buried my head under the covers and cried.

The soft crackle of the fire with a full stomach helped pull me under into a dreamless sleep... at first.

Dark purple eyes danced with green flames. Trees bent themselves low, branches reaching for my hair. Pulling me this way and that.

With swirls of darkness thick as harbor mist, sounds rebounded off the forest canopy. Chanting an unfamiliar language.

I ran. My feet sluggish, like wading through molasses.

Then all went silent.

I could feel eyes pressing in on me, but I couldn't see more than a few feet in any direction.

As one, many voices spoke.

"Soul bound. Unbalanced and mortal. Keeper of the Heart. We seek your audience."

With no idea what the blended voice wanted, panic trembled through my limbs. Fear thumping in my throat.

"What do you want with me?"

My legs wouldn't move. All I could do was hope they didn't have a runed sword at the ready.

The mist let up slightly as more than a dozen souls gathered around me in a circle.

"We are the Balance. We are the Scales. We need you, Keeper of the Heart."

"What could you possibly want with me?" I was no one.

My soul and Xander's had been bound in a past life, but I was mortal now. The bond wouldn't snap into place unless I... wasn't.

"We understand your doubt. We understand your fear. Our lives, our spirits, are left in limbo because the Breaker of the Balance seeks to keep the scales unchecked."

The eerie mist swirled around my feet as they rotated without walking.

"I'm no one. What could I possibly do? I'm a human." Fear rose goosebumps along the tops of my forearms.

The blue streak in my hair lost its color, turning back to its natural silver, bright against my raven black locks.

"Being human means not being touched by the broken balance. You are not untouched, child of the night. We seek your help. Complete the bond. Balance the scales. Maintain the natural order."

With my mind running in crisscrossing laps, I couldn't keep up. The task they'd set before me seemed to be contradictory.

The mist began to thicken. The spirits voices began to fade.

"I have no way to complete the bond, even if I wanted to. They're gone. They're all gone." I shouted into the void.

A singular voice echoed back... *"The way is set. Do not lose yourself to the darkness this time around. We bestow you with our Blessings, Keeper of the Heart. Find your strength. Find your path. Do not surrender the scales of balance to the darkness."*

Awakening with a start, the fire had burned itself out, but I was sweating profusely.

Throwing the blanket to the side, a glint of glass and metal caught my eye from under the coffee table.

Picking up the bottle and tilting it to one side, the contents glistened. Pearlescent with a hint of red throughout.

Opening the top, I inhaled shallowly, scrunching up my nose in case it wasn't pleasant.

The scent of evergreen and copper almost knocked my knees out from under me as that lone voice whispered in the recesses of my mind again. *"The path forward awaits."*

Nothing in the dream made any sense. It had to have been from the grief. *Right?*

Putting the top back on the bottle, the strong scent of coffee beckoned to me.

It was only 10 am. It wasn't supposed to fill the house with that rich aroma until noon, but there was no going back to sleep after it grabbed hold of my senses.

With the bottle of who knew what in one hand, I poured the cream from the other.

Wait! If it was a grief dream, how the hell was I holding a bottle I'd never seen before?

It smelled like Xander. Maybe he'd put it there it before he left, and Aries knocked it off the coffee table before I'd initially woken up?

Opening it again, the smell of the entire forest hit my nose.

There was a draw to it. It called to me in an unnamed way.

With the dream still heavy on my mind, I did the unthinkable. Slipping a couple of drops into my coffee, the draw came from my mug now.

When the first sip hit my lips, I shuddered. My body coming alive.

I still felt the grief of losing Dax. I still felt the chasm in my chest for Xander and Thane and the others... but it didn't touch the surface.

Whatever was in that bottle let me put my emotions into a filing cabinet in my head. They were separate but accessible.

If the dream was real, maybe this was the blessing that last, lone voice had spoken of.

It was time to face whatever came next.

And calling Bitzy was the first on my list of things to do.

Chapter Forty-Two

The next couple of months creeped by through a film of grief and sorrow.

Xander had thought of everything before abandoning me to my fate.

The attorney he'd hired, Mister Eilsel, called to meet with me that first week. He'd shown me everything that was needed of me. Laid it all out in simple, easy to follow terms.

I had money. I owned Eventide. And Doraglia manor was mine as well.

He'd asked if I wanted a moving truck brought to my house to gather my furnishings and I sat shocked, staring blankly with an open mouth.

Imagining myself haunting that enormous house all by myself brought tears to my eyes.

Overwhelmed was an understatement.

I'd told Bitzy to come over that evening after finding Xander's note.

All I could tell her that night was that Dax and I had broken up. Not being able to tell her that my sadness leaked from the absence the vampires and werewolves left in my heart tore at my core.

She didn't push or offer any advice. She'd just held me and let me cry. And after the crying stopped, she cracked jokes to try to make me laugh.

I'd went back and forth. Oscillating between weeping to laughing and back to weeping some more.

The day after they'd all left, I'd gotten a call in the early hours of the morning while she was still at my house.

There'd been a devastating house fire at Dax's place. The fire had raised it to the ground with six bodies inside. All burnt to ashes beyond recognition.

I'd had my phone on speaker phone and when the call ended, I'd dropped to my hands and knees. Real tears streaming down my face.

Bitzy wrapped her arms around me and didn't let me go for hours. And it was all I could do to not give into the guilt of not having told her the truth about everything.

Grieving those who died was only made possible by Xander's fire before departing.

Wondering where they'd gotten a sixth body to fake Cody's death, an even more morbid thought crossed my mind.

Dax's body had been decapitated. Did they use another body in place of his or did they stage a beam falling or... I had to stop myself from the images running through my twisted mind.

Xander had even given a ready-made excuse for his and his "associates" absences as well.

They were off to purchase and establish another business endeavor and get it running like they had Eventide.

I didn't have the first clue about managing a bar or restaurant.

Mister Eilsel suggested that he could hire a qualified manager and leave me out of it all if that's what I'd wish to do and I'd jumped on the opportunity.

Only the manager would know that I owned the place. If I didn't like how something was being done or if I wanted anything changed, they would know to do as I asked.

The young woman he'd found to take over the heavy lifting was named Aisia.

She had long, silky black hair and milk chocolate brown coloring to her skin. Her face was beautiful. Exotic here in Vermont. Especially in Jay.

We weren't exactly what you would call diverse in this area, but we welcomed differences in people like specialty pastries. It made them all that more desirable.

If she were three years my senior, I'd be surprised, but she knew her stuff.

Having put herself through business school by working in the hospitality and the retail business, she understood things that someone fresh out of school might not.

"Just put them over there," I said, pointing to the heavy, soundproof curtains.

One of the only things about Eventide that had bothered me since the vampires left was the "Owners Booth." It brought back memories every time I looked at it.

Aisia told the staff it was to be disassembled, and I was the first to grumble at the extra work.

It'd been a ruse, of course, but Asia winked at me as she'd turned back in the direction of the office.

I didn't know how Mister Eilsel found her, but I had my suspicions that she'd been employed by Xander before.

Waves of melancholy still hit me from out of the blue. A scent. An image. A thought that triggered a memory.

They were a punch to the heart that time hadn't erased. And yet, life went on.

Everyone at Eventide had been given a month of paid vacation under Xander's rule. We were also allotted ten sick days annually.

The only stipulation had been that we couldn't take any more than ten consecutive days in a row off at any given time.

We'd all received raises as well. Everyone started at $25 an hour plus tips. No seniority in play.

Of course, Molly bitched about that. She'd been here the longest and grumbled that she should make more.

I was lucky enough to have been there when Mina laid it on the line to her. Telling her that new owners, new kitchens and services, meant a new employment. And that if she didn't like it she could go find work elsewhere.

It had been the highlight of my week back before my world fell apart.

The raise had done wonders for my peace of mind. It was a few weeks later that Lissie had done even more to ease my financial woes.

Not that I needed my hourly wages anymore, but I'd decided to keep them on the books.

Instructing Aisia to donate them to various charities, it was my way to give back each month.

Luke took full advantage of the funds and the time.

Apparently, he'd put in for his first vacation before we'd lost everyone. He'd left the day after the funerals.

He'd been gone ten days. Back for three days before calling out sick for another four.

I understood being sick sucked but the new kitchen crew and barback weren't in sync with the rest of us yet and I found it too easy to bitch about it with Kamie and Hannah.

He'd taken another vacation last week and was scheduled to work yesterday but called and said he'd been delayed. Something to do with misplacing his passport and trouble getting back into the states.

It only made me more upset with him for no good reason.

Luke had begun to feel like a constant before my world went to shit. Like the big brother I'd never asked for. And irrationally, I'd been mad at him for living his life without regards to the rest of us.

My grief wasn't fully abated. Snipping at my co-workers only made the irritability I felt turn to guilt when I'd snap at them.

Over the last couple weeks, I'd taken to wandering through Xander's manor house.

Rolling in the sheets that still smelled like him. Admiring the artwork on the walls. Missing him more fiercely than I'd ever missed anyone in my life. Including my mother.

No one knew of the tryst we'd had. I'd never divulged any of it to a single soul.

If Bitzy or Luke or any of them suspected, they didn't bring it up. And for that, I was grateful.

I had enough troubles in my mind and aches in my heart for many lifetimes over. I didn't need the headache that would come with Molly's bitchy attitude if she'd found out.

That fact that I'd owned Eventide because of making out with the boss wouldn't be a topic she would ever let go of.

And right now, it was not the time to test my strength of character.

Having bail money and being willing to spend a few nights in jail weren't the same thing.

Though the thought of smacking that pugnacious face of hers brought a smile to my lips.

It had been nearly two months, and I couldn't shake the irritability I felt.

Going home early had become my new way of dealing while I mourned the life that could have been.

Molly had bitched to Aisia about that more than once, but she'd just told her to worry about doing her own job.

Bitzy and Kamie on the other hand, they wore matching worried expressions each time I'd leave.

Their genuine caring about my well being kept me getting out of bed and coming back to work.

Without them, I'd be lost to my own sorrowful ruminations.

It was their faces that I carried with me each time my thoughts turned dark.

They were my guiding light.

After those initial couple months of going through the motions, life started to enter my eyes again.

I'd read and re-read every book I owned, which wasn't but a handful.

Having no money in the past for luxuries, my library card was well worn. I didn't want to wait on the small selection we had at our location.

There was a fully stocked study at Xander's... *ugh*... my manor house, so I'd been making many trips back and forth.

Falling asleep while reading occurred more often than not when I'd snuggle into one of those cozy chairs he'd had.

After going back and forth for weeks, it seemed silly now.

So, with more fortitude than I'd felt, I'd packed the small bit of things that meant something to me and moved myself and Aries into our new place.

I took the contents of that strange bottle I'd found after awakening from that dream every morning with my vitamins.

The scent of evergreen, clove, copper, and something sweet hit me anew each time I'd open it.

Even after two months, the contents never went down. It was a strange magic that I couldn't explain away.

The manor had been lonely when I'd come by myself, but with Aries running around and making himself right at home, it wasn't so desolate.

The first thing he did was run up and down the stairs over and over again. Then he rooted through every room, every crevice, until he put claim on an area in the back sunroom.

I went online and ordered him a climbing tree that looked like a real tree, fit with crawling spaces, hammocks, holes to explore, and plush cushions that looked like tree leaves.

Along with that purchase, I splurged on a robot litter box and automatic feed dispenser that had twenty-four slots.

Programming it to go off at random times throughout the day, it dispensed only a tablespoon or so of pellets at a time.

In true Aries fashion, no matter where he'd been in the house, he'd come zooming into the room the moment he heard it go off.

It had been so entertaining that I'd forgotten my sorrow for brief periods of time.

And for that, I'd gotten him a potted catnip plant to go beside his climbing tree.

Falling into the book I'd been reading for the past few days, my eyes drifted close.

"Wake up, Rori!" The voice was familiar, but no one knew I lived here. Perhaps I'd still been asleep, dreaming.'

A crash sounded from under the window in the front of the room.

Aries hissed from his perch at the bottom of the stairs.

Grabbing one of the swords off a decoration next to the front door, the weight and sharpness of it took me by surprise.

"Who's there?" No one was supposed to know.

Being at the manor for little over a week, I hadn't even told Bitzy that I'd cleared out of my house yet.

"Open the damned door. I'm getting eaten up out here. These mosquitos have brought all of their friends to the party."

With a sigh of relief, I pulled the massive door open.

"Woah! Easy, hon." Luke's eyes went wide.

Realizing I still held the sword, I lowered it to my side but didn't let it go.

"What are you doing here? Better yet, how did you know I was here?"

I hadn't even known he'd made it back in town already, but to be here?

This place was around the bend in the mountain. Down a long, winding gravel driveway that wound through the trees like a snake.

The turn off was hidden. And there were no lamps lighting the entrance or the driveway.

I could barely find it myself half the time.

Which begged the question again, how did Luke even know about this place?

"I went by your house first. Peeked inside. It didn't look like you'd been there for a bit. So, I figured you'd come to the owners place."

He said this all matter-of-factly. Like one plus one equals two.

"Right. The owners place. You mean Xander." Not a question. No one knew I owned Eventide except Aisia and Mister Eilsel.

"Something like that." There was a slight slur to his words. "Look, I know it's been rough on you. With losing Dax and then Xander high tailing it out of town that same week, you've got to be hurting kiddo."

It occurred to me that he might have been drinking. I couldn't smell any alcohol on him but that didn't mean he was sober.

My mind went in a hundred different directions. Why would he care enough to seek me out?

He'd never liked Xander as far as I could tell. And when I could have used a shoulder to lean on, he went on holiday. Twice!

"I'm fine, Luke. I'm reading and then going to bed. So, if you'll excuse me." Closing the door in his face, his foot stopped it from shutting completely. "Luke, really. I want to get back to finish my chapter."

Smacking a bug from his neck, he held up a bottle of booze in the other hand. *That damned grin.*

"I figured you could vent some of that poison from your system." Holding his hands up in surrender, he tacked on, "No judgements."

My book was calling my name, but he was my friend. If he could take the time to try and comfort me, then I'd make the time to hear him out.

Opening the door a bit more, I sighed.

With my small nod, he swaggered in.

Then stopped in his tracks.

Chapter Forty-Three

Aries was hissing like mad. The hair on his back stood on end and he kept advancing forward with a snap of his teeth. Retreating, only to do it again.

"Aries! Stop that!" I shouted, but the cat would not settle down.

I'd never seen him instantly hate someone that much.

He'd never been the friendliest with strangers. And on occasion, he'd hiss and retreat to his own space, coming back in his own time.

... But this. It was something else. Not quite territorial. More protective than anything.

"It's fine. Cats have a way about them. Especially males. It's the nature of living in the in-between." His tone was casual, but something felt off.

Backing up a few paces, he glanced upstairs before his gaze settled back on the cat.

"Did you know they used to be worshipped as gods a long time ago? I don't think they've forgotten it." The slurring that had been in his voice only moments ago completely vanished.

Peeking off towards the study, he then turned to me, raising the bottle.

"Anything to eat to go along with this?"

I pointed in the opposite direction, still watching his sudden sobering.

"Kitchens that way."

Aries slinked up the stairs. Turning at the top step, his paw darted out and knocked the ornamental vase down the stairs as he glared in my direction.

I didn't speak cat, but I was fairly sure he wasn't pleased that I'd let Luke in his house.

By the time I'd cleaned up the broken glass and made my way to the kitchen, there was a large charcuterie board waiting.

I had to give it to him. He was quick and efficient. It's what made him so good at his job.

Buying all of these ingredients earlier in the week, I'd never have thought to chop them and assemble them the way he had in such a short time.

He even made two dips. A sweet one and a savory one.

"That looks great, Luke," I said popping a piece of cheese in my mouth. "It took me longer to figure out the lay of the kitchen than it took you to chop and make all of this."

"What can I say? I'm a natural." The corner of his lips turned up fiendishly.

I didn't understand the devilish grin, but the thought went right out of my head when I tried the crackers with his savory dip.

"By the gods! That's delicious!" It was easily the best thing I'd put in my mouth in weeks.

It tasted of red peppers and herbs. I couldn't place the nutty flavor, but it all blended immensely well.

"I went to Vienna on my holiday. I have a friend who's a chef in a small village outside of the city. She may have showed me a thing or two."

That twinkle in his eyes told me there was more to the story than making food but I didn't feel comfortable enough with him to talk about his sex life.

"Is that where you had problems with your passport?" Maybe it had been an excuse to stay in his *friend's* company a tad longer.

Pouring us both a large portion wine from the bottle he'd brought into two glasses, he handed me one.

"No," he said with hesitation. "That was on the first holiday I had this year."

Remembering he'd been sick after that, it made me wonder what he might have caught from his trip abroad.

It must not have been too bad because a couple of weeks later, he left on another vacation.

Bringing the cup to my lips and sniffing, I was pleasantly surprised. "Sweet?"

"I know you haven't been much of a drinker, but I noticed that whenever Hannah made you the sweeter concoctions, you seemed to like them best."

Why he would notice wasn't something I'd wanted to explore. If he was flirting with me, I couldn't tell.

My only thoughts were getting through each day with as little sadness as possible.

Taking a sip, the flavors exploded on my tongue. There were hints of blackberry, citrus and clove. Maybe honey too.

Something spicy was thrown into the mix but I couldn't place what it was.

"Did you make this?" I said, adding yet another talent to his ever-growing resume.

"Do you like it?" I nodded and took a longer pull this time. "I'm glad. I've had it fermenting for several months now. Potions are sort of my specialty."

My head felt woozy. Either this stuff was the strongest thing I'd ever drank or... *shit.*

"Potions? You mean like cocktails." I tried to sit my glass back on the table but missed.

The glass shattered with a loud peal. Liquid spraying the front of my leggings. The dizziness in my head made me sway.

"Easy there, Heart keeper. I've got you." His arms wound around me before I could fall.

"How do you know that name?" I tried to ask but it all came out slurred.

Setting me to the floor, he went to the other side of the kitchen island and came back with a bundle of butcher's twine.

Binding my hands in front of me. The makeshift rope wasn't tight, but I still couldn't move.

"Why are you doing this? What do you want from me?" I attempted to say but the words weren't coherent in my own ears.

Pulling me to a sitting position, my back rested against the island for support, but I was already sliding down to the floor again.

"This will all be over shortly, Rori." He wrapped a length of twine around my legs. "For what it's worth, I like you, kiddo. I was truly hoping to spare you."

Whatever was in that drink took a hold of me fast. The scene around me faded in and out.

Aries came around the corner and stopped.

"There you are, you rat!" Luke yelled.

Aries hissed loudly and took off around the corner.

"Leaveee hiim allonnee..." I called after Luke's fleeing form as he gave chase.

Then I faded into nothingness.

Chapter Forty-Four

Awakening this time was a struggle.

I'd passed out more in the last several months than in all of my lifetime before.

Whatever had been in that potion was strong enough to keep me under for a long time.

I only knew that because of the tingling in my legs and feet.

Luke must have left me in the same position long enough to cut of the blood to my extremities. The feeling of pins and needles was to the point of pain.

With my eyes still closed, I tried to get my bearings.

It smelled musty, with a hint of wet dog.

Oh gods! I was in the den.

The last time I'd been here was on that hiking date with Dax, when he'd filled me in on everything he could after Dylan died.

We'd talked and ate and slept on the dingy sofa. The very sofa I could smell under me right now.

The sob that I'd thought had been quiet hadn't been quiet enough.

"Open your eyes, Rori. I know you're awake." Luke's voice sounded off. Rougher around the edges.

My eyelids didn't want to co-operate.

Slowly, the left one opened. Then the right.

The den's dim lighting did nothing to dispel my growing angst.

Dawn was on the horizon, but the sun hadn't crested the mountain enough to see its glow yet.

My mouth felt like I'd swallowed sawdust. Gritty and dry.

"What's going on, Luke? Why have you brought me here?" Remembering the events before I passed out, I hissed. "What did you do with Aries?!"

He was facing away from me but spoke over his shoulder. "The little shit got away. Last I saw him, he went running into the woods by the manor."

Thanking the gods that I'd put in a cat door the first day we'd settled into the place, I sighed a breath of relief.

My eyes adjusted a bit, and I could see him more clearly.

A greenish hue peeked from behind him as he turned to face me. The sound of a crackling fire thrummed low in the background.

And then I'd smelled it. The same herbs I couldn't place before.

The scent I now associated with Dax's death.

"It was you!" I shouted. "You killed him! Why, Luke?"

The little I'd eaten yesterday made an attempt to come back up.

Sitting up was difficult with my wrists and ankles bound but I didn't want to chance choking on my own bile if it came up while I was still on my back.

"Maybe the better question is why, in every single lifetime, do you... well, your soul, find its way back to these loathsome creatures? It's been a thorn in my side for hundreds of years now!"

He was fuming after his little rant.

That was when I noticed his eyes. Purple. Purple eyes like the others had described the witch who'd cursed Xander and Thane.

This couldn't be happening. Not now. Not when they'd all left me.

Xander had been looking for the witch who'd cursed him for months, years possibly, and here he stood. The very person he'd searched for to help him end his curse.

"No... No, Luke!" I shouted in disbelief. "You can't be that evil. You've been so nice to me. Please!" I didn't know what I was begging for.

For it not to be true? For this to be some sort of dream? For the reality of the situation to change? This couldn't be happening.

"Oh yes, Rori. I can be *this evil*, as you say." His lips twitched in irritation before he turned towards the makeshift table and picked up something long and yellowing with the smell of rotting meat clinging to it.

Throwing it into the bubbling pot, the green liquid inside hissed and spit. The flame underneath flared brighter.

"I'll do this in your tongue this time. I want you to understand everything." His eyes shifted back to the cast iron pot. "Mortal bone, taken by teeth, I claim your vengeance."

My mind was reeling. Thoughts darting back and forth. Making connections I didn't want to acknowledge.

Shit! We were at the den. He'd brought me here so he wouldn't have to lug his ingredients all over the mountain.

Those mortal bones were... *no. Gods, no!* Dylan's rotting body parts.

"Luke, stop! You don't have to do this!" My pleas fell on deaf ears.

Daybreak brought more light to fill the cavernous space.

The interior of the den was familiar, but he must have brought the sofa closer to the entrance while I'd been unconscious.

"You don't get it, Rori! I'm not the bad guy. Your precious Xander hounded me about his father. Made my meager existence miserable. Then, he strategically tore apart my coven, my family, from the inside!"

Never hearing him yell before. I flinched with every word. My childhood past ingrained on my adult reactions.

I'd known what Xander had done. He'd told me himself. I'd known and overlooked it.

The fact that the witch in question was or had been my friend changed everything.

I could no longer view it in the abstract. I saw the consequences of Xander's actions playing out in real time.

"I'm sorry, Luke," I said, hanging my head.

My bound wrists were beginning to chafe. My throat was dry and course. If I'd been hydrated, tears would have fallen.

"Vincent." He walked to where I sat on the couch and crouched down to eye level.

"My name is Vincent. Do me that respect at least." The edge in his tone frightened me more than the knowledge of who he was.

Vincent Luciant Cazan. The Breaker of the Balance.

Seeing it clearly now, what the dream vision had told me. It was all about the man standing before me.

"Vincent, please. Don't do whatever it is you are planning. You're a good man. I've seen it with my own eyes." The feelings of loss took up more space in my chest.

He'd protected me. Tried to give me money to get away for a while. Gave me advice when I'd never asked for it.

He'd been like a big brother from just about the moment I'd met him.

"Sorry, kiddo. You see, my coven are all dead. Held in limbo for my actions. The gods weren't happy when I refused to end the brother's curses. The balance had been thrown out of whack."

Walking over to the table once again, he came back with a piece of hide. Wolf hide.

Before I could say anything, he'd thrown it into the pot as well.

"Shifting skin, transformed by rage, I take up your cause."

Again, the green bubbles hissed and spit. The flame changed colors from oranges to reds briefly but settled back to orange a few seconds later.

Not knowing his end game, I kept quiet in the hopes that he'd reveal his hand.

Looking to the outside of the den, I pressed my lips shut against the acrid smoke that lingered momentarily.

"Nothing to say? No pleas for mercy on their behalf?"

If Luke had always been a cruel person to me, the betrayal wouldn't have stung so sharply.

I held my remarks tightly against the backs of my teeth.

"Alright then, I'll give you the full picture. They will all be heading this way by now after the message I'd sent."

I couldn't help but to ask. The question falling from my lips before I could retrieve it. "What message?"

Evil was the only way to describe the glean in his eyes.

They traveled over to the corner where I hadn't noticed a cage that hadn't been there when Dax brought me the last time.

From the shadows, I could barely make out a figure.

Hunched over. Bound in chains. And beginning to wake up.

Korrina.

Chapter Forty-Five

"It was convenient for me that the hybrid didn't die with her pack. I needed a vampire for the next part of this spell and the poor, put out girl refused to keep up with her sister." He said all of this while sharpening a sword.

The same runed sword he'd used to kill Dax with. The one that ended an entire pack of werewolves.

"I left evidence behind when I took her. Along with that lock that you always wear. I'd taken when we'd hugged after the funerals. You'd been too sad to notice."

Touching my neck, I couldn't remember the last time I'd thought of it. It had been my mother's and I'd barely registered its absence.

"I figured it was message enough. They should be arriving soon. I'll be gone by then, and they'll be too late of course. But I owe them pain. And this will give me a small amount of the vengeance I've craved."

Everything Luke had done, he'd done with purpose.

I'd thought him a jack of all trades in the past. I was only now seeing the foresight that went along with that intellect.

"Kori!" I shouted. She'd never liked me, but I wasn't so petty that I'd want anything bad to happen to her. "Kori, wake up!"

If she could break free, perhaps she could run with vampire speed to get help.

The chains wrapped around her wrist, her upper arms, her ankles, and the tops of her thighs.

There was a slight glow to them that I didn't understand until Luke threw a bucket of bluish liquid over the top of the cage, drenching her and the chains both.

A potion of some sort. It blazed bright blue and then settle back to that pale color again.

She screamed and I fought the urge to cover my ears. Her suffering was my fault.

The poor girl wouldn't have been in this position if Xander and Anastasia hadn't been mated.

She wouldn't be here in this cave if my soul hadn't sought him out through every lifetime. Wouldn't be chained with metal and magics if I could have just let him go.

"As I was saying," Luke continued as if Kori's screams didn't register any sympathy for her plight. "My coven tried to demand that I end the curses and return the balance, but you see, the vampire and the werewolf turned more humans than I could keep up with. I could never get close enough to end their lives."

He picked at the end of the sword, plucking a stone from the side of the cave wall.

The dream I'd had of his ancestors never spoke of ending the lives of the supernaturals. Only keeping the balance.

"Why would you have to kill them? Couldn't you simply reverse the curse?"

It had sat, niggling in the recesses of my mind for months.

Why would the figure in the woods want to kill Dax and in turn, kill the werewolves under him? If the witch could just end the curse, they wouldn't need to die.

The witch in question stared into my eyes. His face reddening with anger, and he took a step in my direction.

"Why indeed? Back then, I wanted Xander to suffer for all he'd done. Thane was his younger brother and when he'd come to plead that I reverse the curse on Xander, I saw my opportunity to exact some measure of pain. I cursed his brother to be a creature that would serve as his immortal enemy."

Taking a deep breath, he stepped back. Comparing the witch in front of me with the good-hearted friend I'd worked with was a fruitless task. The male before me and the man he'd been over the last half a year couldn't be reconciled.

"When my coven persisted that I end the imbalance, I sought to kill them but that proved to be harder than I'd first thought when I'd set out."

Vengeance was a goal he wasn't willing to give up on, even after all these centuries.

"With all of their creations running amuck, the balance was pushed farther to one side of the scales. My coven shunned me. They told me that unless I could bring the creatures to heel, I would not be welcome home."

Pulling the door to Kori's cage open, she snarled, snapping her fangs out to try and bite her captor.

Yanking hard, he chanted a few words. The chains bit into her skin and she shrieked like a banshee.

"Ah, ah, ah, little lamia. There will be no escape for you." Not an ounce of warmth in his tone.

How could this be the same person I'd come to trust? Come to call my friend?

Pulling hard on my bound wrists only gave me rope burn. My ankles and thighs hurt from the cut off circulation.

Inching my way to the end of the couch, I looked to the vampire who'd coveted my former mate.

The sadness and defeat in her eyes made tears swell in mine.

Leaving hope behind, I committed to being there with her to the end. It was the least I could do. Bare witness to her death.

"So, to answer your previous question..." he continued his story without a thought for the life he was about to take. "With so many new werewolves and vampires sweeping through villages, leaving bloodless bodies and more turned creatures in their wake, my family would forsake me regardless of if I removed the curse from both Thane and Xander. I'd be out my vengeance and have no way to make Xander suffer."

Shaking his head as he dragged Kori's body to the center of the room, a calm replaced the anger in his tone.

"My only comfort through the centuries was that they were brothers. Since I couldn't kill them, they'd suffer a long, miserable life with only each other for family, but be enemies forever."

Pulling out a pair of pliers while he'd spoken, he'd shown no remorse as he yanked Kori's head back and ripped one of her fangs from her mouth.

She let lose a scream, gurgled with blood. Choking the sound off mid shriek as he wrenched out the other fang, flinging them both into the green goo bubbling away in that awful cauldron.

"If I was to be left alone with no coven, no family... I would make sure that they had to suffer the same fate."

I jumped as goo and flames shot from the pot, one ember landing an inch from my ankle.

"That meant leaving them alive after they'd gotten control off the creatures around them." The angry twitch of his mouth set my nerves sparking. "My coven had the nerve to complement their acts altruism as an act of redemption."

That acrid smoke once again shoved itself up my nose. I fought the bindings on my hands and legs to no avail.

"It was not but for selfish reasons that the brothers killed most of the creatures they'd turned. Villages sought to hunt the fiends. And with less prey, they'd starve eventually. Not that it would kill them. It'd make them weak though."

Walking around the shelf, he picked up a handful of herbs and rubbed the sword's blade. The runes embossed there came to life, glowing intensely against the metal surface.

The glowing green let out an inhuman wail that made me cringe, but I kept myself in place. Refusing to leave Kori bleeding and in pain.

"Fate's bite, with teeth and blood, I serve your justice."

Trying to find my resolve, I needed to force niceness into my tone. No room for my usual sarcasm in the face of adversities.

"How are you still alive, Luke... sorry, Vincent? I thought witches only lived a slightly longer life than humans." It was the one thing I'd read over and over again in the books from Xander's library.

"I was angry at my family's decision, Rori. When Xander found you... well, Anastasia, his soulmate, I knew that they'd interfered. Their magics granted the brothers a match, should they come across them in their lifetime. Only the power of my entire coven could have worked that magics."

Kori hadn't made any attempt to move. A low whimper issued steadily from within her chest as she sat, curled on her side in a heap on the floor.

Continuing while he worked his way around Kori's prone figure, he said, "I'm stuck here. Alone. My family all left me. First while they lived. And then again as they died."

His tone turned somber. Haunted as he remembered the pain of their loss.

" The gods themselves cursed me. As long as my mistakes walk the earth, I'm doomed to watch the creatures I'd unleashed on humanity."

Without blinking, Luke stepped forward with the runed sword and plunged it into Kori's chest.

She didn't have a chance to scream. It happened so fast.

Head going limp, the rest of her slumped to the floor. With a swing of the blade, the sword severed her head from her neck.

Chapter Forty-Six

My scream sounded far away in my own ears.

He'd done it. He'd only need her fangs, but he'd killed her anyway.

Gods. The dead eyes that looked back at me told the whole story. Hate and vengeance and villainous loathing swirled in the depths of their purple masses.

I'd thought my biggest problem months ago was Thane and his pack.

How naive had I been to not see the real danger in front of me?

"They soon found their end at tip of my blade. Every single one of them."

I'd been so taken aback by Kori's death, I'd forgotten he was telling me his story.

"I... what? Who?"

The words coming out of my mouth did so without my consent, never wanting to utter another word to this monster.

"My coven. Who else? The ones who pooled their magics to give my enemies a chance at true happiness. All of my strife, my angst. They betrayed me."

Going back over to the counter, I couldn't see what he was doing but something told me I wouldn't like it.

With another handful of herbs, he threw them into the pot and the green glow dulled.

"I've not forgiven them. Even after all these centuries. And when Anastasia bonded with Xander, I may have gone a touch mad."

"A touch? Ya think?" My smart mouth was faster than I was. At only a whisper, he'd still heard it.

The fire reflected in his dark eyes, making the flames look purple as they stared out at me.

Or perhaps he was staring back into the past to her. To Anastasia.

"Lonely is life untouched by another. Hateful is the heart that beats in isolation." His emotions leaked through the space between us as he spoke.

Pain, hurt, and if I wasn't mistaken, envy.

"Couldn't you have used all this time to fall in love? Maybe raise a family? Why choose vengeance when you could choose reclamation? Love is worth fighting for, Luke."

He was in my face in less than a heartbeat, face as purple as his eyes.

"And what if I'd found it, Rori? To have a love and watch them grow old. Watch them wither away as age claimed them. All the while, I stayed young forever? Or even worse... I find love and they notice my not aging. With no mating bond, they'd think me a freak. Leaving me while I still loved them would be worse than bearing witness to their life slipping through the sands of time!"

I couldn't imagine the pain he'd lived through over the years. Now understanding the hesitation when I'd asked about his female friend in Vienna, it tore at my heart.

It wasn't that he didn't want to love. It was that he lived in fear of the loss when it inevitably ended.

What his ancestors did had long term consequences. By providing back the balance in giving the vampires and werewolves the possibility of mates, it kept them from making new creatures unwisely.

They'd only turn a human for love or necessity, like in Cody's case.

The gods cursing Luk… Vincent, to live and bear witness to what he'd created had added rubbing alcohol to a wound.

A revelation hit me like a boulder.

Thane had killed Anastasia when Xander couldn't bring himself to do it.

It wasn't his love for her before she'd been turned that made him do it.

It was his love for his brother that made Thane act. The price of keeping the scales balanced was her death.

She'd killed too many humans and turned too many into new vampires.

Xander's love became was a blind spot, and his brother had stepped up to take away that weakness.

Gods! If I'd realized that Thane wasn't the bad guy all along, maybe things could have been different between us. At least they could have been less angsty.

Shaking his head, he walked back over to me with that cursed sword glowing brightly against the dimness of the cave walls.

The smell of moss and dirt replaced by whatever he'd put in that cursed cauldron.

"I'm done with all of this, kiddo. I meant what I'd said. I wish there was another way."

Slicing the palm of my hand, he shoved a bottle under it to catch the drippings.

It took a moment for the pain to register but once it did, the burning sensation flashed hot throughout my entire body.

When it had filled halfway, he threw it into the pot and the green glow flared back to life, more vivid than it had at any previous addition.

"Blood of the gate, Keeper of the heart, I sacrifice your offering to balance the scales once again."

Turning towards me, the corner of his mouth turning up on one side, the old Luke looked out from that smile.

It could have been my imagination, but I could have sworn I heard a growl come from the forest, a long distance away.

"It's time. Chew this," he said, shoving the herbs in my mouth and clamping my jaws shut around them. "It will help with the pain until the gods come to collect their debt."

My eyes went wide as the sword plunged into my stomach. Pain shoved its way through my body.

Leaning down, his forehead pressed to mine.

"You're not her. I'd wished you were. I'd wished you were ruthless and cruel and a drain on humanity when we'd met. It would have made my guilt lessen. You haven't let that darkness steal your light the way Anastasia gave herself over to it. There will be no more lifetimes for you and for that, I am truly sorry, Rori."

My breathing was slow and raspy. I couldn't think around the pain. The blood ran down my fingers as I grasped hold of the sword sticking out of my gut.

My throat choked on the hot liquid as it dribbled out the sides of my mouth, down my chin.

"I need this to end. My life is tied with theirs. And I will end them soon enough, but I can't leave the keeper of the heart as a tether for either of them."

My vision was beginning to fail. Cold like I'd never known climbed its way through each of my limbs and stole the pain as much as the herbs he'd forced upon me did.

Stepping back, he sighed. "Take a deep breath."

I couldn't but it didn't matter. Again, I thought I'd heard growls echoing through the trees. They were still too far away to do any more than steal my focus.

More air escaped my lungs as Luke pulled the blade from my body. Without waver, he slid it across my throat.

Hot, wet liquid seeped through my fingertips as I gagged on the blood crowding my windpipe.

Waiting for my head to be liberated from my body, my thoughts went to Xander and Thane.

I'd only just found them. I wanted to stay. I wanted to live.

My life had been full of strife and pain but the deep-rooted sorrow that I wouldn't get the chance to know happiness consumed my racing thoughts.

Luke laid me gently onto the sofa.

My mind disassociated from my body trying to protect it-self.

The odd sensation of being held grounded me as I heard a single sob from the male who'd become more to me than simply a co-worker.

With my head still intact, he threw the blanket over me as the blood drained from my body.

Kissing my forehead, he moved to the opening of the cave in my peripheral line of sight as my head swam, blurry and dimming in and out.

My vision going dark, I heard him say, "Thank you for your sacrifice, draga mea. I will put in a word for you with the gods when I arrive. Perhaps they can retrieve you from the nothingness."

Then it was dark. Quiet. No sound, sight, or sense of reality.

Each second felt like a lifetime. Images passed through the shadows of my mind.

Then as suddenly as they'd started, they stopped. Everything stopped.

With a shuddering breath, the last of the air left my lungs with the final beat of my heart.

I was dead.

Chapter Forty-Seven

"Be aware, *Keeper of the Heart. We haven't much time before you awaken.*" The collective said as one, that same dreamlike awareness settling over me.

Light danced behind my eyelids, illuminating my body as I watched on from above. Separate.

Sparks of energy glided over, under, around, and through. They pulsed like a million tiny fireflies with every passing second. The skin of my body glowed brightly.

My hair fluttered on an invisible wave and as I watched on in wonder, it turned iridescent, then back to raven black.

The single streak I'd had of silver became two. One on each side of my face.

"I don't understand. What is happening?" I tried to yell to the coven, but my voice had taken on an angelic quality. I may have well been singing a beautiful aria.

"*You have fulfilled the task we'd set before you.*" The figures turned in a circle around me, limbs never touching the ground or anything else.

It was beyond eerie. Though I held no fear.

Peaceful was the only way to describe the scene around my bloodless, dead body that laid a mere ten feet away.

"You've ingested our magics daily since last we spoke. Your blood sacrifice has satisfied the gods. The scales are once again balanced." Their voices were not as loud as they had been.

One by one they each reached for a light that I could not see beyond. Disappearing the instant they touched it.

"Wait! What does that mean? I don't know what I'm meant to do!"

Why couldn't witches speak plainly? Their intentions were never clear.

That same female from the last time floated towards me.

I had no body to speak of, but I still tensed as she laid her ethereal hand on my shoulder.

While light swirled along her fingertips, I could feel the push and pull of darkness below the surface.

"We gave you the spark of hope and the power of feeling, child. While that may not be the full knowledge of what we've granted you as reward for freeing our souls, all things will come to light in due time."

Her purple eyes shown with unshed tears. Eyes that were so much like Luke's, I cringed.

"You're saying I am an empath? But how? I'm not alive anymore?"

The sense that time was beginning to catch up with us tugged at a string that led from my ethereal spirit to my broken body lying on that blood-stained sofa.

"A streak for each. A gift of the gods with consequences." The whisper of her hand ran through the front of my hair. *"Our part has been played. It is now your responsibility to find balance while delivering justice."*

Her form began to fade as she reached back towards the light beyond my vision.

"That tells me nothing. What do I do? What am I?" Frustration colored my tone.

I'd died. That I was sure of. Luke... Vincent... whatever you wanted to call him, he'd killed me.

And by drinking that iridescent potion his coven had "gifted" me, the gods granted me a boon?

Did that mean I could come back to life?

Vincent's coven had been freed from the in-between for playing their part.

Did that mean he could be killed now? Without harm to Xander or Thane or the rest of them?

Why couldn't they tell me what I needed to know in plain terms? Witches... *Ugh!* They were annoyingly cryptic.

Just when I'd begun to panic at my spirit's inability to move, an electric jolt zinged through my spectral being.

My spirit felt like it was being pulled. The tether that had been a string now became a chain as I was sucked back to my body.

The tinkling of laughter filled my ears as I heard Vincent's matriarch whisper, *"Keeper of the Heart, Hand of the Gods, you Are the Balance. Use the scales wisely."*

That was the last thing I remember before pain exploded everywhere.

It was dark. My mind raced with images.

Images of my life. Images of my past lives.

Everything hurt. Endless pain singed my very soul.

All of the files of my soul crammed their way into my head.

Every deed. Every kiss. Every good thing and bad thing I'd ever experienced.

Reliving my time with Thane. Reliving my life with Xander.

Turning countless defenseless humans into monsters and killing more of them than some of the smaller wars that'd taken place over the centuries I'd been alive as Anastasia.

My death by Thane's hand over and over again. Xander's eyes as he found me this past lifetime.

And Dax. More than a few lifetimes.

He'd been my keeper. The force that kept me alive and out of the reach of Xander.

Vincent was in the images more often than I'd ever thought he'd be. His purple eyes stood out to me now.

I could see him watching. Waiting. Trying to gauge the right time to exact his revenge.

Most of the images had him on the outskirts of my focus, but he was there. Always plotting.

I gritted through the pain. Sharp. Melting hot flames licked through my limbs, burning me from the inside out.

Opening my eyes wasn't something I'd been willing to do as my body repaired its new immortal self while jamming all of the knowledge, all of the **feelings**, I'd need into new filing cabinets in my mind.

There was a tug from inside my heart. From all that information I'd just obtained. I knew it was the bond with Xander. I had felt it as Anastasia.

It smelled of evergreen and copper. The feel of it gentle and full of love, admiration, and pride.

All of our memories, Anastasia through to Aurora, settled into place within me.

I needed to awaken. My mate's fear tore at me through the bond. I was aware of another pull as well, but I had no memory to place it.

Xander was out there somewhere. He'd know I was not mortal anymore.

The tug would call him to me like a bee to a fragrant flower.

I'd almost given in to it. Wanting to open my eyes and look for his beautiful face.

I'd wait though. The pain of burning from within my veins wasn't something I'd want him to endure the sight of again if I could spare him.

It was endless. With my lips pursed together as hard as I could, I clamped down on my screams.

After some time, whether hours or days, I couldn't tell. A new sensation began.

In the same vicinity of my heart, a new thread appeared in my mind's eye.

Where Xander's bond glowed blue, this one glowed red.

It dripped into my being. All sharp edges and snarling whispers.

The scent of cloves and honeysuckle shoved its way into my brain. Forceful and demanding.

The urge to reach out and yank the thread towards me overwhelmed my mind.

My eyes snapping open, pain from the sudden awareness kept place, holding me captive while I adjusted to the new thread.

The intense feelings threatened to overburden my recovering body.

The glowing I'd seen while hovering in spirit form started anew.

Tiny swirling sparks radiated from my head to my toes, only this time I could feel them.

They danced and encircled my fingers.

Twitching the tips of them, the pain receded from that area bit by bit. Up my arms. Through my neck and face.

The slash in my neck tingled and the blood that had remained floated away like it had never existed.

I watched in awe as the same phenomenon occurred throughout my limbs. Running down my chest, all the way to my feet,

Once the pain and blood were gone completely, I stood too quickly on wobbly legs.

It wasn't that I was still weak.

On the contrary. I felt amazingly strong.

The *otherness* **feeling** didn't need but a fraction of a second for my thoughts to calculate the newness.

My body had been remade.

The only thing that called to me more than the threads was... blood.

Before I'd given myself permission to move, I was running.

The forest stretched out before me. Trees and trails in every direction.

A gust of wind lifted my dark hair, blowing long tendrils around my face.

The scent of humans hit my nose from the west, and I was a blur of movement.

I'd never realized how fast the vampires were until that moment.

With every jump, turn, and swing around each tree, my brain calculated it all without me having to think before my body reacted.

Coming closer to the far trail entrance, two hikers were making their way up the sloping hillside to the cliff's edge and beautiful overlook on the mountain.

Speed and stealth were my friend. Catching up to them wasn't a problem in my new body.

I didn't want to hurt them, but the call of their blood made the heat surge in the back of my throat.

Stepping out of the shadows, I slowed my pace to human.

"Hi there. Are you lost?" The bigger male asked after throwing a coy look to his friend.

The tug in my chest came from two different directions, giving me pause, but the wet heat coming from the closer male's veins consumed my mind.

His eyes went wide as I stepped further into the light filtering through the canopy of trees.

A slight glow emanated from my skin. Beautiful and luminescent.

I couldn't stop to consider it at the moment. I needed to quench the horrible thirst that had taken up residence since I'd awoken.

Xander called my name from one side of the forest. Thane from the other.

The vampires and werewolves were all close. Looking for Kori. Searching for me.

With my new enhanced hearing, I couldn't gauge how far away they were yet. I'd need more practice to hone those skills.

If these hikers heard them, they didn't let on.

The burning in my throat was my sole focus. The vein on the side of the closes male's throat beat like a war drum calling me to action.

Batting my eyes, I let my faux naiveté lure them in. Beauty came with the vampire package.

Though I hadn't seen myself yet, I could guess at what they were witnessing.

With my hands up in surrender, I inched forward.

The recently human part of mind screamed at me to stop but it was no use.

"I don't want to hurt you. Please, stand perfectly still."

Before he could reply, move, or scream...

I pounced.

Thane

Finding Kori wasn't on my game card for today when I'd woken up.

I barely tolerated her on a normal day.

Xander came to me himself. My brother and I haven't been civil to one another for centuries.

Not since I killed our girl.

It had to be done. The balance demanded its due.

Anastasia had been my girl first. She would have been my girl forever if he hadn't crossed her path.

When I'd come back from getting my shit together and cleansing the world of my mistakes, I'd found that my brother had taken her to his bed to feed.

Her blood sang to him. Tethered him. She'd been made his mate that very instant.

How she could still want him after he killed her was beyond me. The mating bond seemed more like a noose than a blessing.

After I'd killed her soul in every lifetime since, not once had she looked at me with the love we used to know.

I'd let hope in long enough each time she'd re-incarnated only for bitterness to replace it before killing her.

Now, Kori was missing. Xander's former lover before he'd stolen mine.

It was a message from the witch who'd cursed us.

Xander came to me to help find her because the message was clear. Rori was in danger.

Her necklace was left in place of where the hybrid had been. Blood puddled in a circular pattern on the forest floor around it.

Try as I might, I couldn't shake her from my system.

The emotions she brought forth whenever we were in close proximately always tore at my resolve.

I'd kept her soul from reuniting with my brother time and time again. The fact that it was this lifetime that he'd found her meant something. It had to.

Rori most definitely was not Anastasia.

There was an undimmable light in her eyes.

Even though life clawed and ripped her apart, she'd never given in to the darkness like Stasia had.

She'd been sarcastic and fearless on the surface, but I could sense fear underneath every time I was near her.

Not just fear. Excitement. Longing.

A need she wanted to explore but would never allow herself to think too hard about.

I'd had a little taste of her and that small bite nipped viciously through my willpower. I couldn't keep away.

It had burned through that ice wall around my heart that it had taken centuries to build. All in the matter of a single afternoon.

And now she'd gone missing.

While Xander's brood scoured the west side of the den, my pack searched the east.

The witch wanted something. Dax's death had only been the start.

If Kori and Rori were part of his mission, we had to stop him fast.

The last time he'd fucked with the balance, everything went to hell.

We'd made too many new vampires and werewolves. They destroyed entire villages.

Getting them under control, we'd diminished the population to only a handful.

Now we only turned those worthy of our fellowship for eternity. And we oversaw any vamps or weres who were turned by our chosen ones.

Leaves rustling to the right of the path drew my wandering attention.

The sound was still a good half mile away but with the fur, strength, and immortality came enhanced hearing and an incredible sense of smell.

"Anything yet?" Xander called across the forest.

My annoyance flared its ugly head.

Shifting back to human, I let my naked cock swing proudly as he approached.

"Yup. We're taking our time to enjoy each other's company."

Being a dick to him came to me more naturally than breathing.

He came bounding through the trees and stopped a few feet away.

Smart. My temper could snap its chain quickly when I was frustrated. At least he remembered that much from our human lives.

"Look, asshole. I appreciate you helping but my patience shouldn't be tested right now," he said, with lips curled back and fangs on full display.

My brother and his theatrics. *Typical.*

I shouldn't push him where his former mate was concerned. I knew that. Yet I couldn't bring myself to back down either.

"Maybe if we wait a minute, I'll find that last fuck I was saving and spare your delicate feelings."

Instead of getting mad, the corners of his mouth turned up. The sight cracked my icy heart. Slightly.

Xander was my older brother. Through everything, he'd been my hero.

When he'd been turned, he killed our father, our mother, and half the town but he made himself stop before he could kill me.

I tempered his bloodlust as I grew older.

And when it became too much, I chased down the witch who'd cursed him only to be cursed myself for my troubles.

Xander's and my relationship was ambivalent at best. I loved him. And I hated him.

"She's missing, Thane! That prick took her and..." Stopping abruptly, he dropped to his knees, clutching his chest as he panted.

My hand found his back of its own accord. When I was younger, comforting Xander through pain came naturally to me.

I'd since become a source of that pain. Though now, we shared a common goal.

"What's wrong? What's happening?" I demanded, but I knew.

If he'd felt a tug in his chest, pain and anguish, it could only mean one thing. The bond.

Rori was dead.

It also meant she had been brought back. The bond snapping into place.

"What did you, Xander?" He hadn't been around to give her his blood or his venom.

How could she be turned? *Fuck!*

Looking up at me, the sorrow in his eyes said it all. He hadn't been the one to turn her.

She had died. And neither of us had been there for her. Neither of us was the one to extend her life beyond human.

"What does this mean? Do you think the witch did..." I couldn't finish my thought.

Pain collided against my ribcage as my heart tried to leap from my chest.

The tug wasn't that of a rope. It was a steel chain that demanded I find her.

My mate.

My brother and I had failed Rori. We failed her and she had died.

Her pain was my pain. Her thirst was my thirst. Her pack was my pack.

Jumping to my feet, I growled at him.

I didn't know what the hell was happening but the thought of anyone else having as much claim to my mate as I did didn't sit well with me.

Xander snarled at me as well. He felt the same.

It was hard to explain, but I felt his anger. Not as strongly as Rori's emotions.

More like they were filtering in from her... through her into me.

"You did this!" His accusation flung out of betrayal.

I understood it from his perspective. I didn't want to, but I did.

He'd been her mate before. He'd not given her any means of turning when she'd died.

And now, here I stood, mated to her the same as him.

"I didn't do this! What the fuck is happening?"

Before either of us could make heads or tails of the situation, the tug in both of our chest had our feet moving on instinct.

Somewhere in this forest, Rori needed me.

The sun was going down. Eventide was upon us.

With my pulse racing, I dashed off into the forest to find my mate.

About the Author
Anexa O. Saphire

I was born in Maryland and love steamed crabs. I moved to Florida for a few decades but have moved back to Maryland recently. I love to write, create art, read, and sing. I've become extremely introverted as I have gotten older, but I do still love going out for an occasional night of karaoke. My hubby and I live a simple, quiet life with our furbabies. Life becomes simpler once you let yourself dream and let go of whatever holds you down.

Acknowledgements

A huge shout out to my husband, Tim. With this year's move and turbulent storms of life, he's been the beacon in my lighthouse. Without him, I would have been lost amongst the reeds. He's been the hero I needed and the villain that kept us going.

Thank you to the few people in my life that were always there when I needed an ear to vent to, words of encouragement, and solutions to problems that plagued me.

As one of my closest and dearest friends, Bethipoo has supported my craziness and helped talk me through a lot of my doubts. Thank you for always seeing ME, Beth. Just your silly friend with a no filter personality.

To Keay. Thank you for the hugs whenever one of my characters met with an ill fate. You fall in love with them over the months. Their losses are no less painful than my real-life problems.

To my sister, Misty. Your encouragement and belief in me helped more than words could ever express. Thank you for chiming in with messages just when I needed them most. That sixth sense of yours is uncanny.

I would be remiss if I didn't acknowledge my furbabies. When I was down and needed hugs, they were there as a reminder that I mattered to someone in my quiet times. And whenever I was not willing to push myself to do something, anything, through the stress of the day, they picked up on my needs and dragged me to whatever end.

I've made several friends through social media, and I want to give a shout out to them as well. Thank you all for the encouragement to keep going.

I want to send a special thank you to Melanie Elkins. Without her help, I'd feel like I was going crazy. Her suggestions for correction have saved my sanity.

I am an author, but more than that, I am an avid reader. And a book dragon to boot. It's an addiction that I refuse to kick!

Post Script...

As I am writing this addition, my heart is breaking. My friend, Beth, has passed away.

I am so sorry that she is never going to get to read this. I had named a character after her as a surprise. I now regret not telling her.

Rest in Peace, sweetpea. Bitzy will live on forever within these pages.